Items should be returned on or before the last date shown below. Items not already requested by other borrowers may be renewed in person, in writing or by telephone. To renew, please quote the number of the barcode label. To renew ... This can be requested a ... Renew online @ www.d ... Fines charged for overdu ... incurred in recovery. Dan ... loss of items will be charged to the borrower.

T06658598

Leabharlanna Poiblí Chathair Bhaile Átha Cliath
Dublin City Public Libraries

Brainse Mheal Ráthluirc
Charleville Mall Branch
Tel. 8749619

Comhairle Cathrach
Bhaile Átha Cliath
Dublin City Council

WITHDRAWN FROM STOCK
DUBLIN CITY PUBLIC LIBRARIES

Date Due	Date Due	Date Due

Bondi Bay Heroes collection

The Shy Nurse's Rebel Doc by Alison Roberts
Finding His Wife, Finding a Son by Marion Lennox

And look out for the next two books

Healed by Her Army Doc by Meredith Webber
Rescued by Her Mr Right by Alison Roberts

Available September 2018

Also by Alison Roberts

Sleigh Ride with the Single Dad
The Doctor's Wife for Keeps
Twin Surprise for the Italian Doc

Also by Marion Lennox

Stranded with the Secret Billionaire
Reunited with Her Surgeon Prince
The Billionaire's Christmas Baby

Discover more at millsandboon.co.uk.

THE SHY NURSE'S REBEL DOC

ALISON ROBERTS

FINDING HIS WIFE, FINDING A SON

MARION LENNOX

Leabharlanna Poiblí Chathair Baile Átha Cliath

Dublin City Public Libraries

MILLS & BOON

All rights reserved including the right of reproduction
in whole or in part in any form. This edition is published
by arrangement with Harlequin Books S.A.

This is a work of fiction. Names, characters, places, locations
and incidents are purely fictional and bear no relationship to
any real life individuals, living or dead, or to any actual places,
business establishments, locations, events or incidents.
Any resemblance is entirely coincidental.

This book is sold subject to the condition that it shall not,
by way of trade or otherwise, be lent, resold, hired out
or otherwise circulated without the prior consent of the publisher
in any form of binding or cover other than that in which it is published
and without a similar condition including this condition
being imposed on the subsequent purchaser.

® and TM are trademarks owned and used by the trademark owner
and/or its licensee. Trademarks marked with ® are registered with the
United Kingdom Patent Office and/or the Office for Harmonisation
in the Internal Market and in other countries.

First Published in Great Britain 2018
by Mills & Boon, an imprint of HarperCollins*Publishers*
1 London Bridge Street, London, SE1 9GF

The Shy Nurse's Rebel Doc © 2018 by Alison Roberts

Finding His Wife, Finding a Son © 2018 by Marion Lennox

ISBN: 978-0-263-93364-2

MIX
Paper from
responsible sources
FSC C007454

This book is produced from independently certified FSC™ paper
to ensure responsible forest management.
For more information visit www.harpercollins.co.uk/green.

Printed and bound in Spain
by CPI, Barcelona

THE SHY NURSE'S REBEL DOC

ALISON ROBERTS

MILLS & BOON

For Linda and Meredith, with much love.

CHAPTER ONE

IT BLINDSIDED HIM.

BLAKE COOPER HAD just swung himself off his motorbike in his allotted ED staff parking space at Sydney's Bondi Bayside Hospital and flipped up his visor. He should have been easing off his helmet, now, and reaching for the worn leather satchel in the side pannier but he wasn't moving at all. His fingers felt like they were stuck to the sides of his helmet and his eyes were just as stuck.

On that car...

A gleaming, vintage MG roadster.

Red.

Of course it was red. It was a giant Dinky toy, come to life.

His toy.

And, there he was. Five years old again. Finding that shoebox full of treasure at the bottom of the carton of kitchen junk his mother had bought for virtually nothing from the charity shop clearance sale. There'd been more than a dozen of the tiny pre-loved metal vehicles but his absolute favourite had been that little red MG roadster, even if it did have chipped paint and a missing wheel. He could almost feel the sharp edges of it in his hand right now, as his fingers curled into a fist—the way they had back then, as they clutched the toy hidden in his pocket, whenever something important was happening. Like when he had to change schools. Or when the big boys on the block were following him home…

Blake dismissed the memory of that fear with a soft snort. His upbringing had had its advantages because he wasn't afraid of anything now.

And this real-life toy wasn't anything like his miniature version. Someone must have spent a fortune restoring it. He'd bet it had a completely new motor now, and that soft, red leather upholstery certainly wasn't original. A new staff member, perhaps? Or a visiting consultant who had the means to indulge a pricey hobby? The idea of spending huge amounts of money purely for pleasure was distasteful but he wasn't going to allow that to tarnish a memory that had been a poignant reminder of something very special. It became so much more muted when you were an adult, that bolt of sheer happiness that life could deliver something so amazing. When you could find real treasure so unexpectedly.

He pulled his helmet off. He was tucking it under his arm when the soft, early morning air around him, still blurred with those long-ago memories, was shattered by a sound that lifted the hairs on the back of his neck.

A scream of pure terror.

'*Help…oh, God… Help…*'

It was coming from the adjoining public car park. Blake's helmet bounced, unseen, off the asphalt behind him. He vaulted over the dividing fence with only a touch of his hand to boost him. The heels of his cowboy-style boots beat a tattoo on the hard surface as he ran towards the terrible sound. His peripheral vision caught the movement of others coming in the same direction but he was there first. The young woman standing beside the opened back door of her car didn't appear to be injured or unwell. She just looked petrified.

'What is it? What's happened?'

The question was redundant a split second later, because he could see into the back seat of the car now. Into the baby seat. He could see the blue lips of a baby who wasn't breathing.

The safety harness was already undone and it was easy to lift the infant with his hands under its armpits, his fingers supporting the head. Sometimes, being moved suddenly could be enough to restart breathing but Blake could feel how unresponsive this baby was as he stepped back from the car. He dropped to his knees and cradled the baby in his arms, tilting the head back to ensure the airway was open as he covered the tiny nose and mouth with his lips as he delivered a rescue breath.

And then another. He could see the chest rising so he knew that the airway wasn't obstructed but there was still no response. With two fingers positioned on the centre of the baby's chest he began rapid compressions. A few seconds later, he paused to deliver another two breaths.

Other people had arrived now.

'What happened?'

'How long since he stopped breathing?'

The mother was sobbing. 'I knew there was something wrong, that's why I was bringing him here but I thought he'd…that he'd just fallen asleep… It was just before I turned into the car park…'

'Should I go and get a resus trolley?'

It was a nurse he knew very well who was asking the question. Harriet Collins worked in the intensive care unit but she was also a founding member of the Specialist Disaster Response team that was a big part of Blake's life as well.

Blake had filled the baby's lungs with air again and lifted his head to answer Harriet as he started another set of compressions but then he paused for a second. He could feel the difference beneath his hands. The tension of muscles contracting as the baby took a breath on its own.

And then another.

Blake got to his feet with the baby still in his arms. 'No trolley,' he told Harriet. 'The sooner we get inside the better.'

He was already taking off, heading towards the nearest entrance to the emergency department through the ambulance bay. He could have this baby in their well-equipped resuscitation area in less than a minute if he ran.

He heard the despairing wail of the baby's mother behind him but Harriet was onto it. A swift glance back showed her putting an arm around the still terrified mother's shoulders. 'Come with us,' he heard her say. 'Dr Cooper knows what he's doing, I promise. He's the best…'

He also heard the mother's response.

'But he doesn't even *look* like a doctor…'

'So this is your first day here, dear?'

'Yes, it is, Mrs Henderson.'

'Oh, call me Dottie, dear. Everyone does, you know.'

'Okay, Dottie.'

Samantha Braithwaite smiled at her elderly patient then shifted her gaze to run a practised eye over the drip rate of the IV fluids. She moved the little plastic wheel with her thumb a fraction. The saline drip was only up to keep a vein open—Dottie wasn't hypotensive or dehydrated.

'Is it your first job as a nurse?'

'Oh, no...just my first day here at Bondi Bayside Hospital. I'm very excited.'

'It's a lovely hospital.'

'It is. Maybe you'll get a view of the beach from your room when you're up on the ward. I had a tour a while ago with my friend, Harriet. She works in Intensive Care and she told me about the job coming up here. I couldn't wait to apply for it.'

'It must be a very exciting place to work, here in Emergency. But you're going to see all manner of dreadful things.' Faded blue eyes were full of concern. 'Are you sure that's right for you? I'm sure I couldn't do it.'

Sam's smile was reassuring now. 'I've worked in Emergency for years now, Dottie. At other hospitals in Sydney. I love it. Yes, you can see some dreadful things but it's exciting, too. We get to save lives quite often.'

'And here I am holding up a bed with not an ounce of excitement to offer.'

'You're a treasure.' Sam squeezed Dottie's hand. 'Are you comfortable? I can arrange some more pain relief for you.'

'No...it's fine as long as I don't move. The pillows are helping.' Dottie sighed. 'I can't believe I've been stupid enough to break my hip. You'd think I would have learned to watch my step after ninety-odd years of practice, wouldn't you?'

'These things happen. You're not at all stupid. I'd say you're as bright as a button.'

Sam knew she should be moving on to check patients in the adjoining cubicles that had been assigned to her but she knew they were all low acuity, like the homeless guy who was sleeping off last night's alcohol and the teenager who was being monitored to make sure that his blood sugar levels were stable again. But they had buzzers they could use if they needed assistance urgently and there was something in Dottie's tone that told her how anxious this particular patient was. That she needed more of Sam's attention.

'Is there anyone I can call that could come and keep you company? A family member or a friend?'

'No...my friends are all in the home, now. I'll see them when I get back.'

'Is there anything else I can do to make you more comfortable?'

'A cup of tea would be lovely...and maybe a gingernut?'

'I'm sorry, Dottie. You're nil by mouth at the moment because we're waiting to take you up to Theatre for your operation.'

Yes...that was a flash of real fear in her patient's eyes. Sam squeezed her hand again and this time, she didn't let go.

'I'm quite sure that you'll be fine,' she said quietly. 'It's a straightforward procedure these days. You'll be on your feet in no time.' Her smile widened. 'I wouldn't be surprised if you're dancing again, soon.'

'Oh...we used to love dancing, me and my Bill.'

'Your husband?'

Dottie nodded. 'My third.' She winked at Sam. 'Third time lucky it was, for me. Are you married, dear?'

'No... I'm only twenty-eight.'

'I got married for the first time when I was eighteen.'

'Oh...' Sam widened her eyes. 'Maybe I'm on the shelf, then.'

'No...things are different these days. It's sensible to wait for the right one. I lost my first husband in the war, so that wasn't my fault but the second one was definitely a mistake. I should have kept looking a bit longer.' There was a gleam in Dottie's eyes that suggested she was well distracted from her fear. 'You're such a pretty girl, dear. I'm sure you've got lots of suitors.'

Sam laughed. 'What a lovely, old-fashioned word. I've had a few boyfriends, if that's what you mean. I'm too young to be thinking about getting married. There's too many things I want to do first.'

'Don't wait too long, dear. You might let the right one slip past...'

'I'll keep that in mind. I'd better go now, but I'll be back soon, okay?'

It really was time that Sam checked on her other patients although it was possible that that comment had struck a nerve. Why hadn't she found anyone that turned out to be a contender for the position of the 'right' one? Dottie had been right. With the classic combination of blonde hair and blue eyes, Sam was never short of attracting attention but she'd discovered that being pretty wasn't necessarily an advantage. The interest she attracted tended to be shallow and the end goal blatantly obvious.

'Before you go, dear...do you think you could bring me a bedpan? I've been dying to have a wee for ages now.'

Sam turned back, the curtain still bunched in her hand. 'Of course, Dottie.' She pulled the curtain closed again. 'There should be one under the bed. Yes, here it is. Let me help you...we need to be careful not to move the pillows supporting your leg.'

With the covered bedpan in her hand, Sam left Dottie's cubicle to head towards the sluice room a few minutes later. She swerved to avoid a phlebotomist and her trolley, which put her in line with the doors to the ambulance bay that were sliding open.

'Move,' someone barked at her.

An alarmed glance showed an unusual scenario. She might have expected uniformed ambulance officers pushing a trolley at speed after a command like that but this was different.

Very different.

A tall man, wearing jeans and cowboy boots, with a tumble of dark wavy hair that reached his shoulders was coming in at almost a run. He had a baby in his arms. People behind him were running to keep up with his long strides. A distraught-looking woman. And... Harriet? She should be heading upstairs to start her shift in ICU, surely?

Not that she had any time to wonder what was going on. This was clearly a father on a mission to help his sick baby and Sam did, indeed, have to get out of his way. Her long, blonde ponytail swung wildly as she leapt aside—straight into the path of the phlebotomist's trolley. Racks of glass test tubes rattled and toppled to crash to the floor. A box of vacuum tubes followed, to open and spill its contents over a surprisingly large area. Sam herself was knocked off balance. Not enough to fall onto broken glass, fortunately, but it was enough to send the bedpan in her hands flying. Contact with the floor also spilled *its* contents and all Sam could do for a moment was stare in absolute horror, a hand instinctively coming up to cover her gaping mouth.

The noise made heads turn from every direction, including the man who was now past Sam, on his way to one of the major resuscitation areas. She could feel his appalled glare so strongly she had to turn her head and, for a heartbeat, his gaze held hers.

Dark, dark eyes.

An incredulous gaze. As if he simply couldn't believe that anyone in this department could be so incredibly incompetent. As if his faith in people here being able to help his baby had just been dealt a devastating blow.

And then he was gone.

And there were voices all around Sam.

'Stand back. Stay away from the broken glass.'

'Someone get a mop.'

'I'm sorry. I didn't even *see* you...' The young phlebotomist was looking close to tears.

'It was my fault. I jumped back without looking. I'm so sorry.'

'Just move,' a senior nurse snapped, 'so we can get this mess cleaned up.'

The young technician pulled her trolley clear and muttered something about needing more test tubes as she fled. A member of the domestic staff was already here with a bucket and mop. Sam snatched up the bedpan and kept going towards the sluice room. If nothing else, a quieter space would give her a moment to get over what felt like humiliation.

She couldn't help a sideways glance as she passed the resuscitation area. The curtains weren't completely closed. She could see Harriet in there, with her arm around a sobbing woman. She could see the baby on the bed and staff members busy. Someone had wrapped a tiny blood pressure cuff around an arm and was sliding an oxygen saturation probe onto a finger. Someone else was attaching ECG electrodes. Weirdly, the baby's father—who looked like he'd just come from a gig with his rock band—was standing at the head of the bed, where the person responsible for the airway was supposed to stand. And someone was handing him a stethoscope.

What the heck?

She dropped the disposable bedpan into the rubbish and then turned on the taps over the huge sink to wash her hands. She took her time, using a lot of soap and then paper towels to prolong the process a little longer. Like that young technician, she was fighting an urge to cry.

Her first day on her new job, when all she'd hoped for was to perform well enough to make it obvious that she would be a valuable team member and all she'd done was to make people think she was totally incompetent. Clumsy at best. A liability at worst. She was an emergency department nurse, for heaven's sake. She should be able to cope with an unfolding crisis in her sleep, not jump like a startled deer just because someone was rushing towards her and barking like a guard dog.

Sam took a deep breath and then lifted her chin.

She had patients assigned to her care and she was going to go back and do her job. And, on her way back, she would apologise to the charge nurse, Emily.

'It was an accident.' Emily actually smiled when Sam spoke to her. 'Unfortunate timing but I saw what happened and I can't blame you for getting a fright. It's not like Blake to speak to people like that but he was under a fair bit of stress. He'd just resuscitated that baby out in the car park.'

'Blake?'

'Blake Cooper. He's one of our top consultants.'

'No way…'

What had been intended as no more than an astonished inward reaction must have escaped as a whisper but Emily didn't seem offended. Her lips twitched.

'I know…but he looks different when he's in his scrubs and has that hair tied up. You'll see…'

Sam didn't want to see. She'd never forget that appalled glance he'd given her. It would have been bad enough if he'd been the baby's father but at least she wouldn't have to see him again. That she'd come to the notice of one of this department's consultants in such a humiliating manner was too much to even try and process right now.

'How's the baby?'

'Stable. Looks like he's got a respiratory infection going on but they're also querying an underlying heart condition. He's on his way to PICU at the moment for monitoring and follow up. Oh…your patient, Mrs Henderson? They're coming to take her to Theatre any minute. She was asking for you. Perhaps you could go up with her?'

'Sure. But what about my other patients?'

'The registrar's discharged the ETOH overdose. And the diabetic lad is eating breakfast. We'll discharge him as soon as his mum gets back with his clothes. Don't worry...' Emily smiled again. 'I'll have a whole new list for you as soon as you get back. I might give you some time in the plaster room. And the paediatric corner—just to let you get a feel for the place.'

Or to keep her out of harm's way?

Sam managed to paste a smile onto her face. 'That'll be great. Thanks.'

What a start to the day.

It was nearly two hours later before Blake Cooper felt like things were back to normal. He had a crisp, clean scrub tunic over his jeans, his penlight torch clipped onto his top pocket along with his pens, and his pager and phone attached to a lower pocket. His hair was neatly combed and fastened into the looped ponytail that was appropriate to his work environment and his own stethoscope lay over his shoulders.

The lasting impression of the dramatic start to his day was an odd mix. There was an enormous relief that the baby was going to be fine. A cardiac abnormality had been ruled out and the respiratory arrest seemed to have been caused by difficulty breathing due to a bad case of bronchiolitis, which was now being treated by the specialist paediatric team. The stress levels had been remarkably high as he was carrying that baby into Emergency, knowing that he could have already stopped breathing again on the journey from the car park but it didn't excuse the way he'd shouted at that nurse who'd been right in his path.

So there was an element of guilt to go with the relief. No wonder the poor girl jumped. He'd never seen her before, either, so maybe she was a relief nurse who wasn't even experienced in being in an often chaotic environment like the ED. The sound of smashing glass had made him think that he might have been responsible for causing a nasty injury but when he'd looked, she was still on her feet and all he could see beneath a halo of very blonde hair and horrified eyes was a face half covered by a hand.

A hand with ridiculously polished nails. Polka dots?

Who the hell put polka dots on their nails? Nobody who was serious about working in a place like this, that was for sure.

Emily was near the triage desk, updating details on the huge board that kept track of the whereabouts and condition of all the patients in this busy emergency department.

'Hey, Em...' Blake paused for a moment. 'Thanks so much for sending someone to rescue my helmet and bag from the car park. Much appreciated.'

'No worries, Blake. You can pay me back by seeing how many of these patients can be discharged. Like this asthma attack in cubicle three. Her oxygen saturation levels have been normal for the last hour but she's anxious. Used her alarm to call an ambulance even before she'd tried her inhaler.'

'I'll go and have a chat.' Blake scanned the rest of the glass board, hoping to find something more challenging but the resuscitation and high acuity areas were currently vacant.

The peal of childish laughter made Blake, and everyone else around him, turn. It was a welcome change from the sounds children usually made here and there were smiles breaking out everywhere as a toddler came towards them at speed, crowing with delight. An adult was in hot pursuit, arms outstretched to catch the escapee.

Hands that were almost in contact with the small person whose nappy was now loose enough to hamper chubby legs.

Hands that had fingernails with polka dots.

'*Gotcha…*'

The toddler didn't seem to mind being captured. With another gurgle of laughter he wrapped his arms around the nurse's neck. She planted a kiss on the curly head and then turned to take him back to where he was supposed to be—presumably the paediatric area. The moment she became aware of her audience was very obvious. Her eyes widened and her smile was fading as she caught her bottom lip between her teeth.

Then her gaze collided with Blake's and a flush of colour instantly stained her cheeks.

And, for the second time in a single day, he was blindsided.

She'd had her face half covered the first time he'd seen her so he hadn't realised…

He hadn't realised that this was the most beautiful woman he'd ever clapped eyes on in his entire life.

Sun-kissed blonde hair and the bluest eyes imaginable. A cute little nose and a generous mouth clearly designed for smiling—or for being kissed…

He couldn't drag his gaze away from her.

She was tall and slim, as well. A model masquerading as a nurse. A Disney princess who probably had a tiara and frothy ball gown tucked away in her locker.

He was still staring as she hurried away with the toddler peering over her shoulder. As if mocking him, a small hand was waving at Blake.

'Oh, dear...' Emily murmured. 'She's not having the best first day, poor thing.'

Blake's inward breath made him realise that he hadn't taken one for a while. 'Who *is* that?'

'Samantha Braithwaite. She's come here from Sydney Central with impeccable references including postgrad qualifications in trauma management.'

There was a moment's silence, then, possibly because Blake's tone had finally filtered through to his colleague.

'Oh, no...' Emily sighed. 'Do I have to warn her of your reputation?'

Blake grinned at her. 'Do I have a reputation?'

She laughed. 'Go away. Do your work. What you do in your personal life is none of my business.'

He pretended not to hear her final murmur as he headed for cubicle three.

'And thank goodness for that...'

CHAPTER TWO

'OH, MY GOD, Harriet. I can't go back tomorrow...'

Ignoring the glass of wine her friend had put in front of her, Sam buried her face in her hands.

'Don't be daft. It'll be fine.'

'Everybody thinks I'm an idiot.'

'That's not true and you know it.'

Sam reached for her glass and took a long sip. Okay...maybe not everybody thought that but one person certainly did and he wasn't just one of the senior doctors in her new department and therefore her boss.

He was, quite possibly, the most gorgeous man she'd ever seen in her entire life. Emily had been quite right that Blake Cooper looked different in his scrubs. When she'd seen him later today, thanks to chasing that wayward toddler, his hair was pulled back, sleek against his head, the length of it hidden in a kind of knot at the back. And, without the distraction of those rock god tresses, it was his eyes that grabbed attention. Eyes that were so dark you couldn't distinguish the pupils. Brooding eyes.

Drop dead sexy...

But also capable of delivering a withering glance. As

they had, in that first moment he'd noticed her thanks to that unfortunate bedpan incident.

Sam was staring at her glass of wine, now. 'Has it ever occurred to you that chardonnay looks a lot like urine?'

Harriet let out a peal of laughter that made heads turn in this trendy wine bar with its glorious view of the beach.

'Let it go.' She was grinning.

'I can't. I practically threw a full bedpan of the stuff at the feet of one of Bondi Bayside's top emergency consultants. You were there. You must have seen the way he glared at me.'

Pushing her fingers into her hair loosened strands that escaped the coil she had created so carefully in the early hours of this morning. She pulled the clip from the back of her head and let the rest of it escape as well. Maybe that would help her try and move on from her disastrous day.

'I think he had other things on his mind,' Harriet told her. 'Honestly, he'll have forgotten all about it by tomorrow. And, if he hasn't, he'll make a joke about it.'

Sam finally picked up her glass and took a sip. 'Why *were* you there, anyway?'

'I heard someone screaming for help in the car park. And then I saw Blake leaping over the fence like some hero in an action movie. Joining in was automatic—it was like a training exercise for the team or something.'

'But you don't work in ED.'

'I mean the SDR. I've told you all about that. Wasn't it one of the reasons you wanted to come and work on this side of town?'

Sam nodded. She'd long been envious of Harriet's

involvement with the Specialist Disaster Response team. How exciting would it be to get dispatched as a first response to major incidents like floods or fires or an avalanche, maybe? To be working in the field facing the kind of challenges that you'd never experience in a nice, safe emergency department. She fully intended to try and join the team herself and, given that she wasn't a firefighter or a paramedic, the first step in that ambition had been to become a member of Bondi Bayside Hospital's staff.

Her heart had just sunk a little, however. Had Harriet just made her aware of a possible fly in the ointment? A fly the size of an albatross?

'Blake's in the SDR?'

'Are you kidding? It was pretty much his baby right from the start. He told me once that he'd been planning to join Médecins Sans Frontières. He'd been through the selection process and was just waiting for his first posting but then his mum had a stroke and she's pretty dependent on him now so he couldn't go anywhere. He had a mate in the fire service who got him into USAR and that's when he came up with the idea of a medical team that could add another level of skill to a first response.'

'USAR?'

'Urban Search and Rescue. I've done a course myself. You learn how to find victims in situations like collapsed buildings. It's awesome. I think most firies do it and a lot of paramedics. Not so many doctors or nurses but it's attracting more interest now. You have to do it if you're in the team. Blake's actually one of the regional instructors now. Plus, he's winch-trained for helicopters. I'm thinking of doing that training my-self, actually. Bit scary, though…'

Sam was nodding but her thoughts were skidding off in another direction. Blake Cooper was getting more intriguing with everything she heard about him. He was obviously a born leader. He wasn't afraid of dan-ger.

And he loved his mother.

He was also clearly at the top of the SDR ladder.

'Um… Who gets to decide if someone's allowed to join the team?'

'There's a committee. People have their names put forward by someone who's already on the team and there's a discussion and a vote to see if they're going to be invited to a training session to try out. And then there's another vote to decide whether they get to join.' Harriet raised her eyebrows. 'Want me to put *your* name forward?'

'Sure. But, if Blake gets to vote, I think I might have killed my chances.'

'By throwing a bedpan at him?'

'It wasn't just that. He saw me later today, too. Chas-ing down a toddler who'd taken off from the paediatric area. He must think I'm totally incompetent.'

She knew that for a fact, thanks to the second time they had made eye contact today. The moment the chase had ended when she'd scooped up that adorable little boy, she could feel the intensity of his gaze. And his expression…well, the only interpretation she could put on it was complete incredulity. As if he couldn't believe what he was seeing—that she was still work-ing in his department?

Harriet shrugged. 'He'll soon find out you're not.

He's one of the smartest guys I know and he can read people pretty well. I could tell him myself, just to speed up the process.'

'No, don't do that, Harry. It feels like I'd be trying to get something the easy way. Breaking some unwritten rule for a team that must have to rely on everyone being super competent. I'll just have to impress him at work somehow, if I get the chance. And *then* you could put my name forward.'

'Don't try too hard,' Harriet advised. 'He likes to make his own decisions. If he gets pushed he's likely to walk off and do his own thing. He's a…what's the word for it…when someone's a law unto themselves kind of thing?'

'Fascinating' was the first word that sprang to mind. Or maybe 'irresistible'…

'Maverick, that's it.' Harriet's nod was satisfied.

'Hmm… I guess he is. I mean, that *hair*…'

'I know. Not my thing but it doesn't seem to put other girls off.'

'And he was still wearing jeans under that scrubs top. And…and *cowboy* boots?'

Harriet was laughing again. 'I guess when you're that brilliant at what you do, you can get away with pretty much anything. He's a nice guy, Sam. As long as you don't get too close.'

'Oh? What happens if you do?'

'Well, you don't. That's just it. You get a broken heart, that's all. Oh…speaking of hearts.' Harriet glanced at her watch. 'I've got to run. Pete's taking me out to dinner and that doesn't happen very often. I *think*…' She bit her lip, hazel eyes sparkling beneath her tumble of auburn curls. 'I think he's going to ask me to move in with him.'

'Really?' Oh, my God, Harry. That's almost a proposal. Are you going to say yes?'

Harriet grinned. 'You have *met* Pete, haven't you?'

'Of course I have.'

She'd met Harriet's boyfriend more than once. A tall, very fit fireman who was also part of the SDR, Pete had sun-bleached blond hair thanks to his favourite hobby of surfing and a body that was a testament to the number of hours he spent at the gym. He was undeniably good looking and seemed like a perfectly nice guy but...

Sam gave her head a tiny shake as she reached for her bag. There was no 'but'. Her parents would be rapt if she brought someone like Pete home. They would be horrified if she turned up with someone like...

Like Blake Cooper.

Good grief...one glass of wine on a sunny afternoon and it had gone straight to her head, hadn't it?

'I hope Pete takes you somewhere really romantic.'

'I don't care if it's a fast food joint, to be honest. You coming to the bus stop?'

'No. I left my car at work.' She hugged her friend. 'And I've got some shopping to do. Catch you tomorrow, maybe?'

Luckily there was a pharmacy in the group of local shops near the wine bar. Sam headed in and grabbed an item that had been at the back of her mind all day.

Nail polish remover.

The little red car was still there.

Blake Cooper was finally heading home after a long

shift. He had already worked more than his allocated hours and he would have stayed longer still so that he'd had a chance to get up to the paediatric wing and check on the baby he'd resuscitated this morning but he had another place he needed to be and someone who needed him to be there.

It made him smile to see the car again. He'd have to tell his mum about it, he decided, as he climbed onto his bike and rocked it free of its stand. A trip down memory lane for both of them was one of her favourite things. Maybe he'd even have a dig in those old boxes at the back of the garage and see if that box of toys was still there somewhere.

His smile died as he lifted his head to put his helmet on.

No way…

It couldn't be…

But it was. The woman walking towards the little red car was none other than the new nurse from ED.

Samantha Braithwaite.

The name had burned itself into his memory banks instantly, with a similar lightning bolt kind of finality as what she looked like.

And, if he'd thought she was the most beautiful woman he'd ever seen in that moment, it paled in comparison to what he was seeing now.

She'd been wearing scrubs then. With her hair no more than a lumpy knot at the back of her head.

Right now, she was wearing a gypsy-style, loose white blouse and faded denim shorts with frayed hems that showed off an incredible length of slim, bronzed legs. And her hair… Released from that knot, it was astonishingly long, reaching her waist in a fall of gentle waves that the summer evening breeze was playing with.

Forget the impression of being a princess or a model. What Blake was looking at now was more like an image from one of those magazines he'd hidden under his bed as a teenager.

Every man's fantasy.

And she owned the vintage MG roadster? Apparently so, given that she'd climbed inside and was now rolling the soft top back.

Blake's breath came out in a snort. Of course she did. It was probably a gift from a rich father. Or husband. A boyfriend at the very least. Women who looked like that were never alone in life.

Maybe she'd had those stupid dots painted on her nails to match its paintwork, even.

This was ridiculous. Why was he even giving this woman and her questionable life choices any head space at all? Blake jammed his helmet onto his head and kicked the engine of his bike into life. He took off with perhaps a bit more acceleration than was strictly necessary so it really shouldn't have surprised him that she turned her head to stare at him.

What did come as a surprise was that he rather liked the idea that she was watching him.

'How long will I have to wait?'

'I'm not sure, Jess.' Sam had come into one of the cubicles assigned to her on this shift, to do the obs on a patient who'd been brought into the ED by ambulance earlier this morning. She watched the drip rate of the IV fluids and slowed them a little by turning the small wheel on the line. These fluids were running simply to keep a vein open in case medication was needed at some point. 'I can make a call and try and find out, if you like?'

She knew which of the phones on the main desk she could use. And who to call. After a week in her new department, Sam was comfortably familiar with where things were, subtle differences in protocols and her new group of colleagues, both in the department and the consultants who got called in. They were a great bunch of people and Sam knew she was going to make new friends here. She particularly liked Kate Mitchell, an O&G surgeon, who was apparently also a member of the SDR team although she hadn't had a chance to talk to her about it yet. She lived in the same apartment building as Harriet so maybe she should suggest that they all meet up for a drink one evening, or something.

'That would be great.' Jess nodded. 'I've let them know at work that I'm going to be late but I haven't worked there that long, you know? I don't want them to think I'm a liability.'

'I get it. I'm pretty new here, myself. Let me just do your blood pressure and things and I'll get on it.'

At twenty-five, Jess was only a few years younger than Sam so she already felt an affinity with this patient. That she wanted to impress people at a new job gave them another connection. Sam smiled at her as she wrapped the blood pressure cuff around her arm. Not that she'd managed to impress anybody here yet, as far as she was aware, but at least she'd been able to keep her head down and work hard and had, thank goodness, avoided calling attention to herself for any less than desirable incidents.

She still felt like she was on probation, however,

whenever Blake Cooper was in the near vicinity. Which seemed to be an awful lot of the time. She'd developed a kind of internal radar that alerted her to his presence in the department, even when he wasn't visible, which was a bit weird but she'd proved herself correct often enough to trust it now. It was like some kind of energy that gave a recognisable crackle to the atmosphere.

She wasn't into auras or anything like that, but it wasn't hard to recognise charisma and she'd already been intrigued by this man. When she'd seen him roar off on his motorbike that evening last week, the jolt of what could only be described as pure lust had been shocking enough to explain the crackle she was now so aware of. It was also the reason she was avoiding eye contact with him at all costs. It wasn't easy, either, because that feeling of being on probation came from the knowledge that he was keeping an eye on her.

Watching what she was up to and whether she was doing her job to an acceptable level of expertise.

How embarrassing would it be if he could see how attractive she found him?

She noted a normal blood pressure and then picked up the tympanic thermometer.

'I'm sure I don't have a temperature,' Jess told her. 'I don't feel sick.'

'We're just keeping an eye on things. An infection is one of the things that could be interfering with your anti-epileptic medication.'

'I don't even think I had a seizure. I just fainted or something.'

'You may as well get checked out properly while you're here.'

'I wouldn't *be* here, if that cop hadn't been in the

coffee shop when it happened. He was the one who called an ambulance.'

'I might have done the same thing myself, if I'd noticed your MedicAlert bracelet.'

'But I was fine by the time it arrived. If he hadn't threatened to call my parents if I didn't go to the hospital, I'd be at work now and wouldn't be here wasting people's time.'

'When was the last time you had an EEG?'

'After my last seizure, nearly two years ago. Oh...' Jess groaned. 'I was just about to be able to get my driver's licence back, you know? This really sucks...'

'I know.' Sam wrote the normal temperature onto the chart. 'It's a bit stressful starting a new job. Have you been sleeping okay? Eating well?'

They were all questions that had been asked by the junior registrar who'd been assigned this patient but, sometimes, people found it less intimidating to chat to their nurse and new information could be forthcoming.

But Jess just shook her head. 'You're starting to sound like my mother.'

'Sorry.' Sam grinned. 'Helicopter parent, huh? I know what that's like.'

'You'd think I was still six years old, not a responsible adult.' Jess sighed heavily, leaning her head back on her pillows. 'I don't blame them, you know? My brother died in a car accident when he was seventeen. They've been watching me like a hawk ever since and I know how much they care. That's why I can't let them know I'm in here. My mother would totally panic.'

Sam had frozen for a moment, after clipping the chart back onto the end of the bed.

'I understand,' she said quietly.

Man...she had way more in common with this patient than an age group or a new job.

'And I'm so sorry to hear about your brother. That's really rough.'

She knew exactly how rough. Not that her brother had died in a car crash. No. Alistair had been feeding his adrenaline addiction and climbing a mountain. He'd been twenty-five. Sam had only been sixteen and the loss of her only brother and her best friend had been devastating. Her parents were never going to get over it.

'It wasn't his fault. They said it was, because he was driving but I don't believe it. One of his mates in the car said he collapsed at the wheel but he'd had a head injury and nobody believed him.'

There were tears rolling down Jess's face. 'It changed everything, you know? It was when I had my first seizure and knew how terrified my parents were. We all miss him...*so* much...'

Jess was sobbing now. Sam moved to put her arms around her patient. She needed to comfort her. Emotional distress like this wasn't going to help. It could even possibly trigger another seizure.

And, even as the thought appeared, she could feel the sudden change within her arms. The instant lack of any muscle tension.

'Jess? *Jess*...?'

The lack of any response was no surprise. Swiftly, Sam removed the pillows from behind Jess's head and tilted her chin to ensure her airway was open before pressing her fingers to her neck to check her pulse. The sudden jerking beneath her hand made it impossible to feel anything. All she could do now was to make sure that she kept Jess safe for the duration of this seizure. And to alert the registrar, Sandra, of this new development.

The movements weren't violent enough to put Jess in danger of falling off the bed so Sam took a quick step back to flick the curtain open far enough to call whoever was closest and ask them to find Sandra urgently.

There was only one person close enough to call.

And this was not an appropriate moment to avoid eye contact.

Oddly, she didn't need to utter a word.

And, even more oddly, it felt like she'd known that since the first time she had made eye contact with this extraordinary man. It was exactly why she'd been avoiding this—it felt like he could see anything that she might be trying to hide.

Not that she was trying to hide anything right now. She needed back-up and it took only a split second. With two strides, Blake was behind the curtain with her, his intense gaze on Jess as he took in the uncontrolled movements of her body.

'This is Jess, twenty-five years old,' Sam told him rapidly. 'History of epilepsy. She was brought in by ambulance nearly an hour ago and is waiting for an EEG. She...um...got upset when we were talking. Sudden loss of consciousness and the seizure started maybe fifteen seconds later.'

'Draw up some midazolam,' Blake ordered. 'Five milligrams. We're going to need it if this lasts more than five minutes. Grab some valproate as well, in case the midaz isn't enough.'

Sam's hands were rock steady as she swiftly found the ampoules, double checked the name, dose and expiry date with Blake and drew up the drugs.

He checked his watch. 'Three minutes,' he murmured. He was resting his hand on the arm that had the IV line inserted, to protect it from being knocked out of place. 'What was she upset about?'

'She was telling me about her brother who died in a car crash when he was a teenager. Her epilepsy got diagnosed not long after that.'

'Oh?' Blake slanted a glance towards Sam and, again, there was a moment of communication that went beyond the words being spoken. They both found this snippet of information interesting.

'Apparently, one of the passengers in the car thought he might have collapsed suddenly at the wheel.'

Blake's glance sharpened with what looked like curiosity.

'What are you thinking?'

A lot of people wouldn't have jumped in with both feet the way Sam did. She was a nurse. It wasn't her place to suggest that a doctor's diagnosis might have been wrong. But maybe she recognised the significance of something others might have dismissed and she had the feeling that Blake was on the same wavelength.

'What if it's not epilepsy at all?' Sam suggested quietly. 'But something like long QT syndrome?'

Surprise replaced curiosity in that dark gaze. 'What do you know about long QT syndrome?'

'It's a delayed repolarisation of the heart that can lead to episodes of *torsades de pointes* and can cause fainting, seizures and sudden death due to ventricular fibrillation. It can be hereditary and run in families.'

'She must have had ECGs done.'

'They did a twelve lead in the ambulance this morning. It was reported as sinus rhythm and NAD.'

No abnormalities detected.

Blake checked his watch again but Sam could see
that the drugs weren't going to be needed. The chaotic
movements of Jess's body were subsiding. She could
see their patient's chest heave as she took a deep breath.
Blake quickly turned her into the recovery position,
talking quietly as he did so.

'It's okay, Jess,' he said gently. He pulled up the bed
cover and tucked it around her shoulders. 'You're fine.
Everything's okay. Just rest for a minute.'

Then he straightened. 'Where's that ECG?'

Sam took the manila folder from where it was
clipped behind the observations chart she had been filling in a short time ago. The sheet of pink graph paper
was behind the ambulance officer's report form. She
handed it to Blake and he stared at it for a long minute.

Sam waited, holding her breath, but he didn't say
anything. Instead, he handed the trace to her.

'What do *you* think?'

Her mouth went suddenly dry. All aspects of cardiology were fascinating to her but she was no expert and
traces were difficult to read. Then she let her breath
out slowly. She didn't need to analyse every lead on
this ECG. All she needed to look at was the rhythm
strip at the bottom and to remember what the normal
interval between the downward Q spike and the end of
the T wave was. She started counting the tiny squares,
the figure of ten being in her head.

'Eight, nine…ten…' She was whispering aloud.
'Eleven…no, it could be twelve.' Her gaze flicked up
from the paper. Was she making an idiot of herself,
here?

'Hard to tell without a ruler, isn't it?' Blake's gaze

was steady. He wasn't looking surprised any more. And curiosity was long gone. This look had a very different message.

He looked seriously impressed.

'Definitely long.' One side of his mouth curled up just a fraction. Okay, maybe there was a bit of surprise mixed into that lingering look. He hadn't expected this from her, had he?

She had wanted a chance to impress him but it was kind of annoying that he *was* so impressed that she might have a brain. Blake Cooper might be the hottest thing on two legs she'd ever met but his attitude was less than desirable. It wasn't the first time that Sam had encountered a reaction that suggested she didn't look as smart as she was. What usually followed was the impression that the fact that she could think was just an added bonus that wasn't particularly relevant.

The burning fuse of the potent attraction she'd been so aware of had just been doused with a bucket of cold water and, ironically, in the moment of realising she didn't have to avoid eye contact with this man any more, it became remarkably easy to break it. She turned towards her patient who was waking up properly now.

But Blake had turned as well and they both reached to take Jess's pulse at the same time.

Skin brushed on skin and Sam had to snatch her hand away as if she'd been burnt.

It *felt* like she'd been burnt.

Maybe that fuse hadn't been extinguished as well as she'd thought.

Blake didn't seem to have noticed anything. 'Give Cardiology a call, would you, Sam?' he asked. 'And bring a monitor when you come back. Hopefully this isn't going to happen again, but it would be helpful to be able to record it if it does.'

'Good call, mate.' Luc Braxton paused by the central desk in the ER to talk to Blake. 'I was having lunch with one of the cardiology team and they told me all about your case. Sounds like you probably saved that young woman's life.'

Blake couldn't take all the credit. He couldn't actually take any of it.

'It was a good call,' he agreed. 'She could well have gone on being treated for epilepsy that didn't exist and died from a VF arrest down the track.'

'You should write the case history up for a journal,' Luc suggested.

'I think it's been done,' Blake said. 'What bothers me is that nobody queried whether her seizures could have been due to oxygen deprivation in the first place. And I can't really take the credit...' He lifted his gaze to scan the emergency department. 'It was actually one of our nurses who joined the dots.'

'Wow. That's impressive. Who was it?'

'Samantha...someone. She's new.'

'Ah...' Luc raised an eyebrow. 'The one that looks like a model?'

'Mmm.' The response was meant to be discouraging. He didn't want to find out that any of his colleagues found her attractive. And he certainly didn't want to give anyone the impression that he did. She wasn't his type and never would be.

'Give her a pat on the back then.' Luc turned away but then threw a grin over his shoulder. 'Figuratively, I mean.'

Blake ignored the subtle reference to his reputation with women but the suggestion had already been made by the cardiology team. 'I'll do that.'

Not that he could see Sam anywhere. After a week of being so aware of her in the department, half expecting her to do something else that was clumsy or inappropriate, it was a little disconcerting to realise he might have to go looking for her to pass on the congratulations.

Maybe that had something to do with the impression he'd been left with that she hadn't exactly been thrilled to have him take over Jess's management until the patient was transferred to the cardiology department. She'd barely spoken to him when she'd brought the monitor back and busied herself attaching electrodes and then she'd faded into the background when Jess asked her to contact her parents and let them know what was going on.

What had he done to offend her?

And why did it bother him, anyway?

Okay, maybe she'd ditched those frivolous nails but she still belonged to a world he did his best to avoid. A supermodel clone who drove around in a real-life Dinky toy and had the time and inclination to sit around in beauty salons.

The fact that she was intelligent made no difference.

The jolt of electricity he'd felt when his hand had brushed hers shouldn't make any difference, either.

But it did, dammit.

Against his better judgement, Blake had to admit that he was lying to himself by pretending he wasn't attracted to this newcomer.

He was. Seriously attracted.

Not that he was going to act on it.

So, maybe it wasn't a bad thing if he'd somehow offended her. A useful insurance policy if his body decided it would be worth overriding his better judgement and he was tempted to find out if Samantha Braithwaite was single. Or interested.

And why would she be interested anyway? He didn't sit around in wine bars or treat his dates to great seats for some show at the Sydney Opera House. His spare time was devoted to helping out the less privileged members of society at the free clinic and keeping up with any DIY or gardening at his mother's house. And training, of course. If it wasn't an organised session with the SDR team, he'd be out running or at the gym using the climbing wall or something. Physical kind of stuff for the most part.

The kind that made you sweaty and dirty.

Could break your nails, even.

Nope. She definitely wasn't his type.

And he didn't need to go and find Sam. He'd see her soon enough and he could pass on the message.

Or he could write a note and leave it under the windscreen wiper of the car he couldn't help looking for every day when he arrived at work. Except that she'd think it was a ticket or something, wouldn't she? She might be really annoyed by a gesture like that.

Blake thought about that for a moment. Then he turned to Emily who was working nearby at the central desk.

'Got a bit of scrap paper, Em?'

CHAPTER THREE

THE SUN WAS low enough in the sky that Blake had to shield his eyes as he walked through the car park. He almost didn't see the figure standing beside the little red car.

No. Not exactly standing. Samantha Braithwaite had one hip resting on the bonnet, close to one of the headlights. She looked like she was waiting for something. The roof of the car was down so maybe she was waiting for the interior to cool off?

He had to walk past her to get to his bike. It would have been rude not to acknowledge her, so he nodded.

She nodded back.

'I got your note.'

Blake's steps slowed. Uh-oh...

He'd left that note a couple of days ago. He'd had a day off the next day and he'd barely seen her today with the department having been so busy so he'd forgotten that it could have been annoying. That she might have thought she was getting a ticket for parking in the wrong place or something.

But Sam was smiling now. 'Thanks,' she said. 'It was nice to know that someone was impressed but...'

Blake had stopped walking. He raised an eyebrow.

'But how did you know this was my car?'

Oh, man… She had been waiting for something, hadn't she?

She'd been waiting for *him*.

He shrugged. 'It's a distinctive car. I saw you getting into it. On your first day here, I think it was.'

She slid off the car. The way she caught the length of her hair and pushed it back over her shoulder came across as a defensive gesture. An understandable one, perhaps, and Blake felt a slight twinge of remorse. He hadn't intended to remind her of the humiliating incident of dropping a bedpan in front of everyone.

'Fair enough. And you ride a Ducati.'

His eyebrow still hadn't lowered. Maybe because he remembered that she'd been watching him ride away that day. That he'd revved a bit more than necessary.

That he'd liked that she was watching him.

Dangerous territory, here. It would be oh, so easy to keep talking. To flirt with her a little, even. He willed his muscles to tense, ready to keep moving forward. Oddly, they weren't co-operating.

'That's right.'

'Seven-fifty Sport, I believe.'

Good grief. She knew about bikes? His eyebrow had dropped now. His jaw probably had as well.

'My brother was into bikes.'

'Ah.' Past tense. 'So he grew out of his wilder inclinations, then?'

Sam seemed to have found an interesting oil stain on the asphalt. 'Something like that.'

It was time for him to move. To wish his new colleague a good evening and then go and get on with what was left of his own.

'So…do you know what happened? To Jess, I mean. The girl with the long QT syndrome?'

'She was kept in for some tests but I expect she's been discharged by now.'

'I meant her management. Did she get put on beta blockers? Or is an implantable defibrillator on the cards?'

So she'd been waiting for him just because she wanted follow-up on a case they'd both been involved with?

Very professional but a bit odd to be doing it in the car park when she could have approached him at work at any time. Usually, if women went out of their way to talk to him, they had a very different agenda in mind.

Sam didn't wait for him to respond. 'I guess it depends on the genotype and the exact QT interval when it's been corrected for things like gender and age.'

'Yeah… You got it.' A warning bell was ringing somewhere in the back of Blake's mind. Sam clearly wanted to keep this conversation going.

She wanted…something…

He actually took a step forward to suggest that he had someplace else he needed to be. It could go two ways. Either she'd take the hint and give up or she'd reveal what it was that was really on her mind.

It appeared that Sam could ignore hints.

'Can I ask you something?'

'Sure.'

'I'm friends with Harriet Collins. From ICU?'

'Yeah… I know Harry.'

'She'd told me about the Specialist Disaster Response team. I heard all about that last callout you had, to that bushfire?'

Blake waited politely for the question he was supposed to answer but Sam seemed to be searching for what she wanted to say.

'And?' he prompted.

The movement of her chest as she took a deep breath caught his eye. That hint of cleavage in the low scoop of her T-shirt was even more eye-catching. He looked away swiftly.

'And it's the sort of thing I'd really like to be able to do myself. To be somewhere on the front line, in a crisis. To be part of an emergency response when it really counts. When it can be a matter of life or death.'

If he'd wanted to flirt with her, this was an ideal opportunity. He could make himself look pretty good by sharing a few war stories, too, if it went that far.

But it wasn't going to go that far.

It wasn't going to go anywhere at all.

'You get that yourself. We get plenty of life or death situations in ED.'

'But it's not the same. We've got any amount of backup and resources in ED. It's…'

There was a frown line between Sam's eyes as, again, she tried to find the words that would explain exactly what she meant.

She didn't need to explain because Blake understood perfectly well. Working in a well-equipped emergency department wasn't as exciting. Or challenging. You didn't have to dig deep and find out what you, as an individual, were really made of.

But he didn't want to get into a discussion that could turn personal very quickly.

So he lifted both eyebrows this time. 'Boring?' he suggested.

'*No*... I love my job. But I'd like the challenge of being able to do more. I really admire what you guys do.'

Blake was silent. Was she hitting on him? No. He knew what a woman looked like when that was happening. Sam's gaze was too steady.

Determined, even.

'So that's what I wanted to ask you. How can I join?'

'*What*?' He hadn't seen this coming.

'I'd really like the opportunity to join the SDR team.'

His breath came out in a startled huff. It was only in the silence that followed that he realised it could have sounded a lot like a bark of laughter.

Sam was standing very still. She hadn't broken the eye contact and he saw the flicker of uncertainty that gave way to a flash of something like anger.

'That's *funny*?'

'No... Sorry, I just wasn't expecting you to say that.'

'Why not?'

No. Maybe it wasn't anger. The bright spots of colour on Sam's cheeks suggested embarrassment. Or possibly humiliation? She had been waiting out here for probably quite some time, given that her shift would have finished ages ago and she had done so in order to ask about something that, inexplicably, she obviously felt quite passionate about.

And he had all but laughed at her.

Now he remembered that moment of connection, when he'd known exactly what she was talking about in wanting the extra dimension of dealing with emergencies when you were a long way away from the relatively safe environment of a hospital department.

He was being a bastard, wasn't he?

But the thought of having Sam in the SDR was…

Well, it was unthinkable, that's what it was.

It was distracting enough to have her in his emergency department. Imagine if she was there during team meetings or on training days? They might be serious sessions but they were also the best of times for Blake. Downtime that fed his need for adventure.

For freedom.

And what if Sam was there during a real callout? They were intense enough situations as it was. A simmering attraction could easily explode into something else. He'd seen that happen before, with Harriet and that firie, Pete, who'd joined the team last year. They were a serious item now, despite everyone knowing how he felt about relationships between team members. He'd actually heard a rumour that they had moved in together recently.

Blake was confident that it wasn't going to happen to him but he wasn't about to make it any more difficult to resist temptation. Because he *was* tempted. Of course he was. He just knew how messy it would get. Girls like Sam didn't go for casual relationships that were only ever intended to be fun for a while. She was the type who would expect champagne dinners, dancing to slow music and a misty proposal down the track that involved a diamond the size of a rock.

But what could he say? That he couldn't have her on

the team because any man in the vicinity wouldn't be able to concentrate on the job they were there to do? She might guess that he was talking about himself. But he couldn't really say that she wasn't suitable because she might be worried about breaking a nail without sounding ridiculously sexist.

As his thoughts flashed past in the blink of an eye, Blake involuntarily lowered his gaze to her hands. Those absurd polka dots might have vanished but they were still beautifully manicured nails. On the ends of long, delicate fingers that looked far more suited to playing a piano or arranging flowers than sifting through rubble or messing with ropes.

He didn't like being a bastard, though. He needed to let her down gently.

'Sorry,' he said again. 'It's great that you're interested but...we kind of have a full team at the moment. How 'bout I let you know if we're on the lookout for someone in the future? If you're still interested, we can talk about it then.'

'Sure.' The word was no more than a slightly disappointed monosyllable. Or maybe it was more the sound of someone who knew they were being brushed off. Sam was turning away. Getting into her car. She shot him a quick glance after starting the engine.

'I will be,' she added. And this time her tone was even. Resolute. 'Still interested, that is.'

He'd *laughed* at her.

Worse, he'd brushed her off as not being worth bothering with.

He was going to let her know if they needed someone new? Yeah...like *that* was going to happen...

She'd waited out there in the car park for over an hour hoping to get the chance to talk to him privately. She'd been nervous about it, too. She knew it was probably too soon to say anything but that note that had been left on her car had been an unexpected opportunity she hadn't wanted to waste. Not only had they connected professionally thanks to that long QT syndrome case but he now knew she wasn't incompetent.

So did everybody else. For once, the kind of gossip that went around a hospital department like wildfire had been welcome. Other consultants like Kate Mitchell had taken the time to talk to her about it and say how impressed they'd been and surely Blake must have been pleased that at least one of the cardiologists at Bondi Bayside had complimented one of his department's staff.

But it hadn't made any difference, had it? That look of incredulity on his face when she'd said she wanted to join the team hadn't been all that dissimilar to the look he'd given her when she'd dropped the bedpan in front of him on her first day.

A sound almost like a growl escaped Sam's lips. He'd managed to slide in a reference to that in their brief conversation as well.

It should be enough to quell any interest she had in joining the SDR and make her want to stay as far away as possible from anything that Dr Cooper was involved with. It was, in fact, doing the opposite. Harriet had been quite correct in reminding her that the idea of being able to join this team had been the major factor in deciding to change hospitals. Blake Cooper wasn't the only person who could help her achieve her goal. She could talk to Luc Braxton, an emergency physician who was involved with the team. Or Kate, for that matter. Maybe she should have done that when they'd been talking about Jess's case.

She hit a number on her Bluetooth speed dial.

'Harry? What are you up to at the moment?'

'Not much. I'm clearing out a shelf in the bathroom for Pete. We decided that it was a much better idea for him to move in here than the other way around because I'm so much closer to the beach.' There was a thump as something got dropped or shifted. 'I have no idea how I collect so many bottles of stuff that never get used. What's up?'

'That committee you told me about—the one that decides whether someone gets to try out for the SDR team—does it have to be a unanimous decision?'

'I have no idea. Why?'

Sam could hear more shuffling sounds and the odd clunk as she relayed the conversation she'd just had. Clearly, Harriet was multitasking and still cleaning out her cupboard.

'It's not true, is it? You don't have too many people on the team at the moment?'

'No. We're always open to new members, as far as I know. It might only be a small team that gets deployed on a callout but you need a lot more people available because not everyone can just walk out of their jobs at a moment's notice. You might have firies tied up at a major fire or a surgeon who's in the middle of an operation or something. That's happened more than once to Kate Mitchell. Everyone has a pager but only the people who can respond will answer. The co-ordinator picks the team according to the different skill sets they have on offer at the time so everything gets covered as best they can.'

'Yeah, I thought it worked something like that. He is trying to put me off, isn't he?'

'I dunno. Doesn't sound like Blake.'

'So who should I talk to next, do you think? Kate? Or Luc?'

'Hmm. I wouldn't do the rounds just yet. Might make you look desperate.'

'Maybe I *am* desperate. I really want this, Harry.'

'Give it a bit of time. Show him that you're serious.'

'How?' Sam took the next exit from the motorway and noted the slow traffic ahead with dismay. Her parents were expecting her for dinner and she was going to be late. She'd have to call them, next, so they wouldn't start worrying.

'Um, maybe you could learn to abseil? That's a really valuable skill.'

Sam groaned. 'Imagine how much that would freak my parents out. I haven't even been near a climbing wall in a gym since...well, you know.'

'Oh...yeah... I almost forgot. Sorry.'

'It's okay. Joining the SDR is going to freak them out as well but I'm not going to let it stop me. I've been wrapped up in cotton wool for far too long. Maybe that's why I want this so much.'

'Yeah...they can't expect to keep you in cotton wool for ever.'

'It's not that they've tried to. It was my choice to start with because I didn't want them to worry and it just became a way of life. It's felt wrong for a long time but I couldn't find a way to change things. Joining the

SDR would do that and I'm sure they would understand why I want to do it so much.'

'You could do a course in disaster management,' Harriet suggested. 'It's actually a university degree now, did you know that? You could do it online. Part time.'

'That would take *years*.'

'It would show commitment, though.'

'I need a faster way to show that I'm serious.'

Sam heard a click that sounded like a cupboard closing. Or maybe it was Harriet snapping her fingers.

'I've got it. Do one of those basic USAR courses. An introductory one. That only takes a weekend.'

'Now that's a really good idea. Where do they happen?'

'I did one here but they don't happen that often. I think they have them all over the country, though. Go online and have a look.'

'Thanks, Harry. You're a star. I'd better let you go. I need to call the folks and let them know that the traffic's holding me up and I haven't been squished in a car accident or something.'

Harriet laughed but Sam could almost see her shaking her head. 'They're never going to get over it, are they?'

'No. And I can't blame them for that.'

She wouldn't be able to blame them for being appalled at her desire to join a team of people who threw themselves into dangerous situations like floods or earthquakes or a plane crash.

Having parked in a leafy street in one of Sydney's most exclusive suburbs, Sam killed the engine of her little car and closed her eyes for a moment as she let out a long sigh.

It wasn't just Blake Cooper who presented an obstacle to what she'd set her heart on but the big difference was that she loved her parents. After so many years of protecting them from further worry, she wasn't able to become the rebel and just do what she wanted no matter if it hurt them.

This was going to take some careful management but she was confident it was doable. And, as soon as she got home this evening, she was going to go online and see what she could find out about the urban search and rescue training courses.

Blake clicked on a shortcut link on the iPad he always carried in his satchel, which was now propped up on the windowsill above his mother's kitchen bench.

He didn't check in nearly as often these days. And it didn't seem to instil quite the same level of yearning, either.

The Australian branch of Médecins Sans Frontières was currently helping to deal with a meningitis epidemic in West Africa, an outbreak of cholera in Yemen and providing surgical teams in Iraq amongst a dozen or more projects scattered over the more troubled areas of the globe. Headlines told him that a nurse had been evacuated from Africa with a serious case of dengue fever and a hospital in the Middle East had been bombed. Casualties included several MSF staff, two of whom were doctors.

It could have been him, Blake mused, if his mother hadn't had that stroke. He would have been out there now, probably having moved from one project to another, with nothing more than a quick visit home once or twice a year. With another click, he went back to the music he was streaming and turned back to the task in hand. He drained the pot of boiled potatoes, added some butter and milk and set about mashing them.

He would have died doing something he was passionate about—helping the least fortunate members of the human population—but that wouldn't have made it any easier for his mother to have coped with, would it? And how unfair would that have been for a woman who'd devoted her life to doing her utmost under challenging circumstances to give her only child the best chance of happiness and success.

He spooned the mashed potato over the savoury mix of meat and vegetables in the baking dish, sprinkled grated cheese on top and slid the pan into a hot oven. Then he scrolled down the rest of the headlines of the news bulletin he'd opened online.

He hadn't given up on the ambition to join MSF, of course, and times like this, confined within the four walls of a tiny bungalow in one of Sydney's sprawling outer suburbs, the sharp teeth of frustration would snap at his heels again. It was the flipside of the coin that represented freedom, wasn't it?

An ordinary little house in the suburbs. A wife and kids and a mortgage.

Trapped for life.

A nightmare for anyone who'd dreamed of freedom since he was old enough to understand how limited the choices in life could be for those less fortunate than others.

Searching for, and buying this house had made him break out in a cold sweat, more than once, even though he would never be living here. This house had been his mum's dream. Her own house, with no threat of being evicted or having to put up with the substandard living conditions of something like a blocked toilet because the landlord couldn't be bothered dealing with it. A real home, with two cats, a small garden and even a picket fence.

He'd bought this house for her as soon as he was out of med school and had a salary that could stretch to mortgage payments on top of the rent for his studio loft apartment, and one of the saddest things about the aftermath of Sharon Cooper's stroke in her early fifties had been the fear that she was going to lose the dream of living in her perfect home.

At least he'd been able to do something about that. He'd promised that he would do everything he possibly could to make sure she never had to leave this house. He visited several times a week to take care of things like mowing the lawns or changing a lightbulb and he covered the cost of a home help that came daily to do any housework or meal preparation that his mother hadn't been able to manage.

'You hungry, Mum?' he called. 'I've made your favourite. Shepherd's pie.'

'Starving,' Sharon Cooper called back. 'It smells so good.'

She appeared in the kitchen doorway as she spoke, stopping for a moment to catch the doorframe with her strong hand. Trying hard to disguise her limp. Automatically, Blake reached out to offer her support but she brushed his hand away.

'I can manage. I'm doing better. The physiotherapist says I'm still making really good progress. I'll be back to normal one of these days.'

'You will be. I'm proud of you.' As he spooned servings of the meal onto plates, Blake kept a corner of his eye on his mother's movements as she pulled out a chair and sat down at the tiny table by the window. He *was* proud of her. She'd fought for every inch of her recovery so far and she wasn't showing any signs of giving up before she reached her goal.

And why would she? She'd had to fight for everything in her life from her early years as a foster kid to being a single mother as a young adult, never earning enough to make life any easier. It was heartbreaking that she had had to face yet another huge challenge in this part of her life.

He set the plates on the table and then sat opposite his mother, putting a smile on his face.

'I've made enough to feed an army. You can freeze it when it cools down.'

'I might just eat it every night. It's delicious.' But Sharon's glance was stern. 'You don't need to do this all the time, you know. You've got enough to be doing without fussing about me.'

'You spent a fair few years looking after me, Mum. It's the least I can do.'

'Hmm. I'm sure you've got better things to be doing than making shepherd's pie. When do you get time to do fun stuff?'

'I do plenty of fun stuff.'

'Like helping out at that clinic like you did last night? It's just more work.'

'I like doing it.'

Not strictly true, he had to admit. It was often diffi-cult to keep up his commitment to working two or three evenings a month and sometimes, it was a challenge that left him drained. The free clinic had its share of people embittered by poverty who could become pretty abusive but he also saw people who were grateful for any help and, along with his SDR work, it was another kind of freedom. You could save lives there, too. Like diagnosing a baby with meningitis when there was still time to treat them and an overwhelmed young mother might have put off seeking help that would have cost too much that week.

'And I think it's an important thing to do.'

His mother's gaze had softened.

'It is. I wish there'd been one when you were little. I felt so guilty that time that your eardrum burst when I didn't take you to the doctor in time for your earache just because I was hoping you'd be okay till payday.'

And if his mother had had a free clinic available back then, she might have had her high blood pressure diagnosed and treated before it had caused the damage that had led to her stroke.

'It didn't do me any harm.' He grinned as he reached for his phone as a text message pinged. 'See? I can hear perfectly well.'

'Who's texting you? A girl, I hope.'

'No. I'm not seeing anyone at the moment.' He read the message, frowned for a moment and then tapped in a rapid response.

'What happened to…oh, no… I've forgotten her name. They never last long enough for it to sink in and you never bring them to meet me.'

Blake grinned again. 'I've forgotten too.' He picked up his fork. Of course he never brought them to meet his mother. That was a step along the road to commitment. To having someone dependent on him and a mortgage on a house in the suburbs somewhere.

'That was a request for me to take an introductory USAR course up in Brisbane next weekend. The guy who was taking it came off his mountain bike and will be out of action for a while and they don't have anyone available locally.'

'Are you going to do it?'

'No reason not to. They pay for the flights and a hotel.'

Training weekends were a bit of a bonus. Easy extra money that could go straight into the account that covered Sharon's needs.

'It's lucky I've got a free weekend for once. And who knows? I might need a favour like this myself one day. Don't worry, I'll drop in before I go and make sure you've got everything you need.'

'I'll be fine. You go and have fun.' She looked up from her meal a minute later. 'You haven't had a call-out for a while, have you? Not since that bush fire.' Sharon shook her head. 'Terrible business, that was. I don't know how you do it, love, but I'm very proud that you're one of the people who can. Where would we be without people like your team in the SD... P?'

'SDR, Mum. Specialist Disaster Response.'

'Oh, that's right. I thought it might be P for People.'

They ate in silence for a minute or two. The acronym echoed in Blake's head. In Samantha Braithwaite's voice.

'I'd really like the opportunity to join the SDR team.'

What did she think it was all about? A bit of excitement to break the confines of working in a nice, controlled environment?

It was so much more than that to Blake. A window into the kind of world he'd hankered after when he'd set his sights on joining MSF. A world where you had to rely on every ounce of courage and skill you had and then some, sometimes.

It was freedom, that's what it was. The kind of freedom he'd been chasing his whole life.

People like Sam wouldn't get that. She came from a world full of comforts and the kind of freedom that money could always buy. Full of opportunity to do exactly what she wanted to do and the time and money to do frivolous things that would never have crossed his mother's mind.

'Do you ever get manicures, Mum?'

Sharon laughed. 'That's an odd question. Why would I pay someone else to do something I can do myself?' Then her smile faded. 'Not that I can manage it so well these days. I get Margo to cut my nails when they need it.'

'Would you like to go to a salon? Get a pretty colour or something? Did you know that you can get things like polka dots on your nails now?'

His mother was smiling again. 'I've seen that in the magazines. Nail art, they call it. Ridiculous.'

'Mmm.' About as ridiculous as the idea of having Sam join the SDR team.

'But a pretty colour isn't a bad idea. I'll put some polish on my shopping list and Margo can help me.'

* * *

'Just clear, thanks.'

'What, *no* colour?' The young manicurist looked shocked.

'It really isn't appropriate for where I work,' Sam said quietly. 'I really shouldn't have let you talk me into those dots last time.'

'She's a nurse,' the older woman in the next chair said. 'In the emergency department, did I tell you that?'

The manicurist smiled. 'Yes, you did, Mrs Braithwaite. You must be very proud of her.'

'Oh, I am... Sam, darling, why don't you get a very pale pink? It will still look perfectly natural. You can always go a bit wild with your toes.'

'Sure.' Sam closed her eyes. A muscle in her jaw began to ache as she forced herself to keep her hands very still.

She was so over this spa business but it had become such a thing in her mother's life.

'It's the only way we get to spend some real time together—just you and me, darling. You have to sit still for an hour and there's nothing to do but talk...'

At least she'd escaped from a weekly ritual, pleading uncooperative shift hours or other commitments. These days, it was more likely to only be once a month but, if anything, it had made the sessions more precious to Sarah Braithwaite and breaking free of the constraints of being the 'perfect' daughter was proving to be almost impossible.

And increasingly frustrating.

What had seemed like a huge step forward, in moving into her own apartment a few years ago wasn't enough.

She loved her job but it wasn't quite enough, either. Not now that she was within touching distance of something like the SDR team that could offer so much more.

Sam had her hands under the drier now and her mother was having her nails painted. Bored, she let her gaze drift up to the walls of the salon where it snagged on a picture of a peaceful scene with horses grazing in a mountain meadow. Sarah followed her gaze.

'That grey one looks just like Trinity.'

'Mmm.' A wave of something like grief caught Sam's breath. 'I still miss her.'

'Maybe you should have kept her, darling. Just for trekking or something.'

'She loved eventing, Mum. And she was a champion. It wouldn't have been fair to keep her when I stopped competing.'

It had seemed a no-brainer at the time, to give up her beloved sport. In the months following her brother's death, she had lost any interest in what had been a teenage passion. It wasn't just that she knew how much her parents had always worried about the risk of injury. Sam realised now that part of her lifestyle changes had been due to the notion that she didn't deserve to be having fun. Not when her family was so utterly miserable and her beloved brother could never have any fun again.

'But you might be right. I could start riding again. It would be good exercise.'

'As long as you don't go back to jumping. That's *so* dangerous.'

This time it was a wave of what felt like weariness that washed over Sam. She closed her eyes, mentally hanging onto the bars of an emotional prison. One that she had, albeit, stepped into willingly enough when she was eighteen. When her parents' precious first-born and only son had been so tragically killed. The one that enforced the rule that she was responsible for protecting the people she loved. That she had to protect herself in order to protect them. More than once, she had wondered if her failure to commit to any long-term relationship was, at some level, an unwillingness to strengthen the walls of that prison. To add someone else to the group of people she had to protect.

Her breath escaped in a small sigh. 'Life's dangerous, Mum. You can get killed crossing a road, you know.'

The silence that followed her comment was long enough to make her open her eyes again. A sideways glance showed that her mother was blinking rapidly.

'Sorry... I'm not trying to stir up painful memories. I miss Alistair too. Every day.'

Sarah sniffed and pasted a bright smile on her face. 'You were both such little daredevils. As bad as each other. You with your horses and Al with his mountains.'

Sam reached out to touch her mother's arm. 'You let us follow our hearts and our passions and be who we wanted to be. You can't ask more of a parent than that.'

'Aww...' The manicurist looked up from her task. 'What a lovely thing to say.'

'But...' Sarah was biting her lip. 'You gave up *your* passion.'

'It wasn't fun any more. But...one day, I might want to do something else that has its own risks. I can't promise that I won't do that, if it's something I feel passionate enough about.'

'I wouldn't want you to, darling. If there's one thing

that always gives me comfort, it's that Al died doing the one thing he loved more than anything else. He died instantly in that rock fall so I tell myself he wouldn't have known anything about it. He would have died happy.'

'I tell myself the same thing.' Sam's vision blurred a little with unshed tears.

'And that's all I want for you, too,' Sarah whispered. 'To do what makes you happy. I'll always worry about you but that's just part of the job description of being a mother. And I know you're too sensible to do something *really* dangerous.'

Maybe now wasn't the best time to tell her mother about the new passion that was too compelling to resist. Or the online bookings she had finalised last night.

One step at a time.

This had been a bit of a breakthrough, though. Sam could almost see a shiny key in the doorway of that self-imposed prison. Another step or two and the iron bars of that door could very well swing open.

'I almost forgot,' she said casually. 'I'm away next weekend at a training course. Friday evening to Sunday.'

'Oh? Like that resuscitation course you went to last year?'

'Something like that. A bit more specialised, even.'

Sarah smiled, including the manicurist in the conversation. 'That's my girl. Always having to learn something new and get even better at her job.'

'Good for you.' The young woman didn't look up from the attention she was giving Sarah's final nail. 'I love getting away for a weekend. Hope it's somewhere nice.'

'Should be,' Sam murmured. 'It's in Brisbane.'

CHAPTER FOUR

Nooo...

Sam's heart sank so hard it took her body along with it. She was actually slithering lower on this hard, plastic chair towards the back of a classroom located at a Brisbane emergency response centre that housed both fire service and ambulance vehicles and personnel.

This couldn't be happening.

She'd double checked. Harriet's casual comment that Blake Cooper was involved with USAR training had been a flashing warning sign when she'd booked herself into this introductory course and she'd gone back to check the trainer's name again before she filled in her registration details. It had been Adam Smith. A reassuringly ordinary name. A complete stranger.

Did Blake have an identical twin brother who'd been adopted out at birth and had a different name?

One that wore faded jeans and cowboy boots and had his hair tied back in a casual ponytail?

He hadn't spotted her yet, amongst the dozen or so people settling in here, so maybe she could quietly sneak out while he was busy slotting that memory stick into the computer linked to a data projector. Even as the cowardly thought slipped past, an image filled a large portion of the whiteboard at the front of the room and Sam was transfixed. People around her stopped arranging their notepads and water bottles and the murmur of conversation faded away. They were all staring.

The background of the image were buildings that had been destroyed by an earthquake or explosion, perhaps, and were now a mountain of rubble. Rescuers wearing hard hats and bright vests were dotted over the rubble and in the foreground was a team of people carrying a stretcher. Their faces were streaked with grime and their expressions conveyed a mixture of weariness, determination and satisfaction. In the midst of the horrific destruction, they had found someone alive.

Letters appeared slowly, one by one on the bottom of the image. U. S. A. R. And then words followed rapidly enough to create a sense of urgency. Urban Search and Rescue.

Sam felt herself straightening in her chair.

She was going to be one of those people in a hard hat and high-vis vest. Searching through rubble and triumphantly carrying a survivor away from an unthinkable disaster.

She wasn't going to be intimidated by anyone.

'Morning, all.'

The easy grin from their instructor unexpectedly caught Sam's attention with just as much of an impact as the image had. She hadn't seen him really smile before, she realised. And, man…it was some smile. Confident. Almost…cheeky?

It advertised charm. No, more than that. It was just confirming something she already knew.

Blake Cooper had charisma.

And, in the space of two words and a smile, he had the total attention of every person in this room.

'My name's Blake,' he told them. 'I'm an emergency doctor from Sydney but I've been involved with USAR for some years now. My mate, Adam, was supposed to be taking this course but he had a little mishap with his mountain bike and he's off work for a few days with a dislocated shoulder. You'll have to put up with me, I'm afraid.'

The ripple of laughter, notably from a woman in the front row, suggested that it wouldn't be a hardship. Blake was still smiling as his gaze travelled over the rest of the room.

The moment he spotted Sam was the moment the smile vanished. He actually froze for a moment as he caught her gaze and the intensity of that eye contact made her forget how to breathe.

Okay...maybe she was a *little* intimidated.

She wasn't going to break the eye contact, however. It was Blake who looked away to continue scanning the rest of his audience. It had taken all of a split second. Had she imagined that he'd almost jerked his head to do so?

No. Someone in front of her turned his head to give her a curious glance as Blake started speaking again. A 'what's so special about you?' kind of glance.

'Welcome,' Blake was saying. 'It's great to see so many people interested in finding out what USAR is all about. You won't get to the end of this weekend as qualified USAR technicians but you will get a certificate of attendance and you'll know whether it's something you'd like to get more involved with. And you will be in a position to be a valuable first responder if you're ever unlucky enough to find yourself in a disaster situation. As an ice-breaker, let's go around the room and find out what it is that's persuaded you to give up a weekend to do this course.'

Sam was in a bit of a disaster situation right now. What was she going to say when it got to her turn? Something along the lines of 'there's this guy who thinks he's going to stop me doing what I want and I'm here to prove he's wrong'?

The woman in the front row, who'd laughed so appreciatively at the idea of having to 'put up' with Blake as an instructor was apparently a paramedic, called Andrea, who wanted to increase her skill set.

There were several people who volunteered with the Red Cross and had decided to do this course together.

The young man who'd turned to look at her, Wayne, and his friend beside him, Sean, were both members of a volunteer, rural firefighting team.

'We both want to get into the fire service for real,' Wayne said, 'and doing this course is a prerequisite for starting the unit standards that we'll be doing if we get accepted. We thought it would be a good head start.'

'Good thinking.' Blake nodded. 'The competition to get into training programmes like the fire service or ambulance is getting tougher every year. Doing things like this, off your own bat, will definitely give you an extra tick on the check list for suitability.'

His words stayed with Sam as she listened to more people introduce themselves. By the time he nodded at her, she'd come up with something to say.

'Hi. I'm Sam Braithwaite. I'm an emergency department nurse from Sydney. I've already done a lot of postgraduate studies in things like trauma management and resuscitation, and I want to be able to use my skills in a wider field.'

Blake's smile was tight. 'You've come a long way to do this course, Sam. I hope it lives up to your expectations.'

He was turning away and picking up his laser pointer, clearly intending to get straight into the course overview but Sam hadn't quite finished what she wanted to say.

'I liked what you said—about doing a course like this being helpful when it comes to getting chosen for something you really want to be a part of.' She smiled as she heard the murmur of agreement from the two young men in front of her. 'I'm sure we're all hoping you're right.'

'Mmm.' The sound Blake managed to make in response was merely a polite acknowledgment.

Samantha Braithwaite was here for only one reason that he could think of—to use the course as a stepping stone in her efforts to join the SDR team at Bondi Bayside.

He had to respect her determination and the ability to have identified something that would be a real bonus on her CV as far as the SDR criteria was concerned.

He also had to acknowledge that she couldn't have known he'd be taking the course.

This was karma. Fate had deemed that he needed punishment for the way he'd responded when she'd asked him about joining the team. There was nothing he could do about this situation but it was...annoying. He'd expected a relaxing weekend doing something easy and suddenly it had become complicated. That smile on her face right now told him just how compli-cated it was going to be because he was instantly dis-tracted. It was a hopeful smile, accompanied by what looked like a plea from those huge, blue eyes.

He had the power to give her something she clearly wanted very badly.

Looking like that, he was sure that most men would cave instantly. But he wasn't most men. He turned away, clicking the laser pointer. Part of his brain reg-istered relief that she'd toned down her clothing today, mind you. There were no long, brown legs on display or a frilly, feminine shirt. He'd noticed the practical cargo pants and a plain, loose T-shirt. Her hair wasn't flowing everywhere, either. It lay in a single plait over her shoulder.

She was still a princess, though. Just in disguise.

'There are a lot of other factors, of course,' he added, as he clicked the button. 'But it's certainly a good start.'

A new image filled the screen now and lines of text appeared as Blake began to explain what this two-day course was going to cover.

'USAR is a specialised technical rescue capability,' he told them. 'It's designed for the location and rescue of entrapped people following some kind of structural collapse. Anyone got any ideas what could cause struc-tural collapse?'

'Earthquakes,' Andrea offered. 'You see USAR teams on the news all the time, getting deployed to big earthquakes.'

She was smiling at him as she spoke and it was im-possible to miss the admiration in her eyes. An invita-tion, even, that he might have found interesting under normal circumstances but not today. It wasn't remotely appealing when Sam was in the same room and that was annoying, as well. Maybe that was why he smiled back, as he nodded and turned towards Wayne, who'd raised his hand.

'Floods,' Wayne said. 'We get a lot of those in this part of the country. A decent flood will destroy a lot of buildings.'

'And cyclones.' Sean nodded. 'They often go together.'

'Landslides,' someone else said.

'Explosions?' An older man, Tom, who had a background in Civil Defence, sounded tentative but Blake nodded encouragingly.

'You're right. It could be from an industrial accident or, these days unfortunately, it could be due to a terrorist attack. It's certainly up there on the list of possibilities. Anything else?'

There was a moment's thoughtful silence and despite himself, Blake's gaze settled on Sam, who hadn't contributed.

'Fire?'

Sean gave Wayne a light punch on his arm. 'We should have thought of that one,' he whispered loudly.

Sam blinked. 'Oh...would that be the responsibility of the fire service rather than a specialised rescue team?'

'If it involves structural collapse then, yes, USAR could be involved alongside the fire service,' Blake said. 'It could be in a high-rise building, perhaps. Or secondary to an earthquake. Or a bush fire that involves dwellings. In fact, that was the last deployment I went on, although that was with a specialist disaster response team rather than a purely USAR unit. Anyway…now that we've got a scope of the type of disasters we could be dealing with, let's have a look at our programme and see what we'll be covering.'

He put the timetable up on the screen. He'd be taking them through how a scene size-up was done and how to look for potential voids that could indicate the potential for survivors. He'd do a session on structural hazards and hazard mitigation procedures and then they could move onto location techniques and rescue, including shoring for the stabilisation of damaged structures.

'We'll cover some basic first aid,' he finished up, 'although that's obviously going to be redundant for some of you.' He glanced at Andrea, the paramedic, and then towards Sam. 'Maybe you guys can help me teach that session.'

'Sure,' Andrea said. 'I'd be delighted.'

'The grand finale will be an opportunity to take part in a training exercise. Members of the USAR team in Brisbane—a lot of whom are firies and paramedics who are working at this base—will be preparing a scene for us at a building supplies dumping ground just out of town. You'll get to do a line and hail search and a rescue, if you can find anyone alive.'

An excited murmur ran around the room but Blake raised his hand. 'There's a lot to get through first,' he warned. 'And a test at the end of our classroom time. I won't be letting anyone on site if I'm not confident that you can keep yourself safe. And I should warn you that it's going to be physically challenging. And probably dirty.'

His gaze skated past one of the older women from the Red Cross group who was looking worried to the back of the room.

He was expecting Sam to be looking just as disconcerted by the prospect of something physically demanding but he couldn't have been more wrong. The excitement level in the room might have faded somewhat with his warning but it hadn't left Sam's face.

Glowing...that was the only word for it.

If he hadn't realised just how passionate she was about this, he certainly did now. But it puzzled him.

Why was this *so* important to her?

Maybe it was him who was feeling disconcerted. Why did it suddenly seem so important that he find the answer to that question?

Because he couldn't figure out why a princess would actually want to get down and dirty with rescue work?

Because the idea was kind of...*hot*?

Oh, man...this weekend was going to test his strength of character for resisting temptation big time.

'Let's get into it.' He needed to focus. He picked up a stack of workbooks and began distributing them. 'We'll start at the beginning and look at how we size up a scene. You'll find all the information you'll need in these books and there's plenty of space to make your own notes.'

Sam was getting writer's cramp well before they had their first, proper break at lunchtime. She intended to memorise everything to ensure that she got a hundred per cent on the test they would be having tomorrow.

Maybe it was actually a good thing that Blake Cooper had unexpectedly ended up being her tutor here. She had two whole days to make sure he knew exactly how committed she was to being part of the SDR. She just had to make sure he also discovered how competent she could be.

She was learning a lot. Viable voids were spaces where surviving victims could be located and rescued from. Structural hazards included falling loose debris, shifting of a debris pile or the dropping of higher components like when a damaged wall buckled under the weight of a roof. Risk management meant staying away from dangerous areas if there was no good reason to be there and limiting the number of people going into a hazardous area or the time they spent in there. Hazards could be reduced by removing debris, using monitors to detect building movement or stabilisation, which was costly in terms of time and resources but necessary in high risk areas when the possibility of extricating victims was also high.

Sam listened avidly, studied diagrams and images, joined in the discussions and wrote endless extra notes. She was totally focused on her learning but that didn't stop her awareness of their tutor growing with every passing minute and then hour.

It was his quick thinking at first. The way Blake could instantly catch the thread of what someone was trying to say. And his teaching ability—the way he could ask leading questions that led his students to really think about something and understand the theory behind the knowledge.

And then it was the sound of his voice. The casual confidence in the way he spoke and tones that ranged from an amusement bordering on laughter, a sharpness that advertised a keen intelligence to what she could only think of as a deep—and sexy—rumble.

By that afternoon, Sam was acutely aware of every

movement of his body as well. He used his hands often when he was describing something and her gaze instantly locked on them at the slightest flicker even as she focused on what he was saying.

Big, strong hands. No jewellery, apart from a heavy-looking watch, although those long fingers could have pulled off a ring and still looked completely masculine, and a leather wristband or something would have looked cool and fitted that maverick, cowboy type of vibe.

There was a point, when Blake was explaining the difference between raker shores used to stabilise the outside of a structure and the vertical shores that were then used to create a safer passage internally, when Sam's concentration wavered.

Something twisted deep in her belly as she stared at his hands and her brain just had to go and imagine what it would feel like if those hands were touching her body. And then the twist blossomed into such a kick of the most delicious—and, okay—irresistible desire, that she had to close her eyes just for a second.

How on earth had he noticed that?

'Sam—you want to tell us the difference between a T shore and a double T shore?'

'Ah...'

Had he *guessed* what she'd been thinking?

Good grief...how mortifying would that be? It would hand him confirmation of what he thought about her, wouldn't it? That she was some kind of blonde bimbo who had no right being here, let alone joining his SDR team.

Fortunately, her brain hadn't been completely on

strike. A lightning-fast glance at her notes and she had her response.

'A T shore is quick to put up but is only marginally stable. A double T that uses two vertical four-by-four posts plated to the top horizontal one is the most stable spot support.'

'Hmm...' He held her gaze for a heartbeat longer. 'Good.'

Was she imagining a hint of disappointment? Or was it puzzlement? She hadn't quite figured out what it meant when Blake rubbed the back of his neck like that. She was, unconsciously, building a library of his body movements, though. She could see the way he hitched one hip onto the edge of a desk when he was settling in to make sure his students understood exactly what he was trying to teach. Did he realise how he could encourage people to get to the right answer by the way he moved his eyebrows? And as for the way the tip of tongue appeared to dampen his lips when his enthusiasm was sparked by listening to a question...

Phew...

By the time the intensive, theoretical day had ended, Sam was a curious mix of being both tired and wired. And the buzz wasn't just from all the fascinating information she had absorbed. No. Sam knew perfectly well that the escalating attraction to Blake Cooper had to be responsible for a large part of that buzz.

Lunch had been provided during course time but dinner wasn't. Wayne suggested that the class go to a pizza restaurant within easy walking distance and there was widespread enthusiasm from all the participants that didn't have to get back to family commitments.

'Blake?' he asked. 'You wanna come and have some pizza and a beer with us?'

Sam deliberately didn't look up as she stuffed her workbook and pens into her shoulder bag.

She wanted him to come because that would mean more time being aware of that attraction and...and how alive it made her feel.

But she didn't want him to come because she'd have to be on guard all the time and make sure she didn't say something stupid or...or drop a slice of pizza or something.

She wanted him to come because it would be the first time she'd seen him in a social setting and, while she didn't think it would make him behave any differently, she was curious to find out.

She didn't want him to come because it would mean that the safety barriers of having a professional reason to be in his company would be less visible and...and *anything* could happen.

Okay. Wanting him to come had just resoundingly won the internal battle and, at the same moment, she heard Blake speak.

'Sure...why not? I need to have a chat with some of the guys on station here first, to make sure we're set up for tomorrow, but I'll join you soon.'

Several wood-fired, delicious-smelling pizzas had been delivered to the long, wooden table before Blake joined the group but, for a long time, Sam found it easy to resist the temptation. She was too distracted by keeping a corner of her eye on the doorway that led out to this garden, waiting for a glimpse of those cowboy boots or the shape of that long, lean body heading towards her. Would he have taken his ponytail down so that he looked like a guitarist from some cool rock band again? Like he had the first time she'd seen him in the ED, when she'd made the incorrect assumption that he was the baby's father and not a doctor?

The conversation around her was lively.

'I can't wait for tomorrow,' Wayne said. 'I'm not so keen on all this theoretical stuff. I want to learn about the search techniques. Be out there throwing some rubble around and actually rescuing someone.'

'Yeah...' Sean was nodding. 'What's a "line and hail" search, d'ya reckon? What's the weather got to do with it?'

Everybody laughed and Tom smiled. 'Hail isn't just icy rain, Sean. It's another word for calling out to somebody.'

Wayne shook his head. 'You're an idiot, mate.'

'Hey...and you think you can just *throw* rubble around? You wanna give yourself someone else that needs rescuing?'

But the friends were grinning at each other. And then Sean pushed a platter closer to Sam.

'You not eating? This one's really good. Meat lovers.'

'This one's better...' Andrea held out another platter. 'Vegetarian with extra cheese.'

'Mmm...' Sam took a wedge of the vegetarian pizza and then took a big bite. There was definitely extra cheese. A long string of mozzarella was still attached to the rest of the slice as she pulled it away from her mouth. She lifted her hand up high enough to break the string, which then fell into a coil all over her face. With one hand still holding her pizza and the other trying to pull cheese off her face, it was the worst possible moment to notice that Blake had finally arrived. That Wayne and Sean were moving to make space for him, in fact. Directly opposite her.

He had a frosty bottle of lager in his hand, with a wedge of lime stuffed into the neck, a one-sided smile and a gaze that was firmly fixed on Sam's face.

'Looks like you're getting into it,' he said.

'Mmm...'

With a wave of something like relief, Sam realised she might as well give up worrying about her image in front of this man. She was doomed. And, with that realisation, she relaxed, smiled back at him and broke one of her mother's sternest childhood rules of not speaking with your mouth full.

'It'sh great. Try shome...'

Even Blake looked surprised at her rule breaking. His smile widened to include both sides of his mouth.

'I think I will. That looks like it's got jalapenos on it.' He reached for a huge triangle, expertly dealing with the string of cheese that trailed after it. 'My favourite.'

He took a huge bite and Sam couldn't look away. Wasn't that another note in her mother's etiquette bible—that it was rude to watch people eat?

Why was it that every movement he made was so fascinating?

Clearly Andrea was sharing the fascination. She even leaned further across the table towards Blake.

'I've been dying to ask you,' she said. 'What's the most exciting thing you've ever done, Blake?'

Blake stopped chewing.

The answer to that question that popped—

uninvited—straight into his head was that the most exciting thing he'd ever done was quite possibly 'sitting across the table, right now, from Samantha Braithwaite'.

That jolt of sensation when he'd caught sight of her pulling that string of cheese off her face and then making it disappear between her parted lips hadn't worn off yet, despite trying to distract himself with food.

He'd been doing so well, today, too.

He'd been so aware of her in his classroom. He'd actually been able to *feel* her gaze on his skin whenever he was talking and it had been a conscious effort not to let his own line of sight connect with hers any more often than would have been normal, but he'd never been more aware of what was in his peripheral vision.

He now knew how straight Sam sat when she was listening to something that interested her and that she was inclined to fiddle with something at the same time, like her pen or the end of that long braid hanging over her shoulder. He had learned the timbre of her voice and it had the same effect as hearing a favourite song on the radio when he walked into a café. He just wanted to stand still for a moment and listen. To turn up the volume…

He knew that Sam had the bluest eyes of anyone he'd ever met. Did she wear contacts to get that extraordinary depth of colour?

It hadn't made any significant difference that she was wearing those practical, loose-fitting clothes today. His memory banks had been only too happy to use a kind of mental photo-editing software and superimpose a pair of faded denim shorts over those cargo pants and replace the T-shirt with a soft top that not only revealed a delicious cleavage but had the bonus of being just a little transparent.

And now, here they were in a social situation. With food and alcohol and loud music coming from within the trendy restaurant. A drum beat that was an invitation to break rules and get a little wild.

Oh, yeah…it was exciting, all right.

A damn shame it wouldn't be going any further but it wasn't exactly unpleasant. A bit like holding an expensive gift he had no intention of unwrapping but it was irresistible to pick it up and feel its shape and wonder what might be hidden inside. Not that he was doing that on a conscious level, of course. He hadn't bothered trying to analyse how it was making him feel at all, until Andrea had asked that question.

The shock of realising just how much being this close to Sam was affecting him must have been evident in some facial twitch because Andrea grimaced, apologetically.

'I mean…you know…with USAR?'

'Ah…' Blake finally swallowed his mouthful of pizza as he nodded and then gave Andrea his laziest smile. 'In that case, I guess it's okay to tell you.'

'And how often do you get called out?' Wayne asked. 'For real, I mean?'

'I'm not involved with a dedicated USAR team right now,' Blake said. 'I'm part of a specialised disaster response team at my hospital and we can be called out to almost anything—from a multi-car pile-up to a cyclone at the other end of the country—so we actually get called out a lot. We're a medical response, but we have team members like myself who have USAR qualifications and we work closely with other teams who can already be on scene.'

He risked a quick glance across the table as he took another bite of his pizza. Sam wasn't looking at him but she wasn't eating, either. She was breaking little pieces of her pizza crust off. Fiddling.

She was listening...

'Before we set up our hospital-based team, I used to belong to a USAR unit. A few years ago we responded to a big earthquake in China. There were teams there from all over the world and we were on site for nearly two weeks. I reckon the most exciting thing was finding someone alive who'd been trapped for ten days. I'll never forget hearing the sound of his voice on that line and hail search.'

His peripheral vision told him that Sam's fingers had stilled. And he could feel that gaze on his skin again, as if the hairs on his arm had lifted slightly.

'Talk us through that,' Wayne said eagerly. 'How does it work?'

'The team is in a line, obviously.' Blake smiled. 'And you get assigned an area to cover. There's a safety officer whose job it is to identify and mark hazards and you take turns calling along the line and then stay quiet to see if anybody can hear anything. You'll learn all about this in the morning.'

But everyone around the table stayed quiet. They wanted to hear more now.

'What do you call?' Sean asked. 'Is it like "Can anyone hear me?"'

'Pretty much. Usually, it's "Rescue team above, can you hear me?" Or, sometimes, if there's a bit of metal poking through the rubble, like some reinforcing poles, you can tap on it with a rock or something. Sounds like that can travel a lot further than a human voice.'

'And they tap back? Is that how you found that guy still alive?'

'Actually, I heard his voice. Very faintly. I was on the end of that line and we'd been searching all day and it was the last thing I expected to hear. Nobody had been found alive for the last five days.'

'So what happened then, after you heard him?'

It was the first contribution Sam had made to this conversation and it would have been rude not to look at her but, when he did, his response seemed to vanish and it felt like he was simply staring.

It was only for the space of a heartbeat but he knew that Sam was aware of that tiny pause just as much as he was.

Tom saved it becoming awkward. 'Did you start digging straight away?'

'No. There's a protocol. You have to pinpoint, as best you can, exactly where the sound is coming from. That means changing the position of everybody in the line to try and surround where you think it's coming from. And then you have to plan how to remove the debris and start well away from where the victim is because you don't know what position they're lying in or how stable the void is.'

'That must have been *so* exciting,' Andrea said. 'To get him out…'

'It was,' Blake admitted. 'But I think the biggest thrill was to hear that response in the first place.' He took a long pull of his lager. 'It's weird because you're part of a team but it can feel like you're working alone at the same time.'

Why was he telling them this stuff? He wasn't into discussing feelings.

Maybe it was because he could still feel that prickle on his skin that told him how intently Sam was listening to every word he said.

For some weird reason, he didn't want to stop.

'It's kind of like being lost and walking for the longest time and then seeing a tiny star of light up ahead that tells you that maybe you're not going to be alone for much longer.' He pulled a self-deprecating face. 'It's hard to describe but maybe some of you will actually get to experience it one day.'

Blake helped himself to another piece of pizza. 'Enough shop talk,' he said. 'And eat up, guys. You're going to need plenty of energy tomorrow.'

Wow...

Sam excused herself to go to the restroom a short time later and ended up splashing a bit of cold water on her face.

Who knew that Blake Cooper had a poetic streak? The image he had conjured up was still haunting her—of him lost and alone in some wilderness, pushing himself towards a goal of...what...being rescued or *not* being alone? Or maybe they were the same thing.

He could be in a team and still feel alone?

That broke her heart but she could understand it.

Sometimes Sam felt lonely in the middle of a crowd. And sometimes she was afraid she would feel like that for the rest of her life. Because she was scared to let people close enough that she wouldn't feel alone? Because, even though it was suffocating to be wrapped in cotton wool, it was too scary to imagine existing without it?

Maybe the scariest thing had been that urge to reach across the table when Blake had been speaking.

To take hold of his hand, tightly enough to let him know that he didn't need to feel alone any more.

She knew it would be a bad idea to go and sit back at that table opposite Blake but her feet still took her in that direction. Was it disappointment or relief that washed over her when she saw that he'd already gone?

'I'm going to head back to my hotel,' she told the others. 'I'll see you all tomorrow.'

Pushing through the crowd near the bar, Sam didn't see the man whose arm brushed hers.

But she knew who it was instantly.

'I thought you'd gone,' she said in surprise.

'Only to get another beer. But I'll be heading home soon. Where are you going?'

'Back to my hotel.' She wasn't about to admit to her tutor that she needed some study time to make sure she aced the test tomorrow but sadly, her brain had to find a substitute reason. 'I need my beauty sleep,' she said.

The look Blake gave her was unreadable. Intense.

They were in the middle of a small, noisy crowd but it suddenly felt as if they were totally alone.

Together.

'I know what you meant,' Sam found herself saying softly. 'About being in a team but feeling like you're working alone.'

The intensity of that dark gaze increased. 'Oh? Do you really think that's the best thing to say to someone whose team you want to join?'

Oh, help…was she ruining any chance she might ever have to join the SDR?

'A team is made up of individuals,' she said carefully. 'Being aware of yourself doesn't mean you can't work with everybody else.'

Blake leaned closer as someone pushed past him. His head was much closer to hers now.

'And what are you aware of, Sam? When you're part of a team?'

'That people working together have a power you can never have alone. That that power can make it possible to get past the kind of boundaries that might otherwise hold you back.'

'And why do you want to get past those boundaries?'

'You have to,' she said quietly. 'If you ever want to find out who you really are and what you're capable of. Don't you think?'

The response was no more than a lifted eyebrow.

With a half-smile, Sam turned away and slipped through the crowd. She knew there were a lot of people between them by the time she got to the outside door of the restaurant.

But she also knew that Blake was still watching her.

CHAPTER FIVE

'OKAY... ARE WE READY? You all understand what you have to do?'

There was an enthusiastic, affirmative response from the line of people now standing in front of an impressive mound of hard waste. A lot of materials from demolished buildings got recycled but the rest of it ended up here, in a huge dump on the outskirts of Brisbane. Concrete blocks and bricks and lengths of curly, steel reinforcing rods, corrugated iron and wooden boards, broken doors, window frames and chimneys—even sections of carpeting and odds and ends of smashed furniture.

It was a dangerous environment that wasn't accessible to unauthorised people but parts of this dump were a perfect training ground for urban search and rescue personnel and they had used this particular section as an introductory exercise on many previous occasions.

The current course members were checking that they were the correct distance from each other. Dressed in the overalls and other safety gear provided, some were nervously adjusting items like their hard hats, knee pads, goggles or the dust masks covering mouths and noses. The person standing closest to Blake was holding an extra bit of gear—a can of fluorescent orange spray paint.

There'd been a few disappointed faces when he'd named Sam as the safety officer for this exercise because it was a key role that he would be working alongside. Yesterday morning, when he'd spotted her amongst his pupils, having her by his side like this would have been at the very top of any list of things he would never have considered. This afternoon, however, after an intensive theoretical session on line and hail searches followed by the test of what they'd taken on board so far, he hadn't hesitated for a moment in picking Sam.

It wasn't just that she'd scored a perfect hundred per cent on that test.

Or that he could sense she'd wanted this important role as much as, say, Wayne or Sean did.

No. It was all about what she'd said to him last night. Words that had echoed in his head long after she'd vanished back to wherever she was staying. Words—or maybe it was more like feelings—that had continued chasing him in his dreams.

She wanted to push herself. To find out who she really was and what she was capable of. Well…he could help with that right now. He was going to push her in this exercise.

Because maybe he wanted to find out who she really was and what she was capable of, too?

No, it was more than that. Her words had connected on a deeper level. He'd never tried analysing the effect that being a member of an elite team had had on him but it was true that he'd always pushed himself that bit harder when someone else was in the picture. A team member. Or a patient that needed help. Not that he'd seen boundaries. He'd just known that he had to try harder. Get better at what he needed to be able to do. Had he accomplished that because of the power she'd identified?

Sam also recognised that you could still feel alone amongst others. That battles were private as much as anything shared with even one other person, let alone a whole team.

And that made her different.

Intriguing.

So, yeah…he couldn't have picked anyone else from this group to work alongside him like this.

'You happy if we start?' he asked Sam.

'I can't see any obvious hazards for the first few steps. Oh, wait…what about that bent reinforcing rod there? And that corner of corrugated iron poking out?' The tin of paint rattled in her hand as she shook it. 'I'll mark them as hazards.'

A minute later and the line was waiting impatiently to take their first stride onto the rubbish pile. Blake raised his whistle to his lips and gave one long and one short blast as a signal to commence operations.

Wayne was the first person in the line.

'Rescue team above,' he yelled, when everybody moved forward a step. 'Can you hear me?'

Blake could sense everyone silently counting off ten seconds.

'Nothing heard,' Wayne reported.

Andrea was the last in the line. Had he purposely put her as far away as possible? She'd looked disappointed, too.

Her voice sounded quite faint. 'Rescue team above, can you hear me?'

Blake directed the line to advance a stride and scanned their movements. 'Three points of contact with the debris at all times,' he shouted. 'Don't forget. One foot, one hand, then the other foot and the other hand. Look out, Tom…'

Tom's hand had dislodged a brick that tumbled down to crash onto a sheet of corrugated iron. Everyone froze and Blake's sideways glance at Sam was a question.

'There's an overhang there that might have been weakened by that brick getting dislodged,' she said.

'What are you going to do about it?'

'Mark it as a hazard?' Her gaze was steady. 'Or tell you so you can shift Tom to a safer position?'

Before Blake could respond, there was a sharp blast on a whistle.

'I can see something,' one of the Red Cross attendees called excitedly. 'I think it's a…it's a *foot*…'

'Okay.' Blake redeployed the line. 'Wayne, move forward a metre and then to your left a metre. Sean, come right and down a metre…' He soon had the group surrounding the point. 'Safety Officer—what do you think?'

'We need to move some of the larger pieces of debris. Like that door. And place it somewhere it's not going to cause a problem.'

Wayne and Sean lifted the door under Blake's direction and slid it sideways, uncovering more of the mannequin that had been 'buried'. As the medic for the team, Blake moved in and checked for a pulse.

'He's dead,' he announced. 'What now?'

'Sam's got the paint,' Sean responded. 'She marks it with a V for victim.'

Sam moved carefully, keeping her three points of contact, and sprayed the V on the surrounding debris. And then she remembered to put a line through the V denoting that this would be a body retrieval to be dealt with later, and not a live victim that the team could work to rescue.

She moved carefully back to her position near Blake, keeping her points of contact and clearly testing each point for stability before trusting it with her body weight but he could sense the satisfaction this involvement had provided. When she glanced up, it was an automatic thing to do to nod and give her an approving smile.

This wasn't any kind of question for her to focus on and then respond to so it seemed to catch her off guard. Her eyes widened behind her goggles and held his for a heartbeat. And then another.

Okay, maybe there was a question there—on her part.

And, for the life of him, he had no defences to pull around him. He was the one who was off guard now.

He wanted this woman.

In his life.

In his bed...

Maybe Sam could see straight into his head through that eye contact. She certainly lost her focus for a moment and that made her scramble the order of her points of contact. With no grip for both hands, her foot slipped and she could have fallen onto something that might have hurt her if Blake hadn't reached out and caught her arm. He waited until she'd regained her balance and then he took her hand to help her step over an awkward pile of bricks.

They were both wearing gloves but he could have sworn he could feel the warmth of her skin against his.

And that should have been more than enough of a warning to step away.

The blast on his whistle felt like the first step in doing exactly that.

'Let's re-form the chain,' he called. 'And see if we can find a surviving victim this time.'

The afternoon wore on but there was no sign that the training session was going to be wrapped up anytime soon.

It was hot and Sam was aware of perspiration gluing the T-shirt she was wearing under these overalls to her skin. She could change her clothes before heading to the airport but how likely was it that she'd be able to find a shower? At least she'd chosen the latest flight available back to Sydney. Her plane didn't take off until ten p.m. tonight.

'Rescue team above…can you hear me?'

The call—and then the ten second silence to listen for a response—was so familiar now it was almost boring.

'Nothing heard.'

'Rescue team above…can you hear me?'

Sam's mind wandered a little. She could imagine Blake doing this for real during that earthquake. Day after day of moving over vast piles of rubble, just a metre at a time. Hoping with each call that there would be a response and having that flicker of disappointment every time nothing was heard.

What did he think about when his mind wandered?

This morning, during that intensive theoretical session, she would have said that Blake wouldn't get distracted. That he was capable of a fierce concentration that nothing would dent.

But there'd been a moment a while back, when he'd grabbed her arm after that stupid slip and, even behind the screen of those plastic goggles, she'd seen something completely unexpected.

Something that was very personal. It had felt as if he was seeing her for the first time. *Really* seeing her.

And he liked what he saw…

Oh, man…

Focus, she ordered herself. *Ignore that totally inappropriate shaft of desire. One foot, one hand. Other foot…other hand.*

The single blast of a whistle at the other end of the line was so surprising it made her jump. Turning her head, she could see that Andrea had her arm raised— the signal that she'd heard something. The whistle blast had been to demand silence.

The call was repeated.

'Rescue team above…can you hear me?'

Andrea's arm shot up again. And so did Tom's.

Any hint of boredom after the last hour of slow movements and endlessly repeated calls evaporated instantly. It was ridiculous to feel this excited as Blake redeployed the line to large circle surrounding where the sound had been heard but it was easy to forget the reality that this was a staged exercise and imagine that it was for real.

That she was on the front line in an emergency situation, like an earthquake or a tsunami.

That she was working alongside Blake Cooper in the SDR.

And it was every bit as exciting as she'd known it would be.

It wasn't a voice that had been heard, it was a tapping sound. This time it was a live victim who was buried and they were responding to calls with what sounded like a rock hitting a metal pipe. Larger pieces of debris had to be moved and placed somewhere else under Sam's supervision as the safety officer. Smaller pieces were shifted into a pile that she used as a background to spray a V without a cross through it. This time they were actually rescuing somebody, not locating a dead body.

'I can see a void.' Tom sounded as excited as Sam was feeling. 'There's a window frame that's lying against an old sofa or something. There's definitely a triangle of space in there.'

'Talk to the victim,' Blake suggested. 'See if you can hear a voice now and not just the tapping.'

'Hey,' Tom called. 'Can you hear me?'

'Yes…' a male voice responded. 'Thank goodness. I've been waiting for ever to get rescued.'

'What's your name?'

'John.'

'Are you hurt, John?'

'My arm hurts.'

'Are you bleeding anywhere?' Wayne had moved

closer to Tom and was trying to angle his headlamp into the void.

'Dunno...it's pretty dark in here. How 'bout getting me out, guys?'

'We're onto it, mate,' Wayne told him. 'Hang in there.'

Clearing more rubble to open the void had to be a careful process and Sam had to remind the other members of the team to slow down.

'We can't risk anything collapsing into the space where John is,' she said. 'One piece at a time and watch for any signs of movement in the debris pile around you.'

'The command station has been notified,' Blake told them as they worked. 'There are people bringing a Stokes basket and a first-aid kit to this location.'

It seemed to take a long time until the window frame could finally be tilted to reveal their victim. John was a young man, probably a volunteer from the fire crew based here. Sam looked at Blake, expecting him to examine John in his role as the team medic but, instead, he used this point in the exercise to reinforce earlier teaching.

'Apart from Andrea and Sam, who can tell me what you remember from our first-aid session? What are the three most important things?'

'ABC,' someone supplied. 'Airway, breathing and circulation.'

'What can we tell about John's airway?'

'He's talking,' Sean said. 'So his airway's open and he's able to breathe.'

'What can we do about circulation?'

'Check to see if there's any obvious bleeding,' Tom

said. 'And if there is, we need to put pressure on the wound to stop it.'

'My arm hurts,' John said helpfully.

'If it's a fracture, we need to splint it,' one of the Red Cross volunteers offered. 'That will reduce the pain and the risk of further injuries when we move him.'

Blake nodded. 'Great. And how are we going to move him?'

'The Stokes basket has straps to secure the patient and handles on the sides for lifting and moving it.'

'How many people do we need?'

'Seven,' Sam said into the short silence that followed as people tried to remember. This wasn't a question about basic first aid any more. 'Four people to lift the stretcher and two people standing in front. The front handles of the stretcher get passed to the two people in front and then the two people at the back move around them to stand in front.'

'That's only six people,' Blake pointed out. 'Who's the seventh?'

'The safety officer,' Wayne said. 'No, wait. It's the scout. He's checking to see the best way to go and whether it's safe.' He grinned at Sam. 'Or she.'

'Okay...' Blake was shielding his eyes from the glare of the sun that had dropped much lower in the sky. 'Great job, everyone. We'll call it a day, I think. It's getting late and I know that some of you have to travel to get home. Let's get down and we'll collect up all the gear.' He stretched out his hand to help John to his feet. 'Thanks for your help, mate.'

'Hey, no worries. It's my job to sort the gear and put it away when we get back, anyway.'

It was six p.m. by the time the bus took the group back to the fire station where they'd left their bags. Blake handed out the certificates of course completion to the group and had a few, final words to say.

'I hope this course will have inspired some of you to go further with USAR training,' he told them.

Wayne and Sean nodded enthusiastically. Sam felt herself drawing in a deeper breath. She wanted to nod as well. Instead, she just caught Blake's gaze as it travelled over the group with a steady, determined response. She wanted more than USAR training. She wanted to be part of the action of the SDR team.

'As I said at the start, this course is designed to give you the skills to be a first responder if you find yourselves in a disaster situation. Kind of like a public first aid course as opposed to becoming a doctor or a paramedic. You should, however, now be not only in a much better position to keep yourselves safe in a disaster, but you'll be an asset to the specialist personnel that will arrive as soon as possible. They'll be wanting any information you can give them on potential victims. And, if they know you've done this course, you could well be valuable extra team members. Good luck to you all and thanks for coming.'

People wanted to thank him as well but it was clear that everybody was keen to head home and probably straight into a shower. They were all tired and grubby after their hours at the dump. Sam could feel the grit in her hair and looked down at her stained T-shirt with dismay when the flurry of farewells had died down and the group had dispersed. She picked up her backpack and slung a strap over her shoulder. A glance behind her revealed Blake collecting training manuals and his USB stick. Another glance told her that she was the only pupil left now.

She hadn't thanked Blake yet but she wasn't quite sure what to say. He'd given her more than an insight into a world she wanted so much to be a part of.

He'd given her a glimpse of who he was, as well. Someone who walked alone even in the midst of a crowd.

What she felt about him had changed from being simply attraction.

It was more like a connection now. An understanding, anyway. She believed that Blake Cooper, on some level, lived with the same kind of loneliness that she did. That he had barriers as big as hers that made it impossible to connect with others in a way that made you—or them—too vulnerable.

'Still here?' Blake was moving towards the door. 'Are you staying on in Brisbane or heading back to Sydney tonight?'

'Heading back. I'm on an early shift tomorrow, in fact.'

'Me, too.' The glance in her direction held a note of respect and the tilt of his lips was a genuine smile. 'No rest for the wicked, huh?'

'Mmm.' Sam had to break the eye contact. Somehow, the word 'wicked' when she was standing so close to this man was a little overwhelming. With connotations that were a world away from the kind of activities they had been engaged in this weekend.

Blake held the door open for her and the courteous gesture felt like a gift.

'How are you getting to the airport?'

'I've called a taxi. I've got a bit of time, with my flight not leaving till ten p.m. I'm hoping I can find a shower and get to change my clothes. I'm filthy.'

Uh-oh… 'Filthy' also had connotations that had nothing to do with the dust and dirt she had gathered from head to toe.

Blake was silent as they walked to the front of the building. The taxi was already there. Sam turned and opened her mouth to say goodbye and thank Blake but any words died on her lips. There was an odd look on his face that made her think he was struggling with something. That whatever he was about to say was… important?

'I'm going back on the same flight,' he said, 'and I got a late checkout at my hotel because I knew I'd need a shower.' He cleared his throat. 'Why don't we share your taxi and you could come back to my room and use my shower?'

Wow… This was totally unexpected. And…huge… A gesture of friendship?

And then Sam remembered that look he'd given her when she'd slipped on the debris at the dump and he'd caught her arm to prevent her falling. When she'd had the impression he was really seeing her for the first time and that maybe he was impressed with what he could see.

Attracted, even…

Which made accepting this offer possibly not the wisest thing to do.

But it also made it irresistible.

Incredibly exciting, even…

'That would be awesome,' Sam heard herself saying. 'Infinitely better than an airport shower. Thanks, Blake.'

What *had* he been thinking?

He hadn't been able to stop himself making the offer because it would have been a perfectly normal thing to do with any of the team members he worked with on an exercise. And it *felt* like he'd been working with Sam as a team member out there on the dump.

She'd proved herself, hadn't she? She was smart and committed. And gutsy. Exactly the type of person that they would want to recruit to Bondi Bayside's SDR team. Maybe he'd even had the idea that he might have to rethink his aversion to her trying out for the team.

Except he'd known what kind of distraction she'd be, whether it was intended or not.

And, right now, he was being reminded in the strongest way possible precisely what kind of distraction that could be.

He could hear the water running in his bathroom behind the closed door.

He knew that Samantha Braithwaite was standing in that glass cubicle. Naked. Maybe she was washing her hair and had bubbles flowing down the entire length of her body...

Oh, man... When it came to his turn, he'd need to turn the temperature control right down. A blast of icy cold water might do something towards getting his body under better control. Blake tightened the knot in the towel he'd wrapped around his waist after discarding his dirty clothes. He paced his room, keeping his gaze locked on the tablet he was holding. Maybe catching up on the latest MSF news would help.

It did.

Until the click of the bathroom door being opened made the words blur in front of his face.

A sideways glance showed him bare feet and brown legs beneath a fluffy white towel. He couldn't stop his gaze rising. The top of the towel was tucked firmly across the top of Sam's breasts and she had another towel wrapped around her head.

So she *had* been washing her hair...

'All yours,' Sam said cheerfully. 'It's a *great* shower.'

'Good.'

The need to get into the bathroom and lock the door behind him was so strong that Blake started moving a little more quickly than he'd intended. A single stride brought him right into Sam's path and she swerved to avoid him. Only he swerved as well, at the same moment and in the same direction.

It was a moment that held the same kind of awkwardness that it did on a crowded pavement. Like a dance move that had gone wrong. If they both moved again, it was highly likely that they'd do it all over again, so Blake froze to let Sam choose which way to go.

Only she froze as well.

And there they were. Face to face. Staring at each other as if the rest of the world had just ceased to exist. Wearing nothing but towels that could be removed with a single, casual flick of a hand.

Whatever simmering attraction or interest or whatever it was between them had suddenly exploded into a wildfire that was becoming more out of control with every passing heartbeat.

Blake was certainly losing any ability to control whatever was happening here. He couldn't even *think* about how to make his body move. He was drowning in the scent of Sam's skin, the warmth he could feel coming from her and…what looked like a mirror of his own desire being reflected back from eyes that had darkened to a blue more intense than anything he'd ever seen before.

His voice sounded weird. So strained he couldn't recognise it.

'This…can't happen.'

She was holding his gaze. Her voice came out in a husky whisper.

'Not even…once?'

It was like a 'get out of jail free' card being offered. A one-off. A way to satisfy what was the worst craving he'd ever experienced and for there not to be any consequences.

And Sam wanted it as much as he did?

His voice went from strained to hoarse.

'Just once?'

'Mmm…'

'And what happens here…stays here?'

'Absolutely.'

Sam caught her bottom lip with her teeth as if she was trying not to smile. And then she released it slowly and that was it. Blake lost any vestige of common sense. His gaze was locked onto her lips but he could sense the way her eyelids fluttered shut as he lowered his head to kiss her. The towel around her hair came loose as she tilted her head back to meet his mouth with hers. Long strands of damp hair cascaded over his arm as he cradled her head with his hand but it didn't dampen the fire of desire in any way.

If anything, it made it even hotter.

Nothing had ever felt like this before.

That gentleness with which her head was being cradled made Sam feel like a precious piece of china but the strength in those hands told her that Blake Cooper had a control over his body that was the sexiest thing she'd ever been aware of.

And then his lips touched hers and a very different kind of sensation pushed everything else into non-existence. A featherlike brush and then another and then his lips settled on hers and the first touch of his tongue sparked a flash of need so powerful it was actually scary.

She shouldn't be doing this and perhaps that heightened this desire. She'd never really rebelled in her life. Well...not since Alistair's tragic death, anyway. She'd kept herself safe. Chosen safe boyfriends and resisted any pull towards someone like Blake.

A maverick.

A bad boy.

Someone with whom a relationship would be unthinkable.

But this wasn't the opening dance of any kind of relationship. This was a one-off. Two adults who'd discovered an overpowering attraction for each other that needed...sating.

This was going to be the only time Sam would experience something like this—an encounter that was pretty much in forbidden territory.

And, dammit, she was going to make the most of it.

She kissed Blake back, her tongue tangling with his, a groan of desire coming from her own throat that she might have been embarrassed by in her old life.

Her fingers caught in the now dishevelled ponytail at the back of his head, so she pulled the band free and then raked her fingers through that delicious length of his hair. She pressed herself against the bare skin of his chest and inhaled the musky scent of unwashed maleness. Her hands were moving without any conscious direction now, slipping down his chest to the knot in that towel. It took only a swift tug for it to fall free and this time the groan came from Blake's throat.

A sexy growl that brought a huff of sound like laughter from Sam. And then she squeaked as he broke the passionate kiss only to scoop her up into his arms, carry her to the bed in just a couple of long strides, and practically throw her onto it. The move to pull her towel free a moment later was just as smooth and then, for a long moment, Blake seemed to freeze—simply staring down as he knelt over her.

Her own gaze was just as caught—by the naked, totally ripped and totally aroused body looming over her own.

She'd never seen anything so beautiful.

This was fantasy sex that was about to get very, very real and she'd never wanted anything as much as this.

But then her gaze lifted and locked with a set of dark, dark eyes.

This wasn't just sex, was it?

She was with *Blake*…

The most extraordinary man she'd ever met.

So it wasn't simply sex. This was a connection that suddenly felt overwhelmingly significant.

But she couldn't let Blake know that. She had promised that this was a one-off encounter, never to be mentioned again. It had to be simply about the sex.

So she smiled slowly. Lifted her hands to his head and pulled him down towards her, closing her eyes as she did so, so he wouldn't see anything that wasn't supposed to be a part of this.

When he bypassed her lips to go straight to her breasts, Sam let her head fall back against the pillows as she cried out in ecstasy. Who knew that the touch of a hand or lips or a tongue could be capable of creating such a powerful mix of bliss but also a need for more.

For everything.

She wanted a closer touch. She wanted to feel Blake right inside her. But she also wanted this to last for ever. To build and build this exquisite wanting, until the culmination would be the closest thing to paradise that could be found on earth.

And it was.

For the longest time, a long time later, Sam could only lie in Blake's arms, waiting for her pounding heart to settle and her gasping to become normal breathing again. She had no idea how long they'd been making love but, if they'd missed their flight, she couldn't have cared less.

Maybe the fact that so much of their skin was still in contact gave Blake an avenue for some kind of telepathy because she felt the movement of his arm as he tilted his wrist to glance at his watch.

The sound he made was like someone hearing the

alarm clock sound when all they wanted to do was roll over and go back to a deep sleep.

'We need to get moving,' he murmured. 'I'm going to grab a quick shower and then we need to go and check in.' He kissed Sam's shoulder as he peeled himself away from her body. 'Or do you want another shower first?'

'I'm okay.' Sam kept her eyes closed. 'I can wait till I get home.'

Because that way, she could keep the scent of Blake's skin on her own for a little longer?

He swung his feet to the floor and got up. Took a step towards the bathroom but then paused and looked back. The half-smile and raised eyebrow was an unspoken question.

Another heartbeat and then he spoke, sounding almost surprised.

'You know, don't you?'

Sam let out her breath. 'Yeah... I know. What happened here stays here. I get it. It's fine.'

But he shook his head. 'You know how gorgeous you are, don't you?'

Sam shrugged. Managed a smile. 'You're not so bad yourself, mate.'

A wave of what felt like disappointment dimmed the glow she'd been basking in as she lay there for a minute longer, listening to the sound of the shower running.

This had only been a physical attraction for Blake, hadn't it? It wasn't that she was hoping for more—he'd made it very clear that this was just going to be a one-off sexual encounter and she *was* fine with that. It wasn't as if she was looking for a relationship with anyone and, if she was, he'd be the last person she would have chosen.

Perhaps the disappointment came from realising that he was more like every other man than she'd recognised. He wasn't such a maverick, after all.

And, if she was honest, her attraction to him had been purely physical at first, too. But something had changed over the course of this weekend. She'd seen beneath the gorgeous package. To a man who walked alone.

And possibly didn't even realise how lonely he was.

CHAPTER SIX

WHAT HAD HAPPENED there had stayed there.

And it was easier than Blake could have anticipated.

Okay, it felt a little weird when his path had crossed with Sam's in the corridor outside Emergency on that first Monday morning back at work. He'd avoided all but the most fleeting eye contact and had merely nodded and greeted her the way he would any other colleague, without breaking his forward movement in any way.

She'd been just as casual.

So casual, in fact, that Blake was left wondering for a moment if that steamy encounter in his hotel room had actually happened. Or had he dreamed it?

It certainly felt like a dream in retrospect.

The sexiest damn dream he'd ever had in his life.

The fantasy sex had lived up to any expectations he might have been harbouring. Exceeded them, in fact.

The level of ultimate satisfaction that had stayed with him for the journey home and right through the night had convinced him that it had been the right thing to do. He didn't have to wonder any more what it would be like to have the most beautiful woman he'd ever seen in his bed. What her skin felt like. Tasted like. What it would feel like to have her touching him. What tiny sounds of need or pleasure or ecstasy she might make…

Now he knew.

And that was that.

They could go back to working in the same department just as they had been before the USAR course weekend. Albeit with a secret between them but Blake was not a stranger to such secrets. Sam had just joined a club he wasn't particularly proud of—the women who worked at this hospital that he'd become a little more than friendly with for a brief time.

It seemed to work very well for that first day. And for the next couple of days. But then Blake began to notice something different.

The fantasy sex hadn't stayed in that hotel room.

It was haunting his dreams.

It was in his head, refusing to be compartmentalised into a place that was merely a memory that he could choose—or choose not—to revisit.

The memory popped into his consciousness at unexpected moments. Like when he saw Sam in the department, going past wheeling an IV stand, for example. Or simply standing still, checking the patient board to see what patients she'd been assigned, like she was right now.

It was stronger when he heard the sound of her voice when he walked past a cubicle she was working in. Even worse, when he heard the sound of her laughter. He'd heard that delicious gurgle under such very different circumstances and he'd had to curl his fingers the first time he'd heard it again because they just itched to tickle her in a place where her skin was so incredibly soft and sensitive.

It should be getting easier to get past what they'd both agreed was no more than a one-night stand.

But it was getting more and more irritating that, for the first time ever, he wasn't quite managing to.

Maybe it was because Sam seemed to have done it without any effort at all. In the past, he'd always caught lingering looks from such partners. They'd appeared in his path far more often than could be coincidental. There'd been tears, even. Or, they had gone out of their way to avoid him and, if they couldn't, he'd be on the receiving end of a death glare.

Not Sam. She was here, doing her job, day after day. Competent, cheerful and exactly the way she'd been before their time together. Nobody would ever guess what had happened in Brisbane and it seemed like it *hadn't* ever happened as far as Sam was concerned.

Perhaps that was what was really bothering him. Not that he couldn't move on and forget it but that Sam already had because it had meant nothing.

It was getting harder with every passing day.

How crazy had it been to think that 'just once' would have been enough. That she could have walked away from that hotel room in Brisbane and been able to pretend that it had never happened.

Sam had known that it would be a bit weird on that Monday morning, the first time she saw Blake again, but she hadn't expected how devastating it would feel when he'd just walked past her in the corridor with a polite nod and barely a glance.

As crushing as anything that had happened back in

those teenage years when she had been learning the hard way that dreams of finding true love and living happily ever after were exactly that—only dreams.

She had held her head high, however, and, if her smile had felt a little forced for the rest of that day with both her colleagues and her patients, it had been even brighter than usual. Nobody could have guessed the way her skin prickled at catching a glimpse of Blake on the other side of the department, or the deep twist in her gut when she heard the sound of his voice.

It wasn't as if she was allowing herself to remember how it felt to be touched by this man—not in the daytime, anyway. Nights were a very different story. No, it was more like he had touched every cell in her body and the awareness was no more controllable than, say, being aware of heat if you stepped into direct sunshine on a summer's day.

It should have got easier as the days went by but, if anything, that awareness was growing stronger. Getting laced with a longing to do it all again...

Sam thought she was hiding the struggle perfectly well but Harriet wasn't fooled by that overly bright smile when she finally caught up with her friend for a lunch break a few days into that week.

'What's up?' Harriet asked as they found a shady tree in the grounds to sit beneath to eat their sandwiches.

'Nothing.' Sam tried to look surprised.

She wanted to confess to her best friend—of course she did. But Harriet had warned her about Blake, hadn't she? She'd said nobody got close to him and those who tried only ended up with a broken heart. She'd be able to say 'I told you so' and Sam would have to agree.

She'd have to admit she'd been stupid and, if she started feeling ashamed of herself, she'd feel even worse than she did now. On top of that, the memory of that extraordinary experience would be tarnished and it would change how it made her feel when she lay in her own bed and relived every moment.

And Harriet was part of the SDR team. Sam knew she would keep a secret if asked but what if it just slipped out somehow by a knowing glance or something? If certain other people knew, it might damage her chances of joining the team. Who would want someone on the team that might have an ulterior motive of distracting the team leader?

So she smiled at Harriet again and then shrugged. 'I guess I'm still a bit tired. That USAR course was full on and I've been working every day since.'

Harriet nodded. 'Of course. Sorry, I haven't had the chance to talk to you about it what with being so wrapped up with my new flatmate.' She rolled her eyes. 'I'm a bad friend.'

'Don't be daft. This is a special time for you and Pete. That's why I didn't call *you*.'

That wasn't quite the truth, though, was it? If she'd spoken to Harriet before the thrill of that encounter with Blake had been dented by his dismissive attitude at work, she might well have confessed everything, even knowing that she would have had to field the 'I told you so' response.

'I remember how full on it is. But did you like it?'

'Are you kidding? I *loved* it. Every moment of it.'

Some more than others, mind you. Sam chewed the inside of her cheek for a moment, focusing on peeling the seal from the plastic triangle that contained her sandwiches. It would be weird if she didn't mention who the instructor had been but this was going to be a real test of how well she could keep her own secret.

'You won't believe it, but the instructor was Blake Cooper.'

'No way... In *Brisbane*?'

'He was filling in for someone who'd been injured.'

'Wow. That must have been...um...interesting?'

'Mmm.' A mouthful of bread, tuna and mayonnaise was a great way of avoiding giving anything away.

'I'll bet he was surprised to see you there.'

'Mmm.'

'Was he nice to you?'

'He made me work hard. But...yeah he was nicer than I expected him to be. Phew...' Sam reached for her water bottle when what she really wanted to do was fan her face with her hand. 'It's hot today, isn't it?'

'Sure is. So did you pass the test?'

'A hundred per cent.'

'Go, you. That'll be a feather in your cap when you decide to apply to join the team.'

'I hope so.'

'So when are you going to do it?'

'Um...not just yet.'

Oddly, making the team wasn't first and foremost in her thoughts currently. Blake Cooper had taken that spot. And she couldn't get her name put forward in the immediate aftermath of sleeping with one of the key people responsible for that decision, could she? It might make it seem like that was the only reason she'd encouraged that one-night stand. As if she was the kind of girl who thought sleeping her way to the top was acceptable.

And it might work against her, anyway. If Blake wanted to ignore her and pretend that it had never happened, he might be inclined to keep her out of the team just to underline the fact that it had meant nothing to him. That *she* meant nothing to him...

She could wait. Until it was no more than a memory for her, as well.

She needed to take a leaf out of Blake's book, that was all. If he could simply enjoy a night of the most incredible sex ever and then walk away as if it had never happened, then so could she.

And that might impress him just as much as proving herself clinically capable or acing a test and practical exercise in a completely different arena.

What was it they said? Fake it till you make it?

She was coping pretty well so far, given that Harriet didn't seem the least bit suspicious. Surely Blake must be just as convinced already. Who knew that those drama classes at high school would end up actually being rather useful?

'I will apply,' she told Harriet. 'But, for now, I'll just let Blake think about how well I did in that course.'

And about what had happened afterwards?

Surely he thought about that occasionally? Unless sex for him was always that mind blowing and she hadn't been anything out of the ordinary as far as he was concerned?

She dropped the last part of her sandwich back into the container. Her appetite had vanished.

'I'll know when to pick the right time,' she told Harriet. 'Now...tell me about *your* weekend. What did you and Pete get up to? Some surfing? A fun run or something? Or were you both working?'

* * *

It was inevitable that they would end up having to work closely together.

At least he'd had more than a week to prepare for it but Blake hadn't expected to have to be quite *this* close. The department was stretched and the trauma team was already fully occupied with three victims from a motorway pile-up when another trauma case got wheeled through the ambulance bay doors. He was the consultant who stepped out from the resuscitation bays to assess the new arrival.

And Sam was the nurse standing beside the bed in the treatment room. She was arranging pillows to support the heavily bandaged arm and hand of a middle-aged man.

At least the paramedics were still here, packing up their gear.

'This is Stuart,' one of them told him. 'Fifty-eight years old. He got his arm caught in a conveyor belt at the factory he works in. De-gloving injury to his forearm and hand. Possible fracture. We've just covered it in sterile dressings and splinted it.'

The subtle shake of the paramedic's head warned Blake that the injury was severe.

'Vital signs?'

'All recorded on arrival and en route. GCS has been fifteen throughout. Sinus tachycardia. Sats normal.'

'Pain relief?'

'He's got five milligrams of morphine on board, which seemed to do the trick.'

'Past medical history?'

'He's diabetic. On beta blockers for hypertension and he's a smoker.'

Blake's heart sank a little. They could all complicate the road to successful treatment, especially if delicate surgery was required.

'I can't lose my hand,' Stuart was saying to Sam as the paramedics left. 'Please… I've got six kids at home and my job's the only thing keeping us afloat. You've got to help me…'

'We'll do everything we can.' Her voice was reassuring. 'You're lucky, Stuart.' She was smiling at her patient now. 'You've scored the best doctor we've got at Bondi Bay. This is Blake Cooper…'

'G'day, Stuart.' Blake stepped closer to the bed. It was disconcerting that he had to make a conscious effort to chase the effects of hearing Sam's voice up close into the back of his head. And that smile…

Thank goodness he had a patient to focus on.

'I'm going to give you a quick all-over check first and make sure we're not missing any other injuries and then we'll take a good look at that arm of yours, okay?'

Sam was just as focused. She had wrapped a blood pressure cuff around Stuart's uninjured arm and was checking the IV line to make sure they still had a vein open if needed. She had both the ECG and drug trolleys nearby as well.

A few minutes later and it was time to unwrap the bandages and remove the dressings applied at the scene.

'You don't need to look,' Sam said to Stuart. 'Sometimes it's better not to.'

It was probably just as well that Stuart chose to turn his head away and close his eyes. De-gloving injuries, where the skin was pulled away from underlying structures of muscle and bone, were usually horrendous and this was no exception.

The forearm was stripped to the wrist and the little finger of Stuart's hand was simply bone. The ring and middle finger at least had some muscle still attached and there was an ooze of blood providing reassurance that blood vessels were still intact.

'Can you move your fingers, Stuart?'

The movement was creepily normal so nerves were still intact as well. It was like watching an anatomical model come to life.

Blake flicked his gaze upwards. Even people used to dealing with traumatic injuries could find something like this confronting and he needed to know if Sam could handle it.

Her gaze met his. He could see that she was shocked. He could also see that she could cope. That she was trusting him to know what to do and that she would do whatever was needed to assist him.

And suddenly there was no danger of being distracted by any thoughts about Samantha Braithwaite that were decidedly unprofessional. He had a colleague here that he knew was competent and that he could trust and…he wouldn't have wanted anyone else to be working with him right now.

They could do this.

'We're going to re-cover the wounds with saline-soaked dressings,' he told her. 'We need X-rays and Triple A therapy.'

Sam nodded. She already had a bowl of dressings ready. 'Analgesia, antibiotics and ADT if needed.' She turned her head. 'Stuart, have you had a tetanus vaccination recently?'

'Not that I can remember. How bad is it, Doc?'

'It's not pretty,' Blake said. 'But it could have been

worse. I'm going to get some surgical specialists to come down and see you but we need to get some X-rays first to see if any bones are broken or whether any bits of that conveyor belt got left behind.'

'It was so stupid,' Stuart groaned. 'Something got stuck and I thought that I could just poke it with a stick, you know? The belt grabbed the stick so fast I didn't have time to let go. My wife's going to kill me...'

'Has someone got in touch with her for you?' Sam asked.

'Yeah...but she's got to find someone to look after the kids before she can come in. The twins are only three and they're a real handful, you know? Ahh... that *hurts*...'

'Can you draw up some more morphine, please, Sam? I think we need to top up that pain relief.'

'Got it here.' Sam handed him a syringe with the ampoule taped to the side so that he could check the dose and expiry date.

Man...she was impressive to work with. He had to smile as he thanked her and his gaze snagged hers for just an instant.

They were both being ultimately professional. Blake didn't doubt that in the least but he also knew that the beat of connection he was aware of had elements that went beyond anything he normally had, even with his most trusted colleagues.

Everything about Sam was just that little bit different, wasn't it?

His shift was officially over well before Stuart was passed into the care of the surgeons. Blake knew that Sam had also stayed on, having become so involved with this case. She looked after Marie, Stuart's wife, after she arrived and sat with her as decisions were made about the best course of treatment. X-rays and clinical photographs had been taken and Blake's initial overall examination had been followed up with investigations on all of Stuart's existing medical conditions. The time off work that would be needed for complex reconstructive surgery that could potentially save all his fingers had to be taken into account as well, given that he was the sole financial support for his family.

'I don't care,' Stuart finally decided. 'If losing my little finger and half my ring finger means I can get back to work sooner, that's what I'll do. I'll still be able to use my hand well enough, I reckon.'

'If you stop smoking, you'll recover a lot better and faster,' the surgeon told him. 'It affects blood supply and healing time quite dramatically.'

'I've been telling him to stop for years,' Marie said. 'If losing a finger is what it takes then maybe this is worth it.' She had tears running down her face as she gripped her husband's uninjured hand. 'I can't lose you, Stu. I need you. The kids need you...'

'I'm sorry...' Stuart was crying as well. 'I'll never touch another cigarette, I promise. I love you, honey...'

The emotion in the room was enough to touch everybody. Sam was blinking hard as she walked past Blake, having wished Stuart all the best for the next steps in his recovery.

Perhaps she felt how intently he was watching her because she turned her head and caught his gaze.

And, just for a heartbeat, he saw something unguarded.

Something that suggested a connection that had absolutely nothing to do with the case they'd just spent so much time working on together. Something that made him think Sam knew too much about love…and grief…

It was only the briefest moment of eye contact but it was enough for Blake to realise that pretending nothing had happened between them wasn't going to work any more. Whether he liked it or not, there was something there that wasn't going to fade by being ignored.

If anything, the curiosity and…and this astonishing pull to be close to Sam was just going to get worse.

He was going to have to try something else.

The opportunity to do that came when he fortuitously caught up with Sam as she was walking towards the car park, having finally clocked off.

Okay…so maybe he'd planned his route so that that was going to happen but his decision had been made in that moment of eye contact as she'd left the treatment room.

Maybe it was due to the relief that it was clearly possible to work with Sam without anything that had happened interfering with how professional they could be.

Or maybe it was because he had reached breaking point with not being able to get her out of his head.

Then again, maybe it was what he had seen in that glance that had made him simply want to take her into his arms and hold her close. Very, very close…

Whatever it was, something had to be done.

He needed to know whether what he'd thought he'd seen in her eyes meant that she was also aware of this feeling of connection and was experiencing the same kind of pull towards him or had Sam really moved on without a second thought or backward glance? If she had, fine, he would do the same. Somehow.

But if she hadn't…

Well… Hopefully, he'd know what he wanted to do about that when he knew how things stood.

Sam had known that Blake Cooper was a smooth operator but there was something about the way he appeared so casually and fell into step beside her that made her suspicious that it wasn't entirely a coincidence.

Had he planned this?

Why…because he wanted to talk to her in private?

Her heart stumbled for a beat and then picked up its pace. Her awareness of Blake in a purely professional setting was hard enough to handle sometimes. Walking side by side, she found that awareness was almost unbearable. She didn't dare catch his gaze.

'Thanks for staying on,' Blake said. 'Stuart's wife really appreciated your support.'

'I couldn't leave without knowing what's coming next for them. Do you think amputation was the best choice?'

'I do. Losing a little finger will have minimal effect on his ability to use his hand and, if the replantation and revascularisation of the other areas is successful, he might get full cover for the length of time he'll have to be away from work.'

'It's going to be a tough time for the family.'

'It is.' Sam could feel Blake looking down at her as they neared her car. 'But families can survive if they stick together. If there's enough love…'

Sam swallowed hard. 'I think there is…' She had stopped walking now. She couldn't not look up to meet his gaze. 'Don't you?'

Oh, wow…

Talk about falling into someone's eyes. Maybe it was the echoes of the 'L' word hanging in the air between them.

How was she supposed to keep this casual? To pretend that what had happened had been left behind in that hotel room and forgotten?

But…perhaps she didn't have to…

That *look*… She'd seen it once before. When they had been lying in bed together. When Blake had been poised above her and right about to…

He cleared his throat.

'I…ah… I've been thinking,' he said slowly.

'Me, too,' she whispered back.

'About…you know…'

'Mmm.' Sam could feel colour seeping into her cheeks. 'I know.'

Blake glanced around, as if checking that no one was within earshot. 'And I know we agreed that it was a one-off, but…'

But?

Sam's balance suddenly felt a bit off kilter. As if her legs didn't want to hold her up any more. She focused on Blake's feet to steady herself. On those stupid, sexy cowboy boots.

'I don't do…relationships,' he muttered then.

'Neither do I,' Sam heard herself say.

And it was true, although not because it wasn't something she *wanted*. Eventually. Was it possible that it was the same for Blake? Did he think he wasn't relationship material simply because nothing had worked for him so far? What was holding him back?

She had to catch his gaze again and she knew that

her curiosity would be evident. What surprised her was seeing a reflection of that curiosity in *his* gaze.

'It was a one-off for more than the fact that neither of us do relationships,' she said. 'We work together. It would be unprofessional.'

Blake snorted softly. 'It's pretty unprofessional to be thinking about it all the time.'

Again, Sam seemed to see her own thoughts reflected in those dark eyes. He had been finding this as difficult as she had? Wow...

'And my reputation is bad enough already, I believe.'

She had to smile. 'I believe so, too.' She caught her lip between her teeth. 'So, it wouldn't really change anything, then...'

'No.'

Could Blake hear how hard her heart was thumping right now? 'Um...maybe we just need to get it out of our system, then.'

His voice was a low, sexy rumble. 'Are you suggesting what I think you're suggesting? Another... one-off?'

Sam shrugged, trying to cover the wash of excitement running through her body. Trying to make this seem not a big deal.

'Or a two-off. A three-off, if that's what it takes.' She took a deep breath and then held his gaze steadily as she gathered her words. Yes, she did want a real relationship that was going somewhere but it had to be with the right person and that person wasn't going to be Blake Cooper because she could sense that his demons were even bigger than hers.

But, oh...that didn't stop the *wanting*, did it? The lure of the bad boy...

'We both walk alone, Blake,' she said quietly, 'for whatever reason—and at some point we'll know it's enough. Maybe we just need to agree that when one of us reaches that point, the other walks away too. No regrets. No looking back.'

Somehow, she had moved closer to Blake as she'd been speaking, without realising it. Her head was tilted up so that she could hold his gaze and he was looking down.

Leaning down…as if he couldn't resist the urge to kiss her.

Then he straightened suddenly and Sam could feel the distance increasing between them with a wave of disappointment. Despair, almost…?

But he was smiling. That crooked, irresistibly charming smile of a man who knew exactly what he wanted and was quite confident he was going to get it.

'What are you doing tonight, Sam?'

Her mouth felt dry. 'Nothing important.'

'Give me your address and I'll come and get you. You up for a bike ride?'

Sam could almost hear her mother shrieking in horror at the thought but her rebellious streak wasn't about to be quashed. She might only get one more night with this man so why not add an extra thrill to it?

She could feel her smile stretching into a grin. 'Bring it on.'

CHAPTER SEVEN

WELL...

This was a bit of a turnaround.

Blake had always been the one to call the shots when it came to applying boundaries to any kind of relationships. He was the one to make it clear that it was never going to be anything long term and he was always the one to call 'time' when it was over.

It seemed like he had met his match because there was a real possibility that, this time, it would be Sam who decided when enough was enough.

And it was making him feel...competitive?

He was going to give Sam Braithwaite a night to remember. One that would—hopefully—have her begging for more.

Or maybe it was more a need to gain the usual kind of control he had over situations like this. If she wanted more, he would be back in the driver's seat and he could decide when it was time to pull the plug on this connection.

Whatever...it was a slightly disconcerting position to be in but to walk away from an offer of more of the best sex he'd ever had in his life with no strings attached? An impossible ask.

Could that mean he had already lost control?

Blake pushed that alarming notion into a headspace that he wasn't about to revisit. It was nonsense. If he really wanted to escape, he could end this at any time, however difficult it might be.

He just *didn't* want to. Not yet.

Speeding over the Sydney Harbour bridge later that night, with the sparkling lights of this beautiful city reflected in the expanse of water and Sam's arms tightly wound around his waist and her body pressing against his back, made Blake realise just how much he didn't want this to end.

He wanted this particular night to last for ever.

He knew the best restaurant, with a harbour view. Well, okay, it was only a café but that meant it didn't matter that they were wearing jeans. And it did have the best blues band he'd heard in a long time and he had a feeling that Sam might be up for a bit of dancing.

Slow dancing.

A kind of foreplay that could last for hours and build desire until it was unbearable for both of them.

Who would crack first and suggest that it was time to go home?

He'd changed the sheets on the big bed in the corner of his loft apartment. He'd even thought to put a bunch of candles nearby, ready to provide the kind of romantic light that would be just enough to see every delicious curve of Sam's body. To see the expression in her eyes when he took them both to paradise...

Oh, man...

He was going to crack first, wasn't he? Slowing for some traffic lights on the other side of the bridge, it took a surprising amount of self-control not to turn the bike around right then.

Instead he turned his head.

'You good?'

Sam's gloved fingers pressed more deeply into his abdomen. Her voice might be raised but it was still the sexiest sound he'd ever heard.

'Never better... Can we go a bit faster?'

She'd died and gone to bad boy heaven, that's what this was.

Right from the moment she'd walked out of the door of her apartment block and there he'd been. Sitting there, astride that big bike—like a modern-day Marlon Brando—holding out her helmet and gloves like an invitation to step into her fantasy world.

The sensation of speed, with her body exposed to the elements, was a thrill that was poignant because it gave her an unexpected jolt of connection with the big brother she missed so much. Finally, she could understand his love for this mode of transport—this heady mix of delight and danger. It made her tighten her hold on Blake's body and that gave her another kind of jolt. A feeling of safety.

No...it was more complex than that. She knew this was dangerous but, because she was with Blake, she simply didn't care. She was quite prepared to go anywhere he wanted to lead her.

Even if it turned out it was only for one more night.

She'd expected him to be taking her to where he lived. To where there was a private space with a bed. That was what this was all about, wasn't it?

Just sex. An attraction that apparently neither of them had had enough of yet.

But it seemed that Blake had other ideas.

The smoky, dimly lit, seaside café bar was a place she'd never heard of and probably would never have thought to enter even if she had, to be honest. But the garlic prawns and fries they ate with their fingers was the most delicious food ever. And the dancing…

Who knew that Blake Cooper was capable of dancing like this? It was just as well this place was so dimly lit, because it almost felt like they were making love with their clothes on. Every stroke of his hand down her back that ended in his cupping her bottom. Every press of his forehead against hers so that she could feel his breath on her face. Sam never wanted it to stop.

But she wanted it to stop right now. So they could go somewhere and be alone. To do what had been the intention of suggesting another 'one-off' and sate the need to be with each other in the most intimate way possible.

Blake didn't seem to be in any hurry, however. His body language was totally relaxed but, as the evening wore on, it didn't quite match the intensity she could feel in his gaze.

Finally, she couldn't stand it any longer. She twisted in his arms on the dance floor so that she could see his face properly.

'What time does this place close?'

'I think it stays open all night.'

Okay, there was a twinkle in that intensity now and Sam realised that he'd been playing with her. Waiting…

She shifted her hold, snaking one hand up to thread her fingers into his hair and pull his head close enough to touch her lips against his. Just the softest graze of contact and she kept her eyes open so that she could catch the moment he knew he'd lost whatever game he'd been playing.

He almost pushed her in his haste to leave the dance floor but that only made it impossible for Sam to hide her smile.

Not tonight. Busy.

Blake stared at the three words he had just tapped into his phone. His finger hovered over the 'send' button.

It would be the first time in nearly a month that he hadn't moved heaven and earth to try and make it possible to spend time with Sam.

And it was his mother's fault.

Okay, maybe an alarm bell had sounded a while back—after the third or fourth time, perhaps—when neither of them seemed at all inclined to walk away.

Why would they? The sex was fantastic and they enjoyed each other's company. There were no strings attached. Not even a heavy conversation that pried into his past or demanded forecasts concerning his future. It didn't make any difference to how well they worked together, either. He wasn't subjected to lingering, hopeful glances or 'accidental' meetings and Sam clearly hadn't told anybody about their arrangement because nobody had said anything. He hadn't even noticed a raised eyebrow from Emily's direction.

It felt like a game. Like the one he'd instigated on that first night, when he'd been teasing her on the dance floor and trying to make her crack first and suggest they go somewhere more private.

He'd lost that time. The stakes might be a little higher now but Blake didn't want to lose this time.

It was Sam's turn to crack first. She needed to be the one to walk away.

He'd expected it to have happened by now. They'd had their fun, hadn't they?

Alarm bells couldn't be ignored this time, thanks to his mother. Maybe Emily hadn't noticed anything different at work but Sharon Cooper wasn't so easily fooled.

'So, who is she this time?'

'What do you mean?'

'I know that look. It's not just that I haven't seen so much of you lately. You've got... I don't know...a sort of glow.'

Blake snorted. 'A *glow*? Good grief...'

Sharon sighed. 'You look happier, that's all. And that's a good thing.' She smiled as she got slowly to her feet to carry her plate to the sink. 'Maybe this time I'll get to meet her.'

And that's when it happened.

For the first time ever, Blake actually *wanted* to bring a girl home to meet his mother.

He'd been planning to text her after his visit here and see if she was free later tonight. But Sam had texted first to ask if *he* was free and the timing couldn't have been worse because the message had pinged onto his phone as he was sitting there, shocked at the very idea of inviting his current bed partner into his very private life.

Maybe he just had to take it on the chin and let Sam win again this time.

He was going to crack first.

It took just a tiny tap to send his text message on its way.

Now all he had to do was ease his conscience by making sure he *was* busy later. There were a couple of odd jobs that needed doing for his mother but, after that, Blake decided he would head to the gym. He hadn't had a good workout for far too long.

Not the sort you could do in public, anyway.

It was Harriet's fault.

Sam stood at the bottom of the most daunting climbing wall she'd ever seen but the impressive variety of overhangs and cracks wasn't what was making this so very difficult.

She'd had a go at indoor climbing before and loved it but it was a long time ago and the person who'd been her belayer had been her brother, Alistair. It had been unthinkable to go back without him. Or to play at the type of activity that had led to his death.

What she was grappling with now, as she clipped her belay device to the carabiner on her harness, was a weird mix of emotions.

A wave of grief for Alistair but a sense of pride, as well. She knew that he'd be applauding her right now. Or giving her a thumbs-up, anyway. For being courageous. For breaking through such a huge barrier.

For being so determined not to let it bother her that she couldn't be with Blake Cooper tonight and then doing something about it by grabbing her keys and heading straight out the door.

She wouldn't have thought of coming here in a million years, though, if she hadn't just had that conversation with Harriet.

'I've just had an email about the next training day for the SDR,' she'd told Sam. 'It's a rock-climbing exercise. Didn't you do that when you were a teenager?'

'It's so long ago, I've probably forgotten everything.'

'Nah… I'll bet it's like riding a bike. Muscle memory, you know? Maybe you could get a practice session in first, just to make sure, but I reckon it's the perfect time to put your name forward to try out. Want me to do it?'

Sam's phone sounded her text alert and she put Harriet on speaker phone so that she could change screens, knowing that it could be Blake answering her text.

Not tonight. Busy.

No apology. No suggestion of another day.

It felt like a dismissal. Was this how he was choosing to let her know that it was over?

If it was, there was nothing she could do about it. They'd made an agreement, hadn't they? When one of them reached that point, the other had to simply walk away too. No regrets. No looking back.

Where on earth had this wash of *fear* come from?

It wasn't as if she was in love with Blake. This had been supposed to be fun. A fantasy with the bad boy who broke everybody's hearts.

It certainly wasn't supposed to be threatening to break *her* heart.

And she wouldn't let it.

'Sam? You still there?'

She tuned back in to Harriet's voice. 'Yes…sorry… I was just thinking.'

'That it's time? I can put the wheels in motion for you to get a try out for the team.'

'You know what? I think you're right. And seeing as

I haven't got anything better to do tonight, I'm going to go to that gym near the hospital and see what their climbing wall looks like.'

'Go, you. Hey, if you see Pete there, can you give him a message?'

'Sure.'

'Tell him his dinner's getting cold.' Harriet laughed. 'And I'm getting hot.'

There'd been no sign of Pete when Sam had arrived and organised her climbing session and gear rental. She now had a harness on over her soft yoga pants and sports top, soft climbing shoes with grippy soles and a new chalk ball that she would use to keep her fingers and palms dry.

An instructor checked her harness and clipped the belay device to her carabiner. Her rope was also attached to an overhead anchor because she was doing what was called 'top roping'.

'Are you sure about using the auto belay? Seeing as it's your first time here, it might be better to have someone on the other end of the rope. If you can wait thirty minutes, I've got a free slot.'

'I'll have a go,' Sam told him. 'I have done it before and I'll just go the easiest route. That's the green holds, yes?'

'Yeah… Green, then orange and the most difficult is red. Easy to remember, like traffic lights. You sure you're okay with heights?'

Sam took a deep breath as she glanced up at just how high this wall was. It was safe, she reminded herself. If she missed a hold she could only fall a short distance before the belay device would lock the rope. It might be embarrassing but she wasn't going to get anything more than a bump or a graze from the textured material that looked remarkably like natural rocks. She grinned at the staff member.

'Soon find out, I guess.'

'If you get stuck, someone will be able to help. Main thing is not to panic.'

'Got it. Thanks for your help.'

'I'll check on you. Offer's still open for a training session later if you want it.'

The first few holds were easy with good-sized pegs coming out from the wall or boulders that had plenty of room for a foot or hand hold. Sam took it slowly and carefully but it seemed no time at all before she was quite a long way from ground level.

She didn't look down, however. Or up. She remembered that from those sessions with Alistair so long ago. Her focus only needed to be on the next green marker. One step at a time. There were people here who were at the top of this game and they'd set this route. Beginner's level but it still required physical effort and a determined mind set.

Halfway up the wall, Sam wobbled, clinging to the wall like a crab and pausing to take several steadying, deep breaths.

This was a lot harder than climbing over a huge pile of debris and remembering to keep three points of contact with the surface at all times. An image of Blake filled her head for a moment then, and Sam realised it was the first time she'd thought about him since she'd arrived at the gym.

That had to be a good thing, didn't it?

And maybe it would be a good thing if their time together *had* finished. It would mean less of a complication for when she joined the SDR team. She'd just have to learn to do without him in her life in other ways.

She'd just have to get over this fear that it might be a lot more difficult than she might have expected.

Like this climb was threatening to be now that she wasn't concentrating.

Sam forced herself to focus. *You can do this*, she told herself firmly. *Imagine that it's Alistair holding your rope. That he's yelling at you now to get on with the next hold. Asking if you've fallen asleep or something...*

The thought made her smile. Glance down for a heartbeat, even, as though she would really see her brother down there.

What she did see were other people on the wall below her. Someone was bouldering with no ropes, on a route close to the floor with crash mats beneath them. And someone else was lead climbing where they clipped their rope onto a series of points bolted to the wall rather than overhead. It was a lot harder than top roping and this person was using the red markers as well.

Clearly an expert. For a moment, he was hidden by an overhang and all Sam could see were his fingers as he found a grip that would be enough to haul his body weight through space until he could hook a foot over the edge.

Wow...

If he lost his grip, he'd fall to where the previous clip point was and that could be enough to cause quite a serious injury.

She found she was holding her breath as the foot appeared and then muscles bulged in bare arms as more of his body appeared and then twisted. For a moment, he was in a sitting position on the overhang, but he didn't pause to take a breath, instantly crouching and looking up to see where his new clip point or hold was.

Her breath came out in an incredulous huff.

Blake?

Had she said his name aloud, or had he just heard it anyway?

Or was she just close enough to where his route was leading him?

Whatever. His gaze snagged on hers and then away again, as if he wasn't even surprised.

But he came sideways. As if it didn't matter in the least that he was choosing orange holds instead of red. Or that his clip point was getting further and further away.

'What the heck are *you* doing here?'

'Climbing a wall.'

'I've never seen you here before.'

'First time,' Sam admitted.

'And you're doing it by yourself?' Blake looked incredulous. 'Are you crazy?'

'I've done it before. I just wanted to see how much I remembered.'

'Why?'

For a moment, Sam completely forgot that she was a human spider quite a long way from a solid surface. She held Blake's gaze and tried not to fall into the pull she could feel from his body. From the sweat-slicked skin that his tank top left exposed. From that intense heat in his eyes.

'I heard that the next SDR training session involves some climbing. Harriet's going to put my name forward and I intend to be ready for it.'

The corner of Blake's mouth curled upwards as he shook his head. 'I've got to hand it to you, Sam. You don't give up when you want something, do you?'

'I don't expect you do, either.'

The smile vanished. 'Not unless I have to.'

Was he referring to his dream of joining MSF? Was it a warning, perhaps, that Sam might have to give up on joining the team because he had no intention of allowing her to try out for it?

She held his gaze for a moment longer. *You can't do that to me*, she told him silently. *It wouldn't be fair...*

'Everything okay up there?' The instructor who'd helped Sam had noticed their lack of movement.

'All good, Dave,' Blake called back. His gaze slid back to Sam. 'Or is it?'

'You tell me,' she said. 'Are you going to let me try out for the team?'

'Is that what you really want?' His voice was low. Sexy. As if he was asking about something she wanted him to do to her body and Sam found her lips parting. She had to dampen them with her tongue before she could respond.

'Yes,' she whispered. 'Yes, please...'

His gaze jerked away from hers. Shifted to a point on the wall she couldn't see. And then he started moving away from her. She heard his voice clearly enough, however.

'Guess we'll see you at the training session then.'

Yes...

The excitement his words generated was enough to have Sam conquering the last few holds on her route as if it had only been yesterday that she'd done anything like this. She was still some distance from the very top of the wall but this was the beginner's level and it was high enough. She needed to start going down now and that was going to be slower and harder.

Blake was right at the top. Tackling another overhang.

And, as Sam watched, he lost his grip. For a heart-stopping instant, he was swinging, holding onto the edge of the overhang with only one hand.

Okay, he was clipped in to one side of the obstacle and he wouldn't fall far but that didn't stop the trickle of horror that raced down Sam's spine.

The impact of knowing how she would feel if he got injured. Or killed…

And it was in that instant that she realised just how wrong she'd been.

She hadn't believed that she was in love with Blake Cooper?

Who the heck had she been trying to kid?

CHAPTER EIGHT

THE SMALL GROUP of people looked much bigger once they were clustered together in the limited space available on the top of this cliff.

Members of Bondi Bayside's specialist disaster relief team had carpooled out of Sydney to meet in the Blue Mountains and have an intensive day's training in abseiling under the direction of an outdoor sports education company—a combination of increasing their skill sets and a bonding exercise for the team.

As always, with training days and meetings they had been joined by people outside the core team of medics who were part of the available pool for emergencies and often worked closely with the team on any callouts. Harriet's boyfriend, Pete, was here and so was Jack Evans, a young paramedic who had joined at the same time as Harriet and was passionate about rescue work.

One person had a rather different goal, however. Samantha Braithwaite was here to try out for the team. Harriet had put her name forward and both Luc Braxton and Kate Mitchell hadn't hesitated to second the nomination. This was the opportunity for everybody to get to know her. To see what kind of skills she already had but, more importantly, what her attitude was like and how well she communicated with and respected the people who were already an integral part of the team.

And that was the only reason she was here.

'Does anyone need help with their Prusik loop?'

The extra loop of rope, secured by a double fisherman's knot to link the main rope to a harness, was sometimes called a 'dead man's handle' and it was an essential safety measure.

Sam was nearby and Jack was showing her how to wrap the loop around her rope and fasten it to the carabiner.

'Make sure you've locked it,' Blake told her.

Her glance flicked upwards. 'Sure.'

She looked nervous, he decided. But excited as well. He wanted to give her an encouraging smile. To tell her that she was amazing and she could do this.

Instead, he moved away to check Kate's harness.

Sam was not going to be treated any differently from anyone else who was trying out for the team. Whatever had been between them was over.

Sam's choice.

She'd told him that being on this team was the thing she wanted most of all.

Okay, maybe he hadn't spelt out that nothing could happen again between them on a personal level if she joined the SDR but everyone knew that he disapproved of relationships between team members because they had the potential to interfere with critical decision-making procedures. He was keeping an eye on how Pete and Harriet worked together these days and, if he noticed any hint of them being distracted by each other, he might have to suggest that one of them step away from the team.

And he had the feeling that Sam understood that.

The way she understood a lot of stuff he'd never actually talked about with her.

Like his private life—and his past—being exactly that. Private.

Like the fact that he was never going to have anyone else dependent on him. At some point in his future, although of course he hoped that it was a long way away, he was going to be completely free—to do what he wanted with his life, wherever that might be in the world. To create a new type of prison with a long-term relationship, let alone a wife and children, was unthinkable.

Blake moved past where Harriet and Luc were lining up to be amongst the first people to lower themselves down this cliff. They were laughing about something, totally at ease in each other's company, as good friends always were.

As he and Sam had been?

What about the other things she had understood about him?

Like how deep that driving need for as much freedom and independence as he could find was?

The way she made him feel valued and respected because of it?

The feeling that his life was bigger and better and so much more exciting when he was with her and could see himself reflected in her eyes.

The way she touched him. Not just physically, although missing that was an ache he couldn't escape from at the moment, but somewhere deep in his soul as well. A place that nobody other than his mother had ever really touched.

He hadn't expected to be missing her this much. The shock of wanting to take her home to meet his mother and the conviction that it was time to step away had worn off, taking with it the relief that Sam had made the first move to end things by choosing to try out for the team.

She hadn't texted him since. At work, it was like it had been when she'd first arrived, with no hint of anything personal in any interaction they had. She was professional and cheerful and…

And it had been killing him, inch by inch.

One of the instructors was coaching Harriet to climb carefully over the cliff edge and get into position for the descent.

'Keep your feet wide apart. One hand on the rope above and the other is going to control your Prusik loop. Now lean back into your harness.'

She and Pete had been careful to stay away from each other as the team had prepared for this. If they could manage a serious relationship and both be part of this team, why couldn't he?

Because it wasn't an option, that's why.

The fact that he was even considering bending his own rules to accommodate more than a friendship with Sam as a team member was enough of a red flag. Besides, a serious relationship had never been a consideration, not only for him but for Sam as well. It had been a perfect alliance. Great sex—okay, the best sex *ever*—and not a single string.

So why did he have the disturbing sensation that he was still tied to this woman—not with a string that could be broken easily enough but with a rope heavy enough to anchor a damn battleship?

His problem. Sam didn't seem to be suffering.

If she made the grade and joined the team, she would probably have no issues with dismissing their shared history but, for the first time in his life, Blake was less confident that he could move on so easily.

It might be a relief if she didn't make the grade because keeping a professional distance would be easier in a controlled environment like the emergency department.

But the pull was still there. He *wanted* to see her. To work with her. To be reminded of the person he believed he was when she was close. And he didn't want to be any kind of obstacle to Sam becoming the person she wanted so much to be. She hadn't done anything wrong. Far from it. And she deserved to be treated with the same respect and fairness that he would treat anyone else who came to try out for the team.

Blake could feel the tension in his body.

He needed to step back and deal with his own conflict in his own time.

If Sam was good enough, she could be invited to be a part of this and he would cope. Somehow.

If she wasn't, she wouldn't be invited.

It was that simple.

Sam was one of the last people to take her turn abseiling down this cliff.

Was this a kindness on the part of the group—so that she could watch everybody else manage it and gain confidence for her own performance? Or, and she suspected this might be the case, would they all be down at the bottom watching and assessing how well she could cope with a challenge that was both physical and mental?

Harriet had been down for a long time now but Pete was only just climbing over the edge to take his turn.

The instructors here probably had no idea that those two were a couple but Sam had come here in their car and they'd explained why it would be like that.

'There's an unspoken rule that SDR members do not hook up with each other,' Harriet had said. 'And if they do, one of them might be expected to step down from the team.'

'Whose rule? No, let me guess… Blake Cooper's?'

'Yep.'

'But Pete isn't a staff member at Bondi Bayside. Why would the rule apply to him?'

'Because we go to the same callouts. Because personal relationships can influence decision making. Or be a distraction.'

'Yeah…' Pete had been smiling. 'Harriet might put herself in danger to save me at the expense of victims.'

Harriet had laughed. 'Or you might get overcome with lust and forget what it is you're supposed to be shoring up or something.'

'Happens all the time, babe.'

Sam had tuned out of their playful banter.

Was this why she hadn't heard a word from Blake ever since that night at the gym when he'd agreed to let her try out for the team? Why he seemed as distant as he had been when she'd first started working at Bondi Bayside?

Was that what the intensity had really been about? Had she been making a choice between being on the team and being with him?

Sam cast a quick glance over her shoulder to where Blake was chatting to one of the people who ran this outdoor education centre.

If she'd known that, would she have made the same choice?

The excitement of getting within touching distance of her goal of joining the team should have been enough to fill the gaping hole in her life that had appeared after that night at the gym.

But it wasn't.

'You all set?'

'I think so.'

'Let me just check all the locks on your carabiners.' The instructor reached for the big metal loop that was attaching Sam's belay plate to the centre of her harness. She couldn't help casting one more glance towards Blake. Any moment now and she would be stepping over that cliff.

In front of him. Even more than doing well enough to be invited to join this team, right now what Sam wanted most of all was for Blake to be proud of her.

It intensified the ache that had been with her for over a week now. The ache that was an apparently forlorn longing to be with him again. Not just physically—this went so much deeper than that.

How could she have made a choice between being with Blake Cooper and being on the team? In a way it was impossible to separate the two because, to Sam, Blake was the spirit of this team.

Independent. Intelligent. Brave.

The things she longed to be herself. To be brave enough to get rid of any of the shreds of that cotton wool she had wrapped herself in ever since Alistair had died.

Smart enough to keep herself as safe as possible when they were all gone.

And independent enough to cope with the fears of the people she loved—her parents—but not to let their fears make her less than the person she was capable of being.

So, even if she had known there was a choice, it wouldn't have been a simple one. And, if she could have been strong enough, the choice she needed to make would have still been the same. She would have chosen the team. Maybe being with Blake could have been enough to make her the person she wanted to be but it wouldn't have lasted, would it? He had only done what she had known he would do at some point. He had walked away for no obvious reason except that maybe they had become too close for his comfort.

If she made the team, at least that could last for as long as *she* needed, or wanted, it to.

'You're good to go,' the instructor told her. 'Let's get you over the edge.'

Cautiously, Sam sat on the edge of the cliff, her legs dangling. As she turned her body to lower herself and let her harness take her weight, she could see that Blake had stopped talking and he was watching her every move.

A split second of eye contact and then his lips curved into a smile so subtle that anyone else might not have noticed.

But Sam did.

And it cut straight through her nerves.

Okay…maybe she wouldn't have chosen the team.

She would have chosen even a little more time to be close to the man she loved *this* much...

Blake waited at the top of the cliff, hanging there in his harness, holding his ropes but looking down. The rest of the team were at the bottom of the cliff. Some were looking up, also watching, but others were moving away to get ready for their next challenge—a bit of bouldering.

Sam was doing well. A little cautious with her rope management, which made her slow, but that wasn't a bad thing.

She was about halfway down when Blake felt something odd.

A tremor that he could feel through his ropes that were anchored to a bolt deep in a rock well back from this cliff face.

And then the instructor, who would be the last to follow this group down, let out a warning shout and threw himself sideways—away from the cliff edge.

An edge that Blake could see was crumbling.

Not much. It was just a medium-sized rock that was coming free from those around it but it was having a domino effect on others and, to his horror, Blake found himself watching the birth of a rock fall.

He yelled his own warning to those on the ground, sent out a silent prayer that the anchor for his own ropes would stay strong and then held his breath as his focus sharpened with such intensity he could feel all the tiny muscles around his eyes contract.

'*Sam*... Get in close...'

She probably couldn't hear his shout because the

falling rocks were making their own noise now. A terrifying rumble and crashing.

But she was doing the right thing, not looking up so that her helmet could provide some protection. Flattening herself by clinging to the cliffside so that the rocks were more likely to bounce past. He followed the track of the rocks that were bouncing past her at a reassuring distance, to where those on the ground were running to get themselves clear of danger.

Except for one person.

Harriet was staring up and he could see the horrified expression on her face even from this distance.

Sam was a close friend. She'd been the person who'd put forward the nomination that Sam join this training session.

And now her friend could be in serious trouble. Maybe she felt responsible?

After what felt like the slow motion of watching this begin, it now seemed as if things were on fast forward. The rocks had gone past Sam apparently without injuring her or damaging her ropes but they were gathering momentum as they crashed to ground level.

He could see Jack grab Harriet's arm and pull her away. He saw her start to run.

He saw her trip and fall.

And then he heard someone scream as a rock looked like it landed right on top of her.

A jerk on his rope was enough to reassure Blake that his anchor was still solid. With a sense of urgency unlike anything he could remember experiencing, he let his rope slide and was halfway down the cliff to reach Sam in no more than a few, huge jumps.

He needed to get right down to the bottom to where people were rushing towards Harriet.

But he couldn't go past Sam. She was so still. So frozen. Something had to be wrong and it made him feel sick to his stomach.

This was exactly why he hadn't wanted her on the team in the first place. Because she would be a distraction to whoever got involved with her.

That *he* was that person himself was bad enough.

That he felt the overwhelming urge to protect her above anything else was a wake-up call that hit him as hard as one of those rocks had apparently hit Harriet. Her safety was more important than Harriet's in this instant.

More important than his own.

He *had* to protect her. Had to let her know that she could trust him.

That she could always depend on him.

Dear Lord…he was in *love* with her…

Something he had believed he was safe from ever having to experience.

He didn't get that close to people. *Ever.*

Blake wasn't feeling sick any more.

He felt angry. Angry that Sam had managed to get past his safety walls. Angry that she might be injured.

Just…*angry*…

She couldn't move.

Sam had heard the warning shout from above. She had seen the rocks starting to fall. The terrified whimper that came from her throat was like no sound she had ever heard herself make before.

No…that wasn't true. She *had* made it once before,

hadn't she? When she'd been told the terrible news about Alistair.

Killed in a rock fall.

What she was seeing now was quite possibly exactly what her beloved brother had seen in the last few seconds of his life.

She was about to die herself, wasn't she?

Her poor parents...

Terror mixed with the most astonishingly powerful wave of grief. For her parents, for her brother, for herself. It was too big for any kind of release from something as simple as tears. It was crushing her. Making it impossible to breathe. Blurring her vision so that the shape appearing beside her was unrecognisable. Even the voice could barely penetrate the silent scream that was holding her prisoner.

'Sam... *Sam*... Are you listening to me?'

She tried to focus. To hear what Blake was saying.

This was *Blake*... If anyone could keep her safe it would be this man.

'You have to move. The rock fall is over. You're not hurt but we have to get down. *Now*...'

Sam tried to nod her head but that only triggered a shake that instantly spread to the rest of her body. She knew what she needed to do but she couldn't make her hands co-operate. Or her legs.

So she tried to speak but the only sound that emerged was an echo of the distress that had swallowed her the instant she'd seen those rocks begin to fall.

Blake wasn't saying anything now, either. Sam felt his arm slide around her body as he positioned himself behind her. Somehow, he managed to keep her against his body with one arm as he worked both his own ropes and hers with his other arm.

The first drop was difficult and they stopped with a jerk. The second jerky movement finally seemed to break through what had paralysed Sam. Blake was trying to keep her safe but she had to do that for herself, didn't she?

She always had. To protect the people she loved.

Her parents.

Blake...

'You can let me go.' Her voice was rough. 'I can do this now.'

'I don't think so.'

'Let me *go*, Blake.' She pushed his hand away from her ropes and took hold of them herself. 'I can look after myself. I don't need you.'

'Fine.' Blake's arm disappeared as he swung himself to one side.

A minute later they were both at ground level but any relief Sam felt for finishing the abseil without his assistance vanished as her feet hit solid ground and she crumpled because her legs refused to hold her up. She was still shaking. She wanted to apologise to Blake. To try and explain what had happened to make her freeze like that, even, but any words died on her lips as she looked up at him.

Because he looked...angry?

He held her gaze for a long moment. A searching look, as if he was trying to figure out what was wrong with her. And then he gave his head a single, dismissive shake and turned away. The sound of him unclipping his ropes and discarding them was like a punctuation mark. The sound of his boots on rock as he walked swiftly away made it feel completely final.

Sam had never needed human contact more than she did at this moment. She had never felt more alone.

Where was Harriet?

She raked the scene with a wild glance but she couldn't see her best friend anywhere. Nobody was even looking in her direction. They were all clustered to one side, the group opening and then closing again to swallow Blake.

Sam pulled her knees up and then caught them with her arms. It gave her a space to bury her head for a moment. To try and get control of the shaking. To banish what felt like a tsunami of tears that was trying to relentlessly close in on her.

'Harriet?' Blake dropped to his knees beside the limp figure on the ground.

Her face was deathly pale, which made her freckles stand out. Pete was crouched beside her, one hand resting on her shoulder.

'Sorry,' she whispered. 'I'm really sorry, Blake.'

'What on earth for?' Blake had taken hold of her hand but he was using his index finger to feel for her radial pulse.

'I've wrecked our training day...'

The pulse was rapid but steady enough and strong enough to tell him that her blood pressure was not dangerously low.

'Don't be daft...we get to practise some first aid, too, now.'

His gaze was raking his body but he knew that others would have already completed a primary survey. He glanced up. Jack was looking almost as pale as Harriet and he had Luc right beside him.

'Compound fracture,' Luc told him. 'Tib and fib. She caught a direct hit from a decent-sized rock.'

Luc sounded calm. As though this was nothing that couldn't be dealt with easily. The look he was giving Blake, however, told him that this was more serious and when he dropped his gaze to Harriet's left leg, his heart sank.

It was a mess. An open wound with visible pieces of shattered bone. The risk of infection was huge. The risk of Harriet actually losing her lower leg looked considerable, as well. The potential for irreparable blood supply and nerve damage was obvious.

'Limb baselines?'

'Weak but present.'

Well, that was something. It meant that not all the nerves or blood vessels were damaged beyond repair. 'Is that the only injury?'

Luc nodded. 'Seems to be.'

Jack glared at Blake. 'It's enough, isn't it?'

'It's okay.' Pete seemed to be avoiding looking anywhere near Harriet's leg. 'These guys know what they're doing, babe. It'll be okay, you'll see...'

Someone pushed their way through the silent, horrified group.

'Here's the first-aid kit. And the helicopter's been dispatched. ETA about fifteen minutes.'

Luc was ripping open the zips on the kit. They needed IV gear to get a line in and give Harriet some pain relief. They needed sterile dressings to cover the gaping wound. And they needed a splint. There wasn't much more they could do here. Harriet needed to get to a hospital as fast as possible and into Theatre with the best orthopaedic surgeon that could be found.

They could hear the beat of the approaching helicopter by the time they had Harriet ready for transport. The silent group of onlookers moved back to get out of the way of the paramedics and their stretcher. It took only another minute or two to have Harriet secured but she didn't seem happy. Her head turned from one side to the other and she cried out when the stretcher was lifted.

'No...wait... Where's Sam?'

Blake felt the muscles in his jaw tighten. Sam had not only demonstrated how completely unsuitable she was to join this team, she hadn't even come near her friend who was the one who'd actually been injured in this disaster.

He turned his head to speak to Luc.

'There's no way we're going to let Sam join the SDR,' he said in a low voice. 'She froze up there. Couldn't even follow instructions.'

'*Sam...*' Harriet's call was almost a sob.

'I'm here, Harry...' Sam's quiet voice came from right behind Blake's shoulder.

She moved straight past him. She didn't even glance at him but he knew that she'd heard what he'd said to Luc.

'Oh, God...' Sam was crouching beside the stretcher. 'I'm *so* sorry... I... I messed up.'

'Not as much as I did.' But Harriet was trying to smile. 'Can you come with me, Sam? I'm... I'm really scared...'

'But... I should come with you,' Pete said.

'You hate blood.' Harriet's voice wobbled. 'And hos-

pitals, come to that. I'll see you later...when everything's been fixed, okay?'

'Okay...if that's what you want.' Pete's concerned
frown didn't quite disguise his relief.

'Of course I'll come...' But Sam looked towards the
paramedics. 'Is there enough room?'

'We can take two extras. No more.'

'I'm coming, too.' Blake ignored Sam, turning to
Luc instead. 'Can you take charge now? If people want
to carry on with the next climb, that's fine. It'll be a
while before we can co-ordinate another day like this
but if you decide to wrap things up, that's fine too. Is
there anyone who can get my bike back to town?'

'I can.' Jack stepped forward 'No problem.'

'Don't stop the day,' Harriet said. 'Not on my account. That would make me feel even worse than I do
now. Sam...you don't mind missing the rest of it, do
you?'

'Of course she doesn't.' Blake couldn't help the acer-
bic comment. 'She's probably relieved.'

Sam said nothing but he noticed the way her chin
lifted a little as she followed Harriet's stretcher to the
waiting helicopter.

Any remorse for that less than kind comment, or
that she'd overheard him dismissing her bid to join
this team, evaporated. She couldn't blame him if she
was feeling bad. She hadn't even *tried* to deal with that
situation on the cliff face in any meaningful way—just
pushed him away when he'd been trying to help. She
had ruined any chance of acceptance all by herself.

What seemed worse was that she wasn't the person
that Blake had believed her to be.

Where was the courage and determination he'd seen

her display on that USAR course? The woman he'd inadvertently fallen in love with?

Maybe something good would come from the catastrophe this day had become.

It would be so much easier to move on now.

CHAPTER NINE

SAM CHOSE TO use the waiting room near Theatre to wait until Harriet's surgery was over.

Blake chose not to. It could be hours and there was no way he was going to sit in a confined space—alone—with Sam.

'Please call me as soon as she's taken through to Recovery,' he told the staff member who'd shown them the room. 'I'll be in the building.'

He didn't look back but he knew that Sam had gone into the empty room with its comfortable chairs and water cooler and supply of magazines.

He knew that she was looking almost as scared as Harriet had looked when they'd finally wheeled her into Theatre. Terrified of the possibility that she could wake up and find she was missing half of her leg.

Blake actually stopped before he got to the elevators. Turned around, even.

But then he turned back and punched the button to summon the lift.

He had to fight this...

This *pull* to go back to that room. To comfort Sam. To support her. Just to be there with her and hold her hand.

Because, if he didn't fight, he'd be giving in to the last thing he'd ever wanted in his life. To invite somebody into his world who was so important to him they could shape the whole direction of his future.

He'd be throwing away what had always been his dream.

Complete freedom.

He couldn't do that.

He wouldn't allow himself to do that.

Besides...there were things that needed doing. Like finishing the accident report and other paperwork that had been postponed in order to fast track Harriet through Emergency. And he wanted to have a better look at those X-rays.

A comminuted fracture that made it hard to count the number of breaks in her bones. How on earth were they going to manage to put that back together? That it was already an open wound made it all so much worse. Even with the benefit of IV antibiotics that had already been started, it would take luck to stave off an infection that could destroy more tissue and risk more, debilitating, nerve and blood vessel damage.

He managed to spend over an hour doing that. And then he spent another twenty minutes or more texting Luc to keep him informed about Harriet and to find out what was happening now up in the Blue Mountains. Everybody was worried, apparently, but the consensus of opinion had been that they couldn't waste the resources that had gone into arranging this training session and they were going to see it through.

Still there was no call to tell him that Harriet's surgery was over.

Was Sam still sitting there alone in that room?

Had anyone taken her a coffee? Or something to eat? He didn't like the idea of her being hungry or thirsty.

If he took her something himself, would that mean that he'd lost this internal battle?

No. Blake could feel his frown deepening as he shoved his phone back in his pocket and started walking. It wouldn't actually make any difference if he gave in to this pull because she wasn't about to consider being with him for the rest of her life, was she?

She didn't do relationships. She'd told him that. Or rather she'd agreed with him when he'd said that. When they had been negotiating another 'one-off'. Or a two-off or however many it took before one of them had had enough.

We both walk alone, Blake. For whatever reason...

Why had he never found out what *her* reason was?

It couldn't possibly be as solid as his reason. She hadn't grown up struggling to achieve every step towards a better life or watching someone she loved sacrifice their life for her. She was warm and caring and deserved to be with someone who would reward those attributes by giving them right back to her. And no man in his right mind wouldn't have been attracted from the moment he laid eyes on the most gorgeous woman in the world. She would have had more choice than any woman dreamed of, surely?

So why did she choose to be alone? He didn't understand.

Any more than he understood why she'd lost control so completely on that cliffside. It just didn't make sense. He'd seen her on the climbing wall that night. She knew what she was doing and she had the courage to tackle anything.

He'd seen her at the USAR course and he would have trusted her to face anything and not panic. Blake had been in dodgy situations often enough to learn to trust instincts like this and right now they were telling him that her reaction to that rock fall was completely out of character.

And he had damned her for it.

Guilt was the last straw that tipped the balance in any internal fight that had been ongoing. That, and the idea he'd had that Sam might be hungry.

Was that why his pacing the corridors had somehow brought him so close to the staff cafeteria? There was nothing to stop him getting some takeaway coffees and some food but what would Sam like to eat? There were sandwiches on offer and hot things like sausage rolls and slices of pizza but there were lots of other things like muffins and cookies and he couldn't decide what she would choose if she was standing here herself.

The need to feed Sam had suddenly become the most important thing on his agenda. And he wanted to know what her choice would be so that this wouldn't be so difficult on another occasion. Because there *would* be another occasion in the future. There had to be...

Blake grabbed a handful of paper bags and a pair of tongs to start lifting items from the cabinets.

The worst thing about waiting alone was that there was nowhere to hide from yourself.

No way to distract yourself from thoughts that were dark enough to feed on themselves and become even darker as minutes built into an hour and then started to count down the next.

Nothing to counteract the 'what ifs'.

Like what if she hadn't tried to play down her eagerness to participate and had been one of the first people to go down that cliff? The shock of that rock fall and its effect on her would have been completely private. Something she could have analysed later until she could understand it and excuse herself and then move forward, knowing that she would be able to cope if it ever happened again.

She wouldn't be feeling so disappointed in herself for demonstrating such weakness.

Or so gutted that Blake clearly despised her for it. She could still hear the note of disgust in his voice.

'There's no way we're going to let Sam join the SDR... She froze up there...couldn't even follow instructions...'

And what if Harriet lost her leg? She'd lose everything she loved most about her life. Her job, her work with the SDR team, even the joy she got from surfing and swimming. All the things that made her who she was and the things that she shared with Pete. How would he cope with a disabled partner? Sam had the horrible feeling that he wouldn't cope at all well. He hadn't actually wanted to come with her in the helicopter, had he?

That was incomprehensible. Imagine if it had been Blake who'd been injured? Nothing would have kept her from staying as close as possible. Even if he hadn't wanted her to...

It only needed a split second to change a life, didn't it?

To change many lives, in fact...

How different would her own life have been if

Alistair had not died on that mountain? And her parents' lives.

Oddly, the grief that thoughts of her brother always triggered seemed different now. Because she was so worried about Harriet or sad that things with Blake had ended so badly? Or was it that the extraordinary flood of emotion that had been triggered as she'd been caught in the horror of that rock fall had somehow released something that had been buried for what felt like for ever?

Not that Sam could figure out exactly what that might be but there was a sense that it was something peaceful. Like acceptance, perhaps?

Like knowing that random things could happen to anyone no matter how careful they tried to be. That a life could be lost—or changed for ever—in a heartbeat so you had to make the most of every moment and not let others hold you back, no matter how much you loved them.

Blake was going to hold her back now, wasn't he? Could she fight that and ask for another opportunity to prove herself as competent enough to be considered for the team?

Did she *want* to fight the man she loved?

As if her thoughts had somehow conjured him up, Blake appeared in the doorway of this small room. He was balancing a tray of cups in one hand and held a carrier bag stuffed with smaller paper bags in the other.

'I…ah…thought you might be hungry.'

He put the tray of cups down on top of the pile of magazines Sam hadn't thought to leaf through. And then he started unloading the carrier bag onto the low table.

'I wasn't sure what you'd like,' he said.

Such a casual tone, as if it was a normal thing to buy up what looked like half the contents of the cafeteria. Plastic triangles of sandwiches, the tops of muffins and doughnuts to be seen inside paper bags. The smell of something hot and savoury like a sausage roll or those mini mince pies.

He'd thought she might be hungry?

A single sandwich would have been enough.

This felt like it was far more significant than offering food.

It felt like...a peace offering?

She looked up from the feast that had been set out in front of her. Yes...there was something in Blake's eyes that told her she wasn't imagining anything. That this was more than a peace offering, even.

He wanted to give her food because he wanted to show her that he cared.

A lot...

That...that he *loved* her?

A bubble of something Sam couldn't identify grew inside her chest with such intensity it felt like it was going to explode.

And, just at the point of explosion, two things happened.

The pager on Blake's belt sounded. Three buzzes, a short silence and then three more. Sam knew what that meant. A Code One callout for the SDR. Some disaster was changing who knew how many lives out there in this instant of time.

A nurse appeared in the doorway as the pager was sounding for the second time.

'Harriet's in Recovery. She's asking for you guys.'

Blake was on his phone as they walked towards Recovery.

'What is it, Mabel? No, the team's still out in the Blue Mountains as far as I know… Good grief… really…? I know, but I'm here on my own… Try calling Luc and then get back to me asap…'

He cut the call as they neared the IV pumps and other equipment a phone could potentially interfere with. Harriet was drowsy but she managed a smile.

'I've still got my leg,' she murmured.

'That's a great start.' Sam blinked back tears as she stooped to kiss her friend.

Blake was looking at the external fixation on Harriet's leg. 'That's some impressive scaffolding, mate. Does it hurt?'

Harriet shook her head, her eyes drifting shut. 'Morphine's great stuff…'

'I can't stay,' Blake said apologetically. 'There's been a callout and I'm the only one available. Everyone else is still out in the mountains.'

'What's happened?' Sam asked.

'Explosion and fire on a cruise ship that's just out of Sydney harbour. They're sending the coast guard but they need a medical first response. I doubt that any of the other team members will be back in town soon enough to be useful. Sorry…but I have to go.'

Harriet's eyes opened again. Her voice sounded clearer.

'Take Sam with you,' she said.

Blake froze and Sam cringed. Was he going to tell Harriet that he'd dismissed any chance of her being part of this elite team? That she had made a fool of herself by not even being able to follow instructions?

But his gaze caught hers.

'Do you want to come?'

He knew he was taking a risk. But he was prepared to give her another chance?

He wouldn't do that unless he actually believed that she could do it.

Sam could feel her confidence take the biggest leap ever as she sank into that gaze for a heartbeat. And then one more. If Blake believed she could do it then she *could*.

'Yes,' she said quietly. 'I do...'

If someone had been at all inclined to panic, this scenario would have triggered it.

There were steep, narrow metal staircases to climb down into the engine rooms of this huge ship and it was rolling enough to make it difficult. Power was out, so the only illumination was coming from the lamps on their helmets. It was hot and the air was thick with an unpleasant mix of smoke and oil. To top it off, there were strange noises around them with eeric, muted shrieks and banging from metallic structures that were probably cooling down or had been damaged by the explosion and fire.

Sam hadn't missed a beat so far. Blake paused at the bottom of what was hopefully the last tube-like stairwell and watched her come after him. It had been the longest ladder so far and she had to be getting tired but there was no hint of any hesitation. If anything, she was climbing down faster now. She actually jumped to miss the last rung.

'Is this it? Is this where they're trapped?'

The ship's doctor had met them as they'd crouched and run from where the helicopter had landed on the top deck. He'd briefed them as they'd started their journey deeper into the ship.

'One person's been killed and we've got several others with minor injuries and burns. Most we can manage in our hospital but there's one burns case that needs evacuating.'

'You want us to transport him?'

'If this helicopter can take him back, I've got a nurse who can go with him. There's a bigger problem we need you guys to help with, if you can.'

'What's that?' Blake cast a sideways glance at Sam. She was focused intently on what they were being told. Ready for anything, judging by the serious, determined look on her face.

'There's a couple of people unaccounted for. We think they're trapped somewhere in the engine room behind where the explosion happened. The captain won't let anybody go in there—he says it's too dangerous.'

Blake felt the knot of tension in his gut tighten.

Did he want Sam going in there?

He had no choice now. He had offered her this second chance and this was what the SDR team did. They headed into disasters, not away from them, with the intention of saving lives that might otherwise be lost.

But he was going in first. If it *was* too dangerous, he could change his mind and order Sam to wait on the sidelines.

And now, here they were.

A very challenging environment but it didn't feel too dangerous. Yet.

The man who'd been their guide—one of the ship's fire officers—was still near the bottom of the ladder and he was the one to answer Sam's query.

'We think so. They would have been in that direction. In the next section. We couldn't get near because of the fire but that's all out now and it should be cooling down a bit but...be careful. There's a lot of shredded metal over there.'

Blake nodded. 'Hear that, Sam?'

'Yep.'

'Stay behind me.'

'Okay.'

'Let me know on the radio when you need assistance,' the fire officer said. 'I've got my team ready and stretchers and things available.'

Blake moved forward slowly. The rolling movement of the ship made it even more vital to identify every hazard and the fact that it was Sam who was following him heightened his awareness of anything that could cause harm.

Whenever there was a moment's break or the noise level faded enough, he would pause and call out.

'Rescue team here. Can anyone hear me?'

And ten seconds later, 'Nothing heard.'

'Nothing heard,' Sam would echo.

They squeezed through narrow gaps between enormous metal structures. They climbed over pipes and splashed through deep puddles left behind from the firefighting efforts. The beam of light from Blake's lamp finally raked a warped metal door.

'Rescue team here. Can anyone hear me?'

Another slow roll of the ship happened then and there was a metallic groan as engine parts shifted and scraped. Blake felt Sam touch his arm as she tried to keep her balance. Except she didn't let go.

'I heard something.'

'Background noise.'

'No.' Sam was still holding his arm as she turned her head. 'Rescue team here,' she called loudly. 'Can you hear me?'

This time, Blake could hear the response as well. Faint, but unmistakeable.

'Yes…thank God…' They could hear someone coughing. 'We're in here…'

The door was jammed but the bottom had been bent far enough to create a gap. Not nearly big enough to let Blake get through. Or even one of their backpacks.

'I think I can do it,' Sam said.

'No way. We'll get some more manpower in here. And some cutting gear.'

'That will take too long. What if there's a time-critical injury in there?'

'Hey…' Blake crouched by the bend in the door. 'What's happening in there? Are you hurt?'

'Moz is in a bad way. I think he might be dead. And I'm…bleeding.' The coughing sounded exhausted. 'I can't seem to stop it…'

Sam was pulling her backpack off. 'What's your name?'

'Barry.'

'Try and put some pressure on where you're bleeding, Barry. My name's Sam. I'm going to try and get in to you.'

She knelt on the floor, tilting her head to examine the gap. 'I can't see any sharp edges.'

Looking up, she blinked in the beam of Blake's light. 'Are you sure you want to try this?'

In answer, Sam lay flat on the floor, ignoring the wash of oil-streaked water around her. She lay on her back, her head already in the gap, and then used her feet to push her forward. A few moments later and she had to twist sideways to get her hips through. She felt her overalls snag and rip and could only hope that no skin was involved. Every time she pulled her legs forward she could feel the distance between herself and Blake increase but it didn't matter.

She knew he was there.

And she knew she could do this.

She heard him using the radio to contact the fire officer's team.

'We've found them. We're going to need help.'

Sam scrambled to her knees on the other side of the door. One man lay directly in front of her. Another was slumped in the corner.

'Check Moz first,' the nearest man said. 'Please. He stopped talking to me a while back…'

Barry was gripping his arm. Sam couldn't see any active bleeding from between his fingers.

She crawled swiftly over to the corner but she knew instantly how unlikely it was that she was going to find a pulse on this man. She could see how bad his head injury was.

She checked anyway.

And then she went straight back to Barry.

'I'm sorry,' she said. 'There's nothing I can do.'

Barry groaned. He let go of his arm and Sam saw a

pulse of fresh blood appear. She put her gloved hand over the wound and pressed. Hard.

'I need some dressings, Blake,' she called. 'And bandages.'

He passed them through the gap in the door.

'I'm going to need IV gear as well,' she told him a minute or two later. 'And fluids. Barry? Can you still hear me?'

'What's happening?' Blake's voice was tense. 'Talk to me, Sam.'

'Moz is dead. Head injury.' Sam clipped a tourniquet onto Barry's uninjured arm. 'Barry here has got a deep laceration on his arm but I think I've got the bleeding under control with a pressure bandage. His blood pressure's well down—I can't get a radial pulse and his level of consciousness is dropping.'

'Any other injuries?'

'I don't know. Nothing obvious but I want to get these fluids running and then I'll check more thoroughly.'

'He was coughing. Here's a stethoscope so you can check his lung fields. There could have been a lot of smoke in there.'

'Okay. Give me a second... There... IV's in. I'll just set up the saline and push a bit in.'

She was silent for a minute or two as she worked.

'You okay, Sam?'

'I'm good.'

She could hear the sound of more people arriving behind Blake but the additional sounds didn't quite cover his next words.

'Yeah,' she heard. 'You are...'

CHAPTER TEN

'ARE YOU SURE you don't mind staying behind?'

'No. There's not enough room on the chopper and it's far more important that the rest of the injured people get checked out properly.'

'I'll stay, too, in that case.' Blake's nod was decisive.

'But Barry's your patient.'

'He's stable. And he's in good hands with the paramedics.'

'But the captain says it'll take hours to get towed back into Sydney.'

Blake's eyebrow rose. 'You want me to give up the opportunity for an evening cruise into one of the most beautiful cities in the world? A rare chance to actually relax for a while?'

Sam caught her lip between her teeth. He wanted to stay on board with her? For hours and hours?

It almost felt like a date.

'You're not worried about Harriet?'

'I called the hospital. She's sleeping and probably will until the morning. I left a message to say I'll be in first thing, before I start work.'

Blake's decision to stay behind meant that another crew member with minor injuries could head home to his worried family. As they watched the rescue helicopter disappear into the distance, the captain approached to thank him.

'You both did an amazing job today,' he said. 'And we want to show you our appreciation. I'm afraid I'm going to be a bit busy supervising this towing operation but we want to make one of our staterooms available for you. You can have a shower and clean up. We're a bit limited in what we can offer from our menus, with no power, but we'll do our best.

A shower...

Sam couldn't stop her lips curving into a smile.

It was getting even more like a date. Or rather, like their very first time together, when Blake had offered to let her use the shower in his hotel room. And look how that invitation had turned out...

But maybe he didn't want that to happen again. She risked a quick glance in his direction and something began melting inside her at the brush of pure heat in his eyes.

He was remembering exactly what she was. And he wanted it again as much as she did. Maybe not now. Or here, because that would hardly be appropriate.

But soon...

'Wait here,' the captain instructed. 'Give us a few minutes and then my chief purser will come and get you as soon as we've sorted things.'

It was almost deserted in this area of the top deck where the helipad was located. Sam walked towards the railing to watch the misty outline of the coast becoming clearer. Blake followed her.

'The captain was right,' he said. 'You *did* do an amazing job today.'

Sam smiled. 'Does this mean I'm going to get an invitation to join the team?'

Blake didn't return the smile. 'Do you still want to?'

She caught her breath. She'd been given a second chance to prove herself worthy of the goal that had been so important to her but...was she being given a second chance of something completely different here?

To be on the team—or to be with Blake?

She couldn't tell. But she could sense that the question in his eyes went deeper than whether she still wanted to be a member of the team he was so passionate about.

Sam had to look away. 'You'd really consider that—after what happened today?'

'You mean the way you were totally unfazed by a hostile environment and responded to an emergency without hesitation and pretty much saved a man's life single-handedly?'

'No...' But the praise was doing funny things to her body. Could this glow actually be visible? She didn't dare catch Blake's gaze in case it was. 'I meant what happened on the cliff.'

There was a moment's silence before he spoke quietly. 'What *did* happen, Sam? It wasn't just fear, was it?'

The silence was longer this time but Blake seemed happy to wait.

'A long time ago,' Sam said slowly, 'my older brother, Alistair, got killed in a rock fall.'

'Alistair...' Blake echoed. And then his jaw dropped. 'Alistair Braithwaite was your *brother*?'

'You knew him?'

'I knew *of* him. Who didn't? He was a role model for

a lot of young people. He came to speak at my school once and he was inspirational. Bit of a hero of mine, to be honest.'

Sam's smile was poignant. 'Mine, too. I adored him.'

'It was such a tragedy. My God, Sam… I'm not surprised you got overwhelmed. It must have brought everything back in an instant.'

'Too much,' Sam admitted. 'Like how I thought my parents would just disappear into their grief. How it changed our family overnight. We seemed to swap roles somehow. It became my job to protect *them*.'

'I know that feeling. My mum's been pretty dependent on me ever since her stroke.'

'I heard about that.' Sam hesitated for a beat. She was stepping over an unspoken barrier that protected his private life. It took courage to move past it. Almost as much courage as it had taken to start squeezing herself through that narrow gap in the twisted metal door of the engine room. 'It's what stopped you joining MSF, isn't it?'

Blake didn't seem to mind that the barrier had been crossed. 'I love my mum. And I owe her everything but… I'm not proud of it, but I also resented it. I felt like her dependence robbed me of my freedom.'

Sam touched Blake's hand that was gripping the rail in front of her—an automatic gesture of understanding. 'And I felt like Alistair's death robbed me of doing anything exciting ever again. I had to keep myself safe to protect my parents.'

Blake's hand moved to cover hers. 'You didn't keep yourself safe today.'

'I'm not looking forward to telling them about it.' Sam sighed. 'But…but I felt like *me* today. Who I re-

ally am. The person I really want to be. And that's important, isn't it?'

She looked up to find Blake smiling at her. The look
in his eyes told her that he was about to kiss her but he
had something to say first.

'More than important,' he murmured. 'You're not
only amazing, Sam Braithwaite. You're very wise.'

The glow that his praise had given her paled into
insignificance compared to the one that replaced it as
his lips covered hers. It was just the briefest touch but
that was okay, because they were in a public place, after
all, and were here in a professional capacity.

But life could change in a heartbeat, that was for
sure.

And, sometimes, the change was a good one.

Better than anything you might have dreamed of,
in fact...

The cabin they were offered was luxurious. Crew
T-shirts and track pants had been provided as well,
so that they could get out of their oil-streaked, filthy
overalls. It was only when Sam was turning to head
for the bathroom that Blake noticed the rip in her
protective clothing.

'You're not hurt, are you?' It was weird the way his
stomach knotted so hard at the thought.

'I don't think so. Only a scratch, if I am. It's nothing.' Sam's expression was bleak as she looked over her
shoulder. 'Do you think Harriet's going to be okay?'

'I think infection's the biggest danger now. Let's
hope that doesn't happen.'

'Will she get normal function back again?'

Blake couldn't help his frown. 'It's a nasty injury. That leg is never going to be the same.'

'She'll hate that so much. She loves being on the team so much and every spare minute gets spent outside. It's all the things that she and Pete have in common—surfing, running, the rescue work.'

'Do you think the relationship will survive?'

'I hope so. Harry's got more than enough to deal with already. If you really love someone, going through something like this can make the relationship stronger. What…?' Sam was staring at him. 'Don't you think so?'

'I can't help wondering why he didn't come to the hospital with her.'

'He's not a medic. I think things like that freak him out. And there wasn't enough room in the chopper. Harry asked for me.'

'He didn't jump in his car to follow us, though, did he?'

'No.' Sam was pulling her arms from her overalls. The T-shirt she was wearing underneath rode up and Blake could see the graze on her skin under where the rip had been.

'Let me check that.'

'I'm fine.'

But Blake was already beside her, gently examining the area.

'See? It's just a scratch.'

'It could have been worse.' Blake kept his hand resting on her skin. 'And if it had been, there's no way on earth anyone would have kept me from going to the hospital with you.'

Did she understand what he was trying to tell her?

That he loved her?

The way she reached up to touch his face made it seem like she did understand. And the way she kissed him started to make it seem like she felt exactly the same way.

Until there was a knock at the door and Sam jumped back as though she had been caught doing something unacceptable. Unprofessional, in any case. She disappeared into the bathroom as people started coming into the cabin with trays of food and drink. She was still combing out her hair by the time Blake had taken his turn to shower and change into clean clothes.

'I can't believe this,' she said. 'It's the second time today I've been offered a feast. Oh...' Her eyes widened. 'I've only just realised that we completely forgot about all those things you bought in the cafeteria and it was such a special thing that you did. What a waste.'

'I doubt it was wasted. The nurses would have found it and you know what it's like when there's free food on offer around that place. Besides...' Blake took a step closer to Sam '...even if they didn't find it, it would have been worth it.'

'Why?' This time, it was Sam who stepped closer.

'Because I think you understand why I did it. It said something I couldn't find the words to say.'

Those eyes... The bluest eyes he'd ever seen and right now they were bottomless and he was falling...

'That I need to take care of you,' he added softly. 'To feed you and protect you if, for some reason, it's hard for you to do it for yourself. Because...' He was close enough to touch her now. To pull her into his arms. 'Because you mean so much to me, Sam. I... I love you...'

Those eyes were shining with unshed tears now. 'I

love you too, Blake. And I certainly wouldn't be able to find the words to tell you how much.'

He rested his forehead against hers. 'What are we going to do?'

'You mean because neither of us does relationships?'

'Exactly.'

'But we didn't *choose* to make this a relationship. Does that make a difference?'

'I don't know. Maybe.' Blake tightened his hold on Sam. '*Why* don't you do relationships?'

'I've tried. They just don't work so I kind of gave up.'

'Because it's been enough having to protect your parents? That it wouldn't have left enough room for *you* if you'd had someone else to protect as well?'

'Is that why you don't do them?'

'It's more the idea of having someone else dependent on me, I think. Especially children. If something happens, there's no choice but to sacrifice your life for them. Like my mother did for me.'

'I'll bet she didn't see it as a sacrifice. She loves you.'

Blake nodded slowly. 'I know. And now I'm beginning to understand how you could choose to have a bond like that. How it can make even the things that seemed more important than anything else kind of... well, almost irrelevant.'

'We could always go back to what we were doing,' Sam said softly.

'You mean the one-offs until one of us decides that we've had enough? The secret that nobody else knows anything about?'

'Mmm.'

'I don't want it to be a secret any more. I want everyone to know what you mean to me.' Making it public was suddenly important. Because it would make it feel more real? 'I want my mother to get to know you. She's going to love you.'

Sam was grinning. 'My mother's going to be terrified of you. But she'll learn to love you. So will Dad.'

'And I could never have enough,' Blake added. He knew it was true. He didn't want to be without Sam for the rest of his life. For even a day if he could help it.

Sam's smile had faded completely. She had never looked more serious. 'I couldn't either.'

'So...' Blake straightened so that he could see her face properly. 'Maybe we should just bite the bullet and get it over with.'

'Get what over with?'

He could feel one side of his mouth curling upwards. 'The wedding.'

Sam gasped. 'You've got to be kidding me. That could possibly go down in history as the least romantic proposal *ever*.'

Blake slid his hands down Sam's arms to take hold of her hands. He held her gaze as he took a very deep, slow breath.

'I love you,' he said, then. 'More than I ever thought it was possible to love anyone. I thought that sharing my life with someone would somehow stop me being the person I need to be and take away my freedom but...' He caught another breath. 'You *are* my freedom. You said that you felt like you were the person you're meant to be today and that's exactly how I feel when I'm with you. I can't be that person unless you're in

my life and I'm asking you to promise me that you'll
be there for ever. Will you marry me, Sam?'

Her lips were trembling and those unshed tears that
had gathered earlier were now rolling down her face.

'That's *it*... You've found the words I couldn't find.
It wasn't just that I was doing exciting, scary stuff
today that made me feel like that. It was because I was
with *you*. I've felt like that around you ever since...well,
maybe ever since you glared at me for dropping that
bedpan even though I didn't know it then.' Her words
were tumbling out through a misty smile. 'I don't care
if it means I can't be on the team. I'd rather be with
you. I can't *not* be with you.'

'So...is that a "yes"?'

Sam blinked. 'Didn't I say that already?'

'No.' Blake smiled back at her. 'But I think that's
what you meant.'

'Oh...it was. *Is*... Yes, I'll marry you, Blake. I can't
think of anything I'd rather do.'

Blake could. Their wedding was too far in the future
to think about right now. Not when there was something he'd much rather be doing. Judging by the look in
Sam's eyes, she wouldn't be averse to celebrating this
engagement in a very personal way. Her next words
confirmed that impression.

'Is there a lock on that door?' she whispered.

'I do believe there is.'

'We wouldn't want to get caught, would we...doing
something that team members aren't supposed to be
doing?'

'We're off duty,' Blake said firmly. 'And I think it's
time some of those rules got relaxed a bit, anyway.'

He stepped towards the door and turned the key in the lock.

It didn't feel as if he was keeping something out, however.

It felt like he was letting something in.

A whole new future—for both of them.

It took only another stride to get close enough to Sam to sweep her off her feet and into his arms as he turned towards that deliciously big bed. And now it felt as if he was carrying Sam into that future with him.

And nothing could have felt more right.

* * * * *

FINDING HIS WIFE, FINDING A SON

MARION LENNOX

MILLS & BOON

To Liz and Graham.

With thanks for your support and love over so many years. Should we come and build more shelves?

Love you both,

Marion

CHAPTER ONE

'I COULD USE an emergency.'

Dr Luc Braxton perched himself on the end of Harriet's bed and snagged a chocolate from her stash. He was bored. Harriet was also bored but with more reason. She'd smashed her leg during an abseiling training exercise some weeks back. The break was horrific, there'd been complication after complication and she was struggling to regain any strength at all.

'That's not a kind thing to say to me,' she retorted, but she managed a smile. Yeah, she was bored, but Luc took boredom to a whole new level.

Luc and Harriet were both members of Australia's crack Specialist Disaster Response team. They were based at Bondi Bayside Hospital, and while not wishing disaster to fall on the community at large, Luc was edgy when it didn't.

Disaster response was what Luc lived for. Harriet's accident, with its possible long-term consequences, had left him gutted, but even the damage to his friend hadn't taken the edge off his addiction to adrenaline.

'Was the conference boring then?' Harriet asked, trying to sound sympathetic.

'Who could be bored in New York? And, no, the

emergency medicine component was great. I learned
a lot. But I did spend most of my time on my butt,
listening, and twenty-four hours sitting on the plane
either way. And then to get home and find the team
doing another disaster drill off in the Blue Mountains
without me...'

'Which is why you'd better hope there's no emergency,' Harriet told him, but there was sympathy in
her voice. Harriet was a specialist intensive care nurse.
Luc was an emergency medicine physician. Neither
was good at doing nothing. 'The team can be recalled
fast but it'll take an extra couple of hours to bring them
back to base,' she said. 'And you know they need to
do it. Our last was the disaster when I was hurt, and
they've been trying to get back there ever since. They
return tomorrow. Let's hold emergencies until then.'

'So you're not bored?'

'Of course I am.' Harriet glowered and winced as
she tried to move her leg. 'Give it a break, Luc. I'm
likely to be bored for a very long time. At least you
can do something about it.'

She eyed Luc with speculation. 'Hey, maybe it's
about time you thought about your love life. Word is
that cute little nurse you've been dating threw you over
before you left. Seems you stood her up for one date
too many.'

'Gotta love the hospital grapevine,' Luc said equi-
tably. 'It knows my love life better than I do.'

'You give it fodder. How many's that this year?
Three? Isn't it time you thought about settling? Ba-
bies and a mortgage and washing the car on Sundays?
Not interested?'

'Not in a million years.'

'Word is you were married.'

'Yeah.' He pushed himself off the bed and headed for the door. Personal discussions weren't something he did. 'Eight years ago. I'm not going back there in a hurry.'

'So why the serial dating?' Bored and interested, Harriet wasn't letting him off the hook. 'What are you looking for, Luc? Someone cute, smart, sexy, willing to have nine out of ten dates cancelled because of crises, happy for her guy to dangle from a rope mid-air while the rest of the world thinks he'll break his neck...'

'Harry...'

'Hey, I know, it's none of my business.' She was starting to enjoy herself. 'But you need to quit it with working your way through the hospital staff—it's getting messy. How about you join a proper dating site? I'll help you fill in your profile. What do we have? Six foot two, tall, dark, ripped and just a touch mysterious—or at least he likes crime novels. Yeah, I've seen you reading them between jobs. Super fit. Pulls a great wage. You might need to buy yourself life insurance to cover security issues but, wow, Luc, wait and see how many hits you get. You'll make some girl a wonderful husband.'

'I have no intention of being a husband, wonderful or otherwise.'

'But you've already been one,' Harriet said thoughtfully. 'Want to tell Aunty Harry what happened? Where is she now?'

'And I have no intention of telling you about my marriage, even if you are bored,' Luc retorted through gritted teeth. 'It's past history. I have no idea where she is now. I'm heading down to Emergency to see if I can find someone to treat.'

'The nurses are saying there's nothing doing in Emergency. There doesn't seem to be anything inter-esting happening in this whole hospital. Like your love life.'

'You want to talk about yours? How are you and Pete?'

She winced again. 'Yeah, okay, stalemate. But se-riously, Luc… My offer of planting you in the middle of a dating site still stands. It might even be exciting.'

'I have enough excitement in my life,' he said, and gave her a hug, snagged another chocolate from her oversupply and left.

Harriet was left staring thoughtfully after him.

'You know,' she said, to no one in particular, 'I'm pretty sure you don't. I'm pretty sure there's not enough excitement in the universe to keep Luc Braxton happy. And I'd love to know what happened, and where that wife of yours is now.'

Dr Beth Carmichael was so tired all she wanted to do was sleep. Today had been once crisis after another. She was finally free to head home, but heading home with a toddler and a briefcase of medico-legal letters didn't promise the sleep she craved.

There'd even been a drama when she'd gone to pick Toby up from childcare.

'Beth, would you mind looking at Felix Runnard? He's been listless all day and now he's developed a fever. His mum's not due to pick him up until eight tonight and her boss gives her a hard time if she has to leave early. We've popped him into isolation but…

what do you think? Should we ring his mum?' Margie Lane, the childcare supervisor, was a sensible woman who didn't fuss but she'd sounded worried.

So Beth had put aside her longing for home and sat down with the little boy on her lap.

A slight fever? The staff had taken his temp an hour ago but now he was burning. He was also arching his head and crying when she touched his neck.

Fever. Sore neck. No sign of a virus. Alarm bells had rung.

'Check his tummy for me,' she'd told Margie as she cradled him, and Margie had lifted his singlet and removed his nappy.

The beginnings of a rash.

Meningitis?

The childcare centre was in the shopping plaza, as was the clinic Beth worked from. She sent someone to the clinic for antibiotics and injected a first dose straight away. She could hope her tentative diagnosis was wrong, but she couldn't wait for confirmation. If she was right, immediate antibiotics could make all the difference.

An hour later Felix and his parents were in the med. evacuation chopper on their way to Sydney. Meningitis hadn't been confirmed but Beth wasn't wasting time doing the tests herself. If the infection was moving fast, Namborra wasn't where he needed to be. It was better to bail out early, maybe even terrify his parents unnecessarily, than risk the unthinkable.

Even after he'd left, there'd been things to do. She'd cleaned herself with care, then organised for parents to be contacted, with antibiotics ordered for anyone who'd been in contact with Felix. Finally she'd stripped again—one thing a country GP always carried was a change of clothes. She'd then hugged her own little Toby and carried him out through the undercover car park.

He was whinging because he was tired. She was also tired, but Toby didn't have meningitis and right now she felt the luckiest mother in the world.

'Let's have spaghetti for tea,' she told Toby, and his little face brightened.

'Worms.'

'Exactly. How many worms would you like?'

'One, two, a hundred,' he crowed, and buried his head in her shoulder.

She hugged him tight and headed toward the entrance. Doug, her next-door neighbour, would be waiting to pick her up. Bless him, she thought, not for the first time. Doug was in his seventies, a widower who spent his days making his garden and his car pristine. When she'd first started working at Namborra he'd noticed the number of taxis she was using and tentatively made his offer. At first she'd been reluctant—her hours were all over the place—but she'd finally accepted that Doug's offer filled a need for him as well as for her.

Giving was lovely. She'd realised that a long time ago. It was the taking that was the hardest.

So now…she'd kept Doug waiting for over an hour but she couldn't hurry. The light was dim and she had trouble making out the pillars. Grey on grey was her worst-case scenario.

Sometimes she even conceded a cane would help.

'Yeah, a toddler in one arm, a holdall and briefcase in the other plus a cane…where? Not going to happen…'

And then she paused.

There was a roaring from above, the sound of a plane.

The town's small airstrip was close. It wasn't so unusual for planes to fly overhead, but the approaching roar was so loud it was making the building vibrate.

What the…?

She had a fraction of a second to clutch Toby tighter and duck because that was what she always did when she sensed trouble. Keep your head out of the firing line…

All of her was in the firing line. So was all of the Namborra Plaza.

Luc had finally found something to do. A kid playing hockey after school, no shin pads and a ball hit with force. He'd been bleeding impressively as his teacher had tugged him through the emergency doors. The dressing they'd hopefully taped to his lower leg wasn't doing it.

The kid was ashen and feeling nauseous, mostly from the sight of blood rather than the pain, Luc thought, but eight stitches, a neat dressing and a promise of a scar had him restored to boisterous. 'You're sure it'll scar?' he demanded.

'Just a hairline,' Luc told him.

'You can't make it bigger?'

Luc grinned. 'You want me to re-stitch, only looser?'

The kid chuckled. A nurse appeared with soda and a sandwich and the kid attacked them as if there was no tomorrow.

'Shin guards from now on,' Luc told him, and then the beeper in his pocket vibrated.

The hospital used his phone—or the intercom—to page him. The vibrating pager was used for members of the Specialist Disaster Response.

Three buzzes, repeated.

Code One.

Yes!

Or…um…no. He shouldn't react like this. Code One emergencies meant the highest level of need. It meant that somewhere people were in dire trouble. He should hate it, and a part of him did. After a multiple casualty event, he made use of the SDR's debriefing service and sometimes even that didn't stop him lying awake in the small hours, reliving nightmare scenarios.

But this was what he was trained for, and in a way it was what he needed.

One of the team's more perceptive psychologists had had a go about it once, and for some reason—the nightmares must have been bad—he'd let her probe.

'Your childhood was traumatic and your mum depended on you?' In typical psych. fashion she'd put it back on him. 'How did that make you feel?'

And for some reason he'd let himself think about it.

His mother had walked out on his father when he'd been a toddler. She'd gone from one tumultuous relationship to another, one crisis to another. His earliest memories… 'Is there anything in the fridge? Go next door and ask Mrs Hobson for something. Tell her I'd kill for a piece of toast. And aspirins. Go on, Luc, Mummy will hug you if you get her an aspirin…'

More dramatically, he remembered a drunk and angry boyfriend tossing them out at midnight. He remembered his aunt arriving and scolding him. 'What are you doing, boy, standing round doing nothing? Go back inside and demand he give your mother her belongings. Go on, Luc, he won't hit *you*. Can't you see your mother needs you? You're no use to anyone if you can't help.'

He'd been seven years old. Somehow he'd faced down his mother's bullying boyfriend. He'd pushed what he could see into a suitcase and his aunt had reluctantly taken them in.

And then there'd been his cousin...

Don't go there.

'So you've always associated love with being needed?' the psychologist had asked, but it was too close to the bone and Luc had ended the sessions.

Did he associate dependence with love? There was a germ of truth, he acknowledged, and maybe that's why he and Beth...

But this was no time to think of his failed marriage. His pager was still buzzing.

Don't run in the hospital.

His long-legged stride came close.

After the massive roar of the plane, the shock of impact, then the domino effect as the slabs of concrete smashed down around them, there was suddenly silence.

And then the car alarms started, reacting to the fall of debris.

Beth was on the ground—at least she thought it was the ground. Her back was hard against a pillar.

There was rubble all around her, almost head-high.

Something was across her leg. Something...

The pain was unbelievable.

But worse... Toby was silent.

The air was so thick she could hardly breathe.

Toby.

She was still cradling him against her chest. His little body was curved into hers.

His stillness…

'Toby…' Her voice came out as a strangled, dust-choked whisper. 'Toby?'

And he moved, just a fraction, to bury his face deeper into her breast. A whimper…

Thank you. Oh, thank you.

Her hands were moving over him, searching, pushing away rubble.

No blood. No more whimpers as she ran her fingers over his body.

She was good at this, assessing in the dark. Too good. But her skill was useful now. Her fingers were telling her there seemed no damage. Her arms had been around his chest and his head. He seemed okay.

But for herself…

There was no damage to her hands—maybe scratches but nothing serious. But her leg…

She tried to pull it free from the rubble, and the pain that shot through her body was indescribable.

But Toby was her priority. She was wearing a T-shirt, the one she'd changed into in a rush after treating Felix. Somehow she managed to put Toby back from her, enough to wiggle the hem of the T-shirt up to her neck. Then she pulled it down again, all the way over Toby, turning it into a cocoon to protect him from the dust.

Still he didn't move. The noise, the shock, the darkness must have sent him into panic and for most toddlers the reaction to blind panic was to freeze.

'It's okay,' she whispered, but it wasn't.

Breathing seemed almost impossible. Her mouth was full of grit. The dust wasn't settling.

Toby was safe under her T-shirt, but what was the rule? In a crisis, first ensure your own safety. You're no use to anyone if you're dead.

Okay, Toby had come first but now she needed to focus on herself.

The leg... She needed to...

Breathe. That was top of the list.

She was cradling Toby with one arm. With the other she groped and found the canvas carryall she'd brought from crèche. The clothes she'd just taken off were in a plastic bag on the top. Maybe they were contaminated with meningitis virus but now wasn't the time to quibble.

Oh, her leg...

Somewhere close by, someone started to scream.

There was nothing she could do about it.

First save yourself.

She'd been wearing a blouse when she'd treated Felix and it was at the top of the bag. She tugged it free and a flurry of concrete rubble fell into the bag as she pulled it out.

Was there anything around her likely to fall? How could she tell?

The darkness was total. Her phone had a torch but her phone was at the bottom of her purse and where was her purse? Not within reach.

No matter. She was used to the dark.

Toby wasn't, though. He was whimpering, his little body shaking.

There was nothing she could do until she had herself safe.

She had the shirt free. She shook the worst of the dust out, knowing more was settling every second. Then she had to let Toby go while she wrapped and tied the shirt around her face.

The whimpering grew frantic.

'It's okay.' And blessedly it was. The shirt made breathing not easy but at least possible.

She took a moment to cradle Toby again, hugging him close, blocking out the messages her leg was sending her.

'Stay still, Toby, love,' she whispered. 'I need to see if I can get this…this mess away from us so we can go home.'

Fat chance. She wasn't going anywhere soon.

Oh, her leg…

Was she bleeding? She couldn't tell and she had to know.

Carefully she manoeuvred Toby around to her side, though he clutched her so hard she had to tug. Thankfully the neck of her T-shirt was tight so he was safe enough in there. He wasn't crying loudly—just tiny terrified whimpers that did something to her heart.

But her leg had priority. With Toby shifted to the side she could lean down and feel.

There was a block of concrete lying straight across her lower leg. Massive. She couldn't feel either end of it.

She was bent almost double, fighting to get her fingers underneath, fighting to see if there was wriggle room.

Her fingers could just fit under.

No blood or very little. She wasn't bleeding out, which was kind of a relief.

The pain was…was…there were no words.

She went back to clutching Toby. If she just held on…

She was awash with nausea and faintness. The darkness, the pain, the fear were almost overwhelming and the temptation was to give in. She could just let go and sink into the darkness.

But that'd mean letting go of Toby. He was being so still. Why? She didn't have room in her head to answer. He was breathing, his warm little body her one sure thing in this nightmare.

The sound from the car alarms was appalling. The screaming from far away reached a crescendo and then suddenly stopped, cut off.

There was nothing she could do. Her world was confined to dark and dust and pain—and Toby.

There was nothing else.

Even without the emergency code, Luc would have known there was trouble the moment he walked into the Specialist Disaster Response office. Mabel, the admin secretary, was staring at the screen and her fingers were flying over the keyboard. This was what she was trained for.

Mabel sensed rather than saw him arrive, and she didn't take her eyes from the screen as she spoke.

'Plane crash into shopping centre,' she said over her shoulder. 'Cargo plane. Pilot on board but hopefully no passengers. It's smashed into the side of the Namborra Shopping Plaza. You know Namborra? Five hours' drive inland, due west. It's the commercial centre for a huge rural district. Hot day, air-conditioned shopping centre, Tuesday afternoon. There's no word yet but guess is multiple casualties. It seems the undercover car park and a small section of the plaza itself have collapsed.'

'What resources are on the ground?' Luc asked.

'There's a small local hospital but anything serious gets airlifted here, so there are few resources. I'm bringing the team back, field hospital, the works, but it'll take time to get them there. Luc, I'm trying to sequester med staff from the rest of the hospital but they're not geared up like you are. The fire team's already notified and the first responders will go with you. The chopper's on the roof. Gina's refuelling and ready to go. Resources will follow at need but I want you in the air ten minutes ago. Go!'

And ten seconds later he was gone.

CHAPTER TWO

'MESS' DIDN'T BEGIN to describe what was beneath them.

From the air Namborra looked what it was, a small, almost-city situated in the middle of endless miles of wheat fields. There was a railway line and station, and a massive cluster of wheat silos. A group of commercial buildings formed the town centre, with a mammoth swimming pool and sports complex to the side. But Luc's focus was on the largest building of all—a vast, sprawling undercover shopping plaza.

The scene of disaster.

The plane seemed to have skimmed across the rooftop, bringing part of the roof down and then smashing into the sports oval next door. That was some consolation, he thought, but not much. He couldn't see the plane—what he saw was a smouldering mess.

And the plaza... There was a local fire engine on site, with men and women doing their best to quench a small fire smouldering a third of the way across the smashed roof. There were two police cars.

There were locals, visibly distressed even from where Luc gazed from the chopper, some venturing out onto the collapsed roof, others clustering around people on the ground. Some were simply clutching each other.

They circled first. Gina, the team's pilot, knew the drill. Even though seconds counted, there was always the need to take an aerial assessment. Calculate risks.

'Hard hats. Full gear. You know the drill,' Kev, the burly chief of the SDR fire crew, barked. 'Anyone going in under that mess, watch yourself.' He was including Luc in his orders. SDR medics were supposed to stay on the sidelines and treat whoever was brought to them but it often didn't work that way. In truth firefighters often ended up doing emergency first aid and the medics often ended up digging or abseiling or whatever. No one asked questions—in a crisis everyone did what they had to do.

'Obey orders and keep your radios close,' Kev ordered as the chopper landed. 'Back-up's on its way but it'll take time. For now there's just us. Okay, guys, let's go.

Toby was recovering from the initial shock. Blessedly he didn't seem hurt. One little hand wriggled free, up through the neck of her T-shirt. Tiny fingers touched her neck, reaching up to her cheek. She wiped the grit away as best she could. Toby was making sure it was her.

'M-Mama…'

There were car alarms sounding all around her, a continuous screaming she couldn't escape from, but she heard…or maybe she felt him speak. Toby had been calling her Mama for two months now and every time she heard it her heart turned over. Now, in the midst of noise and pain and fear…no, make that noise and pain and terror, it still had the capacity to ground her.

This little person was the centre of her universe and she wasn't about to let a crushed leg and a shopping centre fallen down around her make her forget that.

'It's okay, Toby, love.' Could he hear above the cacophony? She had to believe he could. Maybe like her, he could feel her voice. She fought to fumble her way into her bag, until her fingers closed on a scrappy, chewed rabbit.

Robert Rabbit was incongruously purple, so garish that even Beth could usually make him out in dim light. She couldn't make him out now—the darkness was absolute—but she felt his scrappy fur and he gave her inexplicable comfort.

She'd be okay. They'd be okay.

If only her head didn't feel…fuzzy. If only the noise would stop and the waves of pain would recede.

She pushed them away—the pain and the faintness—and focussed hard on Toby. And Robert. She put the scraggy rabbit into the little hand and tucked both hand and rabbit back down her T-shirt.

There was one blessing in all this. Because she'd been delayed at childcare, one of the women had given Toby warm milk and changed him into his pyjamas. She'd intended to heat spaghetti at home. Toby would have eaten a few 'worms' and then he'd have crashed. He didn't really need the spaghetti, though. He'd had a full day of childcare. It was dark, he was well fed and he was tired. With luck he'd sleep.

'Heydee, heydee-ho, the great big elephant is so slow…'

The simple child's song was one she used to settle

him in the middle of the night, rocking him, telling him all was well in his world, all was well in her world. She forced herself to croon it now.

The car horns were blaring but he must be able to feel her singing. He was so close. A heartbeat...

'*He swings his trunk from side to side, as he takes the children for a ride...*'

Her throat was caked with dust but somehow she managed it. And she managed to rock, just a little, with both hands cradling Toby.

'*Heydee, heydee-ho...*' Oh, it hurt. Dear God... If she fainted. '*Heydee...*'

And blessedly she felt him relax. This had been scary for a few moments but now...maybe it was no worse than being put into his own cot in his own room. He had his mama. He had his rabbit. He was...safe?

If only she could believe that.

Toby snuggled deeper as she held him and tried to take comfort in him. The shards of pain were growing stronger. The faintness was getting closer...

Do not give in.

'*Heydee...*'

He needed his team!

There was a local paramedic team onsite, plus another from a small town twenty minutes' drive away, but they didn't have the skills, equipment or know-how to try and go underneath the mess. There seemed to be only one available local doctor. She was working flat out in the nearby hospital. That meant triage and immediate life-saving stuff was up to Luc.

A café at the outer edge of the plaza had collapsed, with a group of senior citizens inside, and that's where the firefighters centred their early rescue efforts. One dead, two injured. Luc was in there until the café was cleared, crawling under the rubble to set up intravenous IVs and pain relief.

He was filthy. A scrape on his cheek was bleeding but as the last gentleman was pulled from the rubble he was already looking around for what needed doing next.

There were still no-go areas, smouldering fires, a mass of collapsed tiles where the plaza proper started.

Where to start...

'We're going into the car park.' Kev had been supervising the final stages of freeing the senior cits and he was now staring out at the flattened roof of what had been the undercover parking lot. It was a mass of flattened sheets of corrugated iron and the remains of concrete pillars.

'How the hell did that collapse?' Luc muttered, awed.

'Minimal strength pillars,' Kev commented. 'Concrete that looks like it'll last for ever but turns to dust. The plane's gone in across the top and they've come down like dominoes.'

'Any idea how many under there?'

'We hope not many.' At Luc's look of surprise he shrugged. 'Tuesday's not a busy shopping day. It's too late for after-school shopping, too early for the place to be closing. Most were either in the plaza itself or had gone home. The locals pulled a couple out from the edges but there's reports of a few missing. Don and Louise Penbroke, mah-jong players extraordinaire, had just left the café when it hit. Bill Mickle, a local greyhound racer. One of the local docs...'

'A doctor…' It shouldn't make a difference. It didn't, but still…

'Young woman doctor, works at the clinic,' Kev told him. 'Just picked her kid up from childcare. Her driver was supposed to meet her at the entrance—he's yelling to anyone who'll listen that she's trapped under there. So that's four definites but possibly more. Hell, I wish we could get those car alarms off. To be stuck underneath with that racket…they won't even hear us if we yell.'

Her world was spinning in tighter circles where only three things mattered. Taking one breath after another. That was important. Cradling Toby's small warm body. If he wasn't here, if she'd dropped him, if she couldn't feel his deep, even breathing, she'd go mad. And the pain in her leg…

But she would hold on. If she fainted she might drop Toby. He might crawl away. He was her one true thing and for now she was his.

Dear God, help…

Please…

The firefighters were lifting one piece of iron after another, working with infinite care, taking all the trouble in the world not to stand where people might be lying underneath, not to cause further falls, not to cause dust that might choke anyone trapped.

They found Don and Louise Penbroke first. The third sheet of iron was raised and the elderly couple looked like the pictures Luc had seen of petrified corpses from Pompeii, totally still, totally covered, the only difference being they were covered in concrete dust and not ash.

But as the first guy to reach them touched a debris-coated shoulder there was a ripple of movement. Still clutching each other, the couple managed to sit up. Louise had her face buried in Don's chest and Don's face was in Louise's thick white hair.

Within seconds Luc had their faces cleared. They still clutched each other, their eyes enormous.

'Th-thank…' Don tried to speak but Luc put his hand on his shoulder and shook his head. And smiled.

'You two should thank each other. That's the best way to survive I've seen. What hurts?'

But amazingly little did. They'd been by the ramp leading up to the car park, protected by the concrete sides. They were both shocked but fine.

One happy ending.

A couple of the firies steered them out into the afternoon sunshine where they were greeted with tears and relief.

The firies—and Luc—worked methodically on.

There had to be some way to turn those damned car alarms off, Luc thought. There were fractions of time between the blaring but never enough to call and receive a warning.

At least batteries were starting to fail. The barrage of sound was lessening.

Another sheet came free.

Hell.

This guy hadn't been so lucky. A sheet of iron had caught him. He'd have bled out almost instantly, Luc thought, and wondered how many others were to be found. They were waiting for proper machinery to search the crumpled part of the plaza itself. How many…?

And then…a cry?

The sound was from their left, heard between car sirens.

Kev demanded instant stillness. The sound had come from at least three sheets of iron across. If they went for it, they risked crushing others who lay between.

They waited for another break in the alarms. Kev ordered his team to spread out to give a better chance of pinpointing location.

'Call if you can hear us?' Kev yelled.

'H-here.'

A woman's voice. Faint.

A roofing sheet was pulled up, the rubble lifted with care but with urgency. It revealed nothing but crushed concrete. These pillars were rubbish.

Someone's head would roll for these, Luc thought. They looked as if they'd been built with no more idea of safety standards than garden statuary.

He was heaving rubble too, now. By rights he should be out on the pavement, treating patients as they were brought to him, but with the local doctor working in the nearby hospital he'd decided the urgent need was here. If there was something major the paramedics would call him back.

All his focus was on that voice. That cry.

'Stop,' Kev called, and once again he signalled for them to stand back and locate.

And then… The voice called again, fainter.

This area held the worst of the crushed concrete. Sheets of roofing iron had fallen and concrete had crumpled and rolled on top. They were working from the sides of each sheet, determined not to put more weight on the slab.

'Please...' The sirens had ceased again for a fraction of a moment and the voice carried upward. She must be able to hear them. She was right...here?

Others had joined them now, hauling concrete away with care. Half a dozen men and women, four in emergency services uniforms, two burly locals, all desperate to help.

'Reckon it's the doc.' One of the locals spoke above the noise. 'Hell, it's the doc. We gotta get—'

His words were cut off again by the car alarms, but the urgency only intensified.

And finally the last block of concrete was hauled clear. The sheet of iron was free to be shifted.

Willing hands caught the edges. Kev was there, taking in the risks, assessing to the last.

'Lift,' he said at last. 'Count of three, straight up...'

And the iron was raised and moved aside.

Revealing a woman huddled underneath.

Luc was underneath before the iron was clear. He was stooping, feeling his way in, reaching her. He was lifting a cloth she'd obviously used to protect her face, wiping her face free, clearing her airway. He had a mask on her almost instantly. The initial need was clean air, more important than anything else.

She was matted with grey-white dust. Her eyes were terrified. 'My...my baby...'

And then she faltered as she stared wildly into his eyes. Even with his mask, even with the dust, she knew him.

'Luc?'

* * *

He felt as if all the air had been sucked from his body.

Beth!

His wife.

Not his wife. She'd walked away eight years ago. For a while he'd tried to keep in touch but it had been too hard for both of them.

'Stay safe.' That had been Beth's last ask of him. 'I know you can't keep out of harm's way but, oh, Luc, don't you dare get yourself killed.'

And she'd touched his face one last time, and climbed aboard a train bound for Brisbane.

Stay safe. What a joke, when here she was, trapped by a mass of rubble, so close to death....

The nearest car alarm stopped abruptly. In reality its battery had probably died, but to Luc it felt like the world had stopped. Instinctively his hand came up to adjust his own mask, a habit entrenched by years of crisis training.

His mask was fine. His breathing was okay.

And he wasn't hallucinating.

Beth...

'Leg trapped,' Kev at his side murmured, and just like that, the doctor in Luc stepped in. Thankfully, because the rest of him was floundering like a stickleback out of water.

'You're going to be okay,' he told her, in a voice he could almost be proud of. It was the voice he was trained to use, strong, sure, with a trace of warmth, words to keep panic at bay.

He needed to get the whole picture. He leaned back a little so he could see all of her.

She was slumped against the remains of a pillar.

There was a mound under her shirt, and she was cradling it with both hands. A slab of concrete had fallen over her left leg. Her right leg was tucked up, as if she'd tried to haul back at the last minute, but he couldn't see her left foot.

His gaze went back to her face, noting the terror and the pain, then his gaze moved again to the mound at her chest. A child?

He put a hand on the mound and felt a wash of relief as he registered warmth and deep, even breathing. He slipped a hand under her T-shirt and located one small nose. Clear. Beth had managed to protect the airway.

Beth's child?

This was sensory overload, but he had to focus on imperatives.

'Your baby?' he said, because the fact that a child was breathing didn't necessarily mean all was well.

'T Toby.'

'Toby,' he said, and managed a smile. 'Great name. Beth, was Toby hit? Do you know if he's been hurt?' He lifted the mask a little to let her speak.

'I felt… I felt the fall.' Her voice was a hoarse whisper, muffled by the mask. 'I crouched. Toby was under me. He seems fine. He's fallen asleep and I'm… I'm sure it's natural. It's been…it's been a big day at childcare.'

'Huge,' he agreed. He was acting on triage imperatives, taking her word for the child's safety for the moment as he moved his hands down to her leg. The dust was a thick fog the light was having trouble penetrating. He winced as he reached her ankle and could feel no further.

'It's…stuck…' Beth managed.

'Well diagnosed, Dr Carmichael,' he said, and she even managed a sort of smile.

'I'm good.'

'I suspect you've been better. Pain level, one to ten?'

'S-Six.'

'Honest?'

'Nine, then,' she managed, and then decided to be honest. 'Okay, ten.'

And she wouldn't be exaggerating. He looked at the slab constricting her leg and he felt sick. She'd been under here for more than an hour. Maybe two. What sort of long-term damage was being done?

There was no use going down that road. Just do what came next.

'Relief coming up now,' he said, loading a syringe. There were workers all around them now, shoring rubble. Kev was making his workplace as secure as he could, but Luc was noticing nothing but Beth. If he couldn't block out fears for personal safety then he shouldn't be here. 'No allergies?' He should know that. He did but he wasn't trusting memory. He was trusting nothing.

'N-no.'

'What else hurts, Beth?'

'I... My back...'

She was sitting hard against concrete, as if she'd been slammed there. She had full use of her arms and fingers, he could see it in the way she cradled the bundle on her breast. But what other damage?

First things first.

He should get the child... Toby...away to where he could be examined properly, where he was safe, but for now she was clutching him as if her own life depended on that hold. She was holding by a faint thread, he thought, and he wasn't messing with that thread.

His priority was to do what he must to keep her safe.

And suddenly he was enveloped by a waft of memory. Ten years ago. He and Beth were newly dating, med students together. She was little, feisty, cute. Messy chestnut curls. Big brown eyes. Okay, maybe cute wasn't a good enough description. Gorgeous.

He'd asked her out and couldn't believe it when she'd said yes—and a month later they'd spent a weekend camping.

A week after that she was in hospital with encephalitis, a mosquito-borne virus.

The day he most remembered was a week after that. She was still in hospital, fretting about missing her next assignment. He'd brought her in chocolates and flowers—corny but it was all he could think of. He was twenty-two years old, a kid, feeling guilty that she was ill.

But she was recovering. She was laughing at one of his idiotic jokes. Opening the chocolates.

And then, suddenly, she was falling back on her pillows.

'I can't... Luc, I feel so dizzy... My eyes...'

It was optical neuritis, a rare but appalling side-effect of encephalitis. It had meant almost instant, total blindness.

For weeks she'd had no sight at all, and his guilt had reached stratospheric proportions.

Beth's parents were...absent, to say the least. Suddenly Beth seemed solely dependent on him.

The next few weeks had been a nightmare, for her and for him. His carefree existence was finished. He'd dated her because she was gorgeous, vivacious, funny. Now she was his responsibility.

Blind and bereft, with no other options, she'd agreed to come home with him. He'd cared for her, protected her…and loved her? He still wasn't sure where care ended and love started but her need filled something inside he hadn't been aware was missing.

Her sight gradually returned, not fully but enough to manage. If she was careful. If she was protected.

And as the months went by their relationship had deepened. She'd lain in his arms and he'd known she felt safe and loved. That felt good enough for him. He'd lost sight of the carefree, bubbly girl he'd dated but in her place he had someone who'd need him for ever.

They'd married. And here she was, half-buried in this mess—with a child who wasn't his.

Was there a husband? Was someone else doing the protecting?

This wasn't the time for questions.

He was pushing memory away, years of training putting him on autopilot. Beth was leaning back, her eyes closed as he inserted an IV line.

'This'll make you sleepy,' he told her. 'Relax into it, sweetheart.'

'Toby…'

'You want us to take Toby? Beth, I swear I'll take care of him.'

'How do I know you mean that?' She even managed a smile. 'Of course you will.'

'How old is he?'

'Twenty months.'

'Is there someone we can call who he'll trust?'

Someone to sign papers if he had to be treated? Someone like the baby's father?

She wore no wedding ring. That didn't mean anything. Did it?

And once again his heart did this stupid lurch. This was Beth. His Beth. He wanted to gather her into his arms, hold her, keep her safe...

Which was exactly why she'd walked away from him eight years ago. Into...this.

'Margie,' she managed. 'At the childcare centre. Toby trusts...'

The childcare centre at the plaza? He was pretty sure it had been safely evacuated, but he couldn't be sure of every individual. Right now he could only focus on one trapped woman—a woman who was also his wife.

Ex-wife.

But no matter who she was, she was in trouble and she had no need to be worried by anything else.

Her voice was starting to drag and Luc thought the time for Beth to make decisions was over.

'Right,' he said, firmly and surely. 'Let's get Toby out of here, Beth, so we can concentrate on freeing your leg.'

'You'll look after him? If Margie can't?' Through the haze of pain and drugs, her voice was still fierce. 'Luc, swear?'

'I swear,' he said, and something inside him hurt. Badly. That she could still ask this of him... That she could still trust him...

He'd wanted this, so much, but to happen here, in this way...

And despite the pain and the fear, Beth must have sensed it. Her hand caught his and held.

'Luc, I swore I'd never need you again but I need you now. Thank you...'

His throat was so thick he couldn't speak, and it wasn't from the dust. He squeezed her hand back and then carefully lifted the sleeping child away from her breast. The little boy snuffled against Luc, recoiling a little as his face hit the repellent fabric of Luc's high vis jacket, and then relaxing again as Luc hauled a cloth someone handed him around the little boy's face. Luc tucked it in, giving him a soft place to lay his head as well as protection from the dust.

There were hands willing, wanting to take him, to carry him to safety, and Luc's priority had to be with Beth. But still he took a moment to hold, to feel the child's weight in his arms, to feel the steadiness of his breathing, his sleeping, trusting warmth.

He would take care of him. He'd take care of them both.

He must.

The next hour passed in a blur of medical need. The rest of the team was here now, with Blake in charge. They were panning out through the ruins, removing the need for Luc's attention to be on anything but Beth. Still trapped, she needed constant monitoring.

She was semiconscious, drugged to the point where pain and her surroundings were a haze.

Finally, moving with infinite caution, aware that a break in the concrete over her leg could mean parts of it would topple and cause more damage, the slab was lifted. Finally Beth was extricated.

She'd been wearing pants and leather boots. That had been a blessing—it had stopped lacerations that might well have been serious enough for her to bleed out. There was no doubt there were fractures, but blood still seemed to be getting through. Luc knew the greatest danger was the fact that the leg had been compressed for so long.

He accompanied the stretcher across the debris to the makeshift receiving tent the team had set up.

'Status?' Blake Cooper, ER consultant, had been working on an elderly man as Luc brought Beth in. The sheet drawn up over the man's face told its own story, as did the slump of Blake's shoulders.

'Lacerations, bruises, but priority's a broken ankle and crushed lower leg,' Luc told him.

Blake cast him a fast, concerned look. His voice was thick, Luc realised, and it wasn't from dust. 'Do you need me to assess?' He and Blake had worked together for so long they trusted each other implicitly. Luc knew Blake wasn't asking about Luc's ability, it was all about what he could see in Luc's face.

He shook his head. The stretcher was set down on the examination bench and almost unconsciously Luc's hand slid into Beth's and held it.

Blake saw, and the concern on his face grew, but there was no room for explanation.

Neither was there room for evasion, from Blake or from Beth herself. It would be great to say, *Beth's ankle's broken. We'll fix it in no time*, but the one thing he and Beth always had was total honesty. Sometimes it had broken them in two but it was something he couldn't change. He knew she was listening through her haze of medication. Her medical degree meant she'd recognise sugar coating and he had to say it like it was.

'I've given a peripheral nerve block,' he told Blake. 'There's definitely fracture and dislocation of the ankle, and we need to check for compartment syndrome.' Compartment syndrome had to be considered here. It was caused by extended crushing of the lower limb, forcing build-up of pressure in one section and loss of pressure in another. The long-term damage of sustained crushing was…unthinkable.

'Do what you have to do,' Beth said weakly, and Blake looked down into her face.

'Hi,' he said. 'I'm Dr Blake Cooper. You are…'

'This is Beth,' Luc said hoarsely, and then he added, because it seemed absurdly important for Blake to know. 'Blake, Beth's a doctor. She's also…my ex-wife.'

There was a moment's stillness while Blake took that on board. He searched Luc's face and Luc could see him reassemble priorities. And then it was business as usual.

'I'm very pleased to meet you,' Blake said, smiling down at Beth. 'Though I could wish the circumstances were different.' He took her wrist and felt her pulse, his face set in the lines of someone accustomed to triage, priorities. And Luc knew Beth was a priority. The risk of delayed treatment with compartment syndrome meant the possibility of a lifetime of pain, numbness or even amputation.

'We need to get the pressure in your foot checked now,' he said to Beth. 'You know what's going on?'

He'd accepted Beth's medical background without question. 'I… Yes,' Beth managed.

'Okay, I'm taking over,' Blake told her, with another fast glance at Luc. And Luc knew the glance. It was an order.

Step away, Luc. You're now a relative, too close to be objective and you need to let me take things from here.

'Beth, we need Luc on triage,' he told Beth. 'You know there's a small hospital here? I'm taking you through into Theatre. If I think there's pressure differential—and by the look of it I suspect that's inevitable—then I'll make an incision to decompress. Your ankle will need to be stabilised. That can be done in Sydney but the pressure needs to be taken off now. Is that okay with you?'

'I... Fine,' Beth managed. 'But... Toby?'

Blake looked a question at Luc and Luc managed to haul his attention from Beth to answer.

'Toby's Beth's son. Twenty months old. He was brought out half an hour ago.'

Some of the tension on Blake's face eased. 'A toddler. I saw him. Sam did the assessment and he's fine. He woke as she was examining him, demanding someone called Wobit...'

'Robert,' Beth said faintly. 'Rabbit.'

'Hey, we guessed right.' Blake smiled down at her. 'Apparently he was dropped, but one of the paramedics remembered and scooted over and rescued him.'

'We've also found your bag and purse,' Luc told her, still trying to keep his voice steady. 'How good are we? But now... Is there anyone we can call to look after Toby?'

'He has to come with me,' Beth managed. 'If I need to go to Sydney, Toby comes too. Luc, please... I need you to promise... I need...'

And something settled deep within.

'It's okay,' Luc said, and touched her face. 'I'll take care of him. I'll take care of you.'

And she managed a smile.

And then something odd happened. It was almost as if a ghost had touched him on the shoulder. He was looking down into Beth's grimed, dust-caked, filthy face, but all he saw was the smile. And in that smile... strangely this wasn't the Beth he'd remembered for the long years of divorce, the Beth who'd been his wife, the Beth he'd cared for for so long. Despite the filth, the fear, the pain, somehow this was Beth as he'd first seen her—a fellow med student laughing at him over a bench in the pathology lab. Her eyes had been sparkling with mischief. Someone must have made a joke. He couldn't remember what it was now. All he remembered was how he'd been caught in that smile, almost mesmerised.

He'd forgotten, he thought. In all those years of need and care, and then the long separation, he'd forgotten what a beautiful woman she was. Stunning.

How could he be remembering now? What the...?

'I'll take it from here,' Blake told him, looking at him strangely.

'Thanks, Blake.'

He had work to do. He had to leave—but heaven only knew the effort it cost him to move away.

From...his wife?

CHAPTER THREE

THE SURGERY BLAKE performed was primitive and fast, making incisions to equalise pressure and ensure that blood supply wasn't compromised before Beth could safely be transported. But Luc wasn't involved. With Beth in Theatre, with Toby safe, he needed to be back in the plaza.

In a sense they were lucky, Luc thought as he worked on. The injuries stayed within the scope of what he and the team could handle. If there'd been compromised breathing of more than one patient or, as sometimes happened in these appalling situations, the necessity for amputation in order to get people out, Beth's foot would have dropped on the triage list and Blake would have been needed out here in the plaza. But the efforts of Luc and the rest of the team were enough.

Not enough, though, for the five people pronounced dead at the scene, or the pilot of the plane, but Luc had worked in enough disasters to know how to block tragedy and keep going.

But he couldn't block the thought of Beth. The thought of what was happening in Theatre. The vision of her trapped and wounded in the rubble. The feel of her hands clutching her child...*her child*! Had she remarried? Where had she been all these years?

How could he have let her go? There'd seemed no choice—she'd given him no choice—but the rush of memory from that smile was doing his head in. Did some other man have the right to that smile?

He was trying desperately to focus but when he finished treating a teenager with a lacerated arm, he turned and saw Blake and he almost sagged with relief.

'O-okay?' Hell, where was his voice? And what was he doing, asking if she was okay? She was suffering from an injured foot, not anything life-threatening.

'She'll live,' Blake said, surveying him cautiously. Luc was known on the team for staying calm in any situation. He needed to get a grip now. Now!

'I've done what I can,' Blake told him. 'She has a fractured ankle but seemingly no other significant injury. The main problem is crush syndrome—compartmentalising—but I've done what I can to equalise pressure and I'm optimistic. But she needs an orthopod and a decent podiatric surgeon to evaluate muscle injury. We're evacuating her on the next chopper and I'm sending you back, too.'

'If I'm needed...'

Once again he got that careful, appraising look. Blake and Luc swapped in and out of the role of chief medic on site. They were both accustomed to checking team members for stress, and maybe—definitely—Blake could see Luc's stress now.

'We have enough medics on the ground here,' he said now, roughly.

And Luc thought, Dammit, he's worried. About me?

'I've been talking to the local doc. Apparently this

town has three doctors. Maryanne Clarkson's in her fifties, solid, unflappable. She's working her butt off in Casualty now. There's been an older doctor called Ron McKenzie, in his seventies, and your Beth. Ron and Beth run a clinic in the plaza, right by the car park. Ron's one of the casualties. Maryanne tells me your Beth's a single mum with no family here. Toby, her son, usually stays in childcare in the centre while she works. That's in the plaza, too. The staff did a magnificent job getting the kids out but they're all traumatised. Maryanne says that means there's no obvious person to care for Toby, and no one's stepped forward to be her accompanying person. So in view of that, I'm electing you. Unless the divorce was so acrimonious...'

'I... No.'

'Then you'll do it? She needs medical care during evacuation. I want blood supply to that foot constantly monitored. And she needs someone she knows.'

'And the child...'

'Does he know you?'

'I... No.' How could he know him? Until two hours ago Luc hadn't known he existed.

'Lucky you're good with kids, then,' Blake told him, moving on. 'I'm sending Beth and a guy with fractured ribs and lacerations. Plus Toby. There's room on the chopper and he's breathed in enough concrete dust to warrant twenty-four-hour obs. They're in your hands, Luc.'

'Right.'

Of course it was right. How many times had he done this, accompanying injured back to Sydney?

But Beth.

And her son.

She was a single mum? There'd been someone else. Had she walked away from him, too?

There was something inside him that clenched and wouldn't unclench.

He took a deep breath and struggled to focus. He needed to hand over what he'd done.

'Leave it, Luc,' Blake said roughly. 'Sam'll fill me in on what you've been doing. Your head's with Beth. Sorry, mate, but from now on I need to treat you as compromised. Are you sure you can manage on the plane?'

'Of course.'

'There's no of course about it. Where family's concerned…'

'Beth's not my family.'

'No? Well, maybe for now she has to be because, as far as I understand, she doesn't have anyone else. If it was Sam injured…'

Where had that come from? Blake and Sam—Samantha, SDR's newest recruit—had become an item and were now engaged to be married. They were a couple. There was no comparison.

Or maybe there was.

Until death do us part?

He and Beth had signed the divorce papers but those long-ago vows still whispered in his head. Telling him Blake was right.

Beth was injured. She wasn't family—how could she be? But somehow there were ties that meant that, yes, he'd stay beside her. For as long as he was needed.

'Beth?'

She'd been stirring for a while now, struggling to surface from a drug-induced sleep, fighting down fears crowding in from all sides. She'd been vaguely aware of being carried to a helicopter, being lifted aboard. She remembered the surge of fear as she'd thought she was being taken from Toby, but a paramedic had stooped over her stretcher, showing her a warmly wrapped bundle.

'He's asleep, Beth, but he's coming with us.'

'We even have Robert Rabbit, a bit scruffy but safely tucked in with him.' And it was Luc, a growly voice in the background. He'd been supervising the loading of another patient onto the chopper. She remembered thinking that was what Luc did. He got people out of trouble. He cared…

That care had been so stifling it had ended their marriage, but as she'd been lifted onto the chopper she'd sunk into it. She hadn't had a choice. Let Luc care and be grateful for it.

And now… They were in the air and he was saying her name, touching her shoulder. 'Beth? Stop fighting it, love. You're safe. But if you're awake…there's something you might like to see.'

Love? How long since anyone had called her that? But it was wrong. She should…

She couldn't. She let the word wash over her and insensibly it made her feel…okay.

'This is amazing,' Luc was saying. 'Can I help you sit up a little?'

'Wh-what?'

'This is too stunning to miss,' Luc was saying. 'And it might even make you feel better. You're supposed to be strapped in. Derek's right here beside you but he's fast asleep. He's copped broken ribs and lacerations and the morphine has put him out like a light. Toby's asleep, too, but I know you're awake. We have your glasses. As long as we can do this without moving your leg, you're okay to see. Beth, there's a thunderstorm. Let me help you.' And he was right beside her, gently raising her shoulders, cradling her against him, adjusting her glasses on her nose. 'Look out the window.'

She did—and she gasped in wonder.

The drugs she'd been given had taken away all pain. Confusion and fear faded. She felt warm and close to sleep. She was being cradled by...by...

Yeah, that was too hard to think about. She tried to block out the feel of him and focussed instead on what lay out the window.

It was indeed a thunderstorm, a massive one, enveloping Sydney in an awe-inspiring display.

Lightning flashed across the sky in a mass of jagged forks, splitting and splitting again. The entire sky was lit. The lightning seemed all around them. In the distance she could see the lights of Sydney. The Harbour Bridge. The amazing Opera House. They were lit themselves, but as each crack of lightning sizzled, their lights mingled with what nature was providing.

The drugs were making her fuzzy, weird, stunned. The sky outside was surreal.

Luc was holding her. Luc...

Focus. Lightning. Toby.

Danger? She should...she should...

'You're safe, love,' Luc said again, as if he guessed her fears. Which of course he always had. 'It looks stunning but it's well to the north and moving away. Our heliport's on the roof of Bondi Bayside Hospital. We're giving the storm a few minutes to clear before we land but we'll have you and Toby tucked up and safe in no time.'

So she could relax. She could lie back in his arms and let the wash of what looked like a massive pyrotechnic display stun her into silence. She could look out into the dark, stormy world and know that Luc had her safe.

She mustn't. Once upon a time she'd fallen for that sweet, all-enveloping trust and it had led to heartache and despair. She had to pull away.

But the drugs wouldn't let her and neither would her will. She'd been alone for so long. The fear of the time spent trapped was still with her. The terror.

Luc had her safe and she couldn't fight. For now... once again she had to let him care.

And then they landed and Luc had to take a step back. Blake had obviously forewarned the admission staff and Luc was greeted with something other than professional efficiency. These people were his friends. A barrage of questions was about to descend on him, but not now. He handed over notes and suddenly he was being treated as a relative. Paediatric staff took over the sleeping Toby's care. The orthopaedic team moved in and Beth was wheeled away to Theatre.

She'd been lucky, Luc thought. Or sort of lucky. Most of the crises his team attended didn't have the luxury of an onsite hospital, but Beth had had excellent treatment before transfer. Blake had been able to stabilise pressure, and she was now in the care of one of the best medical teams in Australia.

Bondi Bayside Hospital. The specialists here were world class.

But for now Luc wasn't one of them. Not that he was one of the permanent staff anyway. His role was that of emergency consultant, but he worked here only between medical crises outside the hospital. He couldn't imagine working in the same place day after day. Standing still. Ceasing to need the adrenaline of rescue.

Putting the past behind him.

The past was with him now. He stood in the admissions centre and stared out into the night. They'd been lucky to land when they had. The break in the rolling storms was over. Rain was battering the wide glass windows in the entrance foyer.

Midnight. The place was almost deserted. Ghost-like.

It was at times like this that the ghost of his past reappeared.

Ellen. Seven years old. Bright, bubbly, joyous. Naughty.

'Take your cousin to the playground, Luc.' Those words were still seared into his head. He'd been nine years old. His mother and his aunt had been having a beer or three with lunch, and Ellen's chatter had been interfering with their gossip. 'And take care of her. You know she's a bit silly. You're responsible.'

So off they'd gone, the half a block to the playground.

Luc's best friend, Nick, had been there with his mum. Nick's mum had been immersed in a book, happily reading. He remembered feeling pleased to see her.

He remembered feeling safe. It was a feeling he didn't have all that often with his mum. Or his aunt. But Nick's mum was okay.

So Ellen had raced for the swing, while Luc and

Nick had headed for the see-saw, seeing who could bang the other hardest against the ground as they rose and fell.

He could still see Nick's face laughing up at him.

Then, out of the edge of his eye, he'd seen the swing, suddenly empty, swinging wildly as Ellen jumped off. Then kids on the other side of the road. With a puppy...

'Hey!' Ellen's childish yell was seared into his memory. 'Candy, wait, it's me, Ellen. Is that your new puppy?'

He didn't have time to react. No one did. Ellen was already halfway across the road.

The car had nowhere to go.

And afterwards... The nightmare of adults, screaming, sobbing. 'Who's supposed to be caring for her? Of all the stupid, criminal...'

Nick's mother. 'She's not mine. I didn't even see...'

Then his mother and aunt, haggard, hysterical, dragged from their beer and pleasure to confront a nightmare. His aunt. 'We told you to take care of her, you stupid, stupid boy.'

His own mother. 'It's my fault, Lucy. I thought he was responsible. I thought I could depend on him.'

'It is his fault.' His aunt had hissed it at her, hissed it at him. 'Get him out of my sight.'

What followed was vitriol, recriminations and consequences. His aunt had kicked them out and the cycle of crises and homelessness had resumed.

Until finally... 'I can't care for both of us.' His mother, sober for once, flat and inflexible. 'You got us into this mess, Luc. You face the cost.'

The cost was foster care. Loneliness. Knowing it was all his fault.

Somehow he'd fought his way through it. He'd had a couple of decent sets of foster parents. He'd been smart, and study had been a way to block out pain.

He'd made it into medicine. He'd almost felt...in control?

And then he'd met Beth and taken her camping. The virus. Her blindness.

And now this.

He hadn't even been able to protect Beth. His own wife...

He felt like smashing something. Anything.

He was going nuts here. He had to do something.

He still had Beth's holdall, with her day-to-day stuff. Her phone. Toddler gear. A briefcase of patients' notes shoved on top. Her glasses.

She'd need her glasses.

Thankful for a specific task he headed for the admission desk. The receptionist greeted him cautiously. She knew him—of course she did. Gossip would have reached her as fast as the hospital grapevine would allow, which in Luc's experience was pretty much faster than the speed of light.

'You've admitted Beth...'

'Carmichael? You know she's in Theatre?' She paused while she thought about where to take it, and came down on the side of forgetting about the Doctor before his name and treating him as a relative. 'You know, you might like to pop home and take a shower,' she told him, and for the first time Luc realised he was still liberally encrusted with concrete dust. 'We'll ring you the moment she's out.'

'Right,' he growled. 'What ward's she going to?'

'Orthopaedic,' she said, sounding surprised, and

then realised what he really wanted. 'Whoops, sorry.' She checked a list on her screen. 'Oh. We're almost full so we've had to pop her into a double. She's in with Harriet. Harriet's going to Rehab in the morning so your Beth will have a great room for the rest of her stay.'

Your Beth?

He didn't want to go there.

Focus on the room. Harriet's room was spacious and the admission staff had tried hard to keep it occupied only by Harriet. It would have been one of the last beds left

'But she'll go to Recovery first,' the receptionist said helpfully. She gave him her best reassuring smile. 'I'm sure she'll be fine.'

'I'll take her bag up and leave it for her,' he growled, and the receptionist looked surprised. As if she was questioning why Luc was bothering to tell her.

It was no big deal, he thought. He and Beth hadn't been married for eight years now. She was just another patient.

Except she wasn't.

The nurses had been in and prepared Beth's space. All was in readiness. The room was dark, silent. Waiting. Harriet was asleep.

How often during the last few weeks had he popped in to see Harriet during the night? She wasn't coping well with the new norm of a leg that'd always be problematic. The rock fall had almost been lethal. Lightning reflexes had saved her but she'd been left with a comminuted fracture of her tibula and fibula, and there'd been significant soft tissue and nerve damage. She'd come close to losing her leg. Compared to Harriet's injury, Beth's was minor and he knew Harriet spent hours staring at the ceiling, trying to figure where to take life from here.

So he often came in here and sat, but this night…it was very, very different.

He should go home and have his shower, he thought, but instead he left the bag, then headed for the sluice room, stripped off his filthy outer gear, washed and then returned to Beth's ward.

Harriet's ward, he reminded himself. After all, Harriet was his friend. Beth was… Beth was…

He wasn't sure what Beth was. He sat in the darkened room and waited and tried to settle.

Ha.

His phone vibrated in his pocket and he headed out into the corridor to answer.

'Dr Braxton?'

'Yes.' It was an internal call and his breath caught. Beth was in Theatre. What was happening?

'It's Recovery,' the nurse on the other end of the line told him. 'You're on her form as contact person.'

'Yes. Are things…?' Strange how his mouth was suddenly dry. This was only a fractured leg, he told himself, but still… 'Is everything okay?'

'Beth's waking now. She's asking for you—and for someone called Toby?'

'That's her son.'

'Is he okay?'

'He's fine. He's asleep in kids' ward. Observation only—no obvious injuries.' He'd checked in on the way to Beth's ward. Toby had been bathed and was sleeping with his rabbit.

'She's not really out of it yet,' the nurse was saying. 'But her first words were frantic. I'm wondering…we'll be sending her up to the ward in about half an hour. Would it be possible for her to see her son? I have a feeling she won't settle until she's seen him safe. And you, too.'

'She won't be worried about me.'

'Really?' The nurse sounded dubious. 'She sounded…well, be that as it may, if Toby's okay could you arrange to have him there, just for a moment so she can see for herself?'

'Of course.'

But…

He thought of lifting Toby and carrying him through the darkened rooms to sit with him while he waited for Beth…

It felt like a weird, sweet web was closing about him. A web he'd once embraced and he knew he would again—the web of being needed.

'Luc…'

She was enveloped in darkness, though shimmers of light were breaking through Harsh light. There was something beeping beside her. Her hand…there was something on her hand.

She was trapped. The fear was like a tidal wave, smothering her to the exclusion of everything else.

'Toby.' She heard her own anguish. 'Toby. Luc…'

'Beth?' It was a nurse, speaking in cool, professional and blessedly grounding tones. 'It's okay. You're safe and so is your son. You've been in surgery for a fractured ankle. It's gone well and now you're in Recovery. You're safe, Luc's safe and so is Toby. I promise.'

The light settled. She opened her eyes and it really was light, normal light, reassuring light. A nurse was smiling down at her.

Would she ever get over that fear of darkness?

'It's okay,' the nurse said again. 'They tell me you've been in real trouble but you're safe now. We've stabilised your ankle, we've cleaned up your cuts and bruises and you're going to be fine. And I've spoken to your Dr Luc. Your ex-husband, they're telling me? What a dark horse he is, we never knew. I can tell you now, though, whatever's in your past the reason you married him must still hold true. There's no one more caring, and right now he's caring for Toby. They're up in the ward, waiting for you. As soon as the effects of the anaesthetic fade, we'll have you with them. So close your eyes now, Beth, and let us care for you.'

She let the words wash over her for a moment, settle. Luc, caring for Toby. Of course. He would. And because it was Toby she had to be grateful. Again.

She was. But…

'I don't think I will close my eyes,' she whispered. 'I don't want the darkness.'

'There's nothing to be afraid of.'

You have no idea, Beth said to herself as she absorbed the reality of where she was, the technology-filled surroundings of the recovery suite. With Luc… somewhere. You have no idea of how much reason there is to be very afraid.

CHAPTER FOUR

TOBY WOKE BRIEFLY and whimpered as Luc lifted him from his cot. If he'd woken completely and wailed he might have left him where he was, but he was obviously a kid used to a working mum, odd hours, childcare. He didn't panic. The nurses helped Luc wrap him in soft, cuddly blankets. He had his rabbit. He snuggled against Luc's shoulder and he slept again.

Luc carried him back to Beth's ward—Harriet's ward—and settled into a visitor's chair to wait. Toby slept on, peaceful, supremely trustful. Leaving Luc to his thoughts.

And Luc thought of what Beth had been doing. Working as a family doctor? The difficulties she'd be facing would be enormous, he thought, but to do it with a child...

Where was the father? As far as he could figure she was on her own, and if she was... Toby must be used to being shared.

He held him close and he felt...he felt...

'Want to tell me what's going on?'

It was Harriet, speaking sleepily from the bed on the far side of the room. 'Luc? Is that you?'

'It's me,' he growled.

'Are you holding…a baby?'

'Toby.'

'Toby.' She was speaking as if she wasn't sure where she was going. 'It's true, then. One of the nurses said my new roomie is about to be…your ex-wife? She was under the rubble?'

'Beth.' The whole hospital would know by now, he thought grimly. The grapevine would be in overdrive.

'Beth?' Harriet was suddenly wide awake. They'd both kept their voices low in deference to the sleeping Toby. The lights were dim. It was a weirdly intimate setting. A place for asking…and telling…secrets? 'Is she okay?'

'Lacerations, bruises, plus a broken ankle. She was trapped by falling concrete so compartment syndrome was an issue, but she's had excellent, fast treatment. She's in Recovery now and the surgery's gone well.'

'That's great.' But Harriet's voice still sounded cautious. 'The baby…'

'He's twenty months.'

'Toddler, then. Is he yours?'

And that was a stab from left field. It was a question that required a simple no, but as he held the little boy close there were so many mixed feelings…

Is he yours?

He wasn't. He wasn't anything to do with him. So why did he feel…?

'No,' he managed. 'We've been apart for eight years.'

'Want to tell Aunty Harry about it?'

'I… No.'

'Hey, that's hardly reasonable. How much have I told you about me?'

And he had to concede that was fair.

He and Harriet had worked side by side in situations that'd be enough to give normal people nightmares. They'd become the best of friends. Once upon a time he'd even asked her out and her response still made him smile. 'What? Us? It'd be like dating my twin.'

It was true. Over the years, in the waiting times between crises, evacuating patients together, depending on each other's skills, they'd become a team, but it wasn't until these last few weeks that Harriet had talked about her past. And now... It was his turn?

'So you've been married?'

'I told you.'

'And your ex-wife is about to share my ward. Is she a monster?'

'No!' Unconsciously he held Toby a little closer. 'She's...an amazing woman.'

'The nurses are saying she's a doctor.'

'Yes.'

'And you split when?'

'I... Eight years ago.'

'So Toby?'

'I have no idea who Toby's father is. No one at the scene seemed to know. They're saying she's a single mum. That's why we brought him with us.'

'And it's why the admin staff listed you as next of kin. The nurses told me. Honestly, this is all over the hospital. Luc Braxton's secret love child. Or not.' She was eyeing him cautiously and Luc thought she was using him to take her mind off her own troubles. So when she pushed further... 'Come on, Luc, tell all,' he finally did.

'Beth and I dated at med school,' he told her. 'And

then she copped encephalitis, with complications. Optical neuritis. For months she was almost completely blind. She regained some sight but it's still…not perfect. Not even close. We married and I took care of her, but…she hated it. And it was more than hating the disability. She hated…having to depend on me. I didn't mind—hell, it was me who took her camping. I probably caused the damned mosquito bite, but she fought me every inch of the way. How many times she burned herself, hurt herself because she wouldn't let me help. And then she swore she'd finish medicine. I thought…maybe with help she could get through. She could think about something like psychiatry but she wouldn't accept her limitations. And now…hell, Harry, she's been practising as a family doctor. Plus she's got a kid. What's she been thinking?'

'Wow,' Harriet said softly. 'She sounds like some woman.'

'She's an independent, stubborn, foolhardy…'

'Yeah, just like me saying I want to go back to Specialist Disaster Response.'

'It's not the same.'

'No? But then you have a warped view on what you'd do yourself compared to what you expect the rest of the world to do.'

'Harry…'

'Hey, I think I'm going to enjoy meeting your Beth,' Harriet said, for once sounding almost cheerful. 'We sound like we'll get along. Common enemy and all that. Speaking of which, isn't that the sound of the theatre lift arriving? Pull my curtains, Luc. I'll try for sleep and leave you to your Beth.'

* * *

'One, two, three, lift...'

How many times had she heard that, the phrase used by every paramedic as they shifted patient from trolley to bed, from bed to trolley?

She'd never heard it referring to her, though. Even when the encephalitis had been at its worst, she'd been able to move herself. She could help.

Even if Luke hadn't wanted her to.

'Be careful.'

And the words from beside her slammed her back to a time past, the warning, the voice, the care that seemed to be swinging its way through the fog of this nightmare night. It was Luc's voice. *Be careful?* She held the thought. How could she not be careful when that voice was with her?

'She's in safe hands.' It was an older, big-bosomed woman, talking as the nurses plumped pillows under her head and tucked warmed blankets around her. Beth could hear the smile in the woman's voice. 'I'm Hilda Heinz, orthopaedic surgeon,' she told Beth. 'I should have caught up with you in Recovery but we've had a queue. No matter. We've done a lovely job on your ankle. It's beautifully aligned and should heal really well. The team on site did a great job preventing long-term damage through crush injury and I envisage a good recovery. A few days in here until the swelling subsides, a sexy black boot, compliance with rules, a spot of rehab and you'll be as good as new by Christmas.'

By Christmas... Three months...

'But not to worry about that now,' Hilda was say-

ing. 'All you need to know is that you're fine. Your
surgery's all done and here's Dr Braxton holding your
little boy. Sound asleep. Oh, what a sweetheart. No,
don't you move. Any pain? No? Excellent. If you have
any breakthrough push this button here, PCA—patient-
controlled analgesia—you know how it works? Great.
The buzzer's right by your other hand. Dr Braxton, let
us know when you leave, and the nurses will take over
obs from then.'

And she whisked away with the nurses, and Beth
was left lying in the dim light, trying to regain her
bearings.

Which seemed very shaky indeed.

'Toby...' That seemed important to say, and Luc
gently lifted his bundle across so she was within inches
of her little boy's face.

He was still sleeping.

Toby was a doctor's kid, used to being cared for
by others, used to being lifted in the dead of night
when she finally finished at the hospital and carried
him home.

When she'd first moved to Namborra it had seemed
more than enough that she was finally able to practise
medicine. But then, settled, working hard, living within
the community, she'd allowed herself to think past her
career. Another relationship seemed impossible. After
Luc...well, she wasn't going there again. But a baby...

And one night she'd talked about it to the elderly
doctor she worked with. She'd just given Ron a sky-
dive for his seventieth birthday. He was lit from within.
After years of struggling with the death of his wife,
treating himself as old and useless, he was back in
partnership with her. They both had issues, but be-

tween them they reckoned they made one and a half very competent doctors. After the sky-dive Ron was ready to declare the one and a half description was an underestimation.

'There's nothing we can't do,' he'd declared. 'So, Beth, why don't you have a baby? Use donor semen—whatever? And don't say you can't do it alone. You know this whole town will help you.'

They could. They did, which was why Toby was accustomed to sleeping in strangers' arms. Which was why Luc could hold him and he didn't stir.

Luc… It was eight years since she'd seen him.

He was a stranger.

Focus on Toby.

She wasn't wearing her glasses, but they wouldn't help much in dim light anyway. So she did as she so often did. She saw through touch.

She put her hand out and drew her baby's face, reassuring herself there were no scratches. No tears. His eyes were closed. His little mouth was still…perfection.

'The rest of him's great, too,' Luc said gently as her palm cupped his cheek. 'The paediatric staff have gone all over him. He's perfect.'

Why did that make her want to cry?

Why did Luc's voice make her want to cry?

She had an almost irresistible urge to move her hand from Toby's face to Luc's, to let herself feel what was the same, what was different.

So much was different. She was different. She'd fought for her independence and won, but at what cost?

'Hey,' he said softly as she closed her eyes and stopped trying to see. 'Welcome back to the land of the un-squashed, Dr Carmichael. I can't tell how good it feels to see you on this side of the slab of concrete.'

She thought about that for a while, and the warmth, the doziness from the drugs, the knowledge that Toby was safe—and, yes, the fact that Luc was beside her—faded into the background as memories from the afternoon flooded back. The noise. The fear…

'What happened?' she managed. 'I mean…it was a plane?'

'A cargo plane,' he told her. 'Best guess at the moment is that the pilot had some sort of collapse—maybe an infarct. He ploughed along the top of the plaza, bringing the roof down. The concrete pillars supporting the undercover car park folded—that was where you were. The plane then crashed into the sports oval. No one was on the oval.'

She thought about that for a while. She tried to feel relief, but…

'The pilot?'

'Killed instantly, but maybe he was dead beforehand. That's up to the coroner to decide.'

'And…' How hard was it to ask? 'The plaza? The… the childcare centre?'

'Lots of noise and dust and frightened children. They were trapped for a while but the staff had the sense not to try and shift things to get them out. They're all safe.'

'There's more, though,' she whispered, remembering the crash, the screams, the terror. 'I know…'

'There is.' She could hear the reluctance in his voice and she knew he'd tell her. When had Luc been anything but honest? 'The car park was the worst hit. We're confirming identities now but the locals were sure even before I got on the chopper with you. As far as we know there were five deaths. Bill Mickle. You know him? The local greyhound trainer? Ray and Daphne Oddie. Farmers in their seventies. A woman called Mariette Goldsworthy, a friend of Ray and Daphne's from out of town. And Ron. Ron McKenzie.' His voice grew even more gentle. 'Ron was killed instantly as he walked down into the car park. They tell me you knew him very well. Another doctor. Your partner? Your friend.'

'Ron...' The distress she felt was almost overwhelming.

'I'm so sorry.' Almost unconsciously his hand slipped into hers and held.

She should pull away. She should...

She didn't. He was cradling her son against his chest. He was holding her hand. With the little boy between them they made an island of refuge with the baby enclosed, a nucleus of safety and comfort. It was an illusion—she knew it was—but right now she needed it. Soon she'd have to pull away, as she'd pulled away before, but right now her need was too great. Ron... dead. Her best friend.

She held on for all she was worth.

'You should sleep.' He said it softly but he didn't move and she made no effort to let him go. To let the darkness of the night take over.

The memories were suddenly all around her, that night in hospital so long ago when her world had suddenly grown dark. When Luc had seemed all that lay between her and horror.

'Where's your family?' he'd asked then. They'd known each other for such a short time, he hadn't even known.

'Absent,' she'd told him, shortly. They were always absent. Her clever parents, super smart. When the gravity of her illness had become obvious, when she'd been unable to see at all, her father had phoned from Zurich, barking instructions to the medical staff, offering to fly her to the States for some super treatment a colleague was researching. Her mother had flown in from Glasgow and spent two days with her, most of which had been spent on the phone, reorganising commitments. Both of them had transferred money.

'You'll need carers, at least for the short term, and if things don't improve you'll need specialist accommodation. Your father and I will both contribute...'

But Luc had said no such thing. When the time had come for discharge he'd simply picked her up and carried her home. He'd put his studies on hold for six months. He'd cared for her. He'd told her he loved her.

She remembered the first time he'd said it. 'I love you.' Three little words. Her mother signed off emails with the love word all the time.

Love you, sweetheart. Mum.

Apart from that... She couldn't remember anyone using the words. We're proud of you. That was her parents' equivalent. They were proud that she was independent, that when she'd been packed off to boarding school aged five she'd coped. They loved that she didn't need them.

But Luc... The first time she'd met him her heart had done a crazy backflip with pike, and that feeling had never faded. During that short camping trip she'd kept asking herself, could love happen so fast? And then, when she'd been so ill, he'd never once thought of walking away. He'd held her and he'd loved her and she'd thought he'd be her home for ever. For the first time in her life she'd felt cared for, cherished, safe.

But in the end…it was a sweet, sticky mesh, a trap for someone who'd never had such caring, who hadn't realised…what went with it.

But she knew now. Basing marriage—basing *love*—on need led to disaster. It was a lesson hard learned, but by now it was instilled into her bones. So now she found the courage to tug back. He let her go without a protest and she slipped her hand under the covers, as if it could betray her if she didn't hold it close.

'Can you sleep?' he asked.

'I don't…think so.' She felt tears slipping down her face. Ron…

'Want to tell me about Ron?' he asked, and she knew he was giving her space. That was the thing about Luc. He always knew…

'He's…he was amazing.' She forced herself to focus on her friend. His loss was a gut-wrenching emptiness that'd take time to come to terms with—would she ever?—but for now…for now she accepted the invitation to talk about him. It helped. For Ron's sake?

For hers. It stopped…the other ache. The need for her betraying hand to slip from the covers and take Luc's again.

'I met him five years ago,' she whispered, trying to block out Luc's presence and let herself drift without pain. 'After you…after we split I took a job in Brisbane, with their palliative care unit. My sight was slowly improving but there were still restrictions. I worked with a great specialist staff who used me to the maximum but of course there were things I couldn't do. I was desperate to work in family medicine but it seemed I couldn't. And then there was Ron…'

'Tell me.'

'Ron's wife was a hospice inpatient for about four months. She had bone metastases with spinal collapse and needed round-the-clock specialist nursing. Ron was a family doctor but he was almost seventy. He'd been off work for two years as he cared for Claire and when she died he was…bereft. Stranded. He felt old and useless. After Claire's funeral I found the ad for a doctor at Namborra in the medical journal. It seemed a decent medical centre but remote. Desperate for doctors. Ron loved the country. He and Claire had been aching for a country retirement when she fell ill and he was desperate for something, anything to fill the void. So I pointed it out to him and he said: "I will if you will".'

'I don't get it. Weren't you happy in the hospice?'

'Safe, you mean.' It was impossible to keep the old bitterness from her voice. Even now. 'Yes, I was. I was needed. I was used mostly for counselling, for explaining treatments, outcomes, and I could have stayed there for ever. But that's not what I trained to do. I wanted family medicine and Ron gave me that.'

'I don't understand.'

'We offered Namborra one and a half doctors. Ron was slowing down—he had arthritis and a gammy knee. My sight's a problem but the medical board were satisfied that I had enough to get by. With help. So we made the agreement to run clinics together. Patients coming in get sighted by Ron—more and more it's simply Ron doing a quick visual as he calls his own patients. Anyone looking unexpectedly pasty or rashy he tells me, and if anything needs detailed examination I call him. But I have a magnifying head lamp. I can see for injections and IVs—with the magnifying lamp I'm better than someone with fifty fifty vision. The more I know the community the easier it is, and anything needing young and fit, I'm your man. I've even been known to crawl into a car wreck, with Ron backing me on the sidelines. He trusts... He...trusted...'

But then her voice broke. She couldn't go on.

'Sweetheart, enough.' He ran his fingers gently through her hair, something he'd done long ago. She could feel the mat of concrete dust between his fingers and her scalp and she minded. She wanted those fingers closer. 'Enough,' he said again. 'Grieve for Ron tomorrow. For now you need to sleep. You need to take care of you.'

The feel of his fingers, the feeling in her fuzzy mind, was insidious in its sweetness. She could close her eyes and let go. Relax into his caring. But...

'But Toby...' She forced her mind to think. Toby was still cradled against Luc's chest. 'What...what happens to Toby?'

Would he stay in hospital? Would someone call social services?

'Where's his dad?' Luc asked.

'Not on the scene.' Her mind was doing a stupid, scared spiral. She should have insisted he stay in Namborra. She had friends there. Oh, but to leave him...

'Where are your parents?'

'I have no idea.' It didn't matter. Not in a million years would they drop everything to care for their grandson. They'd thought she was insane when she'd told them she was pregnant. 'I guess…if he can stay in hospital tonight…'

But she hated that, too. He'd have scratches—he must have—and the one thing hospitals worldwide had no answer for was the risk of superbugs. It was a small risk but, oh…

Social services, then? Foster care?

The thought was enough to overwhelm her. She felt sick, so nauseous she felt close to vomiting.

But Luc's hand was on hers again, his grip firm.

'It's okay, Beth. If you agree… I'm due for leave. The service hates it accruing, so there's pressure to take it and I'm thinking this is the time I can. I have an apartment just over the road from the hospital. If you agree, I can hit the paediatric staff for a crib, high chair, stroller, bottles, whatever I need. Then I can take him home with me.'

'With you.' The drugs were really kicking in now. She'd had a jab of pain from her foot and had squeezed the morphine feed. Now she wished she hadn't. The night was hazy enough already.

She couldn't see Luc's face. The light was so dim, even if she had normal sight she might not be able to see it.

She remembered all that time ago, when the darkness had closed in. She remembered Luc letting her—encouraging her—to read his face. To run her fingers over the strong bone structure. To let her fingers see his thick, dark hair, the harsh outline of his jaw, the deep set eyes she knew were almost black, the stubble of after-five shadow that seemed to return about two minutes after he shaved. She wanted that now—but surely it was the drugs. It had to be the drugs.

Luc. Taking Toby home with him.

The same sweet trap…

What option did she have? But her night was spinning.

'Hey, you can trust him.' It was a woman's voice from the other side of the curtain. 'Luc, we need an introduction.'

'Harriet,' Luc said, and rose with his sleeping bundle and drew back the curtain. 'Didn't you promise to go to sleep?'

'I said I'd try, not that I would.' In the dim light Beth could make out a figure in the next bed, a woman, with her leg in some sort of traction. 'Hi, Beth,' the woman said. 'You're doing pretty well for post op, post trauma. I'm your roomie, Harriet. I'm also one of Luc's colleagues, part of the SDR service, and just in case you're lying there wondering whether you can trust this guy with your baby, I'm here to tell you he's good.'

'Luc's good?' She was struggling to make her voice work. Oh, her head hurt.

'Hey, Beth, it's time to let go.' Harriet's voice gentled as she heard Beth's confusion. 'You've had one hell of a day. But before you do… Beth, last year your Luc was caught up in a flood rescue. A pregnant mum with three kids. The mum had gone into labour, which was why she'd been too scared to evacuate. She'd been waiting for an ambulance or for her husband to reach her when the water hit. Luc was lowered into the house just on dark. They were surrounded by floodwater and it was too wild to get anyone else down there. So they were stuck there until mid-morning. At dawn we went in and found them.

'S-safe?'

'Of course safe,' Harriet said, as if there could never have been any doubt. 'They were stuck in the attic but Mum had delivered her baby safely and Luc had everything under control. Mum was snuggled in bedding Luc had dragged from downstairs. She was warm, safe, cuddling her newborn and the rest of the kids were pretending to be the Lilliputians in *Gulliver's Travels*, using the ropes Luc had used descending to tie him up. I don't know who was having more fun, Luc or the kids. Luc had managed to take diapers, wipes, food, everything they needed, upstairs before the flood destroyed everything in the kitchen, and the kids were gutted they were being rescued. So I'm just saying... Beth, you can trust this guy. Let him take care of your baby and go to sleep.'

What was there in that statement that made Beth weep? There was a stupid tear sliding down her nose and when Luc stooped to wipe it away, she couldn't stop. More followed.

And Luc swore.

'Dammit, Beth, you're past exhausted. But you're safe now, and so's Toby. So, please, trust me. Believe Harriet. You know I can cope. Let me care for you both. Go to sleep.'

Let me care...

How hard had it been eight years ago to walk away from that statement? How much pain had that caused? Yet here it was again, a siren song, and she had no strength to resist.

'Let it go,' he told her, and she had no choice.

'Just...just for tonight,' she managed, and he wiped her face again.

'Of course just for tonight. Worry about tomorrow tomorrow. Sleep now, Beth, and trust me.'

She had no choice. She closed her eyes and let herself sink into something she'd sworn never to need again.

Luc.

He'd just offered to take care of a toddler—for how long? By himself?

Was he out of his mind?

But the thought of not offering almost killed him. How could he not?

Here it comes again, he thought savagely. The need to care. The almost overwhelming urge to take on the safety of the whole world.

He'd even talked to the psych about it.

'Luc, do you think every catastrophe in the world is your fault?'

She'd asked that and he'd grinned and pushed it aside but her question hadn't been a joke.

He thought of the squeal of brakes, his little cousin's body lying on the road, the ring of adults screaming, sobbing, his aunt turning to shake him until his head was almost shaken from his shoulders.

Then Beth...lying terrified in her hospital bed, seeing nothing but darkness. The neurosurgeon... 'Encephalitis... It's a rare disease and optical neuritis an even rarer complication, but the mosquitoes this year are almost plague proportion. Didn't either of you have the sense to use repellent?'

His fault.

He had a twenty-month-old baby boy in his arms. He needed to keep him safe.

Another vision…

Beth, her sight recovering, standing in the little kitchenette they'd shared. Her finger sticky with blood after a knife had slipped. She'd been chopping carrots.

'So what?' Her reaction had been loaded with frustration, fury. 'You know my sight's returning. Do you think I'll let you chop my carrots for ever? Everyone has accidents in the kitchen, Luc.'

'You know your sight's not perfect. I can—'

'No, *I can.*' She'd yelled it at him. 'I can and I will. And, sure, I'll mess up along the way but that's the way it is. No, I'm not perfect but who is? I need to take the odd risk. I need to live, Luc, and I can't do it wrapped in cotton wool.'

'I'm only saying it's sensible to let me—'

'I don't want to be sensible.' She'd sighed and swiped a tissue and wrapped her bleeding finger. 'Enough. This isn't ever going to work. I'm leaving. You get to chop your own carrots. I'm off to chop mine, regardless of whatever blood I shed along the way. You've been fantastic, Luc, but your job is done. You've saved me enough. Now it's time for me to save myself.'

But she hadn't been able to. The memory of her crushed under the rubble was doing his head in.

At least she was being sensible now. She knew she had no choice. She was accepting his caring, which meant… He had sole care of the toddler sleeping solidly in his arms.

A toddler. Help.

As if on cue, Toby stirred and whimpered, and Luc's arms tightened around him. Beth's baby.

He should be…

No, that was an almost creepy thing to think. Their marriage was years dead. This was his friend's baby, nothing more.

But still he held, and something about the warmth of the little body, the way the toddler curved into him… Something settled inside him.

It felt right to be caring for him. It felt good to be allowed to help.

Years of crisis intervention had involved years of panicked kids. He was known in the team as the kiddie whisperer, with an innate ability to calm panicked kids. He murmured to Toby and held him closer as he headed to kids' ward. What he needed was equipment. There were all sorts of very capable nurses down there to give him all the advice he needed. He could do this.

For however long it took?

He had no choice. This was for Beth. His ex-wife.

Yeah. The only thing was… Why did it feel wrong to put the ex in front of her title?

CHAPTER FIVE

A WEEK LATER Beth was discharged.

Home?

That was a joke, Beth thought as Luc pushed her wheelchair through the hospital entrance into the sunshine. He paused for a moment as though he understood the sheer sensuous joy of emerging from an air-conditioned hospital into... Bondi Beach.

This wasn't home but it felt amazing.

The hospital was built on a rise overlooking the bay. Her hospital room had had views back over the city, but the street from the hospital entrance ran straight down to the sea.

In the week since her accident the Namborra optometrist had sent her a pair of unscratched glasses, plus a year's supply of contact lenses—*Free of charge, Beth, get well fast!* Now the ocean glimmered, sparkled, sang in the morning light and she had an almost overwhelming urge to ditch her wheelchair and jump straight in.

Sadly, her leg was in a giant moon boot, propped on a frame in front of her. She had crutches but Hilda's advice was to use the wheelchair as much as she could.

Toby was sitting happily on her knee, crowing with glee as they emerged into the sunlight, enjoying this amazing new version of a stroller. Luc was behind her wheelchair. Dictating where she went?

That was hardly fair, she reminded herself. He was being extraordinarily generous. For the last week he'd devoted himself to Toby, bringing him in to visit her two or three times a day, showing enormous patience as his life had been taken over by a toddler.

She'd accepted his offer of help, but her choices had been…well, non-existent. She accepted Luc's help or she handed Toby over to welfare.

And now she was becoming even more indebted. Yes, she was being discharged from hospital but she still needed ongoing rehab. That wasn't available in Namborra.

She could have hired herself a furnished apartment but that left her depending on taxis, on outside help. Toby was fast, beetling around his world with toddler disregard for safety. She saw herself launching across strange rooms to prevent catastrophe—with her leg in a massive boot—and knew she had to accept Luc's offer.

'Home straight away?' He must have sensed her need to take deep breaths of the sea air, to gaze out over the ocean, to let herself come to grips with the fact that she was out of hospital, she was healing, she was safe.

As long as she let Luc take control.

'I… What do you mean?'

'I mean I took your gear over to the apartment earlier. We can go straight there now or we could go down to the beach first. It's a great morning.

'You should be at work.'

'I told you, Beth,' he said gently. 'I'm on compulsory holidays.'

'It's not much of a holiday, taking care of us.'

'It's my privilege. I owe—'

'Don't you dare.' Her anger flashed from nowhere. 'You owe me nothing. I went camping with you and a mosquito bit me. We were having a gorgeous time until then, but ever since, every time you look at me all you see is guilt.'

'That's not true.'

'It is,' she said grimly. 'Luc, you know I fell in lust with you the first time I saw you, and that camping trip…wow. Then afterwards, you were so wonderful I didn't see what was under it. That you needed to be needed. All I knew was that I loved being cared for. I loved being cherished. But in the end it almost killed you to let me do something as simple as chop carrots. Luc, we married for all the wrong reasons and I've more than proved I can handle my life alone.'

'But you're injured now.'

'You're telling me that's your fault as well?'

'If you weren't sight impaired…'

'Right, so that concrete pillar wouldn't have fallen on me if I'd been able to look up and see it fall?' She was trying very hard not to twist and yell. 'Oh, for heaven's sake… Luke, it happened in an instant and no one else injured or killed was sight impaired. And the sight thing… Sure, I have trouble in low light. Yes, I need correction, but technology's so great that now… guess what? I can even chop carrots all by myself. I've been doing it for eight years now and I still have every one of my fingers. As soon as I get this stupid boot off my leg I'll be independent again.'

'But you need me now.'

'I do,' she said through gritted teeth. 'But you know what? I intend to treat you like a friend. And the thing with real friends is that they don't need to be thanked all the time, and they'll also accept when to back off. So back off, Luc. Know that I'm incredibly grateful for what you're doing for me, but for the rest… Let me do what I'm capable of, and accept that where I am is nothing to do with you. I have enough to worry about without accepting your guilt. If you can't manage that then I can organise my own apartment and hire baby-sitters at need.'

'Don't you dare.'

'That's just the problem, Luc. You never let me dare anything.' She glared up at him and then shrugged. 'Okay. I'm grateful. Really I am. Let's go to the beach and forget it.'

And she put her hands on the wheels and shoved, moving the chair forward.

There was a road. A kerb. A drop. A lurch.

She had to let go of the wheels and grab Toby.

Luc caught her before she tilted and fell.

There was a moment's silence while traffic whizzed past. She sat and stared ahead, counting to ten. Then to twenty. She thought about counting to a hundred.

And finally Luc spoke. 'Beth, really, how much can you see?'

Her anger was still with her, but she'd just given her-self a fright. She'd shoved her chair toward the road. Toby was on her knee.

She hadn't been totally stupid. Even if she'd fallen she would have just fallen on the kerb. A bike lane protected her from oncoming cars, but still…she had been dumb.

One of the things she'd found hardest, still found

hard, was accepting her limitations. She took a deep breath, fought for calm, and finally she said it like it was.

'I'm sorry I scared you,' she managed. 'That was stupid. I need to figure this chair out, what I can and can't do, but what I just did had nothing to do with impaired sight. It was temper. My visual impairment is six/sixty without glasses, but my field of vision is around a hundred and twenty degrees. So, yes, I'm impaired but with my glasses or contact lenses I'm close to normal. Not in dull light, though—being honest, that screws me. Colours fade. Under the concrete…that was terrifying. But that's it, Luc. Usually I can do and see almost everything a normal person can.

'What I did was dumb but here's the thing. I'm not all about my disability. I have hormonal flushes, I have temper, I have impatience, I have all the things normal people have. Because I am normal, Luc. Now I have a broken leg, a guilty conscience and an almost overwhelming urge to get down to the beach. As I'm sure Toby does. Don't you, Toby?'

All this while Toby had been sitting on her knee, beaming at the outside sights, delighted with the fact that he was with his mum, on a wheelchair, an amazing wheeled contraption he'd never seen before. There was enough going on around them to hold his attention. Now, though, she'd said the magic word. His little face turned toward the sea.

'Beach,' he said solidly. And then… 'Spade.'

'Spade?' Beth asked, thrown off track.

'During this last week,' Luc said, almost apologetically, 'Toby and I have been learning to dig. We're not quite down to China but we're close.'

And that took her aback, too. All this week while

she'd been struggling with tests, procedures, a mild infection, pain and boredom, Luc had been playing with her son. Playing. She had no doubt of it. Toby had had enough carers in his short life for her to assess how he reacted to them, whether they were full of warmth and fun or whether they treated him as a job.

Whenever Luc had brought him into her room he'd crowed with joy to see her, but the protests when he'd left had been minimal. Sometimes even non-existent. He'd snuggled into Luc as if Luc had known him all his life.

Because they'd dug holes almost all the way to China?

And what was there in that that sent a wash of desolation over her, a wash so great she felt her world was shifting?

It was dumb, she thought. It was because she'd just been released from hospital. Patients often said release meant a weird feeling of discombobulation, emerging to a world that didn't seem to have noticed that they'd stepped out for a while.

And while she'd stepped out... Luc and Toby had formed their own little relationship, and she hadn't been part of it.

She had to accept the new norm and move on. She had to step right back onto this spinning world and be a part of it.

'I would very much like to see you dig a hole to China,' she managed, with forced cheeriness, and Luc sent her a sharp look.

'Are you okay? Pain?'

'Leave it, Luc.' She took a deep breath, pushing away the almost dizzy sense of disorientation. 'No pain. I'm just a bit…befuddled with everything that's happened. I'm sure what I need is sand, sun and maybe even an ice cream. If you could manage that I'd be grateful.'

'But you don't want to be grateful.'

He said it like he was struggling to understand, and she thought, I'm hurting him. Again.

'No one wants to be grateful,' she managed. 'Giving should be two ways, and for me, the balance has always been a bit lopsided for comfort. But that doesn't mean I don't love what you're doing for us. Tell you what. You push us down to the beach and I'll buy the ice creams. Deal?'

And he gave her a look she couldn't begin to understand. A look that said even this tiny thing, letting her pay for ice creams, was hard.

That was dumb. They both knew it was dumb and finally he smiled.

'Deal,' he said. 'Can I have a double cone, chocolate on one side, liquorice on the other?'

'Liquorice? What sort of ice-cream freak are you?'

'A man of taste,' he told her. 'What's your poison?'

'Salted caramel every time. And Toby loves rainbow.'

'Rainbow!' He looked appalled. 'Doesn't that make…?'

'An appalling mess? Yes, it does. And you know what? Sight impairment works just fine for that. All I need to do is remove my glasses and my little boy is just a sticky, Technicolor bundle of happiness. You have a problem?'

'I… Not at all.'

'Then let's go,' she said happily. 'We have work to do if we're to reach China by lunchtime.'

Luc parked the wheelchair on the promenade and, despite Beth's protests, lifted her into his arms and carried her toward the shoreline. The sunshine was glorious. Tiny waves ran in and out. The shallow water made a magical playground for Toby, and a host of tiny sandpipers had obviously agreed to share.

As Luc carried Beth, Toby staggered along by his side, seemingly entranced that it was his mother being carried and not him. He was equally entranced by the sand between his toes so it meant a long carry—which was fine by Luc.

He was holding Beth in his arms and he'd forgotten...how right she felt?

She was holding herself stiffly, though, as if she was afraid to relax. The thought was unsettling. What had he done to make her afraid?

He'd cared. Too much?

How could he limit caring?

He had to, though, or she'd run. He knew it. For all she needed his help, she'd set up boundaries that he couldn't cross. Her body didn't mould against his as it once had. She'd lost...trust.

She'd told him so little of her life for the last eight years. Hell, he didn't even know who Toby's father was, and some gut instinct told him not to ask. She was holding herself tightly contained.

When he set her down by the water's edge she almost visibly relaxed.

'Sunscreen first,' he said, tugging a bottle from his back pocket. And then ice creams.'

'Ice creams when we've done enough to deserve them,' she retorted. 'But hooray for remembering sunscreen. I don't suppose you brought three spades?'

'Two,' he told her. And then at the look on her face he did a fast change of tack. 'My mistake. They sell them at the kiosk. Three bucks fifty each, blue, pink or yellow or red. Toby's is yellow. Mine's blue. Do you have a preference?'

'Pink, of course,' she said happily, and took five dollars out of her purse and handed it over.

He managed to take it. This was a whole new ballgame, he thought as he headed across to the kiosk, and he needed to learn the rules.

When he returned, the hole had been started. Beth and Toby were digging fiercely, a spade apiece.

'Here's yours,' he said, offering her a pink spade with silver sparkles embedded in the plastic handle. 'Plus the change.'

'I've decided I like the blue one,' she said blithely. 'There's been a coup in your absence. Consider the dollar fifty change compensation for the new order. You're in charge of pink and glitter.'

And she chuckled.

It was a good sound. A great sound.

It was a sound that did something inside him he couldn't understand.

But now wasn't the time for asking questions. Toby was digging with fierce concentration, spraying sand as he went. 'Dig,' he said imperatively, and they all dug—and ducked from Toby's sand—and kept right on digging.

Luc got creative. He extended the hole from where

they'd started, down to the reaches of the tide. He dug deep so as the tide started to come in, the water rushed in and out of their hole, making Toby squeal with joy. They dug until the hole was big enough for a toddler to sit in and that was a moment of supreme satisfaction.

And that took Beth aback as well, because Toby started tugging his T-shirt and saying—very firmly, 'In!'. Luc emptied the daypack Beth hadn't even noticed until now, producing towel, spare clothes, spare nappy...

'Wow,' Beth breathed. 'If you ever give up medicine can you come back as a childminder? Dibs I have first chance at employing you.'

'Consider me employed,' he said grandly. 'I have more leave due and it would be my very great pleasure to be your childminder.'

Which silenced her.

They'd been divorced for eight years. After all this time...

'Luc, why?' she managed as he expertly stripped her small son and started massaging in more sun lotion. By the way Toby submitted she knew this had been a daily ritual while she'd been hospitalised.

This man had put his life on hold.

'Because we're friends,' he said solidly, and she thought he always had, sensed what she was thinking. He was wearing shorts and a T-shirt that stretched a bit tight across his abs. His dark hair looked a bit...messy. He rose and looked down at her, smiling that lopsided sexy smile that had made her fall in love ten years ago and that was doing exactly the same thing now.

Except she wasn't a dumb kid, thrown by accident

and disability into falling back into a failed relationship for all the wrong reasons. She was sensible. A mother, a family doctor, a woman who had her own independent future mapped out in front of her. Sort of.

She didn't need to be looking at...abs?

'With no strings,' she managed, and it sounded ungrateful. Or scared. She wasn't sure which but there didn't seem anything she could do about it.

'No strings,' he agreed gravely. 'Just friends, Beth.'

'I... It might be a good time for an ice cream.' She had to break the moment. The way he was looking at her...

The way he was looking...

Toby was done. He was now wearing a swim nappy and nothing else except sun screen. He wriggled out of Luc's grasp and slid into their hole with a resounding splash. An incoming wave filled the hole with foam, and he patted the water with gusto, sending splashes over his mother. He crowed with glee and then caught onto the only word in the preceding conversation he recognised.

'Ice cream!'

And for both of them it was a relief. She could turn away, take time to find her purse again.

'There's a queue at the ice-cream cart,' Luc said, and she could tell by his voice he was as...discombobulated as she was. 'You'll be okay with Toby if it takes a while?'

'Yes.' She shouldn't have snapped but she couldn't help it.

'Of course. I shouldn't have asked.'

'No.' She bit her lip. 'I... Yeah, I have a cast on my

leg so if Toby runs I could be in trouble.' She glanced around the beach and saw a cluster of young mums and their toddlers not too far away. 'But if he does I'll yell for help. I've learned to ask for help if I need it, Luc. So thank you for worrying but I'm fine.'

The ice creams were wonderful. They took turns keeping a hand on Toby's wrist to make sure his ice cream didn't get dunked in his waterhole—that'd be a disaster of epic proportions—and licked their own.

There was little need for words. The sun was on their faces and it was all about sensory pleasure—the warm sand, the hush-hush of the surf, the happy slurps of a toddler in his version of heaven.

People walking along the water's edge turned to smile at them and Luc knew exactly what they were thinking.

A young mum with a broken ankle. Dad taking time to care for her and care for his young son. A family.

It was make-believe, pretend, but for now it felt fine.

Eight years ago... If he'd stayed with Beth... It wouldn't have had to be pretend. He could have been a family man by now. They could have had two or three kids. Living happily ever after.

How could he have kept them all safe?

He suddenly remembered a conversation he and Beth had had, just before she'd walked out.

'I want it all, Luc. I want to go back to medicine. And I want a family. Kids. Maybe even a dog.'

'What the hell...' He still remembered the feeling of panic. 'Beth, I can't even keep you safe.'

'You wouldn't have to keep me safe,' she'd retorted.

'Except in so much as you love me. I'll keep myself safe. There'll be times when I need you—of course there will—isn't that what marriage is all about? But there'll also be times when you need me. And it'll be the same for our kids and this mythical dog I'm proposing. Yes, they'll need us but we'll need them, too. And that's what I'm aching for. Luc, I need to go back to medicine. And I need a family. I've been dependent since my illness and I'm over it. You have to let me care, too.'

He couldn't. The thought of a baby…of Beth being home alone with an infant… For heaven's sake, anything could happen.

'You've told me about your cousin,' she'd said, gently then. 'And I know about your mum. I understand, honestly I do. You know my feelings on it but you can't smother me in caring to make up for it.'

And a month later she'd left.

'You've been wonderful but I no longer need a carer. I need you as my husband but if I can't have one without the other… Luc, I know you can't understand but I need me more than I need you.'

He still didn't fully understand, but as he sat on the sand and watched Toby's unadulterated happiness, he thought maybe he'd been wrong about the family thing. Maybe he could have included children—or at least one child—into his caring. If that could have made Beth happy.

For she was happy now. Toby had misdirected his ice cream and jammed it on his nose. He was snorting rainbow ice cream and giggling, and Beth was chuckling as she tried to sort the situation. She was sitting on the sand, her moon boot protected with a towel so she didn't get sand in her dressings. She was wearing a crimson dress, simple, something the patient welfare people had found her because she couldn't get into the jeans her friends from Namborra had sent. Her hair was still its glorious chestnut. She was wearing prescription sunglasses but they'd slipped down her nose, making her look...adorably cute.

This woman was ten years older than the woman he'd married but she still looked...

'We'd best go home,' she said, breaking the moment. 'I've found with Toby it's best to quit while we're ahead. One minute you have happiness personified, the next you're in tired territory and, believe me, Luc, you don't want to be there.'

'Hey, I've cared for him for a week.'

'You mean you've seen it.'

'Oh, I've seen it.'

'And yet you've stuck with us. You're a man in a million, Luc Braxton. How many men would take their ex-wives in, no questions asked? No strings?' She smiled happily at him, seemingly totally relaxed. 'You're being wonderful.'

'I'm being useful.'

'Yeah, and you love that.' She put a finger on his nose, a gesture he remembered from all those years ago, a gesture that almost did his head in. 'Okay, friend Luc, let's get this baby to bed. Only... I'm afraid you'll have to carry me again.'

So he did. He carried her over the sand while Toby staggered along gamely, clutching his spade and a handful of sand and the soggy remains of an excellent rainbow ice cream.

Friend Luc.

But that wasn't what he felt like. He didn't feel like a friend at all.

CHAPTER SIX

Two days later he went back to work. At Beth's insistence. She had things under control.

Sort of.

Harriet had introduced her to Alice, a lovely, grandmotherly soul who lived in the same apartment block as Luc. Alice was delighted to offer childcare while Beth did rehab. Beth wheeled her chair there easily, taking the lift, balancing Toby on her knee. Despite being well into her seventies, Alice was almost as bouncy as Toby, so he expended his energy there, and Beth picked him up just as he was about to crash. Then she'd bring him back to Luc's apartment and they'd both nap.

Luc timed his work. He was available for Code One emergencies only, and limited time in ER, so he was home early enough to take them both to the beach before dinner.

'There's no need,' Beth told him, but there was a need. She was so close...

He needed to be with her while he could. He was increasingly aware that she was trying to sort her future in her head and that future didn't include him.

'But I don't think I can go back to Namborra,' she

confided, late on the third night. 'I don't think I can work without Ron.'

'Why not?'

'Rules,' she said, flatly, not bitterly. It was simply stating what was. 'My eyesight's not up to standard. Maryanne Clarkson's the other doctor in town and she's a stickler for perfection. When Ron and I approached her to do the combined job she was appalled that we both had health issues. Ron had arthritis that affected his joints—he had to use me to do fine work like finding a tricky vein. Which I could using my magnifying lenses.

'Then Maryanne saw me bump into a post in the car park one night and she rang the medical board the next day and said she doubted my ability to work. I copped a rigid assessment—which I passed—but she's been looking askance at the pair of us ever since. We've provided an excellent service but I doubt she'll support me without Ron, even though the town was desperate for more doctors before we went and will be desperate again now.'

'It'll be a month before you need to make that decision.'

'Yes,' she said bleakly. 'And for that month Namborra will only have Maryanne and she doesn't do house calls…'

'You and Ron did house calls?'

'Don't say it like it's a criminal act.' She glared.

'Beth, working in a clinic where you know where everything is is one thing but—'

'But there's the elephant again. Beth's blind. *Beth is not blind.*'

But he could see Maryanne's view on this one and

it was doing no one a kindness pretending there wasn't an issue. 'You must have trouble,' he said reasonably. 'One of the biggest problems with house calls is that people have lousy lighting.'

'So they do,' she said through gritted teeth. 'And I don't drive so Ron and I did house calls together. And you know what? We had fun. So not only have I lost a friend, I've lost my job and I've lost...fun. Freedom. Dignity. And we did good. No, we did great, so don't you dare imply we were wrong to do it. Leave me be, Luc Braxton. I'm going to bed.'

And he was left, sitting alone watching the moon rise over the sea. Trying to get his head in order.

The phone rang.

Yay for phones, he thought. Yay for work. And it *was* work, a callout to a fire in a holiday rental farmhouse twenty minutes away by chopper.

'An explosion.' Mabel was curt. 'It'll be a meths lab or something like that. It always is. Explosion in remote rented farmhouse. Kids everywhere. What were they thinking?'

'Idea of casualties?' He had his phone tucked under his chin, pulling his boots on as he talked. He wasn't in the business of making judgements. He was in the business of cleaning up afterwards.

'Multiple. Two probable deaths, but no proper count at this stage. It's miles from anywhere. A neighbour rang it in, sounding sensible but overwhelmed. Says most of the kids seem drug affected, even if they're not injured. The local cop's on his way, as are the local paramedics and fire brigade but they'll need backup.'

'I'll be on the chopper in three minutes,' Luc said,

and disconnected. And turned to find Beth watching him from the bedroom door. Leaning on her crutches.

'Trouble?'

'Kids, drugs and fire,' he said abruptly, grabbing his bag. 'An appalling combination and all too common. You'll be all right here while I'm gone?'

'I'll try and hold it together.' Even in his rush he could hear the edge of bitterness in her voice. 'If I didn't have Toby I'd be with you.'

'Yeah, with a broken leg and—'

'Let's not go there,' she snapped. 'Stay safe, Luc.' And before he knew what she intended she hopped across to where he stood and kissed him lightly on the cheek. 'Go save everyone I can't. Do it for me.'

He shouldn't respond. There was no time for anything except getting to the roof to board the chopper.

Except some things were imperative.

Somehow he found himself holding her, gripping her shoulders, looking down into her troubled eyes.

Soldier going into battle? Farewelling his woman? That was fanciful. This was not his woman. Beth was part of his past, nothing more. But still…

Still the need was imperative.

He'd heard the anger in her voice. He couldn't leave her like this, and he reacted the only way he knew how.

He bent his head and kissed her, hard and strong, taking what he needed from the feel of her body against him, the fleeting melting of her breasts against his chest, the instant rush of response. Telling her he was sorry. Telling her his concern was because…because he didn't understand anything any more.

And then he pulled away because he must, and she pulled away, too.

No choice.

'Stay safe,' she said again, but this time it was a shaken whisper.

'For you,' he said, just as shakily, and then he was gone and Beth was left staring at a closed door.

Wondering what had just happened to make her feel her life had changed all over again.

Blake was off duty. Luc was in charge and he flew into a disaster.

What on earth made kids think they could set up a chemical lab a highly qualified scientist would worry about, following dodgy instructions on even more dodgy internet websites, trying to make drugs when they had no knowledge of the composite ingredients—and doing it when they were half-stoned?

The farmhouse was obviously being used as party central. The chopper landed and they could see a dying bonfire in the paddock beside the house, bottles and cans everywhere as if a party had been in full swing for a few days—and a weatherboard farmhouse that had burned so fast that the ruins were starting to smoulder rather than burn.

It looked like it was—a disaster, Luc thought grimly, as they took in the scene from the air.

There was one police car, lights flashing, parked at the gate beside an ambulance—the type used by volunteer, rural paramedics. The local fire engine was on the scene but no one seemed to be trying to put a fire out. The two firemen seemed occupied with injured kids.

The chopper Luc was in was a big one, holding the lead firies as well as the medic crew. Kev looked down grimly. 'This'll be forensic stuff,' he muttered. 'Hell, it must have burned hot. We'll be lucky if we get any-thing for mums and dads to bury.'

Luc cast him a sympathetic glance. Kev had seen everything in a career that spanned over forty years but he still wasn't inured to the sort of catastrophe below.

Nobody in the team was.

They didn't speak as they came in to land. They were shocked at what they were seeing but their silence wasn't caused by shock.

This team was a well-oiled machine, honed by years of response to catastrophes like this and worse. Every man and woman would be doing a personal assessment of what lay underneath them, checking the groups of kids clustered around obvious casualties, seeing how some kids were still close to the fire. For heaven's sake, why hadn't the firies got them back? Even though the fire had burned down, if it was a suspect meth lab there may well be more stuff in there liable to explode. There must be severely injured kids to hold their attention.

'Sam, you're on triage,' Luc snapped as the chop-per finally came to rest and the team unclipped and grabbed their gear. 'Gina?' he called to the chopper pilot. 'Radio in with request for backup, a couple of med. evacuation choppers with every paramedic they can find. I'm seeing ten kids on the ground from here. People, we're dealing with drugs as well as injuries so watch yourself. Even the kids who are uninjured are likely to be volatile. Try and work in pairs, covering your backs. Right, go.'

How could she sleep?

She lay in bed and turned on the radio. The late-night jocks were all over it. Explosion in a remote farmhouse. Casualty count rising. Four dead. How many did that mean injured?

She was lying in bed, warm, safe with her little boy beside her. Her leg was aching. She had the drugs to fix it but she didn't feel like fixing it.

She wanted to be out and doing. In the middle of the action. Working beside Luc, making a difference as she'd longed to all her life.

What chance now? Namborra would be closed to her. She'd have months off work with her leg and then the fight would start all over again to get herself accepted.

While others put themselves in harm's way, doing the work she longed for?

The latest news flash—updating the death count to five.

She felt ill.

At dawn Toby stirred. At least that gave her something to do. She got him breakfast, played with him for a while and then headed to rehab.

Harriet was there, stoically lifting her foot, grim-faced, trying desperately to get her leg working.

It would never be completely normal, Beth thought. Luc had told her just how much damage Harriet had suffered.

Harriet was looking at a lifetime disability, too.

Beth settled herself on the mat beside Harriet and waited while the physiotherapist braced her leg.

Both women concentrated fiercely on their exercises for a while, saying nothing. Then...

'I hate it,' Harriet said, and she sounded close to tears.

'Because you should be out there, too?'

'Of course I should,' Harriet said bitterly. 'But they're saying I'll have to accept a degree of weakness. They'll never let me back on the team. At least your ankle will get better.'

'You think Luc would ever let me near his precious team with my eyesight?'

'Yeah, and he still thinks of you as family. It's a wonder he hadn't put you in a cotton wool climate controller and put the setting to safe.'

'You do understand him,' Beth said cautiously.

'The whole team knows Luc. If there's danger, there's Luc. It almost kills him if someone else has to take a risk. He'd care for the whole world.'

'I hope to hell there's no risk where he is now.'

'Even if there is, you wouldn't be allowed to share.' Harriet gave her leg a savage jerk upward, which earned her a sharp rebuke from the physiotherapist.

'Easy, Harriet. And you, too, Beth. Don't try and walk before you can run. You need to accept your limitations.'

'Of course we do,' Harriet retorted, and Beth grimaced.

'Of course,' Beth muttered. 'And if we forget, all we need to do is ask Luc.'

By early evening Toby was more than ready for sleep. He seemed a bit listless, out of sorts, and so was Beth. No matter how much she hated it, her body needed rest to recover. She'd hardly slept last night, she'd done a decent rehab session and by the time Toby fell asleep Beth was ready to do the same.

There was still no sign of Luc. She'd heard the first

casualties had been flown in but there was still work to be done on the ground.

She had soup on the stove in case he appeared. There was nothing more she could do, for him, for anyone.

She headed for the bedroom she shared with Toby, put her head on the pillow and slept.

And woke as a cat did, at the first sound, as the door opened inward just a little.

'Luc?'

'It's okay.' It was barely a whisper. He clearly had no intention of waking Toby— or waking her? 'Go back to sleep.'

As if she could. She tossed back the covers, grabbed her glasses and crutches and hobbled out.

He was leaning heavily against the kitchen counter. He looked...appalling.

He'd stripped off his protective gear before coming home but there must have been red dust and smoke where he was because it had infiltrated everything. He was wearing jeans and a T-shirt and the coarse sand was caked on. The lines on his chest where his T-shirt had tugged over his pecs, where he'd sweated, formed a road map of red dirt

And the rest... His thick, black hair was matted with dust and soot. He'd have worn gloves but the dust had got through, staining his hands. He stank of smoke and other things that were indescribable. The lines on his face...the matted stubble on his jaw... That was shocking enough but what was worse was his eyes. They were...haggard, mired in fatigue and distress.

'Bad?' she whispered, even though it was a dumb question. His eyes told of a nightmare.

'Kids.' He closed his eyes as if he couldn't bear to go

there. 'Schoolies. Kids who've finished their last exam. They hired the house, told their parents they were going camping…yeah, I know they were mostly eighteen but what parent sends them off without checking? So drugs and alcohol, and more drugs and alcohol and who knew what else besides? And then two imbeciles who thought they were ants' pants in the chemistry world decided they'd make their own gear. They'd bought the stuff on the internet and brought it with them, waiting until everyone was half-stoned to show off their new skill. Half the kids seem to have been in the kitchen when it exploded. Five dead and that's not the worst. There are kids who'll carry the physical scars for life and every one of them will carry the mental scars.'

'Oh, Luc…'

He put his hands up and raked his fingers through his matted hair, then buried his head in his hands. 'What were their parents thinking?' His voice was muffled with pain. 'What the hell…?'

And she couldn't bear it. She dropped her crutches. She had no remembrance later of how she supported herself to reach him. All she knew was that she did. She folded her arms around him and tugged him into her, tight, hard, and she held him and held him and held him.

At first he didn't yield, seemingly locked in his own personal horror. For a moment she thought he'd pull away. Maybe he'd slam out the door as he'd done sometimes in the past when he'd been distressed and he couldn't bear to let her see.

He protected others from pain; he didn't share it.

But holding was all she could do. Of course it wasn't

enough. He didn't need her. This man didn't need anyone and surely she should know it.

But still she held, hard, tight, willing his pain to crack. To open the armour just a little and take comfort...

And then he shuddered, an involuntary spasm that shook his whole body, that shook hers, and he buried his face in her hair and groaned. Or sobbed? It was a guttural sound of total anguish and she thought, Oh, Luc, what have you seen? How are such things bearable? How can you keep caring and caring, rescuing and rescuing and holding the horrors to yourself?

But the sob seemed to have released something deep within. His hands came around her waist and tugged her against him, harder than she was holding him. Pulling her into him. Seeking the warmth and strength of her body.

'Beth...' It was a groan from the depths of need. 'Beth...'

'Hush, love,' she whispered. and reached up and ran her fingers through his hair, through the dust, sweat and grime. She didn't mind—how could she mind? Her hands drew his head down, so she could kiss the dust from his eyes. Her fingers held, possessive. This man was in such pain.

Her man.

And that's how it felt. Ten years ago she'd made vows that should have been dissolved by a divorce court but they were suddenly all around her now.

To love and to honour... In sickness and in health...

I, Beth, take thee, Luc...

And she was taking him now, holding him, willing him to yield to her with every ounce of hope and prayer left in her. Her Luc, her own Luc…

'Beth…' And when he said her name this time it was different. It was like a voice coming from the darkest of places but seeing a glimmer of light. Just a glimmer but that was all she asked.

'Luc,' she whispered, and tugged his head closer, down, so she could touch his lips. Take him to her. Heal with her body.

And take what was hers?

For there was a part of her that knew it was her right to comfort this man, that taking his pain into her was the way it should be.

Had her wedding vows been indeed unbreakable? That was how it felt right now, as if the vows held true. That he was part of her and he was suffering, hurting, holding so much pain inside that she couldn't bear it, and if it was in her to comfort then that's what she must do.

Because his pain felt like hers.

She felt him stiffen again, just slightly as she tugged him down, as her mouth found his, and for a fraction of a second she was terrified he'd pull away. No, she wanted to shout. You have no right to pull away. You have no right to keep your pain to yourself for it's mine, too. She didn't say it—she couldn't because her mouth was claiming his, searching, demanding and every minuscule part of her was a prayer.

Let me in. Luc, let me share…

And she felt it, the moment when the tension eased, as if the pressure had built up to the point where containment was impossible. He groaned again but it was different. This was suddenly not a man fighting himself.

He wanted her. She knew that, she'd always known that, but this was more. For the first time ever, he was drawing into her for comfort.

For need?

But now there was no time for introspection. No time for wonder. Because she was being held, kissed, taken with an urgency, a passion that left room for nothing else.

He was lifting her, and the dreadful blankness in his eyes was changing. His eyes were darkening, with desire, with passion, with need. He held her high, pulling her against his chest. She was wearing…okay, nothing very sexy, in fact the opposite. She'd taken off her dress when she'd fallen into bed and she was now wearing her glasses, a moon boot, a nice, sensible bra and panties, bought from the discount store at Namborra, and an ancient wrap. Not a sexy inch of lace anywhere. But the look Luc was giving her…

So much for sexy negligees. Total waste, she thought with a stab of satisfaction and for some dumb reason she found herself chuckling.

'What?' He'd started striding toward his bedroom, his arms full of her, but he stopped at the sound of her chuckle. His dark eyes gleamed down at her, and her heart twisted with love and with desire.

After all these years… Her Luc…

'The chuckle…' he managed. 'What's funny?'

'I was just thinking of pure silk negligees and…'

'Don't.' He groaned again. 'Beth, you're driving me wild.' And then he stopped as if sense had suddenly reared its head and he had to force himself to say it. 'Love…are you sure?'

'I guess…' Somehow she had to force herself to say it, too. 'If you can… If you have…'

And he got that, too. He'd always had the unnerving ability to read her mind.

'What doctor doesn't carry condoms for educational purposes? But you'll have to wait until I'm showered. If I hit the sheets like this we'll have to buy new linen.'

'Worth it, love.'

'Then worth waiting,' he said, and grinned. 'If you didn't have a leg covered in dressings and a moon boot…'

'And if you didn't have half the outback splattered on your person…'

'All I need is three minutes.' He lowered her onto the bed.

'You can have two,' she told him. 'I've waited for eight years and I won't wait a moment longer.'

She didn't need to.

CHAPTER SEVEN

THEY HAD A night of blessed peace. A night when the work receded.

And then the world flooded back, and then some.

They'd slept after making love, skin against skin, lost in the wonder of each other's bodies.

They were woken by a sound of distress that had Beth tossing back the covers and reaching for her glasses and wrap before she even remembered where she was.

Luc woke, too. They'd been spooned together as they'd slept all those years ago, encased in each other's bodies. At home. At peace. Now he moved with her, his hand still on her thigh. 'Love? What?'

'Toby.'

'I guess that's the new norm,' he said sleepily, as she reached for her wrap. 'Being woken by a baby.' But then he jerked wide awake.

He got it. He'd been looking after Toby for a week while she'd been in hospital. He knew Toby's normal was to wake up happy. As long as Robert Rabbit was in the cot with him he'd burble and chat and play until his mother got her act together and got them both out of there.

If Robert had fallen out, then Toby roared, a full-throated yell of indignation, but what they were hearing now was a reedy whimper, and it had Beth grabbing her crutches and heading for the door fast.

Luc was right behind her, hauling on his pants as he came.

Toby was lying in the cot, uttering little mews of distress. He was on his back, staring at the ceiling. Robert Rabbit lay unheeded by his side.

As Beth reached the cot he registered her presence and held his arms up, as if pleading. Get me out of here?

Why wasn't he standing?

Beth's crutches clattered to the floor as she scooped him up and Luc shoved a chair forward so she could sit with him.

She cradled him against her, a tousle-headed toddler, usually a bright, happy baby version of Beth herself. But now he crumpled into her, limp, miserable. The weak sobs stopped.

Years ago, back when Luc had been an intern, green about the gills, he remembered a child being brought into the emergency department roaring so loudly every head had swivelled to see what was wrong. Luc had responded automatically, turning from the child he'd been treating.

He'd been brought up short by his consultant, an elderly doctor who'd been practising paediatrics since before Luc had been born.

'Stay where you are,' she'd snapped. 'There's no emergency. If a child can roar like that then any damage is superficial. For kids' triage, you see to the silent ones first.'

But now... Toby was silent.

'He's hot,' Beth said, kissing his forehead. 'A virus?'

That'd explain it. Kids got ill fast and they got better fast, too. Nothing to worry about.

Except the silence. And the limpness.

He knelt and put his fingers on Toby's neck. Yeah, definitely hot. They needed to get him cool.

And the way he held himself...he was huddled on his mother's knees but his head wasn't tucked down. He was pulling to one side.

As if his neck hurt?

Luc unzipped his sleeping bag—and froze.

'What?' Beth whispered and Luc rose and pulled back the curtains, flooding the room with dawn light. So Beth could see what he was seeing.

She saw. 'Oh, God...' It was scarcely spoken, a breath of sheer terror. 'Oh...'

'Hey, he's in the right place.' Luc was already heading for his phone. 'I'll ring in and warn them we're coming. It might not be...'

'It is.' She didn't move, stunned with the horror of what she faced. 'Luc...the day of the crash... When I went to pick him up from crèche they asked me to see another child. A rash... A high temp. I started him on antibiotics and got him on a plane to Sydney before the diagnosis was confirmed but I was pretty sure it was meningitis. I left instructions...the minute we had confirmation I wanted the kids he'd been in contact with started on prophylactic antibiotics. And then... Oh, God, Luc, I forgot. I forgot...'

She broke on a sob.

He was on the phone, kneeling beside her, doing his darnedest to be there for Beth, for both of them, even as he barked into the receiver. Marsha was head of Paediatrics and she was the best. At least they were in the right spot. If this was what they thought it was then Toby was in the best place in Australia. 'We have a twenty-month-old with suspected meningitis. We're bringing him in now. Ten minutes.'

'Your little boy?'

Marsha's demand gave him pause even then. The hospital grapevine had indeed done its job. He'd gone to Namborra and brought back a woman who was his ex-wife. He'd taken time off and cared for her child and now he was living with her.

Your little boy?

He looked at Toby, at this little stranger he hadn't met until ten days ago.

He looked at Toby's mother.

'Yes,' he said.

As a doctor he'd always had some inkling that waiting was hard. He'd seen relatives in hundreds of settings during his career, white faced, limp with fear. Often it had been Luc who'd opened the door on that waiting room to give news, sometimes good, sometimes bleak, sometimes terrible.

Now it was his turn.

He shouldn't be here. He was officially on duty. He hoped someone had noticed where he was and told Blake. He'd made one urgent call as they'd arrived, one that couldn't wait, but that was all he'd had time for. All his focus was on Toby.

The way the rash had spread over Toby's small body... The spike in his temperature...the look on the paediatricians' faces as they'd assessed… It had stilled him to numbness.

Was it better to not know the odds? Was it better to not know the risk of appalling long-term damage?

He sat with Beth while they inserted IV lines, set up the antibiotics, maximum dosages. They had fluid lines going in, because by now Toby was too weak to drink. Indeed he seemed barely conscious. The illness was taking over so fast…

Beth sat and held as much as she could of him and Luc stayed in the background. And waited.

He watched the tension of Beth's shoulders, he watched her mouth move in silent prayer, he watched her fingers curl around Toby's as if by sheer force of will she could hold him. As if she could keep him safe. He watched as they insisted on transferring him to a bed so they could work more intensely. He watched Beth watch her baby. He watched for hours.

Finally Marsha ordered him to take Beth out. 'Take half an hour,' she said, and stooped to take Beth's hands firmly in hers. Toby lay on a too big bed, IV lines taped, his tiny face blotched and pallid as he lay among a sea of high-tech monitors. 'Beth, Toby's asleep. For now he doesn't need you.'

'He's un—' Beth began.

'He's not unconscious. This looks a natural sleep.'

'But—'

'But he needs you when he wakes,' Marsha told her. 'And you're no use to him if you fall over. I'm working in here for the next half-hour and the nurses will be here, too. We'll watch him like a hawk and the moment there's any change, the moment he opens his eyes, I'll call you back. Luc, take Beth into the waiting room. There's coffee and sandwiches. Bully her to eat. Bully her to take time out. Do anything, but take a break from the tension. Now.'

So here they were, in the tiny waiting room outside kids' intensive care unit. The room contained a drinks vending machine. An overhead television, turned on but no sound. No windows.

Take a break from the tension? It was impossible. He knew Beth couldn't leave the hospital and he had the sense not to suggest it.

'I can't bear it,' Beth whispered. She'd managed a sandwich and coffee but he knew it had been sheer strength of will that'd got the food down. 'I need to go back.'

'Marsha will have my hide if I let you back in before half an hour,' Luc told her. 'She's good, Beth. The whole team's good. I suspect she'll have half the hospital's paediatric team in there pooling their knowledge while she has a parent-free zone.'

'I wouldn't interfere…'

'But you know as well as I do that a parent's distress can sometimes mess with doctors' heads. Especially with children. We need to give them space, Beth. For the best outcome.'

She picked up another sandwich, stared at it and then set it down again. 'I can't believe… He was so well…'

And then she stood, so fast her empty mug of coffee clattered to the floor and smashed. She didn't notice. Her eyes were huge and her face had lost its last trace of colour. 'The other kids,' she whispered, her voice loaded with horror. 'In crèche. I set up orders to follow up. As soon as Felix's diagnosis was confirmed they were to start… And then I forgot. It won't be just Toby. Luc, the others…'

He tried to hug her, pulling her against him, but she held rigid. 'I can't… Luc, if I hurt them…'

'You haven't hurt anyone,' he said, solidly now, putting her back until he could look into her haunted eyes. 'They're fine. The crèche was undamaged so no other child was hurt. You might not have noticed but as soon as Toby was admitted, I left you for a moment. While Marsha was doing initial assessment and setting up the first IV lines, I rang Namborra. I spoke to Dr Clarkson. She said Margie remembered—the head of your crèche? She had the presence of mind to take the crèche notes with her when the centre was evacuated. Your orders were the last ones written and she realised they were important. By next morning every kid who'd been in crèche was started on prophylactic antibiotics. Dr Clarkson's gutted they didn't follow up on Toby.'

'So Toby's the only one I forgot…'

She was close to collapse. He dragged her back into his arms, holding her, feeling her body shudder with tension and fear. 'Beth, listen. You didn't forget Toby. You sheltered him with your body as the roof collapsed. You saved Toby.'

'What use is that if he dies from meningitis? Or loses his legs or arms? You know what meningitis can do. I can't—'

'Beth!' He put her back again, holding her firmly by her shoulders, forcing her gaze to meet his. 'Firstly, Toby's already been immunised so you did your best by protecting him all you could. We don't know what strain this is but maybe the protection he already has will help now. Dr Clarkson tells me Felix, who you diagnosed on the day you were trapped, has made a full recovery. She's organised parental consent so details of the strain he had have been faxed here. Our medical team's already working with full information.'

'Second, he's been caught fast. I checked on Toby an hour after…after we went to bed.' He touched her cheek, smiling faintly at the memory. 'Things were too new, too overwhelming for me to sleep, and for some reason…' He hesitated. 'For some reason I needed to ground myself and seeing Toby helped. He was sleeping peacefully, clutching Wobit. Therefore, whatever this is, it's come on fast but we've caught it fast, too. We've also caught it within ten minutes of one of the best paediatric units in Australia. The doctors here are the best. He'll be fine, Beth, I know it.'

He couldn't know it, not for sure, but he put every ounce of conviction into his voice, into his body language. His eyes didn't leave hers. She gazed up at him and he saw the moment a faint chink broke through the flood of terror.

'You really think so?'

'I know.'

She didn't break her gaze. 'You checked on him while I slept?'

'As I said, I sort of…needed to. And I've been doing it for the week you've been in hospital.'

'You checked on him through the night when you were caring for him?'

'Before you came home I had his cot in my room.'

'Oh, Luc…' She sobbed and gasped and then buried her face into his shirt, hard, fierce, as if she needed the sheer bulk of him to assure herself all was well. Or all would be well.

'I told myself I didn't need you,' she whispered, half to herself, half to him. 'All those years ago. I thought I didn't need you and how wrong was that? How stupid? Oh, love…'

And she put her hands around him as if she'd never let go.

He hugged her back, solidly, tugging her against him so her breasts moulded against his chest, kissing her hair, saying dumb, meaningless nothings because she didn't need silence.

She needed…him.

And part of him wanted it. Part of him held her and thought his world was settling. He had his woman back in his bed, in his life. She was his wife. And Toby? The little boy already felt like his own.

'Beth?'

'Mmm…' It was a whisper, no more.

'Tell me about…' It almost broke him to say it, but it needed to be asked. 'Toby's father.'

'Wh-why? Her face was muffled in his shirt.

'He needs to be told.' That was the truth, he thought. If it was *his* son he'd want to be told he was in danger.

He wanted it to be his son.

'You mean…he might die…'

'Beth…'

'I know.' She pushed away, shoving her curls from her tear-streaked face. 'I know…the odds. But I don't need to tell him.'

'Why not, Beth?'

'Toby's…from donated sperm. After you…' She shook her head. 'Crazy but after you I couldn't imagine being married to anyone else. But I thought…when I started work at Namborra, I thought I could care for a baby. I thought…' Her voice broke. 'Oh, God, Luc, I was so wrong.'

'You weren't wrong.' He said it strongly. He might not believe it himself but she didn't need a talk on responsibility now. 'You had a fantastic set-up. You had everything in place to care for him.'

'But I couldn't care for him. When I walked away from you I felt so brave, like I could take on the world. But to put Toby at risk…'

'It wasn't your fault.'

'You never would have let it happen.' Her voice broke on another ragged sob and she buried her face in his shirt again. 'Oh, Luc, we needed you. I needed you…'

And wasn't that what he needed to hear?

He held her close as her sobs subsided, as she fought to regain composure, as she fought to regain control of her world. But still she clung.

She needed him.

She'd held him. She'd lain in his arms. She was his wife again, in every sense of the word, and part of him felt like a vast void inside him had been filled. His Beth was where she belonged, and Toby with her.

He would care for them, he vowed. He'd love them and protect them for ever, he told himself as he held her close.

But there was another voice, a tiny insidious crazy voice that told him something was wrong.

Nothing's wrong, he told himself or nothing will be wrong as long as Toby survives unscathed. This was how things should be. This was his family and he could love and protect them for ever.

So why was the little voice niggling?

Why did he feel…something was still very wrong and it had nothing to do with Toby's illness?

For two days Beth and Luc watched and waited, two adults with only one thought between them. That Toby survive with no long-term damage.

For two days he lay limp, almost unresponsive. For two days the doctors fought with everything they had.

And won.

On the afternoon of the third day Luc closed his eyes for a few moments and the miracle happened. He woke to find Beth cuddling Toby. The little boy still had his IV lines attached, but his eyes were wide, he looked alert and he was struggling to pull himself away from Beth's arms.

'Walk,' he said firmly, and Beth closed her eyes for a nanosecond and let him slide to the floor.

The drip lines were still attached but Beth had them organised so he couldn't pull them free.

Toby tried to stand but his legs didn't hold him. The days of desperate illness would have made the strongest individual's knees turn to jelly. So he plonked on the floor in his nappy and singlet, staring at his legs as if he couldn't believe they'd let him down. And then he glanced around the room and saw Luc. He gave a joyful chirp and hauled himself into a crawl position.

Crawling worked. He made a bee-line to his playmate of a week. He and Luc had dug a hole almost to China and his body language said hooray, take him there again. He reached Luc's ankles and held up his hands.

Luc rose and gathered him into his arms, while Beth

wrangled IV lines. And Luc buried his face into Toby's small, bony shoulder and felt…like bursting into tears.

It was okay.

But Toby wasn't in the mood for hugs. He'd had a very long sleep, he was in a hospital room full of interesting *things* and he wanted down. So Luc set him back down. Toby found an oxygen canister he'd really like to unscrew—how did these things work?—and Luc had time and space to hug Toby's mother.

'Over,' he said softly into her hair, and he touched her face and felt tears slipping down. So many tears over the last few days… His strong Beth… Even when she'd been desperately ill herself he could never remember tears, but now… Toby's illness seemed to have undercut every foundation she had.

'I can't say… I can't imagine…if you hadn't been here…if you hadn't taken us in…'

'Not so much of the gratitude,' he growled. 'I think…we're family, Beth. And family cares.'

'After all this time…' She drew back and stared at him wonderingly. 'Is that how you feel?'

'I've never stopped loving you.' He knew that for truth—he'd known it the moment he'd seen her under the rubble. *Until death us do part.* He'd made that vow and it seemed burned into his psyche. Maybe it always had been. Since Beth, he'd never had a serious long-term partner.

Because he already was married?

'I think… Luc, I still love you, too,' she managed.

And he thought, Dammit, she's even weaker than her son. She'd hardly eaten for the last three days. She'd almost worn herself out with fear, and she sure as hell hadn't slept. He hugged her against him and felt her sink into him.

It was where she should be. Where he could care.

And the words were out before he could stop himself. 'Beth, maybe we should think about getting ourselves married again.'

He'd tried—desperately—to keep his voice light but she stepped back and looked up at him. The suggestion hadn't been made lightly at all and she knew it. The bonds between them were still strong and he saw that she knew it as truly as he did.

'Luc...it must be too soon.' She turned away, giving herself space, looking almost panicked. She gazed down at Toby, who was starting to get seriously annoyed that the oxygen cylinder wouldn't open to his command. 'And Toby...'

'I love Toby already. It would be my honour to love and protect you both.'

'And you need someone to love and protect...' She closed her eyes. 'Oh, Luc, if I could be sure you weren't sacrificing...'

'How can I be sacrificing, marrying for love?'

She shook her head as if clearing fog. 'We need you.' She sounded as if she was talking to herself. 'I thought I was so self-sufficient, yet at the first hurdle...'

'It's hardly the first hurdle,' he told her. 'You've completed your medical degree. You found a job you were good at, and you and Ron have been providing Namborra a great little medical service.'

'Little...' She faltered. 'Sorry, I know... I need to accept...' She took a deep breath and went to lift Toby. She was still wearing her protective boot and she staggered, off balance. He was there in a nanosecond, hugging her against him, supporting her, with Toby somewhere in the middle.

'We don't have to decide yet,' he told her. 'Think about it.'

Think.

She should pull away, she thought, but he was supporting her.

She had a broken ankle.

She had a broken will.

It would be so easy to sink into Luc's arms, to let him take charge as he'd taken charge when she'd lost her sight, to admit that she wanted him and...she needed him.

Luc had been right all those years ago when he'd said she should accept her limitations. And it wasn't one way, she thought. Luc needed her to need him. It gave him strength and security to know that he was helping. She knew all about his painful childhood. She knew all about how helpless he felt when those he loved weren't safe.

So why was she hesitating? Why didn't she fall into his arms with a yes when she knew he needed her as much as she needed him?

But she wasn't hesitating, she told herself. She was simply giving him time to figure what he really wanted. To be free or have a permanent millstone around his neck.

A woman who'd tried and failed.

'Hey.' He'd always known what she was thinking and now seemed no exception. He guided her back into the chair and knelt before her. 'Beth, this isn't the end of the world. You're seeing things at their bleakest now, even though Toby's getting better. But your leg still hurts. I bet it's hurting now. You've hardly eaten and you haven't slept for three days. Give yourself a break. Let's do what we need for Toby and then let's get you some rest. In the next few days you can look at this again and decide whether what I'm suggesting is sensible. It's sure as hell not a failure.'

'No,' she managed, and hugged Toby and went to say something else.

Except the door was opening and Marsha entered, followed by a couple of med students.

'I'm here to boast about my success story to my students,' she said, beaming down at Toby. 'I guess you guys are pretty happy, huh?'

'We surely are,' Beth said, and hugged Toby still tighter. 'All is…perfect.'

Luc wanted to marry her again. The concept was mind-blowing.

She could have another baby, she thought suddenly. It would be Luc's this time, not a sperm donor. If Luc thought she'd be able to cope… If he thought it was okay…

'Everything's looking good,' Luc told Marsha but his gaze was still on Beth. 'Our little family's looking safe.'

'Your family?' Marsha's eyebrows did an expressive hike. 'Really?'

'If Beth will have me,' he told her, and Beth shook her head.

'I don't think… I doubt if Luc needs…'

'Hey,' Luc said, and lifted Toby from her so Marsha could check his progress for herself. 'Luc doesn't need, but Beth and Toby do. But let's talk about this tomorrow. For now, Toby's fine and we have all the time in the world.'

CHAPTER EIGHT

WHAT FOLLOWED WAS a week almost out of time. Marriage wasn't mentioned again. It was almost as if they were afraid of it. But every night they lay in each other's arms and knew how right it felt.

They still seemed like a tight-knit family. Toby was recovering, but Beth wanted him close. She was subdued but Toby was anything but. The little boy was a blessing, a happy bubble in the face of Beth's confusion.

Luc was trying his best but she wouldn't have him take more time off. 'We'll be right on our own, Luc. It's enough that you're sharing your apartment, that you're helping at night.'

And she did need him. When he got home from work she seemed almost relieved when he took over childcare for a couple of hours. He took Toby to the beach but she didn't come. 'I'm tired,' she told him, and he knew she was.

And at night...she slept in his arms, but that sleep was broken. He wasn't supposed to know that she slipped out of bed and went out to the balcony to stare sightlessly out to sea.

Once he'd gone out to join her and she'd come in straight away. 'I'm sorry. I didn't mean to disturb you.'

And now... He'd come home from a routine shift and found her staring at her email.

'Luc, the memorial service is happening next Monday at Namborra,' she told him. 'And I'd really like to go. For Ron especially. I was in hospital when he was buried so I couldn't be there. But now... I need to be there for this.'

Of course she did and things cleared in Luc's head. Yes, she was depressed, but the fault didn't lie at his door. She'd been injured. Toby had been desperately ill. But on top of that she'd lost her best friend, her colleague. Of course she was down.

'I don't think I can manage...by myself,' she said, and he thought it almost killed her to say it. The flatness...

And he knew the depression wasn't all about shock and injury and loss of her friend. What else had she lost?

'Of course I'll take you...come with you.' He changed his words but he still saw her flinch. 'We can fly. There's an outback health service operating from Bondi Bayside. The team heads west three days a week. They could drop us off on the way and collect us on the way back.' He tried a smile. 'It's cheaper than commercial flights and if you like you can have a whole bed to lie down on. It'll be better for your leg than sitting up.'

'And if they need to transfer patients?'

'Then we hang around in Namborra until Wednesday. Or take a commercial flight.'

'I still have my apartment at Namborra.'

'Then that's settled. But chances are good we won't need it. Except for a place for you to rest, he thought. She was so tired. She seemed…as if the life had been sucked out of her.

'Thank you, Luc,' she managed, and he hugged her.

'Hey, my pleasure.'

'I know it is. I wish…'

And then she shook her head and managed a smile. 'No. It's no use wishing. It is what it is. You want to take Toby to the beach?'

'I do,' he told her, and let her go with reluctance to pick up the bubbly Toby. 'Would you like to come with us?'

'I might have a sleep if that's okay with you.'

'Of course it's okay. Beth… I love you.'

'I love you, too,' she whispered, but her face was bleak. And he knew that when he left, she wouldn't sleep at all.

The memorial service for the victims of the plaza disaster was held in Namborra's civic centre. It was a magnificent hall, built with community pride, on the only hill Namborra boasted. It could almost be taken for a modern church, Luc thought, with its soaring ceilings and magnificent stained glass. The glass, though, depicted the heart of Namborra, fields of wheat, sheep grazing in lush pastures, the wild birds that frequented the wetlands behind the town. And behind the stained glass were the very things the windows depicted. Luc looked around him and saw all of Namborra within the hall, and all of Namborra stretching away outside.

The flight had been delayed because of a medical crisis. They'd arrived just as the service was about to begin, but the locals had known Beth was coming and had reserved them space near the front. Margie from the crèche had met them off the chopper. She and Beth had hugged for a long time. When Beth had hobbled into the hall, with Luc carrying Toby behind her, there'd been a massive stir. Those in aisle seats had risen and hugged her, and by the time they reached their seats, Beth's eyes were already moist.

Now they sat side by side. Luc cuddled a blessedly sleepy Toby and held Beth's hand with his free hand as they listened to local after local recounting the stories of lives lost.

First they talked of Bill Mickle, family man, retired plumber, passionate about his beloved greyhounds who never did any good on the track but Bill was always hopeful. Born and bred in Namborra. Five grown kids and three grandies.

An elderly lady stood at the end of Bill's son's spiel and told how Bill had chopped her wood every Thursday night. She sat and wept and Beth sniffed and Luc held her hand tighter.

Toby had been playing with a miniature toy truck but he'd gone to sleep in Luc's arms. Beth and Luc seemed…a cocoon in the midst of the community's grief.

Except Beth was grief-stricken, too.

Next in line were stories of Ray and Daphne Oddie. Farmers. They'd produced the best scones in the district, and the best merino sheep.

'Ray used to bring me scones whenever he came for his diabetes check,' Beth whispered, sniffing. 'Daphne was always too busy with the sheep to cook. For Ray it meant cook or starve. They worked it out.' She sniffed again and smiled. 'Scones were his forte but you should have tasted his lemon meringue pie. I'd have married him for that.'

She smiled mistily as those on stage went on to talk of a woman called Mariette Goldsworthy, a friend of Ray and Daphne from out of town, but she'd visited enough to be known and liked. She'd been notorious for cleaning up at the local bingo session.

And then... Ron McKenzie. Beth's partner.

His daughter, Faye, rose to speak. Of Ron's early life, his love of living. Of his grief at the loss of his wife. How Namborra had given him his life back and how the family would be grateful for ever.

And how much Ron had loved Beth. 'We were his kids,' Faye told the audience. 'But after Mum died we could do nothing. He was lost in grief but Beth... Beth, you were here when you were needed. What you achieved was a miracle. You gave us our dad back and we'll be grateful for ever. Beth, on Dad's behalf, we thank you. Our last loving memories of our dad will shine because of the joy you gave him.'

There was a moment's silence and then the hall burst into spontaneous applause. It wasn't just for Ron, Luc thought. It was for the woman sitting silently weeping beside him.

The knowledge was suddenly overwhelming. Beth had done this. Not only had she provided a medical service to this town, she'd spread her love. She'd made a community love her.

A kernel of something he hadn't felt before was budding deep inside. Pride? Admiration?

Awe?

And then she was standing, tugging on his hand until he released her. Heading to join Faye on stage.

He was still holding the sleeping Toby but others rose to help as she hobbled to the stage.

He sat, stunned. After all she'd gone through, to stand and speak in this packed hall…

But she handed her crutches to the people who'd helped her onto the stage and rested her hands on the lectern, supporting herself so every speck of her concentration was on the people she was talking to.

The people of Namborra.

She spoke of meeting Ron for the first time, of his devotion to his wife, of the privilege of sharing his desolation when she died. She spoke of seeing him at his lowest, surrounded by his family and yet unable to see them. Unable to let them help him. Unable to see anything but his loss.

And then she spoke of Ron's face when he'd seen the advertisement for a family doctor at Namborra. Of the awakening. Of the emergence from the dark.

'I was in a dark place, too,' Beth said simply. 'And Ron said could we? Dare we? And suddenly it was light again because we dared and we could. And that light… it seemed to flood our lives. Faye, you talk of what I gave Ron but it was two ways. We've loved the locals of Namborra and you guys…you seemed to love us. With Maryanne we seem to have built a medical team to be proud of. More than that, together we rebuilt our lives. We discovered that we dared lots of things. We dared take on the care of this community and you gave it back in spades. With Ron's encouragement—with your encouragement—I even dared have my little boy. Ron gave me my courage back, and that courage spread to all who knew him. You trusted him, you trusted us, and that trust will stay with me to the end.'

She fell silent for a moment, and a hush fell over the hall.

And finally Beth smiled, that tremulous smile that Luc knew and loved.

'To Faye, to all his family, to those who loved him most, I need to say thank you,' she managed. 'Thank you, Ron, from me, from every one of us in Namborra. Thank you for life. Thank you with love.'

And that was it.

The hall erupted, clapping so loudly the roof almost rose. The local bagpiper, a squat little woman with cheeks the colour of beetroot, lifted her pipes and the sound of 'Highland Cathedral' soared to the heavens.

The service was over.

But Beth was still on the stage, staring sightlessly at the departing crowd.

Margie was suddenly lifting the sleeping Toby from Luc's arms.

'Go to her,' she said, almost fiercely. 'If you're her friend…she needs you.'

Did she?

But Luc made his way swiftly up the steps to the stage. Beth was still standing, mute, tears streaming down her face. Farewelling a friend who'd meant so much to her.

He couldn't bear it. Such pain…

He gathered her into him and she folded, crumpling against his chest. He held, he simply held while the world seemed to settle around him.

They needed to step down from the stage. Most people were leaving the hall but a cluster remained, waiting. Luc recognised a few from the day of the crash, Maryanne, some of the nurses, people who'd helped.

Beth's friends?

They were waiting to claim her.

He gave her a moment longer and then gently put her back from him. He produced a handkerchief—he'd had the forethought to bring several—and dried her off.

'People are wanting to talk to you.'

'I… Yes.' She sniffed and blew her nose and mopped up. 'Sorry. I… Where's Toby?'

'Margie has him.' He smiled down at her. 'I think Margie loves him.'

'That's her specialty. Luc…'

'I know.' He met her gaze. This wasn't the time to say it but it had to be said and it had to be said now. 'Beth, we need to regroup. This hurts but I need to say it. While I was sitting down there, watching you, listening to you, I felt such pride…such wonder… But, Beth, what I also thought, what I realised, was that you don't need to marry me. You don't need *me*. You're an amazing woman, a powerhouse of love and talent, and you don't need anyone to give you wings. You've proved that over and over. We might love each other but that's different. I'm taking back my marriage proposal, my love, because the woman I love…she's magnificent just the way she is. She doesn't need me at all.'

She stared up at him, mutely. Seemingly dazed. And then she closed her eyes and seemed to give herself a mental shake.

'I guess…you're right,' she whispered. 'Of course you are. After all, what basis…what basis is love for a marriage?'

'Beth…'

'Don't go on,' she begged. 'You're right, Luc. I learned to be independent once and I can do it again. I don't need marriage. And, no, you're right. I don't need…you.'

Refreshments were served in an adjoining reception hall. Margie took Toby over, setting up an impromptu play area for the littlies in the corner of the hall. Toby was obviously delighted to see his friends. One of the nurses made her way to Beth, pushing a wheelchair, and Beth was able to sink into it and be as she needed to be—the centre of loved attention.

For the locals loved her. Luc could see it, not just in the way so many were waiting their turn to speak to her but in the way so many gazes gravitated to her. There was community concern and quiet love.

Dr Beth Carmichael had found herself a life in this community. She was as loved and respected as Ron had been.

What had she said? One and a half doctors between the two of them. They'd been so much more. He could see that.

'She can't come back.' The harsh words came from behind him. He turned and Maryanne Clarkson was at his shoulder. This woman was now Namborra's only doctor and she looked grim.

He'd been impressed with her the day of the crash. She'd been unflappable as well as competent. He'd been in the small hospital only briefly that night, but in the midst of chaos of multiple injuries he'd noted her triage system, her fast implementation of rules and the way the staff moved to her command.

Not a lot of emotion, though, he'd thought, which

was good in an emergency, but now, looking at her grim expression, he thought that same lack might be a downside.

'Excuse me?' He was balancing a lamington and a mug of tea and watching Beth at the same time. She seemed okay. She was even laughing at something someone had said.

She seemed...at home.

'She can't stay here,' Maryanne told him, following his gaze. 'At least, not to work. I'll tell her if I must, but I gather you're her friend. It might be kinder if you do.'

Beth had already told him she wouldn't be able to work here but he didn't fully understand. 'Why can't she stay here?'

'I can't work with a disabled doctor.'

There was a table behind him. He turned and set down his tea so he could face the middle-aged doctor square on.

'Disabled?'

'She can't see.'

'She can see.'

'Her vision's six/sixty. That's legally blind.'

'Without glasses. With glasses or contact lenses, she's fine.'

'She's not fine. She told me when she applied for the job here. She has trouble distinguishing colour in low light, and if she loses her glasses...' She took a deep breath. 'The day of the crash...look at the victims. Every one of them was over sixty. And Beth was almost there, too. She wouldn't have been able to see grey pillars crumpling. She wouldn't...'

'Have been able to run with a toddler in her arms,

all the way out of the car park while the roof caved in almost the instant the plane hit? Neither would you.'

'I would have had a better chance and you know it. It was one thing when we had the two of them backing each other up. Together she and Ron convinced the board they could manage. They did manage,' she conceded, 'but alone she can't and I won't take the risks they both did in covering each other. The hospital's liable if she messes something up.'

She paused and looked across at Beth. 'Look at her now. It'll take months for her to get back on her feet. She's already had to take time off when her child was born and as he's copped normal childhood illnesses. She's had Ron to help her but now... You think I can wear that?'

He was staring at her, stunned by her coldness. 'For a competent colleague. For a friend? Yes, I can. Bad things happen to all of us, Dr Clarkson.'

'Yes, and colleagues support when support's needed,' Maryanne snapped. 'Until whoever it is accepts their limitations are long term and chooses a more suitable role. Which isn't here. I was against hiring the pair of them, and look at them now. One's dead and one's even more disabled than when she started.'

'That's not their fault.'

'And it's not my fault either and it's not going to be. I can't spend my time worrying about her.'

'You don't have a choice. She's been cleared by the medical board as fit for practice. How many employment laws are you breaking?'

'I'm not breaking any. I'm simply saying I can't work with her, so if she chooses to return she'll be on her own. You think she can cope, with the load she's carrying?' She gave a grim nod as if the conversation was ended, as indeed it was. 'So there it is. Tell her she needs to look elsewhere for a less demanding job. You tell her—or I will.'

Then came another medical crisis, only not one he had to deal with. The head of the outback clinic was on the phone before he'd recovered his tea—and his equilibrium. 'Mate, there's been a car crash here. We'll be sending the chopper straight to Sydney so we can't pick you up this afternoon.'

'That's okay.' He'd already factored this into his plans. A commercial flight, small but reliable, left every day at midday so they could stay in Beth's apartment overnight.

And then he thought… Beth's apartment was a hospital apartment.

It wouldn't be hers for much longer.

And he watched her face as she talked on to the locals. He saw the rigid set of her smile as she was asked how long it would be before she was back for good, and he thought, She already knows it. She knows Maryanne, she's worked with her for years so she'll know exactly what she's thinking. Maryanne was a competent doctor who wouldn't bend the rules one bit, constantly looking over her shoulder for the bogie man of legal liability. For Beth she must be a nightmare.

Beth was starting to look exhausted. He headed over and told her what was happening with the plane, and she reacted almost with relief. It meant she could have time out in her apartment, rest—have space to come to terms with her lack of future here?

But first she needed to field invitations as the locals realised she was staying.

'Sorry, guys.' She was back on her crutches while Luc held a very sleepy Toby. 'I...' She glanced uncertainly at Luc. 'We need a quiet night.'

'How long do you think before you'll be back for good?' Margie asked directly, and Beth hesitated just a moment too long.

But then she managed a smile and he watched her shoulders brace. Moving on.

'Who knows how long this leg needs to heal?' she said lightly. 'I'll let you know.'

She gave Luc a bright smile that said clearly— Rescue me—and ten minutes later they were back in Beth's cosy little apartment. Beth was putting Toby into his cot, reuniting him with toys he'd been missing, while Luc was pacing the apartment, wanting to punch something.

The anger stayed—but with it came confusion.

Sometime during the service things had cleared for him. Now...fog was creeping back.

Beth headed for the fridge and poured wine for herself, offered him a beer, settled thankfully into a massive armchair and surveyed him thoughtfully. Even with the broken leg she was a woman in charge of her domain, he thought.

Except she wasn't, and it needed to be talked of. But first...the biggie. 'Beth...what I said at the service... about marriage...'

'Luc, that's over.' She met his gaze, calmly, almost challengingly. 'It should never have resurfaced as an option. It only did because Toby was ill and neither of us were thinking. You don't want to be married to me.'

Confusion deepened. Of course he wanted to be married to this amazing woman, but to hold her back...

How to say this? How to explain what he felt?

And what did he feel? How could he move forward from here? There were so many conflicting emotions.

'Beth, I don't want you to have to accept that you need me. Because I'm looking at you now...'

'Yeah, folded into an armchair because I've been tottering about on a broken leg...'

'That's not what I mean. Beth, somehow you've turned into someone amazing. Only maybe that's not true. I'm starting to think you've been amazing all along.' He was struggling here, trying to see inside him. Trying to sort fact from emotion.

'I know I coddled you but you flew the coop and, hey, you knew how to fly all along. You're a competent, practising doctor. You're a great mum. The locals here clearly adore you. With or without Ron, you've made a success of your life. Today...when you stood up and talked about Ron there wasn't a dry eye in the house but it wasn't just about Ron. It was about you. Until one tragic plane crash, you had your life under control and it will be again.'

She didn't respond. She met his gaze, her chin slightly tilted. Defiant?

How hard was all this to work out? How hard was it to say? But somehow he forced himself to continue. 'Beth, I would care for you,' he told her. 'I know that about myself. But I also know I'll risk smothering you, and maybe Toby, too. And I get it. I talked to Maryanne after the service and she's told me how she can't accept your disabilities. She's one cold woman. There's a part of me that wants to really tell her what I think of her, but there's another part of me that wants to agree with her because all I want to do is take you back to Sydney and keep you in cotton wool. Which...' He took a deep breath. 'Which is not what you want. During the awfulness of the past weeks it might be what you've thought you needed but it's not true into the future. Is it?'

'No.' Beth's expression was still calm. Assessing. Watching how he was feeling rather than thinking about herself? 'You're right, Luc. For now... Who knows what I'll do, but remarrying... I know I said maybe, but you're right, I said it for the wrong reasons. It feels like admitting defeat. When Toby was ill that was how I felt, defeated, but now...' She braced herself and tried to smile. 'Wherever I go, I don't need care twenty-four seven. You've been wonderful, Luc, as you've been in the past, but I don't need...constant wonderful. I can't keep needing.'

He was right, then. The thought gave him no joy.

This morning he'd accompanied Beth to Namborra and it had felt right. By some miracle Toby and Beth had been his to protect.

So what had changed? What was making him step back now?

It was because he loved her.

And he got it. In that one blinding moment of clarity, when she'd been on the stage, when she'd been talking to a community who loved her, he'd seen it.

She was wonderful, his Beth—except she wasn't *his* because she didn't need the restrictions he was bound to place on her life.

And she was smiling at him now, mistily, emotion

front and centre, but he knew the smile said that he was right. The last weeks had thrown them back to a place that hadn't suited either of them.

'Can I help you fight to stay here? Can we face down Maryanne together? She's well out of order.' He was struggling to find his voice and practicalities seemed the only way to go.

Once again, asking her to need him?

But she shook her head. 'It's not possible. I thought of it when Ron had the flu last year and we faced the fact that he'd have to retire eventually.' She still had her voice under control, but her eyes were a different matter. They were bright with unshed tears.

'Maryanne's seen my medical records—she actually accessed my past hospital records without asking, but that's another story. She's adamant I'm a risk. We had a car crash here a few months back—a nasty one. I had to crawl under and put in an IV line while the guys were stabilising the site. I cut myself on the way out, quite deep. Maryanne had to stitch me and she spent the entire time she stitched telling me the board couldn't be responsible for my stupidity. The fact that the kid survived because of the line I put in, and anyone else going under there would have been under the same risk as I was, was irrelevant. But she's threatened... If Ron's not here to work—as my guide dog, that's what she called him—she's said she'll leave.'

'Of all the vicious...'

'It's not vicious. It's pragmatic. She'll walk because she can't accept the responsibility.'

'Sort of like the opposite of me,' he said ruefully, and she managed a smile.

'I guess. You need to be needed and Maryanne runs

a mile. Or she makes me run a mile. Maryanne's competent, hard working and she doesn't have a child. She's a much better bet for the town than I am.'

'So the town's stuck with one doctor instead of two.'

'It'd be one and a half…'

'You're a whole lot more than half a doctor,' he growled, and she even managed a chuckle.

'Yeah, but you're biased.'

'Because I love you.'

'As a friend, Luc,' she said softly. 'Please, from now on, that's what it has to be.'

And he thought of what that meant. Tonight. Sleeping on the couch instead of holding Beth's body. The sensation of loss was almost overwhelming.

'Yeah, it sucks,' she said, and he could see she knew what he was thinking. 'But it's the only way, Luc.'

'I could…try to back off.'

'And pigs could learn to fly.' She sighed, her face bleak. 'Luc, I need a rest. Would you mind…maybe wandering down to the supermarket and buying a couple of steaks for dinner? The pub will be packed with locals tonight and I don't want to face them. I'll come back here in a few weeks, when I've finished rehab, so I can pack up and say my goodbyes properly. But for the town, tonight should be all about those we lost, not about me.'

'They're losing you, too. And so am I.' The desolation he felt was almost overwhelming.

'Yeah, but the alternative is me losing me,' she said, striving for lightness. 'And that's a whole heap worse.'

He headed off on his steak quest. Beth lay on the bed she'd slept in for the last few years and waited for exhaustion to do its job. To send her into oblivion for a couple of hours. She ached for time out.

It didn't happen.

What had she done?

And where was her future?

It wasn't here, in this cosy apartment she'd called home for the past few years.

She'd made herself a life here. She'd worked professionally, she'd had her baby and she'd felt a part of this community. But a part of her had always known it had to end. Ron had been nearing the point of retirement and Maryanne was a fixture. She and Ron had even joked about it—making an advertisement for a Ron replacement.

'Wanted, three quarters of a doctor to hold up another three quarters of a doctor.'

'Yeah, but we've been more than that,' she muttered into the stillness. She and Ron had been an awesome team.

Grief was all around her, grief for Ron, the gentle, kindly man she'd called a friend for so long, grief that her time here was over...and grief, all over again, for a man called Luc.

'I should never have slept with him,' she muttered. 'It's made it so much worse.

'It couldn't be any worse.' She was answering herself. 'You've never fallen out of love with him. Couldn't you just...learn to be dependent again? Let him take control?'

But she knew she couldn't.

She imagined Toby, climbing trees, falling off skateboards, doing all the dumb things kids did as they grew.

Would Luc let him take risks that all children had to take in order to turn into independent people?

'It'll never happen.' She knew it but it didn't make her decision less bleak. She took off her glasses and let the world blur.

'I can move on,' she muttered. 'I've done it before and I'll do it again.'

But if she let herself need Luc... How much easier...

'Not going to happen,' she said grimly into the silence, and she knew those four words were the final verdict.

CHAPTER NINE

'So, you and Luc...'

'Friends. Only friends.'

Rehab at Bondi Bayside was intense. There was little time for chat among those fighting to recover what they'd lost, or those learning to make the most of their new norms. Beth and Harriet fitted into a camp apiece. Beth's leg was likely to recover to full use but Harriet was facing a lifetime of weakness.

This morning Harriet and Beth found themselves on the mats together, soft balls between their knees, raising their legs over and over.

Beth was getting better every day. Harriet was struggling.

If anyone else had asked personal questions Beth would have shrugged them off, but Harriet had become a friend. And maybe Harriet was facing long-term issues that almost mirrored Beth's.

'It must be strange, living with your ex-husband.' Harriet was probing gently but Beth glanced across at her and saw the set of her face, the lines of entrenched pain as she raised and lowered her injured leg, and knew she was using Beth's story to deflect thinking of what was starting to be obvious. That the damage to Harriet's leg was permanent.

She knew by now that Harriet's depression was bone deep. Coming to terms with disability...it sucked.

There was little Beth could do to help her but she could at least answer honestly.

'It is weird,' she admitted. 'What's between Luc and I...it's been so intense it's hard to step back, but we're both trying.' She tried for a smile. 'He's too good a friend to lose.'

'He is that,' Harriet said, 'The whole team...they're lovely. But if anything happened...between me and Pete... I don't think we could ever be just friends.'

'Yeah?' Beth had her own views on Pete, aided by Luc's harsh summary.

'Pete's lightweight. Harriet's fallen hard but I can't see Pete sticking round for the long haul. Where is he now? She's injured and he's not exactly playing the devoted spouse.'

'Maybe Harriet doesn't need him...like you assume need,' she'd suggested, but he'd snorted.

'I'm hearing rumours and they're not pretty. I wish she could find someone else...'

Maybe Harriet and Luc, Beth thought as she pushed her ball up and winced as unused muscles screamed their protest. But for some reason... The thought made her feel ill.

So much for just being friends.

She had to get her ankle back to normal and get herself out of here. Make herself a new life.

Learn again to be independent.

He's too good a friend to lose...

He was that, she thought, but the atmosphere in the apartment now... Aagh!

'So what do you do at night?' Harriet asked into the suddenly loaded silence.

And that led to even more loaded silence.

We spend the night concentrating on not jumping each other. That was the honest answer but she could hardly go there. What happened was usually an early dinner, a trip to the beach, time playing with Toby on the sand...pretending they weren't a family? And then home. No. Back to Luc's apartment, not home, she told herself fiercely. And she'd say she was tired and head to bed. She'd lie in the spare bedroom beside Toby's cot and listen to Toby snuffle in his sleep and try not to think about Luc in the next room.

Sometimes Luc was called out to work and then it was easier. Or almost easier because then she kept thinking of what he was doing, putting himself in harm's way. That didn't lead to sleep either.

All in all...friend or not, it would be easier if she was staying somewhere else, she thought, but how would Luc feel if she rejected even that much of his friendship?

'Hard, isn't it?' Harriet said sympathetically.

And Beth thought, I've been silent for too long and she knows. She guesses...

'Yeah, well...'

'It probably is worth fighting to stay friends, though.'

Harriet's voice had turned thoughtful. Beth figured she was using this to distract her from her own problems, so that was okay. She should even encourage it.

Except talking about it was hard.

Even thinking about it was doing her head in.

'How about gaming?' Harriet asked into the stillness.

And Beth thought, *What?*

'Um…gaming?'

'Mystic Killers,' Harriet said. 'It's an online game. Sam…you've met Sam? She's one of the other nurses on SDR and she's pretty much my bestie. She's been researching stuff that might help me kill time, and Mystic Killers does seem to work. Turns out swatting dragons can get rid of a whole heap of angst. Off with their heads. You need to watch the fire spouts, though. And the babies.'

'Really?' She said it with such caution that Harriet smiled.

'Oh, yeah. The ones with forked tongues are the worst. Sam's set me up as Sneak-Swiper and I'm getting better at dodging. It beats lying in bed thinking about what I'm about to do with the rest of my life. Hey, another ten push-ups of this dumb ball and we're out of here. You, too? Do you have time before picking up Toby to learn to play?'

'I…guess. But my eyes… Harriet, I can't…'

'Oh, Beth,' Harriet said, instantly appalled. 'I'm so sorry. I didn't think. I should have…'

'It's okay.' She managed a smile across at her friend. 'That's something I've learned not to flinch at.' She hesitated and then looked at Harriet, at the mess that was still her leg. Did she know her well enough now to say it like it was?

Why not? She'd had enough people tiptoeing around her when her sight had gone, assuming the worst. Luc, front and centre.

'I'm thinking that might be something you need to face in the future, too, now,' she told her. 'A lifetime of people questioning whether you're up to things. Sometimes it's concern and care. Sometimes it's not, it's downright patronising, but if you look for patronising you'll spend the rest of your life defensive.'

'Yeah,' Harriet said grimly. 'I see that. So Luc... concern and care?

'You'd better believe it.'

'And patronising?'

'He doesn't quite get the distinction but he tries.'

'But not hard enough.'

'I don't think he can try any harder,' Beth said bluntly. 'And I have no idea how he can do any better. But that's okay. Another couple of weeks and he can stop trying again. We'll go back to being...'

'Friends?'

'I hope so,' she whispered, and then pushed herself together. 'But gaming...what is this Mystic Killers?'

'Something to play at night if you can't...play at night. And something to vent a little frustration on. Or a lot. But if you can't...'

'I'm not good with fast objects on small screens.'

'But maybe...' Harriet paused for thought and then grinned. 'Hey, there's an enormous screen in the health education unit on the top floor.' She hauled her hospital ID out of the top pocket of her gym gear. 'They hardly use it and I'm officially allowed access. Do you have a big telly at home?'

'I... Yes. Back at Namborra.' Or wherever she ended up.

'There you go, then. Learn here and you'll fly.

Okay, Beth, hold onto your hat, I'm about to introduce you to a whole new world.'

There'd been a minor crisis in the outer suburbs but it was very minor. A recycling warehouse had caught fire. It had produced a frightening amount of flames and smoke, the authorities had panicked and pulled in the big guns, but the team came back to Bondi in a chopper with no patients. There'd been no casualties apart from a bit of smoke inhalation. The local medics had it under control.

It meant, though, that Luc had missed his time at the beach with Toby and Beth, and he'd definitely missed it. It was now almost nine, the time when Beth usually said goodnight, headed into the spare room with Toby and closed the door behind her.

She might already have the door closed.

He had to get used to it. Another couple of weeks and she'd be done with rehab and out of here, he thought, as he rode the elevator to his apartment. It was the way things were, the sensible option.

But he didn't feel sensible. He felt frustrated. He had so few nights left and he'd just missed one. He put his key in the lock and felt tension tighten across his forehead. Please let her still be awake...

He opened the door—and stopped short.

She *was* still awake. She was wearing the soft, blue jogging suit she wore for rehab. Her hair was tousled, she was nestled under a rug on the sofa with her braced leg on a chair in front of her, she was wearing headphones and she was...

Staring at the world's biggest television. It took up almost the entire wall unit.

There were dragons on the screen. Large dragons. As he stared, one lunged forward, all fangs and fire, so real, so vast he almost backed out of the door.

Beth's hand rose on the controller and the dragon exploded into a thousand gory pieces, sliding down the screen and disappearing into the ether.

'Got him! Awesome! He fell right into my trap.' She glanced around at Luc and her grin almost split her face. 'That's Slime Vader taken care of. Let's see what else they can throw at me. Let 'em come. I'm ready.' She typed something fast on the screen and then put the remote aside. 'They can regroup for a while, not that it'll do 'em any good. Sneak-Swiper's in control.' And then she turned her grin to him. 'Hi, dear. How was your day?'

He...blinked. A domestic scene...the little wife bearing slippers and domestic harmony... Not so much.

'Dragons,' he tried, cautiously.

'Mystic Killers,' she said, as if that explained everything. 'Sneak-Swiper and I are on a mission. You want to join us?'

'Sneak-Swiper?'

'That'd be Harriet. She doesn't seem to enjoy it as much as me—she's not bloodthirsty enough—but she's more skilled and I'm improving every minute. Did you see the end of Slime Vader? I'm Mouse-Who-Roared, by the way. That's intentional. Everyone knows dragons are scared of mice.'

'I... Of course.' He ventured a little further into the room and looked around with caution. 'Um...my telly? My sound system?'

'I didn't trade them in, if that's what you're thinking,' she said, and chuckled, and the sound of her laugh was a shock. It was warm and deep and true. It was a sound he hadn't heard…for years?

It made him think…

Don't think.

'They're safely stowed under my bed,' she assured him as if that was entirely sensible. 'With my rubbish eyesight, I couldn't game using your set.'

'So you bought a new one?'

'Hey, I'm sensible.' She stood up and wobbled and reached for her crutches. He didn't step forward and steady her. It almost killed him not to.

'I have a perfectly perfect big telly back in Namborra,' she continued, happily. 'This baby is from the rental place that supplies the hospital. They were a bit stunned when I told them the size I needed but happy to oblige in the end. The console's new, though, bought for me this afternoon by Pete. Harriet's boyfriend?' Her smile slipped a bit then.

'Luc, do you know what the deal is there? I'm starting to have serious reservations about that relationship and I so don't want Harry to get hurt. Harriet was aching for his visit—I could see her face light up with hope every time the door opened. Then when he did arrive… I went to leave but before I could, she asked him if he'd organise me the console. And Pete was out of there so fast… It was like he was aching for an excuse to get out, even though he'd just arrived. Then he insisted on playing here with me when I knew she wanted him. So here he was, looking after the little woman, only it was me and not Harriet who was the little woman. It was nice of him to do it but really… what does she see in him?'

Pete…

There was so much going on here it was making his head spin.

Pete was a firefighter, one of Kev's crew. He and Harriet had been an item for a year now but Luc, too, had reservations. The guy seemed all testosterone-driven ego.

And that he'd been here with Beth... The tension he'd been feeling in the elevator escalated.

'So...is he a toe-rag or am I just imagining it?' Beth was apparently not noticing his...anger?

'As far as I know he hasn't played away.' He tried to haul his mind away from Beth's flushed face and tousled hair, from the cuteness of her jogging suit, from... well, just from Beth. Focus on Harriet, he told himself, and tried. Harriet and Pete. 'My concerns are only instinct.' He sighed. 'With her injuries, I hope I'm wrong. She needs him.'

'Need's not a basis for a relationship,' she snapped, and he flinched. There it was, the underlying reason why he couldn't have this woman. Because she refused to concede...need?

Because he couldn't come to terms with what she really needed. Which was independence.

'Want to play?' she asked, moving on fast, as if she guessed the tensions simmering underneath.

'Play?'

'Mystic Killers,' she said with all the patience in the world. 'I was getting hammered when you arrived. Yeah, I blew up Slime Vader, but there's bigger, scarier dragons in the background. I could use someone at my back. Hey, there's a role that might suit. I need you, Luc Braxton, to kill my dragons. You ever tinkered with online gaming?'

'No,' he said faintly.

'Well, seeing your entire apartment has been taken over, maybe it's time for you to learn. You need a handle. How about…?' She paused and considered. 'Protect-Or-Die.'

'Die…'

'Nobility is your middle name. You don't have a suit of armour in your apartment by any chance? Sword? Chain mail?'

'Um…no.'

'Then we'll just have to use our imagination. Want to share my rug instead? Come on. I need you.' And she tossed back a corner of the fluffy rug someone from Namborra had sent her as a get-well gift and invited him in.

She needed him.

She didn't.

He stood and gazed at her and she beamed back. There wasn't a single sexy nuance in the way she was holding the rug. She was all bounce and excitement. *Let's go slay some dragons together…*

She'd moved on, he thought. That week of clinging, of need, was over. She'd figured it out. From now he was only a friend. But she was offering friendship. On her terms. Her telly. Her hired console. Her rug.

Take it or leave it, her smile was saying, and what choice did he have?

'Give me a minute to find myself a beer and haul my boots off,' he told her. 'How many dragons do we need to kill?'

There was something about blowing fire-breathing dragons into a thousand unidentifiable body parts that settled things inside her—especially when she was blowing things up with Luc snuggled beside her.

He got the gist of the game in minutes, but he played differently from Harriet, or from Pete who'd played for a while supposedly to make sure the set worked. Pete blasted his way in front and ended up pretty much dead for his pains, over and over. She and Harriet played as a team, stalking Mystic World with steady purpose and a certain amount of caution.

Luc played tactical right from the beginning. He slipped in behind her, covering her back. For a start she thought he was content to stay back until he'd learned the fundamentals of the game, but as the night wore on he still stayed back.

And she grew bolder because of it. She found she was moving faster, surer, knowing as each threat emerged she had a solid, safe presence backing her up. When she missed her aim, Luc was there, blasting her way out of trouble. Steady. Intent. Watchful.

But also having a heap of fun. When she hesitated, knowing just over the rise there'd be dragons of truly epic proportions, he was egging her on.

'Go, girl. You can handle hot. Besides, I just won us enough points for you to rise from the dead twice. I wish we had this set up in ER. How about that for a medical scenario? They bring in a crash victim, I go kill a couple of dragons, get my Rise-From-The-Dead points and all's well with the world. And yet they never taught this at med school. Okay, Mouse-Who-Roared. Go!'

And she did, storming the mighty Mystic Gate, sword flashing, fire on all sides, magic and mayhem scattering before her. Luc followed behind, neutralised threats, egged her on, giving her courage. Cheered as she blew things up that needed blowing up. Handed over his points to save her when she was devoured. Joined her in inescapable laughter as they stormed the tower and took on five dragons and their world blew up and they were blasted from the top of the tower, with only Luc's points to save them.

Then Beth headed over a rise and spotted a dragon's nest, complete with adorable-looking, doe-eyed baby dragons. The babies were pecking their way out of their shells and staggering into their new world. Cute as…

She turned her Mystic Blaster to the nest and shot them all into the middle of next week. Leaving Luc… hornswoggled.

'You shot babies,' Luc said blankly.

'Kill or be killed.' She grinned. 'That's twenty less threats we need to face before we gain the Mystic Throne. Besides, grown up they'll threaten our world and I'm all for protecting our world. We're a team, Luc Braxton. Get a grip.'

And then another giant loomed behind them and ethical questions faded. Apparently, you had to pay—a lot— for decimating dragon nests.

Uh-oh. There weren't enough points left in anyone's bank to save them from what happened next.

'We need better tactics,' Luc said, as their online bodies lay crumpled on the dusty plains, with the Mystic Kingdom a mere speck on the horizon. 'I think your sword arm needs a broader sweep. And maybe babies are a no go.'

'The babies need thought,' she conceded. 'Maybe we need to let 'em leave the nest and grow fangs before we pick 'em off. Next time you win points, how about using them for that, rather than all this noble point-saving so you can heal me.'

'I don't like to see you dead.'

'Hey, we survive dead to fight another day. Look at us.'

'Yeah, zero points and back where we started.' He sighed and then cheered up. 'Want to try again?'

'Sorry. Time for a bacon sandwich and bed. Toby'll be up at dawn and he won't take dragons as an excuse.' She tossed back her rug and pushed herself clumsily to her feet. 'But a rematch is certainly in order. Tomorrow night? I reckon in two weeks we could be quite a team.'

'Two weeks.'

'That's when I go.' She shrugged and smiled. 'Back to Namborra for a start, and then back to Brisbane. I've decided. You know Mum and Dad still own an apartment there? It's empty at the moment so Toby and I will stay there until we figure what to do.'

So she had things arranged.

Two weeks. Right.

The emptiness, the desolation, was suddenly so great it threatened to overwhelm him.

He watched as she struggled over to the kitchenette, as she set about making toasted sandwiches.

He should do it for her, or at least offer to help, but he knew by now that she'd shrug him away.

I can do it.

She could, he thought. She didn't need him.

The thought was breaking him in two.

We're a team, Luc Braxton.

Not so much.

He thought of the last couple of hours, of Beth assessing the dragon nest and blasting it into oblivion.

The Beth he'd known—or thought he'd known—would have flinched. Killing cute baby dragons? That wasn't for the soft-hearted.

What had she said?

I'm all for protecting our world.

But he was the protector.

He watched her cook for him and he felt like his worlds were somehow colliding. The impact was smashing something and he wasn't sure what.

He should get up, insist on helping, force her to sit while he cooked.

Or he should relax while she cooked, be grateful that she was happy and helping him.

Neither felt right.

His background was all around him, the need to stay within himself, to be self-contained, to protect, to not need anyone.

He watched her struggle to get to the refrigerator and it almost killed him to let her cope on her own.

But he had to. She didn't want him. She didn't need him. She and Toby would move back to Brisbane and get on with their lives while he went on saving people. Doing what he was good at.

Beth was okay at saving people, too, he conceded. She was skilled, level-headed, practical…and had she really blasted those dragon babies to save the world?

Yes, she had. She was practical.

He wouldn't be so good at living with a practical partner, he conceded. A partner who resented him stepping in. Caring.

So therefore…

'Toastie,' she said, and handed over a plate loaded with buttery, oozy calories. 'And then bed for me, and maybe for you, too? I know you, Luc Braxton. You've been out there saving the world, having quite a day.'

'While you've saved Mystic World.'

'Not yet I haven't,' she said serenely. 'But I will. Tomorrow or the next day or the day after that. And then…there's lots more worlds to save and I'll find some other way to save them than by being a family doctor in Namborra. So don't you worry about me.' She fetched her own toastie from the fry-pan, waved it a couple of times until it cooled and then held it like she was proposing a toast. 'Here's to a future without threats,' she said. 'Here's to the saviours of Mystic World, and dragon exterminators extraordinaire. And here's to you, Luc, exterminating all other threats. We make a great team, you know. It's just…we need to save our worlds separately.'

But an hour later… It was all very well to say that sort of thing to Luc's face, Beth conceded. It was quite another to lie in the dark and think it.

Saving the world separately…

Oh, she still loved him.

She should never have slept with him again, she thought bleakly. It'd brought it all back.

'But it was back already,' she said into the dark. 'It never went away.'

'It has to go away. I have no use for it.'

What?

Love?

Did she still love him?

That was a no-brainer. Of course she did.

She thought of him, playing the game, protecting her back.

'I could do the same for him,' she muttered into the dark. 'We could do the same for each other. Watch each other's backs. Be in each other's corners.'

But it wouldn't be like that. She'd watched him surreptitiously as she'd made their toasties and she'd seen the strain letting her do such a simple task had imposed on him. It'd almost kill him to let her take normal, everyday risks, she thought, and he'd do the same for Toby. He'd wrap them in care, and they'd stifle.

She thought of Harriet with her Pete, Pete who couldn't bear to care. Pete who needed his Harriet to be perfect or he couldn't cope.

'So we have the opposite.' She buried her face in her pillow. Her leg was aching. She should get up and take painkillers but in a sense the pain in her leg was distracting her from the pain in her heart.

She couldn't live with him.

She loved him.

She had to leave.

And in the next room Luc was struggling with demons of his own.

She was going to leave, but how the hell would she cope without him?

Easily.

She had a gammy leg and weak eyesight but neither of those things made her need him. He had no place in her life.

But he wanted her.

So step back, he told himself. Do what he'd done tonight, protect from the rear, let her lead.

Except...did she even want him to do that? He was starting to figure it out. Even tonight when they had been playing…any minute he'd been expecting her to turn on him and tell him to go find his own dragons.

He'd been hunting his own dragons for years now. That was what his job was all about. He'd saved Beth this time. He'd helped her but she no longer needed him so it was back to doing what he always did. Holding himself solitary, unattached, ready to fight whatever needed to be fought and then move on.

But in the next room… Beth and Toby…

They were doing his head in.

He ached for them to need him.

He needed them to need him.

And there was a thought he couldn't get his head around. He had no way of interpreting it.

All he knew was that Beth was right. Being with her when she didn't need him would drive him into a place he couldn't fathom. He had no choice. If he loved her…and he did love her, he knew enough of his head now to accept that fact as irreversible…then he had to let her fly on her own.

He had to let her go.

CHAPTER TEN

BRISBANE WAS BORING.

There were job opportunities—of course there were. She was a qualified doctor with solid experience. Very few employers took the same view of her sight limitations as Maryanne. She was qualified, she wasn't an obvious loose cannon, therefore she was employable. But her leg still needed work. She was still hobbling, still having trouble carrying Toby.

Maybe she should have stayed at Luc's for a while longer, accepted his help, accepted the help of the lovely grandmotherly Alice.

Except she had her pride.

And her fear.

Yeah, okay, she'd been terrified at how close she was growing to Luc. She was terrified she'd become the woman he wanted her to be, a woman who loved and depended on him.

Depended… Yeah, that was the cut. As soon as the rehab doctors had told her she was free to work on her own, she'd run. She'd had no choice.

She'd flown back to Namborra before she'd come to Brisbane. She and Toby had spent a few days catching up with friends and packing up her apartment.

She'd sort of hoped Maryanne might change her mind but it wasn't going to happen. Maryanne seemed tired, overwrought and stressed to the limit as she coped with the workload of three doctors, but it had taken only one short conversation for Beth to realise she wasn't backing down.

'Yes, I'm stressed but do you think having to watch over your shoulder to make sure you're not stuffing things up will make things better?'

She'd tried, for what was to be the last time. 'Maryanne, my sight's not a problem. Not if you...'

'That's just it. Not if I cover for you. It's not going to happen, Dr Carmichael. If Ron had been able to move faster to get out of the way...if you'd been able to see those pillars crumbling...'

'You know that's unfair.'

'Unfair or not, I'm not about to risk a medical negligence suit on my watch.'

There was nothing more to be said. She'd said her goodbyes and left.

Which left her in her parents' elegant apartment overlooking the Brisbane river, working on her rehab, playing with Toby, trying to figure what to do with her life.

She didn't want to be a shift doctor in a city clinic.

She wanted the country. She wanted Luc.

She needed...

No. She wasn't sure what she needed. All she knew was that she didn't need Luc enough to run back to him.

She'd brought Mystic Killers with her. Dragon slaying was good for the quiet times.

When in doubt, kill...

* * *

When in doubt, slay dragons.

Luc had set his own screen up again, and gone out and bought his own gaming console, as Beth's huge screen had gone back to the rental agency and she'd taken her console with her. He played online with Harriet and Sam.

'You know, you can still play online with Beth,' Harriet told him but the idea seemed…

Hard?

Yeah, like watching her limp away hadn't been the hardest thing he'd ever done in his life.

She didn't need him. She was out there slaying dragons all by herself and that was the way she wanted it.

He just had to accept it.

Two weeks. Three weeks. Four.

He was going nuts. He needed catastrophes. Disasters. Anything to make the pain go away.

'You love her.' He was sitting on the end of Harriet's bed—yet again. Harriet seemed almost as morose as he was. Almost? That was crazy all by itself. She had so much more to be miserable about. Her leg was taking its own sweet time to heal, the doctors were unsure if she'd ever regain full strength and on top of that Pete was avoiding her. Toerag. Hell, if Beth needed him like Harriet needed Pete, Luc thought, then…then things would be okay.

He wanted to punch Pete.

He wanted to punch…dragons.

He wanted Beth.

A month. Time to organise crèche. Time to take a job.

So what if the only jobs available seemed to be

working sessional clinics? She could handle that. As long as she didn't try to work in poor light she was fine, and it wasn't as if most sessional doctors did house calls.

She found a good crèche for Toby. It wasn't as friendly as the Namborra childcare but it was the best she could do.

She started working four mornings a week, working on her leg for the rest of the time. And playing with Toby.

Thank heaven for Toby. He kept her sane. He kept her happy.

Almost…

The call came at three in the morning. The worst ones did, Luc thought as he groped in the dark for the phone. He was used to it, though. He was wide awake, reaching for his clothes as he listened.

'A crash on the cliffs north of Illawarra.' Mabel was wasting no words. Like Luc, she'd have been pulled from sleep and the adrenaline would have coursed straight in. 'An eighteen-wheeler, one of those huge double trucks. The driver's lost control for some reason. He's crashed through the barriers and into oncoming traffic. He's okay but a car's been pushed down the cliff. It's hanging by nothing just above the sea. As far as we can tell, there's a woman and three kids inside, too terrified to move. A couple of locals are trying to abseil down to stabilise the car but there's fog and wind. Two minutes to get to the chopper, Luc. Minimum crew as you'll want the chopper for transfer. I'll send backup after you. Gina's heading for the roof now. Chopper's ready. You, Blake, Samantha. Go.'

He went.

She'd seen ten patients that morning and almost all had been boring.

That wasn't exactly a kind thing to think, she conceded as she tried to sleep that night, but walk-in clinics tended to attract boring.

If people had something they were really worried about, they tended to take time off work and make an appointment with their family doctor. If something was urgent, then they'd head to their nearest hospital. Beth's clinic got the rest.

Today Beth had handled five requests for certificates from office workers who'd had to take time off work because of minor ailments. A teenager wanting birth control who didn't want to face the same family doctor her mum used. A construction worker with an annoying rash—wearing polyester while digging in the heat wasn't the wisest move. A young mum who'd popped in on impulse because her baby was having trouble feeding. The last had at least had been rewarding as Beth had recognised underlying postnatal depression, though the head of the clinic had been less than impressed when he'd seen Beth's timesheet for the consultation.

There'd also been two hopefuls who'd seen a new name on the medical list and thought they'd try her as an easy mark for drugs.

It wasn't exactly satisfying medicine.

At least she'd picked the postnatal depression, she

told herself. Left untreated it could have led to disaster, so she had done some good. But this couldn't sustain her long term. She wanted to be a family doctor, someone people chose when they had real problems. She wanted to be a doctor who saw mothers through pregnancies and picked postnatal depression before it did real damage.

'You're lucky to have any job right now,' she said into the dark, and she knew she was. She'd fought desperately hard to qualify as a doctor. And, yes, her time at Namborra had been fantastic but she'd been lucky.

'You make your own luck,' she muttered, and wondered how on earth she was going to make her own luck now.

'So one step at a time,' she told herself. 'Get your leg better.'

And stop thinking about Luc?

Where was he now?

'Out caring for the world,' she said out loud. 'Out setting the world to rights.'

'I could help him.'

'As if he'd ever let you... Get real.'

The car had been hit head on, and then propelled mercilessly over the cliff, the force of the truck smashing it through the metal barricade to plunge almost thirty feet down the cliff.

It hung, seemingly by a wing and a prayer, ten feet above the waves.

The cliff was almost concave, the rock face scooping inward then out to form a slight ledge. The ledge had caught the car—just. It was wedged precariously, its front fender on the ledge, the rest of it seemingly a crumpled wreck.

By the time the chopper landed on the clifftop, the local coastguard boat was in view, beavering through rough seas, heading for the base of the cliff, but the rocks underneath would allow no approach by sea. The night was windy and wild. Gina was having trouble even steadying the chopper to land.

The coastguard's searchlights lit the scene like day as they did their initial assessment but there was no way a boat could get near.

An ambulance was parked on the clifftop, and a couple of paramedics caring for someone they assumed was the truck driver. Minor lacerations and shock, they'd been told. There was also a fire engine, plus about six other cars. There were guys on the cliff face dressed in hard hats, with ropes looped around their shoulders. Local abseilers called on to help? They weren't going over, though. Amateurs?

This wasn't the scene for amateurs, Luc thought, and thanked God they'd had the sense to wait. The look of that cliff... If they'd tried to get down there they might well become further casualties.

There was a moment's silence between those in the chopper as they all stared down at the car. The ledge it was on was so narrow. They could almost see it teetering. 'How many did Mabel say?' Blake asked at last, and his voice was almost a whisper through the headphones. They'd pull themselves together before they landed, but right now the initial reaction from all of them was horror.

'Woman and three kids,' Luc said. His headset was connected to base. 'Mabel's just radioed in what we know. The driver's a Tess McKnight, thirty-four. Kids are Zoe, eight, Tom, six, and Robbie, three.'

'What the hell were they doing out here at this time of night?' Blake muttered.

And Luc knew that, too. 'Anniversary party in Sydney. Driving home late. Husband's following behind, driving Gran and Grandpa and Aunty. He's on the cliff.'

That led to further silence. Scenes like this were appalling but the addition of family watching on...it added tension to tension. The team would need to turn off distress, turn off emotion if they were to have any hope of rescuing anyone.

'Mabel says the firies have called in cranes,' Luc said into the headphones. 'Two, due here any minute. If we can get cables to the car we'll have something to attach them to. She's telling me the boys with ropes are part of a local abseiling group but the cliffs here are sandstone and they don't like their chances.'

'Right.' A moment's further thought while Blake assessed and came to a decision. 'Sam, you're up top,' Blake told her. 'I know you have the skills but you don't have the experience. Luc, you and I head down. Cables, hooks...take thin lines and Sam'll guide down what we need when we reach the car.' The chopper was settling now. They could no longer see the car dangling over the ocean, but the vision was seared into the minds of them all. 'Luc, sandstone cliffs are renowned for nasty surprises. You feel unsafe, you're out of there.'

'Leaving it to you? I don't think so.'

'Same goes for me,' Blake said grimly. 'By the look of that car they might already all be dead and I want no more bodies on my watch. Harriet's proof of what these cliffs can do. Watch your backs, people. Watch everything. Let's go.'

They landed and they hardly talked. Blake and Luc had fitted part of their gear in the chopper but it had to be checked and rechecked before they went near the edge.

'Anyone hear anything from the car?' Blake demanded.

'Nothing.' The chief of the local fire crew, a woman in her fifties who'd introduced herself brusquely as Carol, had things under control. Or as much under control as she could. 'The husband says Tess has her phone on her but it's rung out. I won't let anyone try again. If she's unconscious, if any of the kids try to wiggle to answer it...' She let the sentence hang.

'The abseilers?'

'Friends of our local cop,' Carol said. 'Seems they did a course a couple of years back. Rex called them out but they seemed so nervous I pulled them back.'

'Well done,' Blake said gruffly.

'And you guys can do it?'

'Piece of cake,' Luc said. 'In our sleep.' He was adjusting his Prusik loop, the extra loop linking the main rope to the harness. The loop was sometimes referred to as dead man's handle, an essential backup safety measure. He looped it around his rope and attached it to his carabiner. Making sure he locked it. 'Those cranes you mentioned?'

'They'll be here any second. You get cables down, we'll stabilise.'

'Check?' Blake said.

There was another safety measure, checking each other's equipment, double checking locks were secure.

Blake and Luc checked each other, and Sam did her own check for good measure. She checked Blake first, reaching for the metal loop attaching Blake's belay plate to the centre of his harness.

And then, almost as if it was part of the checking process, almost as if it was part of their normal, professional routine, Sam reached up and kissed Blake, swift, hard on the mouth. It was done almost before it began, before anyone could notice.

But Luc had noticed.

Sam and Blake were practically joined at the hip, Luc knew, a tight-knit couple who worked brilliantly as a team. And for just a moment, as Sam turned to check his locks, he felt a pang of longing so great it threatened to overwhelm him.

If Beth was here…

Right. If Beth was here, in low light, with her gammy leg, there'd be no way he could concentrate properly. All his attention would be on her, when it had to be on the job at hand.

How could Sam bear Blake to take risks? And vice versa? To watch someone you loved walk into peril…

It was far better to be like he was. Alone. Worrying about no one.

He needed no one.

And then a guy broke away from the group clustered around the police car. A big, burly guy in his forties, seemingly capable, steady, intent, and headed towards Luc.

'I'm Mike,' he muttered as he reached him, and he grabbed Luc's hand in his own vast paw. 'It's my family down there.'

'We're doing what we can,' Luc said. And then

he added, 'We're good. If anyone can get them out, we will.'

Carol came up and took his arm to lead him away, but the man wasn't going anywhere. 'My Tess's sensible,' he told Luc. 'She'll keep her head. The kids... Zoe and Robbie'll do as they're told, though Robbie'll cling to Tess. Tom...he's a tense kid and he freezes. But tell him there's a fire engine up top of the cliff and he'll do what you want.'

'That's useful,' Luc said, nodding at Blake to make sure he'd heard it in the wind.

Once more Carol tugged, but the man still had hold of Luc's arm. And the rigid control he'd used to convey information seemed to snap. Capable? Steady? Not so much. This was a man crumbling under a pressure so great it was destroying him.

'Bring 'em back to me,' he said. 'I can't... Tess and I...we've been dating since we were seventeen. She's bossy and independent and she drives me nuts but hell...' His voice broke on a sob. 'My family... They're all I need in the world. Tess is all...all I am. Please...please bring them up safe for me.'

Every nerve-ending, every last fraction of his concentration had to be on the job at hand.

The two local abseilers, plus Gina and Sam, were up top, controlling their lines, making sure any slip wouldn't turn into disaster. He and Blake were descending toward separate sides of the car.

But it wasn't easy, or maybe that was an understatement. The cliff face was crumbling sandstone, and the closer Luc got to the ledge the worse the situation seemed. The nose of the car was almost completely crumpled, and it rested with a tiny percentage of the mangled metal on the ledge.

If he or Blake dislodged any more of the already smashed cliff face...

They couldn't. He had to concentrate on handholds. On trying to find a fraction of rock on which to place his feet.

If it had been a sheer drop it would have been easier, just belaying them both down. But the rocks jutted out just enough to make that impossible.

So concentrate...

And he was, but there was an echo in his head that wouldn't go away.

'They're all I need in the world.'

And while he concentrated he thought...that's what he wanted Beth to feel. That she needed him more than anything.

But not the other way around?

Why was he thinking that now? How did he have room to think it? But it was in his head and it wouldn't go away.

How would she be feeling if she could see him now?

And then he thought of all the times he'd done this job or rescues like it. If he and Beth had stayed married... He would have expected her to stay home and be safe and yet still...need?

The anguish of the guy on the clifftop stayed with him.

She's bossy and independent and she drives me nuts but hell...' His voice had broken on a sob. *'She's all I am.'*

How would he feel if Beth was in this car?

Gutted. Exactly how the guy up top was feeling.

But what if it was the other way around? If Beth knew where he was right now...

She did know. On some subconscious level he knew that she knew. Not that he was hanging over a wild ocean, trying to get into a wrecked car, but she'd know he'd be doing something like it.

He'd place her in a cocoon of safety and not let her care?

'This isn't working.' Blake's voice came through his headphones, strained to the limit. 'I'll have to bail. The car's hit these rocks on the way down and they're already dislodged. It's threatening to shift more. I'll head back up, try and descend further across and come at it laterally. How about you?'

'Still okay.'

The thoughts of Beth were still there but they weren't taking his concentration from the job at hand. Rather they were heightening his senses.

She'd done this sort of work, too. She'd told him about the car wreck she'd crawled into. At the memorial service a couple of locals had spoken of it in awe.

He'd have tried to prevent it.

So he had double to prove, he thought, as he fought to find the next toehold. He had to save these guys for themselves. But also...for Beth?

He had a sudden vision of Beth as he'd first met her, fiery, funny, independent and supremely talented.

She still had that. Sure, she'd lost an edge to her physical ability but as he finally found a toehold, he thought Beth would have found it, too. By feel.

Who needed fifty-fifty vision if you were Beth?

And all of a sudden it was like she was with him. His Beth. Part of him.

What had the guy said?

She's all I am.

'It's teamwork over here,' he muttered to Blake, searching for the next toehold. 'We have it covered.

'We?'

'You have Sam up top, guiding us every step of the way. But somehow… I have Beth right down here, telling me what to do, and bossy doesn't begin to describe it.'

'Are you okay?' Blake said cautiously.

'Yeah, I'm okay,' Luc told him. 'More than okay. I seem to be operating on an epiphany and who needs anything else in the face of such a thing?'

'Cables would be good. Plus medical gear. Plus…'

'Yeah, right,' Luc said, almost cheerfully. He was operating at full strength now, doing what he was good at, every nerve tuned to the job at hand. 'But don't you mess with my epiphany because it seems to be right what I need, right when I need it. You go on up, mate, and stay safe. I'm almost there.'

And then he was there. Not on the ledge itself— some things were a no-brainer—but to the side, hanging from his harness.

Every impulse was to drop further so he could see through the smashed windows into the car but he'd worked in enough situations like this to put instinct aside.

He hovered, toes gripping the cliff just above the car. Steadied.

'Cables,' he muttered, and Sam—or Blake or whoever was at the top of the cliff—attached the first of the steel cables and lowered it down, hooked to his mainstay.

He caught it and then rode his harness in a seated position until he had it fastened under the passenger-side rear-wheel brace.

One. It wouldn't hold.

'Next?'

He could almost taste the tension emanating from the top of the cliff.

Another cable snaked down.

He fought his way across the top—or base—of the car and attached the cable to the rear driver's side.

'You got something up there holding?' he asked.

'Two ruddy great tow trucks parked well back.' It was Sam's voice. 'Blake's trying again but having trouble. More cables?'

He wanted to see what was in the car. If anyone was conscious they must be able to hear him work but there'd been silence.

Were they all dead?

But he had to work on, on the assumption there were people who needed to be saved. At the very least he'd prevent the car—and any bodies—from plunging into the sea.

She's all I am.

The guy's voice was echoing, messing with his head.

And Beth, she was in there, too.

She's all I am.

'Two more cables to be sure,' he muttered, and forced himself to be still and wait until the cables had run down, until he had four hawsers hooked across the car chassis, until he felt the guys up top gently, gently take up the slack so the car wasn't going anywhere.

'Done.' Sam's voice came through his earpiece. 'She's as secure on this end as we can make it. Cables secure?'

She wasn't asking if the cables themselves were fastened. She was asking if the body of the car was still intact enough to hold together.

'Looks as good as we can make it. Keep the pressure up.' It should be okay. From underneath the chassis looked solid.

Time to edge sideways and down a bit.

Time to look through those smashed windows...

He took the pressure from his stay and slipped downward, using the ledge now to steady himself. No weight, though. If the ledge itself crashed the car could still swing...

The rear window was smashed into crystallised glass. He could see nothing.

Down further...

She's all I am.

Beth.

This wasn't Beth. This wasn't personal.

Only it was. Every fibre of his being was pleading...

He had himself secure. He swung around—and a woman was looking out at him. Straight at him through the gap in the smashed glass. Clear-eyed. Conscious.

Alive.

'Tess,' he said, and he saw her face sag, just for a moment. And then some sort of iron control reasserted itself. 'I'm Luc,' he told her. 'And I'm very pleased to see you.'

'You...you took your time.'

'There was a small matter of tying your car up so it wouldn't slip further,' he told her, keeping his voice calm, pragmatic, workmanlike. Emotion right now would help no one. 'There are now four cables attaching you to cranes on top of the cliff. The car's going nowhere. You're safe. We just need to get you out. The kids...'

'I think...' He could hear pain in her voice, and the numbness of shock, but she had herself in hand. 'They're all in the back. Zoe says... Zoe says Tom's knee's been bleeding—a lot—but she's wound her windcheater round it and tied it. She says the bleeding's slowed. I wasn't game to move... I thought...' She caught herself and he could hear the effort she was making to stay calm. 'I told the kids...if we stay really, really still even if we hurt, even if we're scared, then Santa will be so impressed he'll bring double this year. Isn't that right, Zoe?'

'And we did.' A girl's voice, much shakier than her mother's, piped up from the back seat. 'I'm cuddling Tom and Robbie.'

'You know what you are?' Luc said, and for some reason he was having trouble keeping his own voice steady. 'You're a heroine, Miss Zoe. And so's your mum. And you boys...if you can hold on just a little bit longer... There's a fire engine up on the cliff and if you manage to stay still until we take you, one by one, up the cliff in a harness, then you'll officially be heroes in fire hats. The fire chief will give you all helmets.' They'd probably dock the expense from his pay but what the heck.

'Fire helmets...' That was a quavery voice, very young. Not much older than Toby.

Oh, God, Toby...

'It's a promise,' he said, very solemnly, and then Blake was slithering down beside him and tools were being lowered to prise the doors open.

She's all I am.

Suddenly that line was front and centre. He wanted to tell Beth. He needed to tell her.

And in that moment he accepted what he'd been fighting now for so many years.

He needed.

He needed Beth.

'Margie?'

Her phone rang just as she finished morning clinic. The call was from Margie, the head of childcare at Namborra. She saw the name appear on the screen and felt a huge tug of regret. 'Hey, it's lovely to hear from you.'

'Good to hear your voice, too, Beth, love,' Margie told her, but there was a strain in her voice that said this wasn't a social call.

And that brought back the niggle of disquiet. For the last twenty-four hours she'd been fretting...about Luc? Stupidly fretting. There'd been no basis for worry but for some reason she thought...she *knew* that all wasn't well with Luc.

She'd almost rung him but sense had held her back. She was being irrational. Imagining things.

And now... Margie was in Namborra. She'd hardly be ringing about Luc, but the tingle of fear remained. And she'd definitely heard tension in Margie's voice.

'Margie, what's wrong?'

'I didn't... We shouldn't ask.'

'You shouldn't ask what?'

'You're in Brisbane, right? And back at work?'

'Yes.' If you could call it work—fielding requests for scripts from city dwellers popping in to see if the new doctor was an easy target.

'So if I said...we needed you...'

'What's happened?' The fear for Luc was acute—which was dumb but she couldn't get rid of it.

'It's Maryanne.'

Maryanne. She who ruled the medical kingdom of Namborra.

'What's wrong with Maryanne?'

'She's had a stroke,' Margie told her. 'Luckily she was in the hospital when it happened but of course there wasn't even another doctor. They called in the med. evacuation team from Bondi Bayside. They took her to Sydney last night but they're saying it's serious. One of the nurses here knows someone who works at Bondi and they're saying there's left-sided weakness, possible neurological damage. It's...it's too soon to say but best guess is that she'll be looking at months before she's back at work. If ever. And now...there's no one.'

Margie paused. 'Beth, love, we don't know where you're up to, medically, and we know Maryanne didn't trust you to work on your own, but there's not a soul in this district who doesn't trust you to care for them. Beth, would it be possible...just until we can work something out...would it be possible for you to come home?'

Home.

And there was only one answer it was possible to give.

She still had the niggle of fear for Luc but Luc didn't want her. Didn't need her.

Namborra needed her.

And I need to be needed, too, she said, but she said

it silently and she was talking directly to Luc. *I can do this.*

'Of course I can,' she told Margie. 'I'll be there on the next plane.'

CHAPTER ELEVEN

THERE WERE INJURIES—of course there were—but for such an accident the outcome was almost miraculous. Some jobs were better than others, Luc thought as he watched the med. evacuation chopper take off toward Sydney. Blake and Sam were in the chopper but Luc had been left behind. With four patients, plus one tearful, almost unbelievingly thankful husband and father, the chopper was full. Gina would take Luc back in the smaller chopper, but they had to collect their gear first, plus fill in whatever the local rescue services needed to get their reports right.

Normally Luc followed the steps fast and efficiently. Tonight, though, he left Gina to it. He stood on the clifftop and stared out to sea, and Gina had the sensitivity to leave him be.

He was shaking. He, Luc, who never got emotionally involved, was shaking.

There'd been broken ribs. A fractured arm. Multiple lacerations. The accident had been caused by failed brakes, a truck on the wrong side of the road. An ambulance had taken the truck driver to the local hospital, suffering from shock.

'The brakes failed. I put my foot down and there was

nothing there. I couldn't get the gears to hold it. There was nothing I could do, and I could have killed them.'

He hadn't, because one woman had had the sense to keep calm, stay absolutely still and somehow talk her kids into doing the same.

Tess's purse had been in the footwell of the passenger compartment. How tempting would it have been to lean over and fish for her phone, so she could get some contact to the outside world.

She hadn't. She'd assessed the situation and decided the risk was too great.

Beth would do that, Luc thought. Beth was just like Tess, a practical, sensible woman who wouldn't crack in a crisis.

He thought of her calmly holding Toby under her T-shirt in the concrete rubble, waiting for help. Knowing it would come.

Knowing he'd come?

How could she?

He thought of Sam and Blake tonight—Sam deferring to Blake's overall command, watching Blake abseil into danger. Staying on the clifftop, ensuring both Blake and Luc stayed secure, feeding equipment down the lines. He and Blake had both needed Sam.

The cliff where Blake had been trying to descend had crumbled—he knew that now. Sam must have felt it as Blake had lurched, as the line had gone taut with strain, but there'd been no panic. Blake depending on Sam's skill to keep them safe.

And there was a deeper level. Sam depended on Blake.

Their wedding was to take place in two weeks. It

was a marriage of equals and Luc knew in his bones that they'd be gloriously happy.

They needed…each other.

There was a touch on his arm and he turned to find Gina watching him, looking worried. Gina was an amazing chopper pilot and they depended on her absolutely.

They needed Gina.

He was thinking suddenly of his mother, fragile, brittle, demanding. She'd needed, over and over again. She'd even needed her little niece's death to be his fault, so she and her sister wouldn't have to take the blame.

'It wasn't fair.' He said it out loud and Gina's look of concern deepened.

'Luc, love? Are you okay? You did great. Really great but everyone's safe. Thanks to you.

'Thanks to all of us.'

'We're a great team,' she said, and suddenly she hugged him. 'Come on, mate. Let's go home.'

'Back to Bondi?'

'Where else?'

'I'm not sure,' he said slowly. 'Yeah, for now, Bondi. But home… Hell, Gina, I've never had one.'

'Hey, I've seen the view from your apartment.' He had her seriously worried—he could see that. 'Your home's amazing.'

'The telly's too small.'

'Really? You can fix that.'

'I might have to,' he said slowly and then, because she was still looking worried and she was part of his team and he loved every single one of them, he hugged her back. 'But that's for tomorrow. For now...you're right, let's go home. Wherever home is.'

The commercial flight from Brisbane to Namborra left at ten the next morning and Beth was on it. With Toby.

The head of the clinic had been annoyed when she'd rung to quit, but not surprised. He was a man in his seventies, an entrepreneur who wanted to make money from medicine.

'I knew you wouldn't stay,' he said gruffly into the phone. 'You guys who want to save the world drive me nuts. Me, I just want a quiet life making a decent nest egg for retirement.'

A decent nest egg. She thought of the fortune the man was reputed to have and she almost choked.

'So I'm heading to Namborra, the outback town the plane crashed into a few weeks ago,' she told him, and then cheekily added, 'You want to make a donation to the rebuild fund?'

'You're telling me I'm losing a doctor to them—and you want money?'

'Would you rather donate money or come and do the hard yards with me?'

And amazingly he'd chuckled, and promised a bank transfer.

That was great but as soon as she disconnected she stopped thinking about him. About Brisbane. She had to get on that plane. She had time to think of nothing else.

Except... Luc was still in her mind. In her heart?

Why had she been worried last night? Why the niggle?

For that's all he is, she told herself firmly as she carried Toby up the steps onto the plane. 'A niggle. My life's about to get very busy and that's just the way we want it. We have no time to worry about Luc. We're on our own again, Toby, love.'

She was about to be Namborra's only doctor.

That was taking alone to a whole new level.

Luc had a couple of minor scratches that needed attention—hauling kids and mum one at a time out of the wrecked car and harnessing them up the cliff had involved a scratch or two. Blake insisted on a full body check and told him to go home to bed.

As if he could. He showered and checked again on his rescued family—all present and correct—and then headed up to annoy Harriet.

'Hey, well done,' she told him. 'The guys are saying you did good.'

'It's the mum who did good,' he told her. 'Having the presence of mind to freeze and get the kids to stay frozen…they saved themselves.'

'So that dressing I see on your hand…'

'I gotta have something to show for a night's work.'

'It sounds as if it was awesome. Oh, I wish I'd been with you.'

'I know you do.' He stooped and hugged her. 'But your rehab is going great. You'll be back as part of the team…'

'You know my leg won't let me,' she said, flatly now. 'You're mouthing platitudes, Luc Braxton. Me and Beth. Perfect or nothing, and perfect's not going to happen. And if we're not perfect then you can't take it. You'll spend your life worrying about us.'

'That's…'

'True,' she finished for him. She put her head to one side and considered. 'Tell me I'm wrong then. You don't want to wrap Beth in cotton wool?'

'I… What she does is her business.'

'So if she ever decided she wanted to hang from ropes and save people?'

'She'd never be able to.' It was a gut response, and he saw Harriet wince.

'Yeah, like me. No rope hanging for us because we're *not* perfect.'

'Harry…'

'It's okay. I understand.' She tugged his hand so he had to stoop and then she hugged him, hiding her face for a moment in his shoulder. Using the moment to re-group? 'I'll just…figure it out. My way. I hope.' She moved back and seemed to have herself back under control. 'By the way, have you been in contact with Beth?'

'I… No. Why should I?'

'Why not indeed,' she said speculatively.

'There's nothing wrong?'

'There you go again. Protective mode.'

'I'm not.'

'Yeah, you are.'

He held up his hands in surrender. 'Okay, Harry, I admit it. I messed up our marriage. I love her. I…' He stopped. How to say it. But in the end it just happened. 'I need her.'

'Even if she doesn't need you.'

'She's proved she doesn't need me.'

'She might.'

And panic slammed back. 'What…? Harriet, what are you…?'

'It's okay. There's nothing wrong,' she said hastily. 'Or not with Beth.'

'Toby...'

'Will you stop it? If you're going to be any use at all, you need to get over that mind set.'

He paused. Took a breath. Eyed Harriet with caution.

Yeah, he was overreacting. He needed to work on that.

He needed to work on a lot of things.

'So why are you asking if I've been in touch with Beth?' He flattened his voice. Tried to make himself sound only vaguely interested.

Failed.

'Because of Maryanne,' Harriet told him.

He had a feeling Harriet was playing games with him and he needed to stay calm and ride it out.

'Maryanne.'

'Namborra's doctor.'

'That's who I thought you meant.' He hesitated. 'So... Maryanne... She hasn't cracked and offered Beth a job?'

'I don't know about the job but it seems she has cracked.' She was watching him, he thought, assessing his reaction. He felt like an insect in a specimen jar but there was nothing he could do about it.

'Explain,' he said sternly, and she took pity on him and did.

'She's ill,' she said. 'The med. evacuation chopper brought Maryanne herself in yesterday. Sue from the flying squad popped in to see me late last night. She knows Beth's from Namborra and she thought maybe

I might let Beth know. I have Beth's number but... I thought I might wait. And talk to you.'

'The med. evacuation chopper brought Maryanne in...'

'Stroke,' she said, briefly, back in medical mode. 'She has some cognitive impairment, hopefully transient but it's too soon to tell. She's still in Intensive Care and of course that means Namborra's without a single doctor. Anyway, it occurred to me that if your Beth found out about it...'

'She will have.'

'Yeah?'

'She has friends at Namborra. Of course they'll tell her.'

'There you go, then. No need for me to tell her. No need for you to even contact her.' But she was looking at him again in that same way. Head to the side. Inquisitive.

Summing up the possibilities.

What were the possibilities?

There was little love lost between Beth and Maryanne. He knew Beth would be concerned but he doubted she'd be rushing back to Sydney to see her.

But then...

He thought of Namborra, of how remote it was, of how long they'd taken to find doctors in the past, so long in fact that Maryanne had had to accept Beth and Ron.

He thought of how Beth felt about Namborra. She'd given but...she'd felt the community cared.

There it was again. She'd needed Namborra and Namborra needed her.

'Hell,' he said, and saw Harriet's curiosity step up a notch.

'Hell? Really?'

'She'll go.'

'That's what I thought,' Harriet said in satisfaction.

'She can't.'

'She can't what?'

'You know as well as I do. She can't cope on her own.'

'Because?'

And he took a deep breath and fell silent. He walked over to the window. Now Harriet was in permanent rehab, she'd been moved to one of the few rooms in the hospital with a sea view. He could see the bay. He could see...

The future. Beth working her butt off in Namborra.

Bringing up Toby alone.

The urge to fly to the rescue was almost overwhelming.

But...

She wouldn't want him.

He wanted her.

'Luc?' Harriet's voice from behind him was almost tentative. 'What are you thinking?'

'I don't know,' he said, and he didn't. 'But...hell, Harry, I need to go take a walk. A very long walk. I think... I think I have a whole lot of thinking to do. A lifetime's worth of thinking and that may take quite some time.'

CHAPTER TWELVE

BETH'S DAY HAD been crazy, from beginning to end. It had started at three in the morning with a false alarm: *'I was sure it was a heart attack, Doc—Stevie told me I shoulda let that curry alone...'* She'd been running on catch-up all day. And now, when she should be heading home for dinner, she was stuck in a bathtub with a three-year-old.

It sucked.

There wasn't a lot of choice, though. Three-year-old James Hollis trusted her. His mum, Millie, was eight months pregnant and had finally been persuaded to take a few minutes out and give her body a rest. Someone had to sit in the bath with her little boy.

For James Hollis's toe was firmly stuck in the plughole.

Beth had given James as much tranquilliser as she dared but he didn't seem sleepy. He was bundled in blankets and pillows. She was holding him tucked into her. His toe was inconveniently stuck but she'd given him a digital nerve block. He wasn't upset. They were watching some ridiculous cartoon about a cute wombat on Beth's laptop.

Walter Wombat's moralising antics were making Beth want to throw up.

She still had a ward round to do—plus when the firefighters currently cutting pipe under the house finally got James out of the bathtub there'd still be the not so small matter of giving anaesthetic while she cut the plug from his foot. She doubted he'd stay calm enough for her to do it under local.

And there was another worry. Anaesthesia. She needed to be two doctors.

She was currently weighing up sending James to Sydney when they finally had him free—but that'd mean another hour at least with his toe constricted. Or do the thing herself?

And Toby... Margie had him in care and would be giving him dinner. He'd be having fun. He wouldn't be missing her but, oh, she was missing him.

'We're cutting through now,' one of the firemen called from under the house. 'We've got your end of the bath stable but don't move, Doc. We're cutting through the floorboards so we can see to cut the enamel from the side.'

'Fine,' she called back. James had headphones on—thankfully—so she didn't have to compete with a cartoon wombat telling her not to litter.

Her leg was aching. Of course it was. 'Stay off it as much as possible,' the orthopod back in Sydney had told her and she thought, yeah, right, she was off it. She was sitting in a nice bath at the end of a long day.

Joke.

'Done,' the voice from below said in satisfaction as she heard a clump of masonry fall away. 'Coming up. You respectable, Doc?'

Ha.

She sighed. Two weeks as Namborra's sole doctor and she was exhausted.

Two weeks and the rest of her life to go?

Without Luc.

Stop it. Stop-it-stop-it-stop-it.

The mantra in her head wasn't working but she had to make it work. She'd spent years teaching herself that she didn't need Luc, and here she was, pining like a teenager.

An uncomfortable teenager. In a bathtub.

But she couldn't keep doing this. Two weeks doing the work of three doctors had made her see sense. It wasn't fair to Toby.

It was impossible.

'The firemen are coming back in,' she told James, lifting a corner of his earphones. On her instructions, the firemen had donned their uniforms and were keeping them on. James had been told if he was very still then he and his mum could ride to the hospital in the fire truck as soon as he was free. It was pretty exciting for a three-year-old, and he was being extraordinarily good.

It was only Beth who wanted to drum her heels and yell.

Or weep.

She felt…she felt…

Like she had to get a grip. She did—sort of. She held James tighter and put on a cheerful professional face as the door opened and a couple of firefighters trooped in.

And…oh, for heaven's sake…

Luc?

Luc. Here he was again, riding to her rescue, and it wasn't even Beth who had her toe stuck.

He was casually dressed. Faded jeans. Open-necked gingham shirt. Smiling?

At her.

The urge to weep was almost overwhelming.

She didn't, though. She sat in the bathtub and held James and didn't say anything at all.

'We've cut it right out.' Troy, the head of Namborra's fire service, sounded almost cheerful, talking over his shoulder to Luc. 'A great hunk of the floorboards and we've cut the pipe below. Once we rip these side tiles off we'll have full access—we'll cut that plug right out and they'll be free. This is young James Hollis. His mum's about to pop another baby out, his dad's doing a bit of interstate truck driving and James here decided he'd make life more interesting by sticking his toe in the plughole.'

Then Troy turned to her and the little boy she was holding. 'How you going, young James? Doc Carmichael? Here's Doc Braxton come to help. He's one of the docs who was here during the plane crash. You remember Doc Braxton, Doc? Hey, wasn't he the doc who came with you to the memorial service? Of course you know him.'

Of course she knew him.

She stared up at Luc in stupefaction. His smile had slipped. He was looking at her as if he saw the tears she was struggling to hold back.

He was looking at her with concern, with a look that said she'd be cared for and cherished...

Yeah, been there, done that, got the T-shirt.

'What are you doing here?' It was a snap, out before she could stop herself, and his smile returned.

'That's not a very polite way to greet a friend. Mind, greeting friends from bathtubs does put you at a disadvantage. I can see that. I stopped at the hospital and they told me I could find you here. So I thought I'd pop right over and help.'

Of course he did. That was what he did. Riding to the rescue. Luc, the hero.

She'd had it with heroes. Hadn't she made a decision to stay clear of this man? For ever?

But right now… It would be petty—and unprofessional to say she didn't need him.

As well as untrue.

'I… Great. Could you…could you check on Millie?' she said, grudgingly. 'I… She's thirty-seven weeks pregnant and she's been sitting in the bathtub for longer than I have.'

'Where is she?' And he'd clicked into medical mode, just like that. Which was also what he did. He was no longer Luc, her ex-husband, her nemesis. He was a colleague and right now she could have fallen on his chest and wept.

Only you didn't do that to…nemesises? Nemesi?

Maybe she was close to hysteria?

'I hope she's in her bedroom. I sent her there twenty minutes ago.'

'Right,' Luc said. 'But we might do a bit of role swapping?' And before she could argue, before she could say that James trusted her and might disintegrate with strangers around him, Luc was kneeling beside the bath and producing his phone.

James, who was finally wearying of Walter Wombat

and his nauseous prosing, shoved back his headphones and looked at Luc with wobbly suspicion. The sedative was keeping him back from the edge of toddler panic, but he was reaching the limits of his endurance.

Any minute now he'd disintegrate.

'Hey, James. I'm Dr Braxton. I'm a doctor who's very good at getting toes out of plugholes,' Luc told him. 'But first, would you like to see what you look like?' And he lifted his phone, snapped a fast picture of James and handed the phone over.

What child could resist seeing a picture of himself? James stared at the screen, fascinated.

'Let's take a picture of Doc Carmichael holding you?' Luc said, and did, then gave the phone back to James.

Another moment. James's attention was totally caught.

'And now…' Luc said with all solemnity. 'We'll make a movie. Watch.' And he took the phone, stepped back and took a quick clip of Luc and Beth in the bath with Troy stooping to knock away the tiles.

'We can do even better,' Luc told him as he replayed it for James's benefit. 'If I hop into the bath we can make pictures of everything that's happening. I'll show you and then I'll teach you how.' He handed the phone to James and held out a hand to Beth, a hand that told her she was coming out of the bath right now.

So she could object—or she could do what he said.

It felt like giving in.

It felt like sense.

She went to push herself out but she wasn't permitted. He stooped, tugged her upright, then put his hands on her waist and lifted her bodily from the bath. Then he swept her against him and hugged, a brief, strong hug that had nothing to do with professional anything—but if they sold that sort of comfort in bottles…

Um…not. She'd be professional even if he wasn't.

'I… Thanks.' But he'd already released her and was sliding into the bath behind James, attention back on his phone.

'Now, James, we press this button. That lets us see ourselves in the camera. If we hold it right out here we can even see what the firemen are doing under the bath. You can hold it while we take pictures of just us, but if we want the firemen I might need to hold it because my arm's longer. Dr Carmichael, can you please go check on anyone else who needs checking? We'll call if we need you, won't we, James?'

'M-Mummy,' said James, uncertainly.

'Dr Carmichael's going to give your mummy a cuddle,' Luc told him. He'd been recording while he talked so now he turned the phone around and hit replay. 'And the firemen are going to get your toe free. James, I think you might need to wiggle your ears to make our picture more interesting. Can you wiggle your ears? I can. Why don't I wiggle and you hold the camera?'

And twenty minutes later one toe—with metal plug and James attached—was ensconced on the front bench seat of the fire engine. With Millie. Troy even obliged by using sirens and flashing lights as they headed for the hospital.

Luc followed in his car.

Beth followed in hers. Dazed.

Luc had his car. That meant he hadn't flown here.

It was half a day's drive from Sydney.

That meant…no flying visit?

Her mind was in overdrive. Here was Luc, dashing to her rescue again. She should tell him to turn around and go straight back to Sydney but of course she couldn't. She needed his professional help.

Nothing else.

Liar.

What was he doing here?

'Just rescuing,' she said wearily. 'Just being someone I need. Oh, Luc, how am I going to learn not to need you?'

With two doctors the procedure to remove one toe from one metal ring was relatively simple. Beth gave the anaesthetic, really light as James was already sedated. Once the adrenaline of the rescue and the fire engine ride was done he'd slumped into his mother's arms and hardly noticed as Beth had set up a drip and administered what she needed to put him under.

Luc did the actual removal of toe from metal. If the plug hadn't been so bulky he could have used an orthopaedic pin-cutter, but for this they needed heat shields to protect the underlying skin, then the specifically designed surgical cutter with grinder attachment.

And good eyesight.

Yeah, she could have done it, she conceded. Her magnifying glasses would have worked.

Except…she was bone weary. Her hands were starting to shake and the cutter required eye-watering precision. To be safe, she'd have had to send him to Sydney. Instead she monitored breathing and watched while Luc expertly freed one toe.

It was a five-minute job. The toe wasn't compromised. James surfaced from the anaesthetic and almost instantly drifted toward normal sleep.

There was swelling because of initial tugging, but by tomorrow he'd have nothing more than a slightly sore toe, a memory of firefighters and fire engines—and a heap of pictures to show his dad when he got home.

One of the firefighters had stayed on to take Millie and James home. Beth walked out to the car park to see them off and then walked back inside.

To face Luc.

He was helping the nurses clear equipment, chatting as if he'd known them all their lives—and gently probing as to what else needed to be done tonight. For a moment she stood back in the doorway of Theatre and watched. Barb and Dottie were the nurses on duty—middle-aged, sensible women. The clearing was finished. Neither of them actually needed to be in Theatre any more but she could see they were attracted to Luc as moths to flame. She stood and watched and thought… Yeah, why wouldn't they be?

And then Luc turned and saw her. He smiled and she thought moths and flames had nothing on her.

'All done, Dr Carmichael?'

'Thanks to you,' she said, and was cross that her voice quavered a bit. 'I… Thank you.'

And Barb nudged Dottie and Dottie nudged Barb and they disappeared.

Which made her feel even more…even more she didn't know what.

'Think nothing of it,' he said, and his smile became a caress all on its own. And before she knew it, he was across the room, enfolding her into his arms and holding her tight.

Just…holding her. Nothing more. Just holding.

She could feel the beat of his heart. She could feel the strength of him.

Her Luc.

'Beth,' he whispered into her hair, and somehow it sounded like a vow.

She had things to do. She needed to move on. She needed to back away, thank him nicely for what he'd done, ask what the hell he was doing here, tell him she no longer needed him but it had been very nice of him to come check on her.

Instead she simply stood and let her heartbeat settle to his. And pretend for just this moment that this was how it could be.

Luc…

Her phone rang. Of course. Her phone had been ringing pretty much nonstop since she'd returned to Namborra. She'd flicked it off in the bathtub and then again as she'd put James under, but the moment she wasn't urgently needed, she'd flicked it on again, ready for the next problem. It was what she did.

Like Luc responding to need.

But instead of letting her answer, Luc lifted the phone from the back pocket of her jeans and answered it for her.

'Namborra Medical Service. Dr Braxton speaking.'

'Give it to me,' Beth tried, but he smiled down at her, used his spare arm to hug her even closer, and went on speaking.

'Right. I can see why you're worrying, but the incubation period for meningitis is well and truly over.

If your little boy caught it from Felix he'd have had it by now. But tell me the symptoms.'

He listened, his face grave and attentive, but while he listened his fingers started playing with her spine. Doing...doing...

She should listen. She should...

Oh, the feel of those fingers...

'You know, that sounds very much like a cold to me. Thirty-seven point seven? Yes, that is a slight fever but it's very, very mild. And he has a runny nose? Is he alert? Did he eat his dinner? Yes, I agree we can't be too careful but I think, given the symptoms, that we can wait and watch for a while.

'What I'd like you to do is pop him in the bath— watch the plughole, by the way—there's been a bit of a problem with toes and plugholes and we don't want that to go around. Pop him in pyjama bottoms with no top and put him to bed as normal. Don't put too many covers on him. Take his temperature again before you go to bed and if it's over thirty-eight then I want you to ring me again. No, not Doc Carmichael. I'm the doctor on duty tonight but this number reaches us both. That's great. Get some sleep yourself and feel free to ring if you have any concerns. Goodnight.'

And he flipped the phone closed and tucked it back into her jeans pocket.

And she stared up at him, stunned. What had he just said?

'You're what?'

'What, love?' The fingers started their magic again. He was smiling down at her. Lovingly? Oh, Luc...

Back off. Back off! This was terrifying.

'You're the duty doctor tonight?' she managed.

'I thought I'd start tonight—if it's okay with you. I agree, as junior partner I should have asked you first, but seeing as I—'

'Junior partner... Luc, what are you doing?'

They were right by the sinks. She could feel the bench at her back. Luc was in front of her. The bench was behind.

The bench felt solid. Luc felt...terrifying.

'I'm here to stay,' he said, and even the bench stopped feeling solid.

'You can't.'

'I can't stay?'

'No.' She was hovering between tears and laughter. 'Luc, you know you can't. You'll go nuts. A family doctor...'

'I think I might like it.'

'You wouldn't. You won't.'

'Why not?'

'Because it's not dangerous,' she said, feeling desperate. 'Because it's not filled with adrenaline. Because you don't get to swing on ropes and dive into burning buildings.'

'No?' He appeared to think about it. 'You know, I've never considered family medicine until now, but I've spent a lot of the last couple of weeks talking to Maryanne. She sends her regards, by the way. They're pretty fuzzy regards. She has residual left-sided weakness so her speech is a bit impaired but she's fit enough to tell me exactly what this job involves. And why it's unsuitable for someone like you with a bit of sight impairment. Because she says there *are* times when you need to hang off ropes.'

'I never have...'

'But you crawl into wrecked cars. You head into unknown homes at the dead of night. Maryanne says you've talked people out of suicide. You watch kids grow, dealing with every dumb accident kids fall into. You cope with unexpected babies... Why is Millie still here, by the way? Are you seriously proposing to deliver her? No matter, we'll talk of that later. All I figure is that family medicine can be routine and I think I'm ready for that, but it also seems that it can be very exciting indeed. There'll be dramas here and we're first responders. Like stuck toes with fire engines attached. How can I return to Specialist Disaster Response and miss that?'

'You can't be serious.' She could hardly breathe. 'Luc, you can't. Honest, you'd go nuts.' She took a deep breath. 'I've figured...tonight in the bath I thought it through. You're right, I can't cope here on my own. It's not fair to anyone. Namborra will need to find someone else. I don't know who but it can't...it can't be me. And as for you coming here, too, you know it's impossible. You'll go crazy trying to stop me taking a fair share and I can't watch you go crazy. Luc, I don't need you that much.'

'No,' he said seriously. 'You don't. That's what I figured. It's taken me a while—ten years, in fact. I'm a slow learner but I have it now.' He took her by the waist again and tugged her into him, hard and strong. 'You don't need me that much but I need you at least that much. No. I need you more.'

'What...what...?'

He kissed her hair, a feather touch, a touch she should hardly have felt but it was a touch that sent shards of heat running through her entire body.

'I get it,' he said softly, into her hair. 'Finally...'

'You get...what?'

'That I need,' he murmured. 'That I've always needed. You know my background. You know my crazy mother. She was damaged herself and she spread that damage. I was only worth anything when I was needed. If I wasn't needed, I wasn't loved. I've done enough hard thinking over the past few weeks—in between fighting fire-breathing dragons—to accept that I need to change. But, then, I guess I've always known that. It's just that I haven't wanted to change enough to do it.'

Her heart was hammering but so was his. Two hearts beating as one. How corny was that?

She didn't do corny. She couldn't hope for corny. Hearts and flowers? Violins playing soppy love songs?

Her heart was screaming, Yes, please.

But she needed to listen. She had to listen. Luc's voice was little more than a murmur and every nerve-ending was attuned to every syllable.

'I've spent the last ten years thinking you needed me,' he was saying, even softer now as if he could hardly believe what he was saying, as if there was some deep part of him surfacing that had to struggle past barriers that were a lifetime deep. 'But you know what? I've watched you dispatch dragons, and there hasn't been a single time when you haven't whirled and coped with your own threats.'

'That's not to say... I mean, there will be times...'

'When the dragons get too much?' He kissed her then, properly this time, and it was a kiss that was so sweet, so tender that she almost melted on the spot. 'Of course there will. Those dragons will be there for me, too, and when they are, I want you to be the one looking out for me. That's because I need you. But you know what I've finally figured? I love you first and need comes second. So, Beth, I'm hoping…no, I'm gambling my life here on the one big thing. That you love me regardless of need.'

She couldn't speak. She was having trouble breathing. She didn't…she wasn't…she couldn't respond.

But he hadn't finished. He had both her hands in his, smiling down at her in a way that made her heart turn over, that made joy build to a point where she felt she might turn into a puddle of happiness. That the world was somehow transforming into something new and bright and magnificent.

Listen, she told herself fiercely. Listen…and breathe.

'Beth, you have damaged eyesight and sometimes you need help,' he was saying, holding her tight. 'Right now you have a damaged leg so you need help there, too. Maryanne's desperate to get back to work but she'll probably be left with residual weakness and she'll need help as well. But maybe my disability is worse. Beth, I was a lonely kid who never got taught the basics of loving, and how does a little eyesight loss or leg injury or even left-sided weakness compare to that? It's huge. So of the three of us…'

'The three of us…'

'Yep,' he said in satisfaction. 'Because our future needs to include medicine. I've spent the last two weeks trying to sort this out. I needed to get all my ducks in a row before I talked to you. This isn't a half-baked idea, love. It's a full-blown rest-of-our-lives proposition. Maryanne wants to come back after rehab but she'll face restrictions. She knows that but she's accepting—

very humbly, by the way—that if we give her space she can manage. That makes a country practice of three doctors. It'll be three doctors who all have different needs but, hey, no one's perfect. And maybe together we can provide what this town needs. And…what we all need?'

'I…' Where had her voice gone? The lone syllable came out a squeak and she had to breathe a few times before she could try again. 'Luc…are you talking medical practice here or…or us?'

'I'm not including Maryanne in the marriage,' he admitted, and he chuckled and drew her closer. 'But I am talking marriage. Seriously now. The way a man should talk marriage.'

He put her back from him then and held her at arm's length but his eyes still caressed her. 'For that's what this is all about,' he said softly. 'This is the single biggest thing I've ever said. We married once but I know now we married for all the wrong reasons. The love was there but there were too many ghosts. I hadn't sorted them—and maybe you hadn't sorted yours, either. But finally our ghosts seem to have been dispatched and I can't tell you how grateful I am. So…'

'S-so?'

'So, Beth Carmichael, I love you with all my heart. Would you do me the very great honour of marrying me? Properly this time, though, Beth. Marrying for love. Not for need, though need's there because, God knows, I need you more than life itself. But, Beth… I've never stopped feeling that you're my wife. I want to slay dragons with you, not for you. I want to have a family. A dog? A brother or sister for Toby? I…whatever… Will you…?'

And he stopped. He could go no further.

And neither could she.

He was looking down at her with all the anxiety in the world. He didn't know, she thought. He didn't understand…

So say it, she told herself. Just say it.

One little word.

One vast, soaring ode to joy.

'Yes,' she said as he gathered her into him.

'Yes,' she said as he raised her and swung her round and round until her heart felt like it was swirling out of her body.

Yes, she said again, but this time her yes was silent because his mouth had found hers.

Because two people had found their home.

* * * * *

COMING SOON!

We really hope you enjoyed reading this book. If you're looking for more romance, be sure to head to the shops when new books are available on

Thursday
23rd August

To see which titles are coming soon, please visit
millsandboon.co.uk

MILLS & BOON

MILLS & BOON

Coming next month

THE NURSE'S PREGNANCY MIRACLE
Ann McIntosh

Nychelle tried with all her might to say they shouldn't go any further, but couldn't get the words out. Knowing she needed to tell him the rest of her story battled with the desire making her head swim and her body tingle and thrum with desire.

'Tell me you don't want me,' he said again, and she knew she couldn't. To do so would be to lie.

'I can't. You know I can't. But...'

He didn't wait to hear the rest, just took her mouth in a kiss that made what she'd planned to say fly right out of her brain.

Desire flared, hotter than the Florida sun, and Nychelle surrendered to it, unable and unwilling to risk missing this chance to know David intimately, even if it were just this once. Was it right? Wrong? She couldn't decide — didn't want to try to.

There were so many more things she should explain to him, but she knew she wouldn't. Telling him about the baby when she knew he didn't want a family would destroy whatever it was growing between them. It was craven, perhaps even despicable not to be honest with him, and she hated herself for being underhand, but her mind, heart and body were at war, and she'd already accepted which would win.

She'd deal with the fallout, whatever it might be, tomorrow. Today—this evening—she was going to have what she wanted, live the way she wanted. Enjoy David for this one time. There would only be regrets if she didn't.

His lips were still on hers, demanding, delicious. She'd relived the kisses they'd shared over and over in her mind, but now she realized memory was only a faded facsimile of reality. The touch and taste and scent of him encompassed her, overtaking her system on every level.

Her desperate hands found their way beneath his shirt, and his groan of pleasure was as heartfelt as her joy at the first sensation of his bare skin beneath her palms. His hands, in turn, explored her yearning flesh, stroking her face, then her neck. When they brushed along her shoulders, easing the straps of her sundress away, Nychelle arched against him.

Suddenly it was as though they had both lost all restraint. Arms tight around each other, their bodies moved in concert, their fiercely demanding kisses whipping the flames of arousal to an inferno.

Continue reading
THE NURSE'S PREGNANCY MIRACLE
Ann McIntosh

Available next month
www.millsandboon.co.uk

Copyright ©2018 Ann McIntosh

LET'S TALK
Romance

For exclusive extracts, competitions
and special offers, find us online:

 facebook.com/millsandboon

@millsandboonuk

@millsandboon

Or get in touch on 0844 844 1351*

For all the latest titles coming soon, visit
millsandboon.co.uk/nextmonth

*Calls cost 7p per minute plus your phone company's price per minute access charge

Want even more ROMANCE?

Join our bookclub today!

'Mills & Boon books, the perfect way to escape for an hour or so.'

Miss W. Dyer

'Excellent service, promptly delivered and very good subscription choices.'

Miss A. Pearson

'You get fantastic special offers and the chance to get books before they hit the shops'

Mrs V. Hall

Visit millsandbook.co.uk/Bookclub

and save on brand new books.

MILLS & BOON